# BROKEN & BURNED

## THE SACRED HEARTS MC BOOK TWO

### A.J. DOWNEY

# COPYRIGHT

ISBN: 978-0692333891
Book Design by Maggie Kern
Cover Art by Dar Albert at Wicked Smart Design
Editing by Barbara J. Bailey

# DEDICATION

*To Barbara, for your amazing editing and proofreading superpowers... and, you know, your ability to keep up with me... You're amazing! And to Andres Delgadillo for being an inspiration when I was stuck on Dray. You're still my favorite Marine. Lastly, to Dar Albert of Wicked Smart Designs, for bringing my characters to life with some amazing cover art! Thank you for putting up with my particulars. You're always so patient!*

# 1

Worst.
Day.
Ever.

It started with me being late to work, cue ass-chewing from my manager. I finished my day job burning myself with the steam from the espresso machine, only to find out the first-aid kit was out of burn gel. What's more, I didn't understand a goddamned thing in my statistics class, which I was pretty sure I was going to fail; my boyfriend won't answer his phone; and now my car was wheezing its death rattle and I was terrified I wouldn't make it into the mechanic's lot!

I could barely afford to keep a roof over our heads and me in my classroom, I had no idea how I would afford to fix my car and if I needed to call a tow truck to go two blocks I was going to implode.

The mechanic's shop was *right there...*

"Come on baby, come on baby; come on baby..." I chanted under my breath as if it would help anything.

I cranked the wheel and pulled into the lot with a little shout of triumph and my car just died. I stepped on the brake, stopping with a little lurch, and one of the mechanics, a man about my age, looked up in my direction from under the hood of an ancient old brown Ford pickup.

Tears pooled in my eyes. I was frustrated, embarrassed, stressed-out, and just everything all at once. I took a deep breath and grabbed the strap of my overloaded backpack to heave it off the passenger seat. The zipper gave way at the seam and with a mighty ripping sound my textbooks, notes, pens, and pencils all spilled out onto my shabby, if tidy, passenger-side floorboard.

That did it.

I burst into tears.

The mechanic, a Hispanic man with chin-length, stick-straight black hair looked on with detached interest as I bent and tried to scoop everything back into my bag.

*God, Everett, get a grip, girl!* I thought savagely to myself.

I shoveled everything back into my bag and as I went to straighten, my driver's-side door opened. I jumped and let out a little startled shout. My hand, moving unbidden, pressed to my chest.

I looked up into a pair of intense dark eyes, so dark a brown you couldn't differentiate where the iris left off and the pupil began. The mechanic raked me once over with that smoldering dark gaze of his, from my head to my feet, and his lips quirked up on one side. I swallowed hard, my heart doing a somersault in my chest.

"Having a bad day?" he asked and his voice was even and deep without a trace of an accent.

"Yeah." I nodded.

"Put it in neutral and steer," he commanded and disappeared around the back of my forlorn little Toyota. I did as he told me to and put the gear shift in neutral, taking my foot off the brake. He pushed, and I steered, which was a lot harder without power steering.

"Pull up in front of the center bay!" he called and I put some elbow grease into cranking the wheel in that direction.

"That's good!" he called and I braked, put the gearshift into first and threw the parking brake.

I sighed. This was going to take the last of my savings and then some. I didn't know how I was going to do it, but I would just have to cross that bridge when I came to it.

"Come on into the office." He started walking that direction and I hung my head for a second. I pulled my permanently-open backpack into my lap and, holding the overstuffed bag like a toddler in my arms, shuffled to the office dejectedly.

Could this get any worse? Any more humiliating?

I set my messy pack onto one of the old scruffy waiting room chairs. The office was small but neat and smelled heavily of stale engine grease and metal.

"The diagnostic is fifty bucks and includes a full vehicle inspection," he said and was filling out a carbon-copy sheet listing out everything that was included. His printing was neat and orderly, flowing out from the Bic stick pen in block letters. He only used capitals. I fished out my phone and sent yet another text to my boyfriend, Jerry.

"Name and address?" he asked me.

"Oh yeah, sorry." I was kind of blank. I went to my ruined backpack and unzipped the smaller front pocket, glaring at the gray canvas-like material for its betrayal, although I suppose I shouldn't be *too* hard on it; it had served me pretty well since my sophomore year of high school.

I extracted my small black leather wallet and pulled out my driver's license and handed it to him. He looked down at it and then back at me then back down at the small plasticized cardboard rectangle.

"Something wrong?" I asked. His intense dark eyes raked over me and I swallowed as the hair stood up on the back of my neck. I felt a slight blush brush my cheeks with a kiss of heat.

"No," he said simply, but that didn't stop his stare, so I boldly stared right back at him in a vain attempt to give as good as I got, which of course, only made him smirk at me. It was a sexy smirk and judging by the gleam in his eyes, he knew it too.

He was a couple of inches taller than me. Maybe five-eight to my five-six. His black tee shirt hugged his muscular shoulders and was tucked into the light blue grease stained coveralls, the arms of which were knotted around his waist. His black hair shone with blue highlights under the bare overhead bulb and I realized that even though it was fall it was awfully dark for early afternoon.

I dragged my eyes from his bronze skin, noting as I did that his jaw was just barely kissed with the beginning shadow of dark stubble. I turned with some difficulty; I didn't want to stop looking at him. I looked out the window behind me with some effort. The uniformly neutral colored Venetian blinds were in the down position but the slats were open to let in the natural light from outside. The sky hung heavy with dark rain clouds, threatening a deluge. I sighed. *Of course.*

I tried Jerry one more time, but after several rings his phone just went to voice mail. I hung up without leaving a message. I would try again when my business with the hot-as-hell mechanic was concluded.

"What kind of name is Everett?" he grunted.

"It's where my dad ended up. A city north of Seattle." I sighed. Not much of a name but my dad had kind of been stunned and when they'd asked him what to put on the birth certificate it was the first thing to come out of his mouth and I was forever branded.

"Long way from home," he commented. I rolled my eyes.

"Grew up here, well not *here* specifically, but in the state." I looked him over.

"What's your name?" I asked, noting the lack of a name tag. Likely it was stitched on his coveralls, but in their current position that wasn't a lot of help.

"Folks call me Dray," he said and I tilted my head to the side. An unconscious gesture.

"Dray? That short for Andre?" I asked.

"Naw, short for Draven." He made a face.

"What kind of name is Draven?" I echoed his earlier question and he smiled.

"My mother's last name is my first, I carry my dad's surname. She wanted me to have both names and my dad wasn't on board with a hyphenate." He looked up and a flicker of surprise crossed his features. "Not sure why I just told you that," he said gruffly, and dare I say, looked a little embarrassed himself.

"Secret is safe with me, so long as you don't tell anybody mine." I held out my pinky finger and he looked at it like it was an alien being from another planet. I self-consciously tucked my hand back over the edge of the counter.

"Well, Ms. Moran," he said, oddly formal all of a sudden, "You can pay when the diagnostic is complete, should know what's up with it tomorrow afternoon. Got a number I can reach you at?"

I wrote down my cell number on the paperwork and thanked him, handing over my car key. My house keys and key ring I stuffed into my jeans pocket. The spiky metal lump was unfamiliar and uncomfortable there, but it was only until I got home. Dray-the-mechanic handed me back my driver's license and I tucked it back in my wallet and my wallet back into my traitorous bag.

"Thanks," I muttered and picked up my torn backpack, attempting to crush it closed at the top. Talk about an exercise in futility. I went back to carrying it like a toddler and walked out to the street. I looked up at the forbidding steel gray autumn sky and scraped my bottom lip between my teeth. I juggled the bag and got my phone to my ear.

"Pick up, Jerry," I swore under my breath and stood at the edge of the shop's driveway by their sign.

*"Hi! You've reached Jerry, I'm doing something right now, leave a name and number and I'll get back to you."* The recorded voice of my boyfriend of four years played out of my phone and was immediately followed by an obnoxious tone.

"Jerry! It's Everett, I'm stranded at..." I looked up at the sign, "The Open Road Garage on 39th street. Please come get me? I love you. Thanks, bye." I ended the call and my shoulders slumped as the first fat drops of cold rain began to fall.

Great.

I looked back towards the garage but the open sign was out and the bay door was inches from the ground and closing fast. I hugged my bag to my chest and tried to keep the top closed as the rain fell faster.

Frustrated tears stood out in my eyes as the first trickle of cold water ran down the back of my neck. I was cold, I was tired, having been up since three thirty that morning and my left hand hurt from my thumb to my wrist where it was burned just shy of blistering. I glanced over at my car and sighed... Can't wait there, key was in the shop. I looked up and down the street for some cover.

Nothing. All the buildings were industrial and warehouse-like with flat fronts in brick or stucco, not an awning to be seen. I sighed and hugged my bag tighter. I was soaked through to my skin in a couple of minutes but longer than that dragged by.

What the hell was Jerry *doing*? He didn't have any afternoon classes and it was his scheduled day off from his non-existent job. I rolled my eyes. I loved him dearly, I really did, but he couldn't stay employed for longer than a couple of months and when he lost whatever piecemeal dead-end job he'd had, it was always someone else's fault. His mother coddled him, and honestly, at least his dad paid his portion of the rent, that was something... I sniffed. My nose was starting to run from the chill. I was going to kill him when I figured out how to get home. I tried his cell again. Voice mail... again.

A sleek and shiny, black, fully-restored 70's Trans Am, complete with gold firebird on the hood pulled up beside me. The engine was growling in that rumbling purr that declared *'I am a mechanical bad ass, just step on the gas and I'll prove it.'* The passenger door popped open and I bent. My lip was trembling with the chill and I gritted my teeth to keep them from clacking together.

"Get in. I'll take you home." Dray, the sexy-as-sin mechanic, was leaning over the center console. His dark and burning gaze straddling the line between brooding and angry. I swallowed hard.

"That's okay my boyfriend Jerry will be here any minute." I forced a smile onto my face and he scowled.

"You can't bullshit me, Sweetheart, get in the car. You're freezing and your boyfriend ain't comin'." I debated for one heartbeat, then two. The man made a harsh, impatient noise and I got in, shoving my bag on the floor between my knees and shutting the door firmly on the cold downpour outside.

"Thank you," I murmured.

"No problem," he said as I fastened my seatbelt.

I turned to look at his profile as he drove. He'd taken off the coveralls and he wore butter-soft, light-colored blue jeans that clung to his muscular thighs, falling straight-legged, the frayed cuffs covering the tops of the laces of his well-worn steel-toed work boots. The leather was pitted and scarred from use, a patch of the shiny steel showing through a ragged hole in the leather.

Watching those worn boots work the gas and clutch suddenly became really fascinating if it meant I didn't have to meet those deep dark eyes that were casting sidelong looks at me. His hand interrupted my view of his feet as it reached out and hit the switches on the heater console. Warm air blew over my feet and legs and the feel of wet denim against my skin made me grimace. I hated being in wet clothes; the sensation bothered me, the clinging dampness just ...eww.

His hands were clean, I noted, and the leather of his jacket creaked with the movement. My eyes traveled up the well-worn black leather sleeve, the leather turning brown and scaly with too much time spent in the elements. He had a vest on over the jacket, hiding the shiny silver snaps and zippers behind equally well-worn leather bearing patches for a motorcycle club. I shifted nervously in my seat and my eyes continued flowing up that sleeve, past his elbow to his shoulder to his smirking sensual lips.

I shivered.

"She'll warm up in a sec," he said but his lips twisted and I just knew he knew that little shiver hadn't been from the cold.

"I live in an apartment above Vale's dry cleaning with my boyfriend. He should be home, I don't know why he didn't answer the phone." I swallowed. Dray's presence was, in a word, intimidating as he steered the growling muscle car through the rain-slicked streets.

"Yeah. I know where you live." He muttered and I blinked. The sound of the pounding rain and the *swish-shush* sound of the wind-shield wiper blades filled the sudden silence in the interior of his car.

*Swish-shush.*

*Swish-shush.*

*Swish-shush.*

"You gave me your license, I just wrote it down, I have a knack for remembering things I read." He shifted uncomfortably in his seat.

"Oh." I said.

"Sorry, didn't mean to make it all creepy and awkward." He gave me a lopsided grin that made his face go from harsh to endearingly boyish and handsome and I couldn't help the shy answering smile of my own.

We lapsed back into silence and it was comfortable enough that I didn't feel a need to fill it if he didn't. He piloted the old muscle car deftly through the streets and I felt myself stealing glances at his vest, secretively trying to read some of the patches nearest me. One over his breast declared him the vice president and I felt my eyebrows raise. He was young... Maybe twenty five to my twenty, wasn't vice president usually a position reserved for a grizzled older biker with a big beard, who was going soft around the middle?

I turned back to the window and stared out as we turned onto my street. He pulled smoothly up to the curb in front of the dry cleaners and I gripped my bag together at the top, shoving some damp papers in at the side where they'd tried to spill out sometime during the short ride.

"Thank you for the ride, Dray," I said softly. He looked me over one more time, face serious, half smiles and smirks fled from his lips.

"No problem, give him hell," he grunted, and I opened the door and got out. I shut the door behind me and dashed to the glass door to my apartment. I slipped inside, bypassed the four mail boxes set in the wall and took the shabbily carpeted steps two at a time up to my apartment door.

I fished my keys out of my pocket and opened it.

Did I mention that this was the worst day ever?

"Jerry?" My voice sounded small and wounded, and I hated it. I blinked slowly and heard my bag hit the floor just inside the door, the contents spilling out over the tired brown carpet in a slosh of paper and books.

I blinked slowly as my boyfriend stood up from the couch, spilling the woman who'd been straddling his cock to the living room floor. My face felt hot and flushed and I shook, tears traced their way from my eyes to my chin in twin hot lines.

"Shit! Everett! What are you doing home!?" he demanded.

"That's what you have to say to me!?" I screeched outraged.

"Baby, who is she?" the girl asked. I blinked at her as she pulled her too-short jean skirt down over herself, her long legs terminating in a pair of clear plastic platform stripper heels. She wore a fire-engine-red lace bra and her matching thong lay in a damp puddle on my coffee table. I shuddered with revulsion.

"I *was* his girlfriend! Who the fuck are you?" I demanded.

"Girlfriend!? I thought you said you lived here with your sister!" She glared over at Jerry, who was trying to fasten his pants.

I put my hands on my knees and doubled over and tried to breathe. I gagged both on the smell of sex permeating the air and the fact that he was decidedly *not* wearing a condom as he shoved himself back into his pants.

"Oh, my God, this isn't happening," I heard myself say.

"Baby, come on, she doesn't mean anything; she's just some chick I met when I was out with the guys last week. Let's talk about this." I straightened and raked him with a cold hard glare.

"You want to *talk about this!?*" I shrieked.

"God! Fuck you, you fucking jerk!" the girl pulled on a tight-fitting red top and grabbed up her panties and her purse from the coffee table. "I'm out of here," she muttered and I closed my eyes.

"God, yes, please... get out," I said, swallowing hard to keep my gorge from rising.

She made a derisive noise.

"Shit, maybe if you were a better lay he wouldn't have had to come to *me*," was her parting shot as she brushed past me and went out the door. I crumbled a little on the inside but I would be damned if I would let it show.

"Seriously, Jerry?" I demanded. He leveled me with his unremarkable brown eyes and ran a hand through his sex-mussed dark hair. I closed my eyes so I didn't have to see him standing there shirtless and barefoot, but closing my eyes just brought the image of the woman with the long dark hair riding him on my couch. I shuddered in revulsion.

I *so* needed to get tested.

"Babe, it's not like that, I was weak. I mean, she has a point, I have needs and it's not exactly like you've been there to meet them." Cold laughter filled the small apartment and I realized it was pouring out of me. I snapped my mouth shut.

"For the last two or three years I've been getting up at three o'clock in the morning to *go to work* Jerry! To keep us in this shitty apartment. When I'm not working my ass off to make ends meet, I'm in *school*! I'm fucking *tired* and it's not like you do anything to make it better! You sit on your ass playing video games and live off your daddy's money! So excuse me if after putting in sixteen hour days for weeks on end my fucking panties won't drop for your half-assed notion of foreplay!" I crossed my arms more to hold myself together, hold myself in, than anything. I felt blasted apart, angry, hurt, and exhausted like a piece of rope frayed to its last string and that last string was at its limit.

I stared across the small space at the man I'd loved since high school and wondered when and where it all went wrong.

This was easily the worst day of my life so far.

## 2

Dray...

I watched Everett Moran slide behind the glass door and take the stairs to her apartment two at a time like she couldn't get away from me fast enough and felt myself frown. She was the kind of pretty I could get used to looking at, despite the drowned-rat look she was sporting right that second. Long, light brown hair with golden highlights braided over her shoulder, the end curling tantalizingly over her full breasts. Wide steel blue eyes and a lush mouth... Shit, the girl was hot!

I'd fully expected her to be gone by the time I'd closed up shop and the rain had really started. It had surprised the hell out of me, seeing her standing there soaked to the skin by the time I'd gotten out and fired up Sadie. I racked my neck back and forth to pop it and listened to and felt a satisfying crunch in either direction.

She'd gotten nervous and tense all of a sudden and I'd caught her eyes roving my jacket and cut. Wasn't her fault. She didn't know any better. A lot of people look and see biker and it's like their brains shut off or something. Once upon a time, Sacred Hearts were in among the one-percenter's, but that was a long time ago. We were firmly in the top ninety-nine now but you wouldn't know it by the uniform.

I gave my passenger seat where she'd been sitting a cursory going over and spotted something rectangular, plastic, and electronic-looking on the passenger side floor board, the gray case barely standing out against the black carpet and mat. I bent over and picked it up. I slid it apart and my eyebrows went up. A graphing calculator. Hadn't seen one of these since high school.

I sighed. She'd probably need it for whatever classes she was taking. I couldn't say I was entirely disappointed that I had a chance to look her over one more time, so I shut off my car and ducked out into the downpour. I dashed for the entrance she'd disappeared into.

She was in apartment 2A. I have what they call a photographic memory. The scientific term is eidetic. Once she had shown me her driver's license it had been all over. Couldn't forget it if I wanted to. *Everett Mary Moran, born November first nineteen ninety-three.* Twenty, a little under two years younger than me. I'd turned twenty-two over the summer. Her twenty-first was coming up in just a few weeks. A leggy brunette crashed down the steps and knocked into my shoulder on her way out as I was going in. "Watch it, jerk!" she cried before she dashed down the sidewalk in her stripper shoes. I glared after her and wondered where the fucking fire was at.

I heard it as I headed up the stairs.

"Come off it, Evy!" a male voice scoffed. I heard a choked incredulous noise.

"Oh, you are not putting this off on me!" Everett shouted. "You're the one that couldn't keep your dick in your pants, Jerry!"

"And I'm telling you I wouldn't have to have gone elsewhere if you weren't such a frigid cunt!" he shouted back. I cleared the doorway, scowling and looked into the small, dilapidated apartment. Everett stood, back to me, arms crossed over her chest, hugging herself; she was dripping onto the carpet and from the looks of where it was saturated hadn't moved from that spot since she'd gone through the door.

"How long?" she demanded and the cheating bastard smirked at her.

"Long enough," he said and his voice was haughty.

"You son of a bitch," Everett whispered and he scowled. Took me a second to realize he was scowling at me.

"Who the fuck are you?" he demanded and Everett whirled. Her face was a study in raw naked pain. Tears slid from her too-wide steel blue eyes and she looked like she was ready to fly apart any second. Water dripped from the end of her not quite blonde, not quite brown, braid and tendrils of it stuck to her face and clung to the side of her neck. She was shivering but I couldn't tell you if it was from shock, the cold, anger or a combination of all three. Our eyes met and I felt my lips thin. Her mouth hung open slightly in surprise and then she closed it and her eyes. Her shoulders dropped slightly in defeat and when her lips parted again it was to say,

"He's Dray." Her voice was hollow, empty…

*He's Dray.*

Not, '*he's the mechanic*', or '*he's nobody*' or '*just the guy that gave me a ride home when your punk ass wouldn't answer the phone*'… I don't know why, but her acknowledgment of my name gave her a few points in my book.

My eyes cut back over to her boyfriend and my lip curled in derision. His dark brown hair was sticking up at every angle and he was shirtless and barefoot, the button on his jeans undone. His narrow chest spoke of a lack of time spent at the gym and in a split second I had his measure.

"You mind? My bitch of a girlfriend and I are trying to have it out over here," he said, and I felt my lips curl into an unfriendly smile. I put some heat and purpose into my gaze.

"Go ahead. Call her a bitch in front of me again. See what happens," I voiced tonelessly and I swear the fucker flinched. I was a scary man when I wanted to be. I was shit-your-pants terrifying when I needed to be. I settled somewhere in between for this particular assclown.

"Dray, I'm so sorry you had to see this. What… What can I do for you?" Everett asked, voice barely above a whisper.

"You forgot your calculator, fell out of your bag." I held it out to her and captured her eyes with my own. They widened, again, too much white around those baby blues for my tastes.

"You want to stay here with this assclown?" I asked her softly and he choked incredulously and started spouting off. I ignored him and kept her eyes pinned with mine. I could see it all over her face. She was a hurtin' unit and she didn't want to stay.

"Are you fucking kidding me, Everett?" He yelled at her when she'd been silent too long. "Do you even know this guy?" he railed at her, and that snapped her out of our silent exchange.

She jerked as if she'd been slapped and turned on him slowly. "Up until I walked in here and saw that hooker riding your cock on my couch, I *thought* I knew *you*. Turns out I didn't know a goddamned thing!" Her voice was level and low and I smirked at the assclown. I felt a little thrill of pride at her words.

"Everett," I said and she turned back to me.

"Go pack your shit. I'll take you out of here." I crossed my arms and leaned a shoulder against the door frame and nodded at her to go do what needed doing.

"This is fucking unbelievable," the douche-du-jour uttered and I hit him with another scary look.

"I'd G-T-F-O if I were you. At least until she's done," I said. Everett hadn't moved yet; he was standing between her and their bedroom. Place was a fucking one-bedroom. He crossed his arms and looked smug.

"You're going to have to come back sometime," he told her. I took a step into their space and watched as she raised her eyes to meet his, a look of steely determination crossed her face.

"Did you fuck her in our bed?" she asked him and his nasty smile was pretty much all the answer she needed.

"When I get back you need to have your shit out of here," she said, voice cold.

"Uh, you're forgetting something, baby. My name's the one on the lease." He crossed his arms over his narrow chest and had the balls to look smug.

"You're forgetting something too... I was the one paying the majority of the rent and bills." She made to go past him and he caught her by the upper arm. She recoiled and I took a step forward. His eyes cut to me and he let her go. She passed him by and I heard her rummaging through her closet and drawers. I saw her fling a suitcase open on their rumpled bed and she started stuffing things into it, a laptop, a photo album, some yearbooks... I sighed. This was going to take a minute and fuck if I knew if Sadie was going to hold it all.

She tossed clothes into the suitcase, zipped it closed and went into the kitchen, returning with one of those white garbage bags. The rest of her clothes went into it. She turned to me, and, tears tracking unhindered down her smooth cheeks, said, "Thank you for getting me out of here." Her eyes swam with gratitude as well as moisture and I nodded and took her suitcase from her. The thing was heavy but not too bad.

She stooped and picked up her falling-apart backpack, giving it a bit of a boost with her knee like you would when picking up a small kid. She hugged the mess to her chest, with the trash bag dangling forlorn from her hand. I stood aside and let her go ahead of me. I followed her down the stairs. I didn't want him trying anything and if he came after me I could beat the brakes off him and neatly claim self-defense.

I watched Everett's tense shoulders, her head held high as she went down the stairs in front of me. I wasn't in the business of taking in strays but what the hell why not? I mean, look how it had turned out for Trigger.

She ducked into the pouring rain and I went out behind her. I opened up Sadie and put the seat forward shoving her shit into the back. She got into the passenger side when I put the seat back down and I got into the driver's seat. Her boyfriend didn't even try to come down stairs and stop her or to even argue. Fucking little cock-bite. I scowled and fired Sadie up.

"Where can I take you?" I asked her, and she turned wide and frightened eyes to me. Scared, sure, but I didn't think it was of me, more of the unknown.

"I don't know, just... just – away from here – please." She got onto her phone and was doing something. I scowled and pulled out onto the street. I glanced over and caught her swiping at the tears leaking out of her eyes. She was still soaked to the skin, so really she was just smearing the wet into other wet on her face. I felt a twinge of sorry for her.

"Texting a friend or relative?" I asked.

"Transferring money from the checking account he has access to, to the savings account he can't touch," she answered quietly and my eyebrows went up. Smart girl.

"Where your folks live?" I asked her.

"Mom died giving birth to me, dad passed from a heart attack last year," she murmured.

"Grandparents?" I asked.

"Dead both sides," she said.

Shit.

"Who's your BFF?" I asked her. She looked at me, sky blue eyes clouding with some undefined emotion.

"Can you pull over?" she asked.

"What?" I frowned.

"Pull over!" she cried and I jerked the wheel toward the curb. She jerked on the door handle and stumbled out of the car, landing on her knees in the mud and grass between the curb and the sidewalk. She heaved and whatever she'd eaten that day came up.

I totally appreciated that she did not just puke in what I considered my second born. My firstborn was my bike, would be until the day I ever really *had* children of my own. *If* I ever had kids of my own. I sat as patiently as I could while she puked and cried, and let my thoughts wander in every which direction I could that would keep my mind off of her pitiful heaving. I so did *not* do puking well, be it from the boys, or pretty lost orphan girls who wandered into my garage.

It was about this time it hit me.

*Oh my fucking god what was I doing!?*

I sighed and scrubbed my face with my hands. Shit. In for a penny in for a pound, whatever the fuck that even meant. I frowned.

My head was all over the map since meeting this chick. I wondered vaguely if Trigger had felt half so panicked or confused when he'd picked up his Sunshine Girl on the side of the road last March.

My thoughts were wrenched back to the present when she dry heaved loudly a couple of times causing me to wince in sympathy. I opened up the glove box and pulled out my emergency toiletry kit. Had one in here and one on the bike. It held the bare minimum. Travel toothbrush, mini-tube of toothpaste, mini-thing of mouth-wash, those little hotel bottles of shampoo and conditioner, and a sliver of a foil-wrapped bar of soap.

She was in luck, I'd never actually had an occasion to use this one, but if I had a mouthful of puke going on, I wouldn't care if the toothbrush had been used by someone or not. Not sure if she held the same principle. Everybody was different when it came to their toothbrush habits. I was trying really damn hard to concentrate on anything other than the sounds of her retching and thankfully, by the time I rounded the front of my car, she seemed to be over it for the most part and was staggering to her feet. I fished out the toothbrush and loaded it with paste.

"Here, never been used. Promise." She took it from me and stuck it in her mouth, swishing it around. She spit on the ground and I gave her a half smile and a few more points for not being embarrassed about getting the job done. She tilted her head back and opened her mouth wide for some rainfall, swished it around in her mouth and spit again. I uncapped the mouthwash and handed that to her too. She poured a slight mouthful past her lips, swished it and spit.

"Thanks," she said, eyeing me speculatively.

"Yeah." I crammed everything back into the little clear vinyl case and zipped it shut. I shrugged and handed it to her. "Yours now," I said, and she took it with shaking fingers.

"I don't have any place to go," she blurted. I'd never been in her position, I never would be with the MC at my back, but I could see where it would take paramount concern over just about anything else she'd be thinking. I gave her a grimacing smile.

"I guess I kind of figured as much when you started puking," I said and she barked a harsh laugh that was so much bitter broken glass it almost hurt to hear it come out of her. I grimaced a little harder and smiled a little less. Man, no one deserved to be in her position. Nobody.

"Get in the car," I told her.

"I already told you I don't have any place to go," she said steadily.

"Fine," I said and shrugged. I wanted to help her, but I didn't really know how to do it gently and fuck, if she didn't want to go, there wasn't anything I could do to make her. I got into the car, my hair plastered to my skull and turned on the defrosters full blast to clear the steam from the inside of the windshield. She got in quickly.

"You have my stuff," she said hollowly. I looked over my shoulder at the meager pile of possessions in my back seat.

"Yeah," I said and with a check to make sure nothing was coming, pulled back out onto the rural street.

"Um, I guess take me to a hotel?" she said.

Yeah... what had been seen could not be unseen, leastways not by me. She barely had enough to afford the diagnostic I was supposed to do on her car, let alone any repairs that would need to be made for her to live in it. I tightened my grip on the steering wheel and huffed out a harsh breath. This was so not my usual M.O. but fuck it...

"Stop worrying about it for right now. I've got a spare room at the house." It was a total lie but my dad was out on a run and she didn't need to know the particulars. I could at least give her a place tonight, get her dry and let her get her shit straight. She was staring at me unabashedly now.

"Why are you doing this for me?" she asked and it was like her true-blue eyes saw right through me so I didn't try to bullshit her.

"I don't know." I said honestly, and truth was I didn't. The man I was a year ago, hell, of a little more than six months ago, would have been like *sucks to be you!* and would have driven right on by while she stood in the rain waiting for a man that would never show.

I flashed back onto the spring memorial lake run, of Ashton Granger's wide, frightened eyes as I'd forced that kiss on her. On the naked disappointment in my father's eyes when he'd had to intercede. That's what killed me. The look on my dad's face. A man that had always looked on his only son in pride. I'd fucked that up. Dashed it upon the rocks and choked the everliving shit out of it and I'd realized that he was the only parent I had left and fuck, if *he* was disappointed what would my mom have thought? That had been a turning point and a half for me.

"Uh, Dray?" Everett's husky voice interrupted my thought pattern and I glanced at her.

"What?" I asked.

"Where did you go?" she asked frowning, an edge of fear crowding her fine boned features.

"Nowhere why?" I asked.

"You just ran a stop sign, didn't you hear that driver honking?" she asked, frowning.

I shifted uncomfortably in my seat. "Sorry," I muttered. "Thinking too hard, I guess."

"Okay, but in case you hadn't noticed, I'm having like a *really* shitty day. Like the worst, and I really don't want to top it off by dying." She put her head back against the seat and looked so drawn it was borderline scary and the laugh that had been bubbling up died in my throat. Still, I couldn't help the genuine smile that took over my face.

"So your car breaks down, your guy is a total douche and you *still* can crack a joke?" I asked. Her expression darkened.

"I was also late to work, got chewed out by my boss, and burned myself." She turned her hand in my direction to show me the angry red mark on it.

"That and I'm pretty sure I'm going to fail statistics, which I need to graduate; I'm pretty much homeless; borderline destitute; and with no way to get to work in the morning, probably fired." She sniffed and her eyes welled up again.

"Jesus, girl, one thing at a time," I said, pulling onto my street.

"Sorry," she uttered and more tears slipped down her creamy skin.

"Naw, I just don't want you to puke again. That shit's nasty." She blinked at me and I tried a smile on her. She almost smiled back but then turned her head to look at my house as I hit the signal to turn into my driveway.

My house was a squat one-story with a basement and a detached garage in back. White with hunter green trim and well kept, my mother had loved this house so my dad and I kept it in good repair right down to the lawn and flowerbeds. Inside it was small but cozy, a two bedroom one bath built in the 1920's with enough hidden nooks and crannies to make it worth it to my dad when he'd bought it for them during his more illicit activities for the MC.

I pulled up into the driveway. The garage was really only big enough for the tools, lawn equipment, and the bikes so Sadie stayed out here. I killed the engine and looked over at Everett Moran. She was only a couple of inches shorter than me, so about five foot six, but she was slender and fine-boned but not too thin. She had a lithe figure, all graceful curves and, sue me, some tits to die for under her camisole and soggy form fitting sweater.

She looked pretty wrecked. Makeup mostly washed off by the rain and tears, skin pale and clammy. Eyes bright with yet *more* tears. Her hair clinging to her face where it escaped her braid... I had half a mind to get her settled and go pound the shit out of her ex-boyfriend. Not sure what it was about her that tripped my trigger with the protective instincts and all, but she had. It was pretty damned uncomfortable to be honest. I sat up, my leather jacket making a wet tearing sound against the leather of my seat where they'd adhered to each other with rainwater. The sound startled Everett who jumped and I frowned. First time ever I wished I looked a little less scary. That was new.

I got out and came around to her side. I opened her door and she got out stiffly. I pulled the trash bag stuffed full of shoes and clothes and turned for the house.

"Come on. I'll get the rest in a minute," I unlocked the front door and she trailed into the house. I went to my room, glad I made the bed every morning. I wanted her to believe it was a spare bedroom. I set the trash bag on the floor by the bed.

"Find something to wear that's dry," I ordered and went out into the hall to find her some fresh towels. She set the toiletry bag from my glove box on the bed and knelt into a crouch, keeping her muddy knees off the hardwood. She scored a few more points with me.

I found two large towels that smelled freshly laundered and I handed them to her. She had some things over her arm and picked up the bath kit.

I pointed towards the bathroom door between the bedroom doors.

"Through there, take a hot shower and get warm. Take your time." She nodded mutely, subdued and just drained.

I went to go get the rest of her crap but her voice stopped me from the bathroom door.

"Dray..."

"Yeah?" I asked.

"Thank you," she murmured and I could see that she meant it.

"Yeah, sure. No problem," I answered and I was surprised to find that *I* meant it.

**3**

______

Everett...

I shut the bathroom door firmly and rested my forehead against it for a moment. I breathed out a long slow breath and turned the old fashioned lock with my fingers, satisfied with the click it made. I turned around and eyed the old claw-foot style tub. It looked really inviting for a bath but I didn't dare impose like that. Instead, I started the shower.

It took me a minute to get the shower going. There seemed to be more knobs than I was used to. I was used to hot and cold and pull up on the thingy, but this had three knobs. The center one is what started the shower. I got out of my wet clothes and folded them neatly on the closed lid of the toilet rather than leave them in a sodden heap on the black and white tile floor. The bathmat was cushy beneath my bare feet and I stepped over the high edge of the bath tub, the shampoo, conditioner and sliver of soap clutched in one hand. I set them down and unbound my hair.

The small vials of hair product smelled like white citrus which wasn't so bad, but were barely enough to get the job done with as thick and long as my hair is. I used the sliver of soap until it was gone.

It too smelled like white citrus. Usually I used bath soap that smelled like lilac but I hadn't thought to grab any of that out of the apartment... just clothes and some other sentimental items.

I washed my face, then everything else twice, using the sliver of soap until it was gone. I was sure I would never be able to shower off my sheer revulsion at Jerry, and Lord knows, I would never be able to scrub away that image of him with that other woman straddling his lap on my couch, his bare cock disappearing deep inside her. I heaved again and did my best to banish the image from my mind. It was my number-one prerogative to get into a clinic as soon as possible and get tested for every STD known to man.

I washed up quickly, despite Dray's admonition to take my time and still felt just as dirty as when I'd stepped into the shower. I dried myself completely, dressed in my pajamas which I was now ridiculously self-conscious in, and set to doing the best I could at getting all the water out of my hair. Satisfied that it was as good as it was going to get, I dragged the mass over my right shoulder and braided it swiftly, efficiently, and tightly, reusing my hair tie to bind it at the end.

I stood in front of the fogged-up mirror, my reflection pale and indistinct. I looked down at myself. I wore a black ribbed tank top with a racerback and a pair of men's blue-and-white-striped boxer shorts. I looked down at my pale pink chipped toenail polish and sighed, taking in a deep breath, holding it in before letting it out slowly and completely. I gathered my things and the towels and opened the bathroom door uncertainly.

"Um, Dray?" I called out softly.

"Kitchen," was his terse, one word reply. I rounded the archway leading from the small hall into the living space and looked right into the open kitchen. Dray stood at the stove and I blinked at his profile.

He was naked from the waist up, his lower half clad in a pair of loose-fitting black cotton lounge pants that were slung low on his hips. He was muscular, the definition in his arms as he stirred a pot on the stove spectacular, as was the muscle definition along his back and ribs. He turned his head to the side and his dark gaze landed on the dirty clothes and towels in my arms.

"Go ahead and ditch those in the hamper." He jerked his head towards the small mud room behind him. I skirted around the counter and put the towels in the proper receptacle and found an empty plastic grocery bag on top of the recycling bin. I put my clothes into it and tied the top as I reentered the kitchen. The tile was chilly under my bare feet and Dray was watching me.

His upper arm on the side closest to me was taken up by a black and white tattoo of a lifelike human heart wrapped in barbed wire. The valves of the heart seemed to morph into cold steel pipes which belched flames, hovering above the image, seemingly suspended in the air. He flipped something in a skillet and the way the muscle moved beneath his skin caused the heart to throb once as if it were beating. I found the image captivating and found myself moving closer to get a better look.

"What does it mean?" I asked softly.

"Symbol for the MC," he said and nodded towards his jacket which hung on the back of one of the dining room chairs.

I glanced at it, and sure enough the big patch in the center was a white background with a red bleeding heart on it. Wrapped around the blue veined heart was barbed wire and the valves morphed into gray steel, which I belatedly realized, were supposed to be tailpipes. Orange, red, and yellow fire hovered above the heart; a crescent patch arching above the heart read 'Sacred Hearts'; another curving below it, cradling the image, bore the state we were in.

"Oh." I said.

"Go put that down," he grunted and I nodded and went into the guest room and set the bag with my soiled things next to my small pile in the center of the hardwood floor. I returned to the kitchen just as he was plating a grilled cheese sandwich.

"What's on your back?" he asked and I turned around and brought my shirt up, keeping my front covered , letting the ribbed cotton material ride on the back of my neck. The air in the room was cool against my naked skin. Dray gave a low whistle.

My back bore a set of grayscale angel wings, the Irish trinity knot between my shoulder blades where the lifelike wings sprouted from. The ink I displayed dipped below the waistband of the boxer shorts I wore, the tips of the wings ending midway down each ass cheek.

"Had it done after my da' died," I said, pulling my shirt back down.

I heard the plate click against the table and turned around. The sandwich sat next to a steaming mug of tomato soup. I smiled and sank into a chair, tears springing to my eyes.

"Miss him?" he asked softly.

"Yeah but it's not that... he used to always make me grilled cheese and tomato soup this time of year." I sniffed and smiled up at him. Dray looked surprised.

"Oh, it's just what we had in the house." He shrugged a shoulder nonchalantly.

"You even made the soup with milk instead of water," I observed. I raised my eyes to meet his, he arched one dark eyebrow, his full lips twisting up on one side.

"Isn't that the way it's supposed to be done?" he asked and I smiled.

He brought over his plate and soup and took the seat at the head of the table, where his jacket hung, so we were sitting at a right angle to one another.

"Where do you work?" he asked blowing on a spoonful of soup.

"Quick-Stop Coffee, it's that 24-hour coffee shack over on Allen Road," I murmured, timidly sipping my soup from its mug so I wouldn't burn myself. Warm, rich tomato flavor slid across my tongue and I felt some tension ease from my shoulders and back.

Dray eyed me sideways and took a bite of his grilled cheese after dipping it into his soup.

"What time you gotta be there?" he asked.

"Four." I said and he shrugged.

"That's not so bad," he said and I smiled to myself.

"In the morning... I get off work at twelve thirty and two days a week have class at the community college. Not tomorrow though," I sighed.

Dray was looking at me like I was some sort of fascinating alien creature.

"What the hell time do you go to bed?" he asked.

"Well, I get up at three so usually I'm in bed and asleep by eight if I want to get enough," I explained.

"Shit. You're making me a free goddamn coffee," he muttered, then, "I can't believe I'm going to do this." I blinked at him.

"Do what?" I asked.

"Get my ass up the usual time I go to bed to take you to work," he groused.

"I... You don't have to do that," I said taken aback.

He looked me in the eyes, his dark gaze burning and intense as it bore into my own.

"You're right. I don't," he said. He left the *'but I'm going to anyway'* silent but his eyes communicated it all the same. We finished our small meal and I felt marginally better, but exhausted.

"Come on," he stood up and nodded towards the guest room. I stood and began to clear my plate but he took it from me and set it down.

"Bed, Everett," he intoned gravely.

"Okay." I nodded and rubbed my eyes.

"Good night, Dray," I said to him, and "Thank you for everything."

He pursed his lips and looked me over, nodding once and I slipped off to the guest room, shutting the door softly behind me. I switched on the light and looked at the room. The walls were a tasteful slate gray, the hardwood floors dark with a black area rug. The bed was dark wood, and heavy, queen-sized and filling the small room. There was an armoire and a dresser that matched the bed and, curious, I eased open one of the drawers, blinking at the overabundance of socks in it.

*Since when does guest room furniture contain clothing?* I wondered. I opened another drawer after sliding the sock drawer shut. Tee shirts. Another held jeans. I shut everything carefully and quietly and sat on the end of the bed. I wasn't in a guest room... I was in Dray's room.

*But why would he lie to me?* I closed my eyes. *To make me more comfortable?*

I thought about it and came to the conclusion that thinking about it was just going to give me a headache. I switched out the light and pulled back the blankets. With a soft sigh I slid between the high-thread-count, black sheets. I closed my eyes and lay on my side breathing in Dray's scent which enveloped me. It was spicy and masculine with a hint of wind and road. I lay there, lulled by the sound of the rain in the eaves, trickling down the drainpipe. My thoughts drifted back to Jerry, to everything that had happened today. I'd been burned in more ways than one, and it *hurt*. I sniffed and curled in on myself. I shuddered and dragged in a tortured breath. A low moan emitted from my chest and broke on a sob. I wept bitterly; scared, angry, and alone.

*Had Jerry given me something? How could I not have seen what he was doing? Who was Dray really? Was this the stupidest thing I'd ever done or what!? What was I going to do? How was I going to survive? I couldn't call Mandy... Couldn't impose on her and her folks, could I? No... God, how could I have been so stupid!?*

I lay in the bed of a man I didn't know the first thing about, these thoughts and more chasing around in my head and I cried myself to sleep to the sound of the pouring rain.

# 4

**D**ray...

I lay flat on my back on my dad's bed with my hands behind my head staring at the ceiling. She'd tried to cry quietly but the problem with old houses was the walls were paper-thin. I didn't know how to comfort her. I couldn't fix it, so I'd finished the dishes and had come in here and listened to her cry, which bothered me.

Trouble was I didn't know what bothered me more, the fact I didn't know what to do to help her feel better or the fact that I didn't know what to do about *wanting* to. These thoughts and ruminations kept me awake, staring at the ceiling for a long damned time. Now it was only a couple of hours until she'd be up and I hadn't slept at all. The door swung open and the light flared on and I threw up my hand to shield my eyes.

"The fuck you doin' in here, Boy?" my dad asked, annoyed. I sighed. Water dripped from his riding leathers and I sat up abruptly.

"Shhhh!" I hissed and his eyes, a mirror of my own, burned a hole right through me. If I were a lesser man, I'd be shitting myself, but I wasn't a lesser man. I was my father's son, so I gave him his own look right back. I got up and motioned for him to follow. I eased open my bedroom door and he looked over my shoulder.

Everett was on her side, facing the door, a slight wrinkle between her brows but at least she slept. I didn't think she was getting much rest out of it though. I eased the door back shut and scowled at my father and MC President and he scowled right back, but he wasn't pissed at me.

"What happened? Where'd you get her?" he asked.

I motioned for him to meet me in the kitchen.

"She came rolling into the shop today, her car dyin' half way into the drive," I murmured when he joined me. I set the coffee to brewing.

"So why is she in your room and what're you doin' in mine?" he asked.

"She kept trying to call her assclown boyfriend and he wasn't picking up. She went out talkin' on her phone, shit all spilling out of her ripped bag and I thought she was on the line with him. I closed up shop and didn't think anything of it, but here it is like a half hour later and it's pouring down rain and she's standing out at the street by our sign looking like a drowned rat. He never showed up, turned out she'd been talking at his voice mail." I poured us each a cup of coffee.

"Still doesn't explain what she's doing in your bed and why you ain't in there with her," he grunted and I smiled thinly.

"So I take her home," I shrugged, took a drink of my coffee and kept going, "Thing is this calculator dropped out of her bag onto Sadie's floor so I go to give it to her and walk right into the middle of this domestic dispute." My father's eyebrows went up.

"He hit her?" he asked.

"Naw, didn't get the chance," I thought about how he'd grabbed her arm, "But it was headed that way." My dad raised his eyebrows at me and I went on, "He never answered his phone, because he was banging some other chick on their couch. She caught 'em at it when she walked through the door." I hung my head and scratched an itch behind my ear.

"She pays the majority of the rent and bills, he sits on his ass and then has the balls to tell her that him banging this broad is *her* fault for her bein' too tired to put out on the regular." I crossed my arms. My dad leaned back in his chair and let out an explosive breath.

"Assclown," he said.

"Yeah. So *she* reminds *him* that she pays the rent and bills and he turns around and says to her that his name is the only one on the lease... It wasn't going anywhere, so I tell her to pack her shit and I'll take her anywhere she wants." He looked me over.

"And she wanted to come here?" he asked.

"Mom died giving birth to her, her dad died of a heart attack last year. She says take her to a hotel, that she doesn't have anybody, but she says it as she's moving what little cash she has out of her checking into her savings where he can't get to it," I said.

"You saw how much she's got?" I gave him a flat look and he waved me off. He knew damn well about my memory for things I'd seen.

"Hundred and twenty bucks," I affirmed and his eyes widened.

"She tells me she got up late for work, got an ass-chewing from her boss, burned herself at work, is in danger of failing one of her math classes, her car takes a shit, her boyfriend takes an even bigger one on her... all in the same day. I felt sorry for her. All her shit fits in one trash bag, one suitcase, and a ripped backpack. It was fucking ridiculous." I uncrossed my arms and raked a hand through my hair.

"Doesn't hurt that she's easy on the eyes." He gave me a sly grin, his teeth white in his black beard.

"Naw," I said in agreement.

"So what time is she getting up?" I grimaced and checked the clock.

"Forty-five minutes or so. She works four in the morning to twelve-thirty at that coffee place on Allen," I grimaced.

"Well, sorry to piss on your parade," he said getting up. "I'm home early and I'm going to bed. Have fun on the couch." He trudged into his room and I gave him a sour look. He shut the door behind him with a chuckle.

Ten minutes later, Everett peeked around the corner, rubbing her eyes.

"Guest room, huh?" she asked softly.

"Figured it out then?" I asked her.

"Didn't take much." She slid into the seat my dad vacated, "Was that your dad?"

"Yeah." I wondered how much she'd heard.

"Tell him what a pathetic charity case I am?" she asked and I shook my head.

"No," I said and she smiled and it did something to her face, she went from sweet and pretty to fucking beautiful.

"Liar," she said and I scowled; the smile disappeared and fear slid behind those steely baby blues of hers.

"I told him what happened. You had a shit day. I am a liar, at least about my room, so I'll let that slide," I gave her. "But know this, I don't lie about the important things." I leaned back in my seat and contemplated her.

"Why *did* you lie about it being your room?" she asked thoughtfully.

"Wanted you to be comfortable. Didn't think you would be if you knew you were sleeping in my room. He wasn't supposed to be back until tomorrow night." I shrugged.

"Why?" she asked.

"Why'd he come home early? Fucked if I know."

"No, why are you being so nice to me?" she asked softly. I looked her over.

"Couldn't tell you," I said and I was being honest. Maybe in some small way it was my atonement for being a dick to Ashton Granger when Trig had brought her in off the road last spring, beat to fuck and bloodied by her now-dead husband.

Though I suppose helping Reaver kill that twisted fuck had been atonement enough for that particular sin, even if it meant putting a blacker one on my busted-ass soul. I searched Everett's face while she searched mine. I liked that this chick was cool with silence.

She stood up abruptly and padded back into my room. A moment later the bathroom door shut. I sighed, got up and went into my room and pulled on some clothes. When the bathroom door opened again I was sitting on the edge of my neatly made bed lacing up my boots. She padded in in her sock-covered feet and sat on the floor, pulling on her knee high black riding boots and zipping them up on the inside of her leg.

She wore form fitting dark jeans that kissed her legs like a second skin. Over them she wore a black long-sleeved shirt that hugged her curves, the neckline low; a simple silver necklace chain with that Irish tri-knot thing hanging from it graced her long throat. Her hair had been reworked into a fresh braid and she wore subtle, tastefully-done makeup that made her eyes stand out larger-than-life from her face. She was feminine without being small and she carried herself well. I realized I liked what I saw the more I looked at her but still, she'd been through hell in a handbasket yesterday and I was nobody's rebound.

I went to the closet and dug into the bottom of it. I pulled out an old army backpack and handed it to her.

"It's not pretty but it'll work," I told her. She looked at it and stood up.

"Are you sure?" she asked.

"I don't use it anymore." I shrugged. It had some old Sacred Heart MC patches on it but I didn't think it would matter much.

"Thanks," she murmured, taking it from me. Her blue eyes met mine and were still full of pain. I sighed.

"It'll get better," I grunted and as I brushed past her and out into the living room, I almost missed it when she answered.

"I know, it already is..." She spent several minutes transferring things from her torn pack to my old one and came out with it slung over her shoulder.

"Ready?" I asked her.

"I'm not sure what to do with my stuff," she said, shifting from foot to foot.

"Leave it. We'll talk after you get off work," I said and she nodded.

I shrugged into my jacket and cut and followed her out of the house. I didn't bother locking up. Whoever wanted to break in with my pops home would have a real bad time. I opened her car door for her and then wondered what the hell I was doing. She slid into the seat and tucked the bag between her knees, and I closed it shaking my head. It was still dark out and I was tired by now, but there was nothing to be done about it. I backed out of the driveway and hit my lights.

"Twelve to one is when I take my lunch, I'll come by and get you," I said.

"Actually, can I just meet you at your shop?" she asked softly.

"Why?" I asked frowning. I wanted to make sure she wasn't going back to assclown's place by herself. She was quiet too long and I turned to look at her, her head was bowed, just when I thought I was going to have to repeat myself she took a breath to speak.

"I need to go to the clinic," she said flatly, her voice filled with tension.

"Let me see," I said, assuming she was talking about her burn. She turned wide blue eyes, the color wrung out of them in the dark, on me.

"I'm sorry?" she said.

"Your hand. Let me see it," I said. She held out her left hand as we rolled up to a stoplight and I flipped on the dome light. I resisted the urge to touch her. I could have taken advantage of the situation, taken her hand in mine to find out if her skin was as soft as it looked, but I didn't. Instead, I looked over the red mark on her skin. It didn't look bad.

"Doesn't look bad," I said and she laughed a little nervously.

"Jerry wasn't wearing a condom yesterday." She swallowed hard and rushed out, "I need to get tested..." her voice fell off at the end and she wouldn't look in my direction, fixing her gaze out the tinted glass. I felt like a grade 'A' fucking idiot. Duh. Of course she would want to get tested.

"Shit. Sorry," I said and flipped out the overhead. I pulled smoothly through the intersection when the light allowed for it.

A long silence fell between us. Just as I caught sight of the neon sign for her coffee shack I came to both a realization and a decision. I was crap at this. Being a supportive-type person had never really been my thing, especially for a chick, but something about Everett Moran made me want to try. So I decided then and there that I would do my best.

I turned to look at her, following the long graceful curve of her throat, her pale skin glimmering in that flat expanse of skin left bare by the plunging neckline of her top before the lovely curve of her breasts took over. The trinity knot necklace set at the center with what I guessed to be an emerald winked in the watery street light as she shifted to drag the pack I'd given her into her lap.

I know she'd been through a shit storm because of her assclown ex, but I couldn't help my gaze slipping lower over the generous swell of her breasts. I liked what I saw. What red blooded male wouldn't? She had a nice rack, the seam of her cleavage flawless. She didn't catch me looking, so what was the harm?

"I'll pick you up at twelve-thirty," I said as she opened her car door, "Drive you to the nearest clinic unless you had one in mind." She looked me over, searching my face from hairline to chin.

"There's a Planned Parenthood over on Twentieth Avenue West. I went there last year," she said softly.

"Fine, make an appointment if you can. If you can't we'll wait," I said. She nodded thoughtfully.

"How do you take your coffee?" she asked.

"Surprise me," I said and she got out. I waited and she came back a minute later and handed me a can of energy drink. I grinned.

"Good guess." I told her and got her to smile.

"Um, I forgot a bag of stuff in the trunk of my car," she said, and it was like she was afraid to ask... I nodded.

"It'll be in the back when I come to pick you up," I said. She nodded carefully.

"Thank you," she said and I watched her walk across the dark parking lot.

I didn't leave until she was safely inside the little shack, couldn't bring myself to do it. This wasn't the most upstanding neighborhood during the day, let alone in the dark of night. Once she was inside I put Sadie in gear and pulled out of the lot. I went to the garage. I was tired, sure, but it wasn't like I couldn't make my own hours. My dad and me, we owned the place and he'd either be in to put in some work or he wouldn't. Gypsy, an older, near-toothless club member and one of our other mechanics would be in by eight and could close the place if need be.

As long as I put in eight hours, five days a week, nobody really cared when I was in and when I wasn't. We usually had Darlene in the office to deal with people, but her kid had gotten sick and she'd had to bounce early yesterday which was why I'd been on my own when Everett had rolled in.

I let myself into the shop and looked down the row of lifts to figure out what I wanted to do first. I punched my timecard on the old-as-hell timeclock and stepped into my coveralls after hanging my jacket and cut on their usual peg. I punched a button on front of the old shop stereo and plugged my phone into it, cranking up the Alice in Chains.

I thought about Everett while I got to work finishing up installing the rebuilt carburetor on the old '63 Ford I'd left off doing the night before. The girl was in a hell of a mess. No family, jackass boyfriend she'd probably been stayin' with on account of the familiarity. Only way to dig out of the wreckage she was sitting in was to give her time... Time to save money for first last and deposit at the very least.

I cracked the monster can of energy drink she'd given me and downed half of it in three swallows. It was going to be a long day and I'd better do what I'd said I would before I forgot to. I went out to the sorry old Toyota and I moved the bulky midnight blue gym bag from Everett's trunk to Sadie's back seat. I wanted to look in it but resisted the urge, still, I could tell just by handling it that there was at least one pair of shoes in it, maybe two.

I set back to work still feeling like a jackass for not putting two and two together when it came to her wanting to go to a clinic. Suddenly her heaving her guts up on the side of the road made a whole lot more sense. I felt a little ill myself thinking that his asshattery may have far-reaching consequences. She seemed like a genuine and hard working person, for all I knew absolute dick about her. I guess that would change in time. I wasn't exactly sure when my mind had made itself up that she was *sticking around* but it had and now I just needed to figure out the logistics of it. That would require an in-depth conversation with my pops, in both his incarnations as my dad and my Pres.

I worked until nine when the man himself strolled into the shop. By now, Gypsy and Darlene had shown up and the bay doors were open and the sounds of a garage in full swing were clashing with the music coming from the speakers. He leaned across from me inside the open hood of Everett's tired ass mid-nineties Toyota which I had finally gotten around to trying to diagnose.

"Hey," I grunted.

"Hey," he grunted back. I continued doing what I was doing and he didn't say anything for long minutes, just watching me. It was the way we were. Eventually he would be critical of something I was doing and I'd make some smart-ass comment and he'd make one back and then we'd start talking about what he really wanted to know.

"Should use the extension on that, you're going to bust a knuckle," he said. I made a derisive snort.

"Doin' just fine, old man... Ow!" I cracked a knuckle on an exposed piece of casting and jerked my hand back shaking the smarting finger. He laughed, a distant roll of thunder in his hacking smoker's way.

"Shut it," I muttered.

"That's what you get for callin' me old," he said. I scowled at him.

"So," he said after a long silence.

"Yeah?" I looked at him and he looked back.

"What're you going to do with her?" he asked. I sighed.

"I have no fucking idea man," I said. He raised an eyebrow. I shrugged and got back under the hood.

"She's broke, got nowhere to go... Looks like she blew a cylinder, it's gonna need a new engine. She needs time and a place to regroup, save money for first, last, and deposit or for her car, though I don't much like the thought of her living out of her fucking car," I straightened and scowled. My dad was watching me, amusement sparkling in his eyes.

"What?" I asked.

"Nothin' just proud of my boy. Your mamma would be too if she could see you now," he said and the edge of my annoyance softened. He hadn't said that since the lake. Since the spring, and the bit about my mom... he didn't talk about her, period, at least not with me... Ashton had changed a lot of things, for a lot of us. Not just Trig. I swallowed hard.

"Yeah?" I asked carefully, on guard. I suddenly felt cracked wide open. All it took was my pops making one mention of my mom and suddenly I felt sixteen, lost and alone all over again. I looked at my dad, cautious, hoping for a bit more.

"A year ago you wouldn't have given her situation a second thought," he shrugged.

"Yeah, I'm not sure I want to be that guy anymore," I said honestly. He eyed me critically and nodded slowly.

"I'll pull some of my shit together and stay out at the clubhouse for the time being," he said judiciously, sucking his teeth. I blinked, taken aback.

"Really?" I asked.

"Hell, I hardly stay at the house as it is," he said voice gruff with emotion. It was true. He spent more time at the MC than he did in the house my mother had so loved. "Ain't no thing," he went on, shrugging, "Who knows, you might get an Old Lady of your own out of the deal, you play your cards right." I snorted and he gave me a cutting look.

"Not sure I'm ready for nothin' like that, pops," I said and he raised his eyebrows. I frowned at him and went back to my special brand of dry sarcastic humor. "Yeah, because she's totally going to want to hook up with the guy taking her to the STD clinic the day after finding her boyfriend barebacking some skeez on her living room couch," I said.

His expression went dark and stormy, likely a mirror of my own. Not over my hardcore denial about life and love and all that happy horseshit, but over what'd happened to Everett. We traded looks and I nodded, we were on the same page again. I mean really, it wasn't a matter of if I were ready or not for anything, granted it'd been more than a minute since my last relationship, but the particular girl in question, that girl being Everett... Well, she was part of the equation too and she may be pretty as all get out but she'd been burned *but, good*.

"Exactly," I said when my dad's expression relented. "She's a hot piece but no way am I going there." At least not with the way things were, not that quick. I'd never say *never*... I frowned. Why was I even thinking about this!? I'd just met her *yesterday* for Christ's sakes!

"Who is this guy again?" my dad asked and I stopped chasing the white rabbit of my thought pattern for a second to come back to the conversation.

"Don't know his last name, first is Jerry. Why?" I asked.

"I want the club girls to steer clear of a guy like that. I'll put out the word," he straightened.

"Probably a good idea. Might want to put it out at Sugar's too. Pretty sure the broad he was bangin' was a stripper." I shrugged.

"Shoes?" he asked grinning, turning to walk away.

"You know it!" I called to his retreating back. His booming laughter filtered back to me. My dad had taught me a long time ago you could tell a lot about a man by the shoes he wore. You could tell much the same about a woman. The more shoes, the more high maintenance, for instance. As far as I could tell, Everett didn't have a lot of shoes, but then I thought about the gym bag. I thought about looking for half a second but decided she didn't need me being nosy and invading her privacy. Not a good way to get her to trust me.

My thoughts drifted back to the day before, of her standing in that living room, looking all destroyed, throwing her few belongings into what the two of us could carry out. I didn't need to violate her privacy or trust, she'd been violated enough. What did I need to do? Well, I needed to ask her if she'd gotten everything she wanted or needed out of that place. That was as good a place to start as any. I didn't want to believe that what she took was all she had. One suitcase, all though it was a good-sized one, one kitchen trash bag and one backpack did not a life make.

I was losing steam. The next time I looked at the clock it was twelve. I punched out. I needed to pick up Everett and I didn't want to be late. She knew where the shop was, but after being left on the curb like so much trash in the pouring rain yesterday, I didn't want her to even *think* I would be late.

Back when I was a kid, I mean a small kid, like second grade, my pops wasn't doing so hot. He was addicted to something, booze, coke, didn't matter. My mom asked him to pick me up from school. He'd forgot. It had been like the second coming when my mom found out but let me tell you, I still remembered the feeling of sitting on my elementary school's front steps, waiting and waiting and believing any second he'd pull up. The school had called my mom and she'd been there as fast as she could.

She'd kicked my dad's ass out of the house that night and wouldn't let him come back until he was stone cold fucking sober and he *hadn't come back* for over a month while he'd detoxed the hard way. But he'd done it. For her, for me, for his little family of three. Still, it took a long time for us to get to where we needed to be, to heal, to trust. And the illegal shit went on until my mom paid the ultimate price. My bitterness over that surged so completely that I could taste it and I swallowed it back down as hard as I could when I pulled up outside Everett's little coffee shack.

I closed my eyes, resting my head back. I could still hear the shots, could still feel the booze running down the back of my collar. The smell of tequila even today brought with it the undertone coppery tang of blood. The passenger door opened and I jumped; Everett slid in but it didn't look like she'd noticed.

"Hey." She froze, her blue eyes roaming my face, her eyebrows knitting together. Well, if she hadn't noticed me jump, apparently it was written all over my face. "What's wrong?" she asked.

"Nothin'," I said, mouth turning down at the corners. I shook my head as much in denial as to clear it.

"Please don't lie to me," she said gently and her voice was so solemn the truth slid right out of my mouth before I could even think to stop it.

"Thinkin' about the day my mom died." She searched my face and nodded sadly.

"I think about my dad a lot too," she said quietly. I fired up Sadie and pointedly changed the subject.

"Where we going?" I asked and cleared my throat. I so did not want to have a fucking moment over our dead parents here. I instantly felt a pang of soul-wrenching guilt over thinking about my mom that way. Everett was talking and I turned my thoughts to what she was saying, burying all the shit from my past back down deep again for the time being.

"Planned Parenthood on Twentieth. No appointment necessary, first-come, first-served, but they said they were usually slow this time of day." She looked ashen.

"I don't think you have anything to worry about," I said and I winced inwardly at her stricken expression. Shit, way to make it sound like it wasn't a big deal or that it didn't matter. Her look settled into simply being withdrawn and she nodded mutely. I sighed and thought, *way to go Trujillo*. That was so not what I had meant to accomplish with that statement but there it was anyway. I didn't know what to say to fix it so I just drove us over to the low profile medical office complex in silence. It was painted a nondescript light earth tone and I parked right out front. Everett got out before I even shut off the engine and I could see she was a bundle of nerves. I wanted to kick the fucker's teeth in all over again.

I followed her into the clinic and stood behind her as she checked in. The woman behind the counter looked at me, "It's always nice when couples come in together!" she exclaimed and I saw Everett blanch. I wanted to make up for my earlier fuck up and so I picked up the pen and signed in right behind her to save her any explanations and by default, embarrassment. It'd been a while since I'd been tested, might as well since I was here, right?

"Have a seat, we'll call you when we're ready for you and get you all taken care of." She smiled sweetly at us from behind her lavender framed granny glasses and I went and sat down beside Everett who was looking at me like she'd never seen me before.

"Thanks," she whispered and she seemed more relaxed. I shrugged.

"Sure." I said and left it at that.

**5**

―――――

Everett...

I sat on the examination table in my stupid pink paper gown and tried not to freeze. The doctor was filling in some notes on her tablet. I'd already given a urine sample and had blood drawn, which was never fun. The paper tape and cotton ball was pulling on my skin at the crook of my elbow uncomfortably. All of this had been done by the nurse, *and now it's time for the main show! I thought bitterly.*

"So, Everett, what brings you in today?" she asked. She was a plump woman in her forties, maybe fifties. Her blonde hair was going gray and was pulled into a neat French twist with one of those plastic claw clips. Her face was free of makeup and she wore a lavender sweater over a white button down blouse. Her gray slacks were pressed with a sharp crease and fell over sensible black shoes. She had a gentle manner and was, in a word, placid. It felt easy to trust her and that took some of the bite out of this whole humiliating process.

"I want a full STD panel," I said, and my voice sounded hollow even to me.

"It says here you had your last pelvic three months ago at your regular doctor's." she said, confusion tinging her voice.

"I walked in on my boyfriend sleeping with another woman yesterday and he wasn't wearing any protection," I said.

"The man who was in reception with you?" she asked frowning.

"No! No. Dray is... I just met Dray, he uh... I guess he's a friend." Truth was, I didn't know *what* Dray was, but if I had to put a label on it, I guessed "friend" was accurate enough. I didn't even think about it and before I could stop myself the whole story came pouring out from start to finish. The doctor handed me some Kleenex and I wiped my eyes and blew my nose.

"Do you feel safe with Dray?" she asked gently, and I was surprised to find that I did. I mean he was built and intimidating as hell but my dad had always taught me, actions speak louder than words and his actions spoke volumes at this point. I mean who *does* what he did for me? What he was *continuing* to do for me?

"Yes," I said and my tone brooked no argument.

It had surprised me when he had signed in to be tested too, rather than make me go through explanations about who we were to each other in front of the whole waiting room. I'd thanked him for it, at least back here the explanations could be kept private. No one had to know about what an idiot I'd been in trusting Jerry.

"Okay, Everett, lie back and put your feet in the stirrups," the doctor said, her voice gentle. I complied and felt like my humiliation at the hands of Jerry was complete. She made quick work of the exam and rolled back on her stool, pulling off her gloves with a rubber snap.

"Okay, all done." I sat up.

"How long?" I asked, voice unsteady.

"Typically results take one to two weeks, but given your situation I am going to put a rush on these and see about getting them in around three days. It's the best I can do, I'm sorry," she said and I nodded.

"Do you want a paper copy?" she asked and I nodded.

"Where would you like it sent to?" she asked.

"I... I'm between homes," I said.

"Okay, we will call you with the results and you can come pick them up here. How does that sound?" she asked and I nodded.

"Okay, you take your time getting dressed and pulling yourself together before going out if you need to. Keep taking care of yourself, Everett. It was nice meeting you," she said and slipped out into the hall, shutting the door behind her.

I sat by myself in the tiny examination room and wiped my eyes. God, I hated feeling this weak and shaken and insecure! This wasn't who my da' had raised me to be. I missed him something fierce. He always knew what to do no matter what the situation and not for the first time in the last year I wished like hell he was still here.

I got dressed carefully and meticulously. I know it was just an exam but I felt gross, like I needed a shower and I wondered when my next opportunity to get one was going to be; where I was going to go from here. I pulled the olive drab backpack with its frayed random motorcycle patches up onto my shoulder and checked myself one last time in the mirror. Satisfied that I looked all right, I stepped out into the empty hall and slipped out into the waiting room.

I sat by the door leading out of the clinic to the parking lot and to all appearances, looking from the outside, I waited patiently for Dray. Honestly though, I was as impatient on the inside as I could possibly be, and it was through sheer iron will alone I kept my knee from bouncing erratically with that impatience. When Dray stepped out into the waiting room at last, he looked stormy; I guess he'd gone through with the whole test. He stopped beside my chair and I stood up. He nodded once and went out the door, I followed.

Warm he was not. If I had to pick one word to describe Draven...

Oh.

I didn't know his last name.

Still, if I had to choose a word to describe Dray, I would pick 'distant' or maybe 'guarded'. His affect may be cold but the burning looks he gave with those smoldering dark eyes couldn't be mistaken for anything icy. He was a puzzle, but made it clear by his mannerisms that he didn't wish to be poked at and I was happy not to for now. I had the feeling I wouldn't like to see a for-real angry version of Dray, motorcycle gang jacket aside. He opened the door for me again and I set my bag on the passenger side floor board.

"I uh, made enough tips today that I could probably afford a cheap hotel room for tonight," I said and his reaction took me by surprise. He frowned, hard.

"My room not good enough?" he asked gruffly.

I blinked, startled. "No! No! I didn't say that!" I hadn't meant to come off as insulting!

"Okay then, get in the car," he said and smirked.

"Look, I didn't mean to be insulting, I just... I..." I finally settled on, "I'm sorry."

Dray swung the door back and forth on its hinges a little to signal his impatience and I got into the car. He shut the door and my eyes followed his leather-and-denim-clad form as he went around the hood and got in too.

"You know how to cook?" he asked, firing up the muscle car. Odd question but I would play.

"A little," I said.

"Good, because I'm starving and I'm exhausted so you're cooking." He drove us back towards his place and I stared blankly out the window for several blocks.

"You're letting me stay?" I said turning back to him.

"My pops is moving some of his crap to the clubhouse, so, yeah. You can stay until you're on your feet. Your car is dead, needs a new engine. One of your cylinders is shot," I closed my eyes but he kept talking, "I'll drive you to work in the morning, school in the afternoon, adjusting my schedule doesn't matter much. In a month we'll see where you're at and go from there."

I opened my eyes, my throat growing thick with tears. "Why would you do that for me?" I whispered, not trusting that I could keep it together if I spoke any louder.

He looked over, his hard features softening as his gaze swept over my face. He quickly turned his head back to the road, though.

"Who knows?" he said, adding "Ask Trigger, maybe." Which he muttered so softly I almost didn't hear him above the growl of the engine as he accelerated through a four-way stop. He cleared his throat before I could ask who Trigger was, assuming it was some kind of a nickname. Didn't all bikers have some kind of nickname?

"Option is open. Take it or leave it," he grunted and I looked him over again. I nodded slowly.

"I'll take it," I said softly, my curiosity winning out. Dray was one big walking contradiction and I'd be lying if I said he wasn't in a very attractive package. He was the quintessential bad boy. All hard planes and angles wrapped in leather and shrouded in dark good looks and I wanted to know more about him, especially after everything he'd done for me in the last... It hadn't even been twenty four hours yet! I was startled to realize.

He pulled onto his street and I wondered briefly what else might be expected of me aside from cooking. I decided that I would cross that bridge when I came to it. He turned off the car and searched my profile as I pulled the pack into my lap. He let out a brief sigh and pushed his hand through his hair.

"Why you look like that?" he asked.

"Like what?" I felt my face smooth, setting into lines of surprise.

"Like you just sucked on a lemon or something," he said and I thought about it.

"Truth between us without you getting offended?" I asked.

"Wouldn't have it any other way, Princess, shoot." I frowned at his obviously sarcastic use of the pet name. Princess indeed... maybe Cinderella since I moved in with Jerry.

"I was wondering what else might be expected of me in exchange for my staying here," I said softly. He barked a laugh and it sounded bitter.

"Look at you all polite and shit!" he said but his open and friendly grin belied his words. He had the most heartstoppingly adorable dimples when he smiled like that. "Never been asked so politely if I were a sex predator or not," and his grin turned wolfish. I felt a little green.

"Look, I'm sorry, I didn't mean..."

"Yeah, you did," he interrupted me and his look had turned

serious and considering. "But it's okay, you're just being smart and safe and I get that. Nothin's gonna happen to you here that you don't want to have happen." He leveled me with a stern look and I swallowed, nodding.

He got out of the car and shut the door. I sat for a moment to think about what he'd said, watching his leather and patch-clad back as he rounded the front of the car and started for my door. I got out and he reached behind the seats and brought out my dance bag.

"You brought it!" I said, pleased to no end, the mere presence of it making my heart lighter.

"Said I would," he passed it to me.

"It means a lot. I'm glad with everything going on yesterday that I left it in my car and not at the apartment. I would have been *really* upset if I had to try and replace these." I smiled at him and resisted the urge to hug him. The bag held both sets of my dance shoes and several costumes that would have been irreplaceable.

"So you didn't get everything of yours?" he asked, searching my face. I blushed.

"I got the important things," I mumbled.

"Come on," he said with an exasperated sigh. I followed him into the house.

"Put that in my room, empty the suitcase in a pile on the bed if you have to; let's go get the rest of your stuff."

I blinked. "I don't need –"

He snorted. "*Not* the point, babe," he said and I frowned, he ignored it. "That guy is a royal class douche. He doesn't get to hold on to your stuff and you don't get to let him keep it."

I set my stuffed dance bag on the floor of his room. "It's just stuff," I said. Then I confessed, "What happened yesterday was beyond humiliating, I don't ever want to go back there."

Dray stood stock-still and looked me over with those intense dark eyes and I fought not to shrink under the scrutiny. He took a tentative step forward and then another. I went completely still. He surprised me when he pulled me against his chest and hugged me. I didn't know what I expected but that certainly wasn't it. What surprised me more is that I let him hug me. The leather of his jacket was slick and warm beneath my hands where they rested at his sides. Over the leather smell was that spicy masculine scent that permeated his sheets the night before. I closed my eyes and took comfort from him, I don't think I realized just how much I needed a hug until I was in his arms, his hands splayed against my lower back and the back of my neck. He smoothed a thumb along the side of my neck and it was an oddly tender gesture that was at odds with his hard looks and sharp and reserved personality.

"Let's go get the rest of your stuff, Em," he said.

"Em? Who's Em?" I asked, jerking back out of his arms.

"Everett Mary Moran... E.M.M., Em, you're Em. Sorry." His skin turned dusky with what I was sure was a blush but he turned away and was out the door before I could be sure. I didn't know what to make of him giving me a nickname but there would be time to analyze it later. I zipped my empty suitcase closed and picked it up by the handle and followed him out. I found him smoking a black cigarette out by the car, and found the source of the sweet spicy smell he carried in his clothes and left behind in his sheets.

"I didn't know you smoked," I said.

"There's a lot you don't know about me," he said, with one of those burning scrutinizing looks.

I frowned. "Are you trying to scare me with a comment like that?" I asked quietly.

His eyebrows went up in surprise as if he hadn't considered it. "No. Just stating a fact," he said.

"Well, fact is that makes two of us, you don't know much about me either," I said. He took my bag from me with a smile.

"Guess living together, we're going to find out," he said.

"I guess so... and likely pretty fast." He shoved my empty suitcase into the back seat before he turned back to me and nodded.

"Come on, I really want to get some sleep." He passed a hand over his eyes and I blinked.

"I'm not the one that wants to do this, you are!" I reminded him.

"I'm well aware of that, Princess," he said sarcastically, "And the sooner we do it, the sooner I can get back here and get some shut-eye, so if you don't mind?" He put the seat back and stepped aside so I could get into the car. I got in and he carefully shut the door behind me. Then he stood outside and finished his cigarette. I huffed out a harsh sigh, he wanted sleep and I had homework I had to do. I buckled my seat belt and waited, just when my patience was about to give with the ridiculousness of it, he flicked the cigarette butt out into the street and rounded the car. He got into the car with me, carrying with him the spicy sweet smell of the clove he'd been smoking mixed with the scent of impending rain. I closed my eyes and breathed his smell in, finding it oddly calming.

"I don't want to see him, or deal with him," I said softly.

"I know, but I *do*," He said and his voice was steely and underlying the hardness was the heat of his anger.

"Why?" I asked.

"Because I want him to give me an excuse to pound his fucking face in," he said simply, in the same tone of voice. I was quiet for a moment while I processed what he said.

"Is it wrong of me that I wouldn't mind so much if you did?" I asked and he turned a feral grin in my direction.

"Is that permission?" he asked.

I stayed quiet. My da' had always told me that what had never been said never needed to be unsaid, so I thought that would be a good policy to adopt for this particular situation. Dray gave a dark little chuckle at my silence and I smiled a little to myself. I snuck a glance in his direction and surreptitiously studied his profile. He had his hair drawn back under a dirt-and-grease-smudged gray bandana. Having the raven-wing locks back away from his face served to show just how sharp and angular his cheekbones were, sweeping into slightly shadowed hollows before being rescued from looking gaunt by an equally strong and defined jaw.

"Like what you see?" he asked, teasing, and I felt myself blush, but my da' had always taught me to give as good as I got for the most part so with a stubborn set to my chin I told him, "Yes." He laughed and gave me a slow careful sweep of his gaze.

"Good to know," he said and I wondered when the hell we'd started flirting. *No, no, no and no!* Flirting was such a bad idea! A *really* bad idea! I wasn't even twenty four hours out from the disaster with Jerry. I shouldn't be flirting!

"Dray look, I'm sorry, I don't mean to flirt I shouldn't..."

He barked a laugh. "I'm the VP of an MC, trust me Sweetheart, I *know* when a woman is looking at me to get some and when one is just admiring the view. You're fine." he said, pulling up to the curb in front of the dry cleaners.

"Arrogant much!?" I exclaimed laughing.

"Am I?" he asked and turned that dark, intense gaze full of so much raw heat on me. I felt things low in my body uncoil with a spark of lust that so should not be there.

"Maybe a little," I said honestly, "I can't really tell yet." It could be arrogance or it could be false bravado, I really *couldn't* tell. Dray, from what I'd been able to see so far, was often times withdrawn and mercurial. He shut off the engine and I got out of the car before he could get the door. I pulled the suitcase out of the back and contemplated the glass door that led up the narrow staircase and ultimately to my apartment. I so did not want to go up those stairs.

"Maybe I should have called first," I said.

Dray made a rude noise.

"Naw, fuck that. You paid the rent, you live here. Let's go get your shit so you can be done with him." He opened the door for me and I got the mail. I needed to get a PO box or something. I slid my mail into the front pocket of the suitcase and put Jerry's mail back. Dray followed me up the stairs, a resolute presence at my back, pressing me inexorably forward. With him at my back I almost felt like currents of wind being pushed forward by a dark thunderhead. I was a little mixed up over it, being both grateful and resentful in the same breath. When we reached my apartment I stared at the door for too long I think, because Dray took my key ring which hung limp from my fingers and slid the correct one home into the lock for me. He opened the door.

"Evy?" Jerry called and he sounded hopeful. I closed my eyes and went through the door. He stood up from the couch, his game controller forgotten in his hand. He looked at my suitcase and smiled. "I knew you'd be back. Ready to talk?" he asked and it was Dray's voice from behind me as he followed me into the apartment that saved me from having to shriek my outrage.

"Think again, asshole. She's here for the rest of her shit." I blinked, and swept down the hall to go for more of my belongings before Jerry could say anything or move to stop me.

*Was I ready to talk?!* Really!? As if *I* was being the unreasonable one! Un-fucking-believable. My eyes swam with tears, the hot and angry kind as I lined the bottom of my suitcase with the rest of my shoes and pulled the hanging things out of my closet. I had just made off with socks, underwear, jeans and shirts out of and off of the dresser yesterday. I finished cleaning out the dresser, grabbed my framed photograph of me and my da' off the night table and my phone charger.

Jerry was in the living room, squared off with Dray, who was as unmovable and unflappable as a small dark mountain. I went into the kitchen determined to get the last of my things. I returned with two trash bags for clothes and bathroom essentials and gave Jerry a dark look before sweeping into action.

"Evy, what are you doing with this guy!?" Jerry demanded, "I mean shit, I forgive you if you fucked him, Christ... You need to stop. Ev, just stop!" He was following me from room to room. I threw all of my toiletries, and I mean *all* of them into my first trash bag. Shampoo, conditioner, toothbrush and paste, tampons, all of it haphazardly into the bag. Razors and refills, even the Q-tips, my makeup, all with Jerry standing in the door way shouting at me to fucking say something, anything to him. My anger boiled over.

"You want me to say something!? Fine Jerry! How about fuck you and get out of my way!?" I shouted. He stopped talking and blinked at me.

"You don't talk to me that way," he said imperiously and I shoved past him.

"I just did, what are you going to do about it?" I scoffed and he grabbed my upper arm. It was a mistake. He'd missed Dray stalking up the hallway behind us quietly, like some kind of black-leather-clad panther or something. Dray grabbed him around the back of his collar, fisting his hand in Jerry's tee shirt and ripped him off of me. I turned my back on them and went into the bedroom and finished getting all of the rest of my things. Dray was talking, low and controlled barely inches from Jerry's face, who looked like he was going to take a swing. He didn't. Smart move, I was pretty sure Dray could have, would have, taken him apart. His dark eyes tempestuous, he pinned Jerry to the spot with his gaze, his hands clenched into fists at his sides.

"This is it Jerry, I'm done. We're leaving and I'm not coming back. Don't call, don't write, have a nice life." Dray's fingers uncurled from the fists he made as he took the over-full suitcase and a trash bag from me. I hauled my hangars full of stuff over my shoulder and hefted the other trash bag with my other hand. Jerry glared at me and crossed his arms over his narrow chest.

"Stupid bitch, you think he's going to treat you better?" Jerry asked but when he opened his mouth to say more he swallowed Dray's fist. Jerry fetched up against the wall and slid down it, his hands going to his mouth, blood smearing his fingers. I gaped, open-mouthed at Dray. I hadn't even seen him drop the trash bag let alone move! Violence crackled around him like heat lightning as he stood over my now very ex-boyfriend.

"I told you, last time I was here, that you'd see what'd happen if you called her a bitch again." Dray picked up the trash bag and transferred it to the hand my suitcase dangled out of. He put his free hand on the back of my shoulder to guide me out of the narrow hallway. I shivered and stepped over Jerry. He did the same and we left the apartment and went down to the car. He shoved the suitcase in the back seat and the rest in the trunk. Jerry spilled out of the entryway, blood coating his chin and teeth.

"I'm calling the cops, you asshole! I'm pressing charges!" he shouted and I felt myself pale. Dray motioned for me to get into the car and I complied.

"Wouldn't be my first time," Dray shot over the roof of the Trans Am. He got in and fired it up, leaving Jerry behind on the sidewalk gasping like a landed fish. I closed my eyes and leaned my head back against the headrest.

"Don't sweat it," Dray said and I opened my eyes and pinned him with a look.

"Thanks," I said and his lips curled into a nasty little smile.

"Really, it was my pleasure," he stated rather simply.

"You didn't have to hit him." He gave me a sidelong look. I rolled my eyes, exasperated. "I'm not feeling bad about it, or for him, he deserved it. I'm more worried about you," I said and he nodded.

"Don't," he grunted and we finished the rest of the ride in silence. I ignored him and worried about him anyways. I was pretty sure Jerry wouldn't call the cops. He'd have to explain and he wouldn't want the wounded pride but I had been wrong about him before. Dray gripped the steering wheel tightly to the point it creaked and my gaze flicked to him.

"How the fuck a girl like you land with a guy like him?" he demanded and I opened my mouth to reply and closed it.

"We went to high school together, he was on the basketball team, star player, and I was a cheerleader." He looked me over.

"I can believe it," he grunted and I raised an eyebrow and wondered just what that was supposed to mean.

"He was sweet, persistent even. Walked me to every class, would leave notes and flowers at my locker until I agreed to let him take me to homecoming. We had a few things in common... we were different but it was good. Then it was comfortable, and then it wasn't but I guess by then it was normal." Dray looked at me and I lifted a shoulder in a shrug.

"He was my first," I whispered, "I suppose it was naïve of me to think he would be my only." I leaned my head back and watched storm clouds of emotion cross his face. He gripped the wheel with the strength to make it creak and I looked at his hands. The knuckles of the right one were starting to swell and turn purple. A cut, likely from one of Jerry's teeth, was bleeding freely, a trickle of crimson disappearing between his ring and middle finger.

"You had plans for him and you?" he asked and I thought about it, I mean really thought about it.

"I have plans for me," I said, startled to realize that I had stopped believing Jerry would be a part of them a long time ago.

"Good," Dray said and turned onto his street. He didn't ask what my plans were and so I didn't volunteer them. I had some things to sort out, that was for sure. This was definitely an unscheduled detour on my life's highway. He pulled the old muscle car smoothly into his driveway just behind a motorcycle parked in front of the garage. He left plenty of room for the bike to get around his car.

"Dragon's home," he uttered.

"I'm sorry?" I said.

"My Pops, he's here," he said.

"You call your da' Dragon?" I asked curiously. Dray shrugged.

"That's his name. You say "dad" funny," he remarked.

"I say it the way I was raised to say it, my da' was full-on Irish, accent and all." I felt myself slip into my half-brogue and smiled.

"Accent is hot. You might want to use it to pick up dudes when you're ready." He got out of the car before I could say anything to the smartass comment. He began extracting my suitcase from the back seat as I shut my door and the front door of the house opened.

If I ever wondered what Dray might look like in twenty or thirty years, now I knew. I looked from father to son and back and shut my mouth.

"Alright, boy. You're good to go," said the president of the Sacred Hearts MC and father of Draven... damn it, I still didn't know his last name. Well, I could try to fix that. Anyways, there stood Dragon, who was more built than Dray and a few inches shorter. His leather was time- and care-worn and looked comfortable. He came down the steps in blue jeans and used faded black leather chaps. He looked me over with the same intense burning gaze as his son, although it was different somehow, friendlier than Dray's. He had a dark, full beard where Dray usually went clean shaven or at the worst, with a little more than a five o'clock shadow. His smile was very white, set in the deep black whiskers and his hair was long, but pulled into a low pony tail that hung down his back.

"You must be her," he said.

"You must be him," I said back and smiled. I stuck out my hand.

"Everett Moran, pleased to meet you, Mr..." I trailed off in hopes he would supply his last name.

"Dragon," he said and shook my hand firmly but carefully. I smiled and shook his back.

"Dragon," I repeated and said, "Most people call me Ev or Evy," I said. I heard Dray snort behind me.

"The assclown calls her that. I call her Em," he said. Dragon's eyes shifted to his son and I could see the love and pride radiate from the older man.

"Em, huh? I like it. Pleased to meet you, Em." I took back my hand.

"Pleased to meet you too, sir," I murmured then haltingly, "I really can't let you move out of your own home for me. I can get a hotel room, there's an inexpensive one that..."

"Naw!" he said. "It's nothin'. I've got a lot of business to take care of and a room over at the clubhouse. I'm hardly ever here anyways. You take the boy's room, he can have mine till you get back on your feet. It ain't no thing."

"I don't know how to thank you or your son," I said and the tears welled up again. I dashed at them with my fingers, embarrassed.

"You need to introduce her to Sunshine," Dragon muttered, and Dray nodded.

"See yah, Pops," he said.

"You coming to the clubhouse tonight?" he asked. Dray frowned and shook his head, he looked exhausted and it was all my fault.

"Naw, if I don't get some sleep soon I'm gonna pass out anyways," Dray answered, and I winced.

"Right. Nice to meet you, Em." Dragon nodded and slung an old army green backpack higher on his wide shoulder. He went for his bike and Dray ushered me into the house. I went inside and to Dray's bedroom and he followed, depositing the suitcase onto his bed. I made my way past him and into the kitchen.

"Still want me to feed you right?" I asked.

"Fuck, I don't even care anymore," he said and shrugged out of his jacket and hung it on the same chair as yesterday. He slid past me and disappeared into Dragon's room. I heard him flop onto the bed with a groan.

I sighed, weary as well, and went into his bedroom. I shoved everything into an inglorious pile in the middle of the floor with every intention of figuring it out later and pulled off my boots. I lay down and was asleep the minute my head touched the pillow.

# 6

Dray...

My suspicions about her not getting enough rest were confirmed when I heard her moving around in my room and then silence. I couldn't bring myself to feel one way or the other about it as I slid the rest of the way into sleep. I slept hard, and when I woke up it was in the same position I'd flopped down in. I hadn't budged. The house smelled like food and my stomach growled. I got up and took off my boots, stripping off my socks. My feet were hot as hell after sleeping in 'em. I padded out to the dining area and looked into the kitchen. Em was pulling something carefully out of the oven with pot holders and setting it onto the stove top. When she was clear of anything that might burn her, I spoke up.

"Smells good." She startled something fierce, arms snapping in to protect her chest, one leg coming clean up off the floor as she bent at the middle and turned her side to me, and let out a short shriek of fear. I couldn't help but smile at the same time I noted that every movement she'd made, even unconsciously, was elegant, graceful and precise.

"Sorry," I said as she gasped for breath.

"You scared the life out of me!" she panted and her accent was thicker.

"You sure you grew up in the states?" I asked her. She nodded.

"Just mostly with my da' around other of our people." She straightened and looked me over.

Yeah, I was sleep-rumpled but I was home so I didn't much care. She wore some of her pajamas which made it hard as hell to concentrate on anything else. Her nap looked to be much shorter than mine by the laptop and piles of papers set out on one end of the table.

"How long was I out?" I asked, gruffly.

"A little over six hours," she said.

"How long were you?" I raised an eyebrow.

"A little under two. I tried to be quiet, did I wake you?" She bit her lip and roved me with her bright clear eyes. I shook my head and pulled out a chair so I could face her, dropping into it.

"Naw," I said. It was dark outside the windows and the dim glow of the lamps she had turned on made the space more intimate. She moved around the kitchen and by the smell of things I had lucked out and rescued a stray who could cook.

"What'd you make?" I asked her.

"Guinness and steak pie, traditional Irish Soda Bread and some salad." She moved around dishing up two plates. My eyebrows went up.

"We had all of the stuff to make that?" I asked.

"I walked to the grocery store and picked up what you didn't have. Like I said, I had some good tips today." She set a plate in front of me along with a paper towel and some silverware. I looked up at her.

"You're supposed to be saving money," I said.

She smiled and shook her head. "You can't expect me not to pitch in *at all*." She sat down with me and sighed.

"Fair enough, try to keep it to a minimum though. You've got a life to build, and didn't you say you had plans?" I raised my eye brows and took a bite of food, and Christ as a cracker, the girl could cook. Bet she could even give Ashton a run for her money. Score.

"I did," she affirmed, but the way she said it, the glimpse of deep sorrow in her eyes had me wondering if that's what she really meant. Was that an affirmation or was she giving up?

"What are they?" I asked, then added, "If you don't mind my asking." She looked over at me, chewing carefully, considering.

"I want to open a coffee and chocolate shop," she answered. Not what I expected.

"Okay, coffee I get, and chocolate, I get, but together? Like how together?"

She smiled. "Coffee drinks, drinking chocolate, but also specialty chocolates, truffles, bonbons and the like." She set down her fork and got up. "Something to drink?" she asked.

"Need to go anywhere?" I asked her.

"No," she said, frowning.

"Then gimme a beer," I answered. She nodded in understanding and went to the fridge and pulled out two bottles. She opened them both and returned to the table. My eyebrows went up. Didn't know a lot of girls that would drink beer, let alone a dark one. She crooked a smile.

"I'm Irish," she said and tipped the bottle to her lips. I laughed a little. She had her hair swept up into a high pony tail leaving the line of her neck and the curve of her shoulder bare. I had a sudden and strong urge to put my lips to that sweet spot where the two came together. She held herself with perfect posture, back straight, shoulders thrust back, and I wondered if the girl ever got the chance to relax. We finished our meal in comfortable silence and when she reached out to take my plate my fingers closed gently around her wrist.

"You cooked," I said and looked up into her pretty blue eyes. She had really long eyelashes and I wondered how come I hadn't noticed before, I mean shit, I'd been spending a fair amount of time staring awestruck into those baby blues.

"So?" she asked and swallowed hard. Her eyes dilated and I fought down a smirk. So she found me attractive and my hand on her skin did something to her. Interesting. I let her go but it was reluctantly. Her skin was smooth, soft beneath my work-rough hands. She set my plate back down.

"So you cook, I clean. Fair?" I asked. She nodded and I got up and cleared the dishes.

"You should let me have a look at that hand," she said.

"What hand?" I asked.

"The one you punched Jerry in the face with," she said without a trace of judgment or reproach.

I looked at it. The one knuckle was pretty swollen and the split from his tooth pretty angry looking. Who knew where his mouth had been? I flashed on the skeez from the day before and then flashed on Everett's fresh face stained with her tears. I wanted to hit him all over again and keep hitting him until he couldn't get up.

"Sure," I said and she got up. I rinsed the dishes and put them in the dishwasher. My dad's gift to my mom one year had been a full kitchen remodel to bring all the modern conveniences into the small Prohibition-era home. Everett had disappeared into the bathroom but now she was back and motioning for me to retake my seat. I sat down, amused, and she took my hand gently between her own. I sucked in a silent breath and held it. Her hands were warm and silky and even though I wouldn't be going there, I let my thoughts drift to what they would feel like wrapped around my cock. She picked up a brown bottle of liquid and soaked a cotton ball with it and I wondered where the hell we had cotton balls in the house.

"This might sting a little at first," she warned and dabbed the cut with the solution. It started foaming and bubbling. It didn't really hurt at all but the bubbling sensation was foreign and unexpected and my hand jerked. She started blowing on the cut and looked at me and those blue eyes made my mouth go a little dry. They were clear and just so bright and I think made all the more dramatic by the fact that on the outer edge of the iris they were ringed by cool steel. She averted her gaze, back to cleaning the cut, and I resolutely told my dick to settle down.

She dabbed at the cut with the solution until it stopped foaming and smeared it with some antibacterial ointment before sticking a cloth band-aid over it. She pressed a tiny kiss over the band-aid, her lips grazing the skin around the bandage and murmured so softly I barely heard it,

"There. All better." She smiled at me but it wilted at the edges when she caught the look on my face which I felt had gone to stone.

"Why did you do that?" I asked. She swallowed.

"Do what?" She feigned innocence but I wouldn't have it ignored.

"Kiss it." I flicked my tongue over suddenly-dry lips. "Why'd you kiss my hand?"

"My da' used to do it to me whenever I had a scrape or an owie. Habit, I guess?" She rose and gathered the band-aid wrappers and soiled cotton balls in one hand. *Owie?* Could she be any more innocent or adorable? I captured her wrist and jerked her down into her seat. She sat heavily.

"I'm only going to say this once and then we're never going to speak of it again," I said, needing to get one thing clear. She took a fortifying drink of her beer. "You're cute, pretty even, but I'm nobody's rebound." I kept her stare pinned with my own and she didn't as much as flinch. She nodded slowly.

"I wasn't trying anything," she said evenly, and after a brief moment of searching her face I believed her.

"Okay, then," I said and let her go. She got up from the table, clearly rattled, and I couldn't say I was sorry for it. She threw away the trash and put the rest of it back wherever it had come from. I got up and pushed in the chairs, heading off into my room to grab something comfortable to lounge in. She had everything neatly folded on the floor against one wall, as much as she could and I went into one of my drawers. I extracted a pair of black straight legged sweats and went back out.

"Need to pee or anything you better do it now. I'm going in for a shower." She nodded and slipped into the bathroom, did her business and came back out. I shut the door and turned on the faucets with a gusty sigh. Hot water poured from the tap and I twisted the center knob to get the shower going. Steam rose around me in a soft plume and I stripped down. I washed the garage and the rest of my day off quickly, but stood under the punishing hot soak to ease some of the tension out of my shoulders before I got out. I felt clean and more relaxed and pulled on some sweats, tying them where they were comfortable, low on my hips. I ran a comb through my hair and sopped the water off my shoulders and chest the act of combing my hair had rained down on my skin. I gave the bathroom a once-over look to make sure I had everything before hitting the light and coming out. She sat at the dining room table in front of her laptop, wearing these hot-for-teacher black-framed glasses, one leg tucked gracefully under her, the other swinging idly back and forth.

The whole image was a pretty intimate view of Everett Moran and not going to lie, one I probably wouldn't get tired of looking at. I went out into the mud room and dumped the laundry into the hamper. When I stepped back into the kitchen her eyes were boring into mine through those hot nerd glasses of hers over her laptop screen. I stopped midstride.

"Do you know anything about math?" she asked. I smiled and sauntered over.

"Maybe," I said leaning down over her shoulder to take a look at her screen. It looked like she was doing some kind of algebra with symbols I'd never even seen let alone heard of. I frowned.

"What is this shit?" I asked.

"Alien translated into Greek," she complained and rubbed her forehead. She was online so she'd figured out the Wi-Fi password, which was impressive.

"At least you figured out the Wi-Fi," I muttered.

"It was the network key on the bottom of the router, the first thing I looked at," she said like it was child's play. I nodded.

"I'm putting on a movie. Come join me if you'd like," I said and straightened. She sighed and went back to her figures. I sat in the living room and turned on the television. Lounging back on the couch, I put my feet up and went through the cable listings. I landed on something from a premium channel through on-demand. A gusty sigh came from the dining area and I glanced up. She closed the lid to her laptop and joined me, curling up on the love seat, hugging herself. The movie went through its opening sequence and I got up.

"Beer?" I asked.

"No, thanks," she said. I pulled the throw blanket off the back of the couch and put it over her. She murmured her thanks and smiled up at me. I smiled back and went and got another beer. I sat back down, wishing she weren't so far away then wondering *'What the fuck?'* at myself as the movie started.

"Batman, huh?" she asked.

"Yeah," I answered.

"I'm a Marvel girl," she confessed, "But if I have to watch DC, Batman is who I would pick." I quirked a one sided grin.

The movie was the third in the Dark Knight trilogy and went longer than I remembered it being. By the time it ended Everett was fast asleep and I was fairly sauced, more than a few empties sitting forlorn on the coffee table. The credits were rolling and I let myself have a minute or two to just look at her. She had her hands tucked under her cheek and was sleeping so peacefully I didn't have the heart to wake her. Instead, I went into my bedroom and pulled back a triangle of blankets and sheets, noting that she'd made the bed the way I like it. I went back out and gently unwound her from the throw and put it back where it belonged.

I bent at the knees and power-lifted her frame into my arms. I couldn't do it forever, I mean she and I were nearly equal in height with only a couple of inches of difference. While she wasn't fat, she had some solid muscle to her, especially her long legs. I turned sideways through the door and she jolted awake as I stooped to set her on the bed. Her arms locked around my neck and shoulders in reflex.

"Shhh, just me. Just Dray," I said, and the confusion cleared from her eyes and the tension in her body eased marginally. Her reaction secretly pleased me. I set her down and slipped my arms out from under her, reaching up to untangle myself from her arms. She let me go and I situated the blankets up around her.

"Get some sleep," I whispered into the dark and her eyes fluttered shut. I wondered briefly if she had even woken up at all.

"Don't close it," she said when I had my hand on the door knob and I had my answer.

"Why not?" I asked.

"I'm afraid…" She muttered but her voice fell off, and I couldn't understand what else she uttered. I let go of the door and reentered the room, crouching down by the bed.

"What are you afraid of, Everett? Why can't I close the door?" I asked softly.

"If you close the door, I won't hear or see them coming." She sounded stricken, sad…

"Who are they?" I asked.

"I don't know," she sighed and sounded impatient and frustrated. I wanted her to rest so I let it go for now.

"Okay, okay, sleep. We'll talk about it later." I adjusted the blankets around her even though I didn't need to and let her sleep.

What she'd said bothered me. Her voice had sounded small, almost childlike but whatever had happened, it had left an impression. I lay on my Dad's bed and stared at the ceiling for a long time before drifting off myself.

I woke up and I couldn't tell you what time it was. Clouds hung low in the sky threatening rain outside the window and I groaned. I wanted to get a ride in today. I sat up and thought I heard water running. I went out into the hall and found the bathroom door shut tight, which wasn't helpful when I had to go this bad. I stood outside it and waited impatiently.

"Em!" I called out.

"Yeah!" she called back from the shower.

"Stay behind the curtain, I'm coming in!" I called.

"Wait! What?" but I was through the door and the lid and seat were up before she could finish her exclamation. She poked her head out, caught sight of me bringing myself out of my pants, said, "Oh god!", and ducked back behind the curtain.

The curtain was clear but in that frosted sort of way and I tried very hard not to look at her nude silhouette as she rinsed her long hair. I failed, her body was one long sleek line as she tipped her head back under the spray. I couldn't pick out any details, the curtain kept everything vague and indistinct, and I was grateful for that. I finished my business quickly and closed the seat and lid.

"Sorry, Em, wasn't about to go outside like some kind of mutt," I said and left the bathroom quickly. I didn't flush, the old plumbing would scorch the hell out of her. She finished her shower quickly and emerged from the bathroom dressed in jeans and a sweatshirt that had the neckline cut, the straps of her bra peeking out at the shoulders. She was drying her hair briskly, rubbing it back and forth between her towel-covered hands.

"Sorry I didn't check first, I didn't know what time you would be getting up and I didn't want to wake you." She rubbed her hair more vigorously with the towel and the smell of lilacs drifted over to me.

"Is there coffee?" I asked her, and she nodded and went into the kitchen. She ditched the towel in the hamper and poured me a cup.

"Thanks," I said.

"It's an Ethiopian dark roast. Might be a bit much, black," she warned. I sipped and a rich, bold smoky flavor trickled across my tongue.

"It's good," I declared.

"Thanks," she murmured and sat at the table to pull on her socks and sneaks.

"Got somewhere you gotta be?" I asked, raising an eyebrow.

"Yes, actually. It's Saturday, I'm going here," she handed me a note she'd left on the table.

"I'll be done in about three or four hours, if not longer. I called a cab to come get me to take me but if I could get a ride after, that would be really awesome." She bit her lip and looked so hopeful I laughed.

"I'll pick you up," I said and she gave an excited little squeal, and I winced.

"Correction: I'll pick you up as long as you swear you'll never make that sound again," I said and sipped the dark coffee. A horn blared outside and she picked up the mystery gym bag.

"Thank you, Dray," she said solemnly and coming forward, she kissed my cheek and dashed out the door before I could say anything about it.

Whatever.

I pulled my own gym bag together, took the chance, and rode out to the 'Y' to hit the gym. I changed once I was there, and it was as I was warming up, I realized what she'd said. Three or four hours if not longer... who exercises for that long?

I did an hour of weights and an hour of running. Reaver and Trigger came through the door just as I was finishing up. I nodded to them and they came over to my treadmill.

"Dragon says you picked up a stray of your own." Trigger, the big blonde bastard, was grinning from ear to ear. I slowed it down to a walk, caught my breath and nodded.

"Something like that, man," I said.

"That why you were MIA last night?" Reaver asked and he was all smiles. Creepy fucker. I nodded.

"Yeah." I told them what was up and their smiles turned to more sober expressions.

"She'll do all right if she's got you watching out for her," Trigger commented and it meant a lot that he'd say it. He and I weren't always on the best of terms. His woman Ashton had changed a lot of things for the better since he'd picked her up from the side of the road last spring.

"Just tryin' to do the right thing," I said.

Reaver and I exchanged looks and he smiled a little one-sided and nodded. "We're here for you if you need anything, Brother," the slimmer man said. Reaver was muscled without being bulky. He was more about speed and endurance than power. Any man that preferred knives rather than a gun was half-cracked in the head and off his rocker. That was Reaver, still, all in all, he was a good guy.

"Wanna lift with us?" Trigger invited and I shook my head, stepping off the treadmill.

"Naw, man, I did that before. Time for me to hit the shower. I only have around an hour to kill before I have to go pick up Em."

"Em, is that her name?" Reaver asked.

"Naw, its Everett. Everett Mary Moran. Her initials stuck out at me and I've been callin' her Em," I explained.

"Sounds serious," Trigger teased.

"What?"

"I nicknamed Ashton 'Sunshine' in my head the first time I saw those eyes of hers. I think that was when my caveman brain branded her mine." He winked at me and I snorted.

"I'm nobody's rebound and she wouldn't want to have anything to do with a broken fuck like me," I said, looking at Reaver, the things we'd done were standing out fresh in my mind. He and I traded knowing looks.

"Never say never brother," Trigger said and he was grinning. I knew he wasn't oblivious, he'd just found his be all and end all's in Ashton, and was deluded into thinking that because he could find it, then the rest of us would too. I almost wished that line of thinking were true but life wasn't a fucking fairy tale for all of us. Some of us didn't deserve what he and Ashton had together.

"See you tonight?" Reaver asked, pulling me out of my dark thoughts.

"Yeah. We'll see," I said.

We parted ways and I showered, dressed, and rode home. I got Matilda, my bike, into the garage just as the first fat drops of rain started to fall. I smiled and thanked the weather gods for their kindness and finished closing up the small free-standing garage, locking it. I dropped some laundry in the washer in back and got it going before I headed out and fired up Sadie.

It had been over three hours, pushing four, and I wanted to know what was up with little Miss Everett and the mystery gym bag. I drove into town and found the address she'd written for me. I pulled into the lot next to the old brick building and wondered what the hell it was. There was no sign outside declaring it this or that. I got out of Sadie and locked her up and strode up the cracked sidewalk to the glass door and let myself in. It smelled strongly of dust, and floor wax, and cleaner. Random clacking and banging could be heard. I went into a doorway and found a huge room, the walls lined with mirrors and bars. A row of little girls in dance gear and some kind of tap shoes stood in a bundle around Everett.

"Please Ms. Moran!? Pleeeeease!?" one girl was begging. Everett laughed.

"Okay! Okay! Tabitha, music." One of the little girls tapped-ran to a stereo in the corner. I shrank back; Everett passed the doorway and took up a place in the center of the large expanse of beat-up floor. She stood, legs straight, hands on hips and nodded once. Music, Irish folksy crap, slow at first, flowed out of hidden speakers and I watched as Everett's one foot tapped, faster than lightning, faster than the eye could see. *Rat-ta-tat!* A long pause, then again, *Rat-ta-tat!*

She was making music with her feet as much as anything and when the music from the stereo hit a certain portion of song, she *danced.* Her hands stayed glued to her hips but her feet and legs — they moved and she bounced and floated across the room, spinning and kicking and the whole damn thing was magical and mesmerizing. She danced the whole song through and I ducked back out of the doorway and plastered my back against the wall.

She was a *dancer,* and a damned fine one, so why the hell was she going to school to open a coffee and chocolate shop? The girls streamed out giggling and laughing, and I heard her drop into a seat. I caught sight of her in a mirror in the next room across the hall, changing her shoes from the hard tap shoes to something softer, almost ballet-like but not. She stood and turned the song to something else, still Irish, still folksy but slower, more melodic and I tucked myself to the side in the doorway to watch.

She wore black tights and over it a short maroon dress with long sleeves and a short flowing skirt that fluttered easily in any stray passing breeze. Her hair was half up and fluttered around her shoulders as she raised up on her toes and bounced across the floor in short leaps. Her arms were stick straight at her sides and her legs did all the moving. It was some kind of Riverdance shit. I'd seen it on television a time or two and it had been cool as hell, but this, in person... her body, her legs and heart and mind behind it. I was just plain blown away.

**7**

———

Everett...

I loved to dance. It was my way of burning off steam, of letting go and my way to feel free. My da' had insisted on traditional Irish step dancing for his only daughter. When I was a child I had no appreciation for it but as I'd grown older I'd grown to embrace it and love it. I stretched my body into sleek lines, twirling and spinning.

I came up on point and swayed like a pendulum and heard a gasp in the doorway, I turned and smiled when I caught Dray's deep dark eyes mesmerized by my little solo performance. I danced my way over and held out my hand pulling him into the center of the room. I made him my personal Maypole and laughing, stepped around him to the light, airy, and positive music. He turned to follow me with his eyes and I was surprised at his slack-jawed look of wonder. I lifted his hand and spun underneath it and as the song finished pulled myself close and then spun out far and curtsyed. He smiled, a slow curve of lips and I think my heart melted just a little. I straightened and smiled, chest dewed with sweat and heaving.

"So what do you think?" I asked, swinging his hand back and

forth. He extracted it from mine gently and ran a hand through his hair.

"That was," he gave a little incredulous laugh, "Wow, I don't know what to say."

I smiled.

"Been dancing since I was six. Da' made me do it. I volunteer to teach here every Saturday both so I can stay in shape and because by doing it, I can come and dance whenever I want." I wiped my face and neck with my towel,

"You should be doing this. Not making people coffee," he said decisively.

"I love doing this; if it were a job, I wouldn't love it anymore," I explained.

He was looking at me like he'd never seen me before. I went over and sat down to pull off my shoes.

"I want to ask you something," he said and sat down next to me.

"Sure," but the look he was giving me made me still.

"Last night, I put you to bed," he started and I smiled. He went on, "You wouldn't let me close the bedroom door, seemed to think you wouldn't see or hear them coming... Who is 'them'?" he asked and I laughed.

"The English," I said.

"What?" he asked confused.

"My da' was a card-carrying member of the IRA. He came to America on the run before I was born. Met my mom, got married, she died having me and he never got remarried. Anyways, when I was small, I had a lot of aunts and uncles that talked like my da'. Other members that ran Stateside when the shit hit the fan or whatever. They would tell stories and I would listen to them even though I wasn't supposed to. My bogey man was different than other kids, I guess." I shrugged.

Dray blinked.

"Seriously?" he asked.

"Seriously," I affirmed, "I don't know everything that my da' was into but I know that he did things to support the cause, when I was growing up." I put 'support the cause' in air quotes with my fingers. Dray blinked at me.

"You don't seem to have a problem with that," he said. I shrugged.

"He was my da' and I loved him," I said quietly, "Besides, you honestly want to tell me you and yours haven't ever done anything against the law?" I leveled him with a look and he roamed my face with those dark eyes which for now, were calm and considering. Still dark pools rather than burning embers.

I smiled and nodded. "That's what I thought," I said at his silence. I pulled on my street shoes.

"You hungry?" he asked, changing the subject but he was looking at me like he'd never seen me before, like I was brand-new to his eyes. I'd had an unconventional childhood for sure, but my da' had always kept me safe and made sure I was loved.

"Starving, take me back to get a shower and I'll heat up the rest of our dinner," I suggested. He nodded slowly. I bit my lip, worried that my little revelation had somehow possibly damaged something between us.

I got up and pulled my iPod from the stereo and put it in a pocket of my gym bag. Dray seemed distracted, lost in thought as we walked to his car and my concern grew. He opened the door for me and I smiled, the gesture somehow reassuring. I shoved my bag into the back seat. He drove us back to the house in silence, which I was comfortable with, and when we pulled into the driveway he shut off the engine.

"I ran into a couple of brothers at the gym today, they asked if I was coming to the clubhouse tonight. Feel like going?" he asked. I thought about it and secretly let out a relieved breath. Perhaps my revelation about my upbringing hadn't changed anything after all. I hoped not.

"Sure," I said.

"If we drink, it's cool, I have a room there so feel free to cut loose. Like I said. Nothing is going to happen that you don't want to happen." I nodded and thought about it. *I have a room there... Hmm.*

"So what typically happens at the clubhouse on a Saturday night?" I asked as we got out of the car.

"Same shit that happens at your typical biker bar." He shrugged and I imitated my father, dropping into a familiar Irish brogue.

"Now, don't be thinkin' of e'er goin' to a place like that, Evy. Highway men, th' lot o' them. I want my little girl safe, not turnin' into a monster like meh." Dray turned around and looked at me, giving me one long slow blink. "My da' would be rolling in his grave if he thought of me casting my lot with a rough and rowdy crowd like a bunch of bikers," I said and smiled, "Then again I don't think he'd ever met a biker quite like you... So I'll ask again, what typically happens at the clubhouse on a Saturday night?" I cocked my head to the side and Dray, who had momentarily looked stricken, gave me that heart-melting boyish grin. I raised my eyebrows and he laughed.

"Drinking, smoking, dancing, cards... laughter and conversation, sometimes live music, mostly whatever is on the stereo. That's usually what happens at the clubhouse," he said and opened the front door to the house. I felt better about it already. I dropped my dance bag in Dray's bedroom and gathered things for a shower, opting for comfort for now.

"What do the girls usually wear?" I called out.

"Wear what you would out to a club!" he called from his father's room.

I showered quickly and fixed us both lunch from last night's left overs. Dray watched television while I did some homework. Finally, about an hour before leaving, I went to get dressed. I chose some black footless leggings that looked painted on and wet. Over that I wore a silvery top that cascaded in the front, held in back by strings like a bathing suit. One halter style around the neck, the other across the back. I figured a biker bar may have an appreciation for the tattoos. My hair. I swept over my shoulder and braided, anchoring it with a silver hair tie. The top hung low in front showing off my trinity knot necklace.

I added my Mt. St. Helens Obsidianite post earrings; the stones were a deep emerald green and matched my necklace. They were my mother's. My father had bought them for her when they were dating. He'd met her while living in Washington state and he had saved them for me until I was eighteen. He'd given them to me as a graduation present; as a way of having my mom there with me too, as I'd walked and gotten my diploma. I wore the necklace every day; the earrings I brought out when I felt like being dressy.

I did my make-up, to bring out my eyes and slipped on a pair of silver high heels that matched the backless halter top. I gave a little shimmy in the mirror to make sure everything was secure and I wouldn't fall out anywhere and, satisfied, added a touch of clear gloss to my lips. I slipped out of the bathroom, shutting off the light. Dray was on the couch, texting someone, and looked up when I made myself visible. His eyes widened.

"Too much?" I asked meekly. He stared open-mouthed and I nodded. "I'll go change," I said and he stood up abruptly.

"No! No, it's fine," he said and gave me a once-over with those burning, dark eyes of his that made me want to shiver. My inner wanton goddess perked up and said *'Oh, yes please!'* and I told her to shut up. Until I had those results in my hand declaring me all clear of any diseases I was strictly hands off, and even then, I wasn't about to jump into anything. *But oh God* the way Draven was looking at me, I really wanted to jump into something with him, like his bed, or his car, or the shower, or wherever he would have me.

"Let me grab my phone off the charger and we can go," I said. I turned around and heard his sharp intake of breath and smiled to myself. That right there, if anything, confirmed that he found me desirable, and after everything that had happened with Jerry, well, having any man, let alone one as delicious as Dray, find me attractive was worth its weight in gold.

I felt my self-esteem re-inflate a little as I snatched my phone from the charger and slid my debit card and ID into the back of the case I had on it, one of those ones that was made to hold such things. I didn't really have pockets in this get up so I held my phone in my hand and went back out. Dray was a cutting figure in his jacket and form-fitting black tee-shirt. His legs were encased in light denim that was worn butter-soft with age, frayed at the cuff and the edge of the pockets but miraculously free of holes. He had on those black biker boots with the silver buckle on the outside of the ankle peeking out from beneath the cuff of his jeans.

He held himself in that way that spoke softly that this was a man who was used to violence, a subtle warning to anyone who looked at him. He'd pulled half his hair up and tied it off with a black hair tie that disappeared against his raven's wing locks. His dark eyes swept over me one more time as I shrugged into a dark gray sweater. It was light and didn't afford much protection from the elements but it covered my back and draped in the front falling to long points at my thighs, matching the halter top quite nicely.

"Stay close to me tonight," he said, and it sounded almost ominous.

"Okay," I agreed and we left the house. He opened my door for me and I smiled, slipping into the passenger seat.

"You, uh, you look incredible," he said as he started the car and I smiled, pleased that he would think so.

"I hope you realize what a total fucking moron that assclown ex of yours is," he said derisively. I looked out the window and must have been silent for too long.

"You do, don't you?" he asked and his tone had shifted to incredulous.

"I've been wondering if some of it was somehow my fault," I said quietly. "Maybe if I *had* tried a little more with my appearance or tried to spend time doing things that he liked..." he snorted.

"I don't know what the hell he was thinking, Baby, but you deserve a hell of a lot better than he gave you. Don't worry about it. Someday, someone is going to see you for the awesome, brilliant, gorgeous, and hardworking chick you are and it'll be all over. You'll be treated well and be loved and pretty much worshiped the way you deserve to be." His hands tightened on the wheel, making that creaking noise. I stared at him agape.

That was probably the sweetest, most genuine, most beautiful compliment I had ever in my life been given. He kept his eyes resolutely on the road, his jaw tight with tension. I looked out the window as he pulled onto the highway. We weren't on it for very long. He flipped on his blinker and got into the center turn lane. When traffic was clear he cranked the wheel and we lurched into a steep gravel driveway with one of those chain link rolling gates open to one side.

He pulled up and off to the side in front of a squat one story gray cinder-block building. The roof was rusting corrugated steel, and high windows blocked by Venetian blinds lined the front. A big picture window was set by the door, a black flag with the MC's logo on it hanging in it ominously, the blinds behind the flag closed. For anyone stumbling in off the highway, the building didn't exactly exude 'friendly', which I suppose is what was intended. The window and door trim were painted a muddy brown but even though the whole thing gave off an unwelcoming and shabby appearance, it was remarkably well kept.

Nothing was falling down or sagging and the *bikes* – good Lord, the motorcycles lining the front of the building were a study in beauty, all shining chrome and personalized gas tanks, some glossy with paint and wax, some a matte finish, satiny in the dim light of the parking area's lights. The leather of the seats looked buttery and soft from use but there was not a crack or a tear in sight. All of the machines lovingly cared for by their owners. Dray looked wistfully at them and I smiled.

"Miss riding?" I asked tentatively.

"That obvious?" he asked.

"Kind of," I admitted.

"You ever ride?" he asked as we got out of the car.

"No," I said.

"No?" he asked and his tone was light, playful.

"Mm-mm," I said and shook my head.

"Good to know," he said and held out his arm for me. I hugged it and we carefully traversed the gravel minefield, or at least I did in my heels, Dray was sure-footed in his motorcycle boots.

"Thanks," I said when we were back on solid ground, but I neglected to let go of him. I liked the feel of his strong arm beneath my own and he didn't try to take it back. He opened the door to the clubhouse and I was hit by a wall of sound and heat.

I slipped my phone into my sweater pocket and stepped through the portal into Dray's world. The first thing that struck me, other than the shouts and cheers thrown in Dray's direction, was the tickling sensation of cigarette smoke in my nose. I fought the urge to sneeze as one leather clad man after another stepped up to him to shake hands, pound fists or to hug him. I was forced to let go of his arm for that and I have to admit, I felt a bit cast adrift for it.

I let my eyes roam the dimly lit interior of the clubhouse. The room was big and looked a lot like the interior of an older bar. To the left as you came in the door there *was* a bar. Scarred wood that had seen better days was clean and polished with mirrors and rows of colorful liquor bottles lined up behind it. There was a doorway that led back into a stainless steel industrial kitchen off to one side behind it.

I turned my head to look around the rest of the room.

A large archway led back into an open area with doors that opened into what were obviously bathrooms. A hallway led back into the dark, and likely the rooms Dray had spoken of earlier. There was a glass fishbowl at the back wall across from the front door with black curtains hanging in the window. The door was open and a long scarred metal table took up the center of the small room. In front of that was a pool table and to the right on a back cinderblock wall was a mural of the club's logo.

A dance floor was raised and in the center of all the tables and chairs, and music played loudly over large speakers against the back wall with the mural. There was a stage in front of that back wall with it's mural for live performances and I noted the pool table was on locked casters so it could be wheeled away if need be.


"WHAT DO YOU THINK?" Dray asked, and he was smiling with pride.

"It's comfortable," I said and smiled.

"Come on, I wanted to introduce you to Trigger and his Old Lady

Ashton; Reaver's over there, too." He took me by the elbow and we threaded our way through the tables to a large one near the dance floor, which had a couple of enterprising girls my age already getting down on it.

The first thing I noticed was a big behemoth of a man sitting at it. He was taller than Dray but they were about equal the way their bodies looked; all hard lean muscle, broad through the shoulders and tapering into a narrow waist. Trigger had long blonde hair to Dray's black, and the only thing missing to make him absolutely scream 'Viking' was a braided beard. He was clean-shaven with silvery blue eyes and had a pretty, small woman perched in his lap.

She had long, long auburn hair that hung loose around her shoulders and flowed down her back. Her eyes were a bright golden color and I'd never seen their like. She had freckles scattered across her nose and wore minimal make up. She didn't really need any, she had that natural beauty most women would kill for. The looks of love and adoration that she and the Viking were trading were unmistakable and I wondered how long they'd been married.

"Dray! Is this your stray!?" a man in his mid-to-late-twenties asked Dray.

He was more slender than either Dray or the Viking and had rich milk-chocolate brown hair that was shorter on the sides and a bit longer in the middle which he had smoothed to a point between his eyes. I think they called the style a faux-hawk. His bright blue eyes sparkled with mischief and laughter, crinkling good-naturedly at the corners. He had a dark blue teardrop tattoo at the corner of his left eye and very nearly vibrated with barely-contained energy and enthusiasm. He was the kind of guy you meet and instantly take a liking to. His smile was infectious and I smiled back while Dray made introductions.

"Everett, that's Reaver," Dray said indicating the man with the sparkling blue eyes and happy disposition.

"That's Trigger and his woman Ashton, but everyone calls her Sunshine on account of her eyes." Dray pulled out a seat at the table and I shrugged out of my sweater and hung it on the back before slipping into the seat.

"It's nice to meet you all," I said and turned to Reaver, "I'm Dray's what?" I asked and he laughed.

"His stray. That's what happened isn't it? He took you in like some stray cat?"

I blinked and blushed. "Uh, yeah, I guess it is," I said, flustered.

"Don't worry," The woman on Trigger's lap murmured, "I'm sure it isn't so bad. Ethan found me on the side of the road." She cuddled back into Trigger and looked content to be there. I raised my eyebrows. *The side of the road?* I thought to myself, but made no judgment or comment.

"It's true, her husband left her out there and I come along and the rest was history," the big Viking explained. I blinked. That wasn't what I had pictured at all and I felt properly chagrined, maybe I *had* been judgmental. When she said "the side of the road", I'd thought prostitute, which was really unfair considering she was dressed classier than me by a long mile. She wore black leather pants and riding boots, with a tight-fitting baby-doll tee shirt bearing the MC's logo on the breast. If anyone looked like a hooker it was me, by comparison.

"So spill, how'd you and Dray meet?" Reaver asked. He hung his arms on the back of the chair he was straddling and rested his chin on them. His piercing blue eyes searching my face. There was something cold and calculating below his happy, clowning around exterior and I swallowed, mouth suddenly gone dry. He had the look of one of my childhood 'uncles', a man I had overheard speaking to my father one very late night about killing another man for 'the cause'. It was strange how seeing that look on this man Reaver's face brought me back to my childhood; to a time where I felt the most safe.

"Worst day of my life ever," I said truthfully, though admittedly I wasn't counting the day my da' died. Nothing compared to that pain.

"Then you need a drink before you start to tell this story," Trigger said. Reaver jumped up.

"What's your poison?" He asked me.

"Irish whiskey, neat," I answered and he looked surprised. Dray was looking at me with that expression he sometimes got, the one that said I had mysteriously somehow earned points with him or something. Like his respect had gone up a notch. Reaver looked at Dray.

"It's a Scotch night," he answered.

"Comin' right up." Reaver went off to the bar.

"So where are you from?" Trigger asked in an attempt to make some small talk. I smiled.

"I was born in Everett, it's a small city north of Seattle. My mom died, and my da', he moved us out here shortly after. Been around here ever since," I answered.

"I'm sorry about your mother," Ashton said and I could barely hear her over the music. I shrugged.

"I never knew her. My da' made sure I was looked after, did all right I suppose." I smiled fondly.

"Where's your dad live?" Trigger asked and I felt my smile flee.

"Died last year. Heart attack."

"Oh, no!" Ashton's face crumbled into deep sympathy.

"It's okay, he's with me ma; he never even tried to date after her. Her dying broke him as a man. I'm pretty sure he carried on just for me and when he knew I'd be okay, when I left the nest, it was like it was okay for him to go home, to be with her." I shrugged gently. Dray didn't know it but I had his ashes at his house. I didn't want to weird him out. I knew beyond a shadow of a doubt that my da' had died of a broken heart. He was as fit as ever there were a man to be seen, so heart attack simply didn't fit the bill.

"Here we go," Reaver set down glasses in front of me and Dray. I picked up the amber liquid and breathed the aroma and smiled at the familiar smoky sweet scent.

"Sláinte!" I said, raised my glass and took a sip.

"What's that mean?" Dray asked, brow furrowed.

"I means 'to your health'," I smiled and Trigger, Ashton and Reaver raised their glasses.

"To your health!" they chorused and I laughed.

"So you're named after the city you were born in? How did that happen?" Ashton asked and my smile widened.

"Caught that did you?" I asked and she smiled happily and nodded.

"A fine story if ever there was one," I said and let out a gusty sigh. I sipped my whiskey and let a smile curve my lips even if it was just a little bit sad. I slipped into my father's accent with the telling... I couldn't help being just a little theatrical, it was how my da' had been and his blood coursed through my veins sure as anything.

"So there was my da', his wife had just died and a new nurse is placing me in his arms. She asks him, 'What are you going to name her?' but my da', he's looking at my poor mother and somehow he thinks that she's asking him those questions. You know the ones, 'Sir do you know where you are? Do you know what day it is?' *Those* questions. And me da', he doesn't hear her, so he asks 'What?' and she asks him 'Do you know what her name is?' and in his grief he hears, 'Do you know where you are?' so he says 'Everett' and he's staring at his wife..." I pause, just as my da' had done a thousand times before in the retelling of the story of how I got my name. I used to love hearing the story when I was a child, and I still did. Telling it the way he would made me feel closer to him, so I pressed on.

"Now the nurse just takes him at his word and writes down 'Everett' and then she asks him my middle name and he looks at her and says, 'I want to name her after my wife Mary...' so she writes that down and before you know it, there I am a wee babe in my father's arms, 'Everett Mary Moran.' Which, it's not a bad name, really." I polished off my whiskey, the four faces around me thoughtful and somber. Silence stretched between the lot of us.

"So! How'd you meet our boy Dray?" Reaver smiled and levity returned with it. I looked a little sadly at my empty glass and launched into that story. My Irish accent disappeared.

"Well, it all started when I got up late for work on Thursday..." I told them everything, sparing no detail, right up until the first time Dray took me the hell out of the apartment I shared with Jerry.

Reaver reeled back in his seat.

"Please, tell me you punched this little cockbite in the mouth!" he said to Dray.

"Yesterday." Dray held up his fist which was still sporting the band-aid I'd put on it. Reaver raised his fist and they bumped them together. I laughed.

"Good," Trigger grunted and Ashton nodded happily, which surprised me.

"So did you divorce your husband?" I asked Ashton, and Dray and Reaver went very still, exchanging a look. I was surprised to see the same cold darkness my 'uncle' had borne in his gaze, and that I had caught in Reaver's, slide behind Dray's dark eyes.

"I didn't have to. He committed suicide," Ashton said, but her chilly smile belied her words. Trigger looked grim, his silvery eyes going positively glacial. I smiled.

"I'm sure he did," I said simply and looked at my glass for more alcohol. I settled back into my seat and watched the four of them trade spooked looks. Dray was looking at me with worry in his eyes. I mouthed 'IRA' at him and shrugged. He seemed to relax marginally but his look grew to one of considering. Reaver cleared his throat and got up.

"Another drink?" he asked.

"Absolutely," I smiled and nodded and he picked up my empty glass and meandered through the tables and crowd to the bar. Everyone at the table was rather subdued and quiet. Dray was looking me over as if he were trying to decide something. I smiled at him and gave a luxurious stretch.

"Dance with me," I said in an effort to dispel the tension gathering over our little group like a dark cloud. He looked me over.

"Not me, I suck at it," he said and I could tell he was slightly intimidated by the prospect after having seen me that morning.

"Oh, please," I rolled my eyes, "Traditional Irish step does nothing for me when it comes to contemporary dance. It's like expecting a classically trained ballet dancer to know hip hop." I stood up and he stood up with me smiling.

"Hey! Haven't you ever seen that Julia Stiles movie where she's the ballerina and moves to the inner city and learns hip hop from that one dude after her mom dies in a car accident?" Reaver asked, setting the drinks on the table and joining the conversation late. Dray raked him with one of his burning dark looks.

"Dude," he said simply, his tone laced with disgust.

"What?" Reaver asked.

"Pussy," Trigger said, trying to keep a straight face and failing. Ashton was even staring up at him agape.

"What!? Chicks love a dude in touch with his feminine side." Reaver bounced his eyebrows up and down at me and smoothed a hand down the front of his white tee-shirt.

"You just showed off a little bit too much of your man-gina for my tastes," I said flatly and drank my whiskey in one swallow. I was just this side of pleasantly buzzed and feeling a little braver than normal. I captured Dray's hand and pulled him onto the dance floor without so much as a backward glance at Reaver, who had this mock-wounded look plastered to his face. Trigger was laughing uproari-ously at him and even Ashton was giggling from behind her hand.

Dray had that gorgeous boyish grin on his face complete with dimples and I smiled a small victory that I'd put it there. It quickly disappeared when we stepped up onto the floor; I drew close to him and swayed to the beat. He looked me over and the unmistakable lust in his eyes left my skin tingling wherever his gaze landed. His arm went around my lower back, the leather of his coat sleeve cool and slick against my skin and he pulled me tightly up against the front of his body, one of his powerful thighs sliding between my own. I gripped his well-defined shoulders and we moved to the beat, in a dance that wasn't bordering on indecent, it was miles past the line. I breathed deep his spicy, masculine scent and lost myself in the music and his presence, our bodies pressed tight. He was smiling, I was almost his exact height in the heels and our eyes were locked, his lips a bare inch from mine.

"I know I shouldn't, but I want to kiss you, Everett," he said, and his breath tickled across my skin, the peaty warmth of the scotch he'd drunk teasing my nose.

"I know I shouldn't, but I really want you to kiss me, Dray," I said back and he closed his eyes, the war clear on his face. He opened them and my heart gave a painful squeeze in my chest.

"Just a kiss," he said, "Doesn't have to go anywhere, doesn't have to mean anything..." his lips drew closer.

"Right," I said and my voice was breathy, "Doesn't have to..." I said and his lips touched mine. Our bodies stilled as our lips took over and heat raced across my skin. He stole the breath from my lungs and the world narrowed to the press of his lips, tight against mine. My hands came up, trembling, to cup his face as he deepened the kiss, his tongue flicking lightly against mine. Sparks leapt between us and I finally understood what it meant when people declared a kiss to be electric. I must have kissed Jerry a thousand times and more, and never, *never* had he ever kissed me like this.

Dray's mouth was warm and succulent against my own. His hands drifted up from my ass to slide along the naked skin of my back, kneading as he went. I melted against him and kissed him back with a wild urgency. Some whistles and appreciative shouts went up around the room and I smiled against Dray's insistent lips. I felt his hand leave my back and go up, he waved it around the room in the direction of those whistles and calls and I caught that he was flipping the spectators off.

I laughed and he swallowed the sound, his tongue plunging past my lips, demanding, conquering, and it was so incredibly hot my knees felt weak. My hands drifted into his hair and I held his mouth tight to my own and felt the vibration of his moan through our tightly pressed bodies. The kiss didn't have to go anywhere, it didn't have to mean anything... but we both knew that it would and it did.

The conversation died and the sounds of chairs scraping back suddenly, the sharp sound of some of them crashing to the floor, disrupted everything. Dray jerked his mouth back from mine and I felt the loss keenly. We turned our heads in unison towards the door and Dray's hold on me tightened. Two uniformed Sheriff's deputies stood in the open doorway. The music cut out and the hushed silence that descended on the room was deafening.

"Sorry to interrupt the festivities," one of the deputies said, "But we're looking for a Dray." I closed my eyes and felt my muscles go loose with defeat.

"Fucking Jerry," I muttered under my breath.

"I'm Dray. Draven Trujillo," Dray spoke up. I sighed, this was a hell of a way to find out his last name, although I probably could have just asked, like a thousand times over, by now. I made to take a step back but his arms tightened imperceptibly around me. I stayed put, it wasn't hard to do. I loved the feel of being pressed against Dray's hard body.

"What's going on here?" Dragon, Dray's father, pushed his way through the crowd. He was shirtless and the MC's logo was tattooed in full living color, size and detail in the center of his chest, right over where his actual beating heart was. I swallowed.

"You are?" The deputy asked, eyes flicking from Dragon to Dray and back again.

"Jose Trujillo, you can call me Dragon, I'm the president of the club. My boy, Dray, is Vice President." He motioned over to where we stood. "What can I do for you, officers?" he asked.

"I'm sorry to say, sir, we're here to arrest your son on a charge of assault and battery." The deputy did look genuinely sorry but I think it was more the fact that he and his partner had drawn the short straw and had to be the ones to come out here.

Dragon looked over to Dray. "You know the drill, Son. Don't say nothin'. Wait 'til I get you a lawyer." Dragon gave Dray a crooked grin and I looked Dray in the eyes from mere inches away.

"I am so sorry," I murmured, "This is all my fault."

Dray grinned crookedly at me. "Divine intervention," he said with a smirk and let me go. I frowned, not comprehending. He put his lips against my ear.

"If I weren't being arrested, I'd be taking you someplace to fuck you with or without no damned test results," he whispered harshly. I felt butterflies take flight in my stomach and my panties definitely grew moist. That was the hottest thing anyone had ever said to me, and it wasn't *what* he said, but rather *how* he said it. I found myself nodding rapidly.

"Reaver!" he called.

"Yeah, VP?" Reaver appeared next to us as if from thin air. Dray handed him his keys.

"Get my girl home for me, yeah?" Reaver nodded grimly.

"Yeah, boss," he said.

I felt my eyes well with frustrated tears. I had really cocked it up this time, hadn't I? I should have dug my heels and left the rest of my crap. I shouldn't have gone back there; shouldn't have let Dray talk me into going back there. He walked over to the officers and turned around, presenting his wrists. They handcuffed him. I sniffed and small arms went around my waist. Ashton was hugging me.

"Don't cry. The club has a good lawyer," she murmured.

I didn't know how to explain how I felt like a walking disease in more ways than one now. First because of Jerry, now because of... well... Jerry. I think I was crying more because I was angry than anything. I turned my eyes to the ceiling as they led Dray outside.

"Call my lawyer for me, Pops? I'm saving my phone call for someone more important," Dray called over his shoulder as they disappeared out the door with him.

"I feel you. Right behind you, Son!" Dragon called. He looked at me with his much older and much wiser burning gaze and I sniffed.

"I am so sorry," I said mournfully. He laughed abruptly.

"I'm not. He gave that puta barata his just desserts for what he said to you. I've never been prouder of my boy." He grinned but it was quickly replaced with a dark look. "Had to be a Saturday," he mused darkly, turning around and disappearing down the hall into the maze of rooms in back.

"At least it wasn't Friday night," Reaver commented.

"Why does Saturday matter?" I asked, turning to him.

"Can't post bail until he's arraigned and one is set. No arraignments on the weekend, he's stuck in there until Monday." Reaver shrugged inelegantly.

"Oh," I said, watching the police car turn down the driveway through the clubhouse's open door, taillights disappearing over the rise.

"Come on. I'll take you back to Dray's." I nodded, a little numb at the prospect of Dray spending the entire weekend in jail over me. I gathered my sweater and Ashton reached out. I hugged her back this time and felt better. Trigger engulfed me in a hug next and I hugged back, a little surprised.

"Known Dray a long time and never seen him do that," he said, looking me over.

"Do what?" I asked.

"Kiss someone like he kissed you," Ashton said, and she looked a little excited.

"Welcome to the family," Trigger said and shot me a half-assed little salute. I laughed incredulously. I turned to Reaver.

"Yep, he licked you. You're his," he declared and looked pouty.

I laughed. "Is that how that works around here?" I asked.

He nodded solemnly. "That's how it works," he said and walked with me out into the parking lot. The music came back to life as we swung the door shut behind us. I negotiated the gravel drive carefully in my heels and heaved a sigh as he unlocked my door.

"It'll be fine. Not Dray's first time being arrested and he hasn't served more than a little bit of jail time yet." He smiled beatifically at me and I rolled my eyes.

"That is *so* comforting," I said and got in. Reaver leaned down and all trace of humor had been whisked off his face.

"This club turned a new leaf a long time ago. We aren't like that anymore, but no one, not a single one of us has a problem with Dray going to jail for punching that assclown in the mouth for calling you a bitch. That shit simply does not fly with this crowd." I nodded slowly and noted the stiletto knives tattooed along his inner forearms.

"Okay," I said carefully and the mask simply snapped back into place. Reaver was all smiles again and quipped, "Glad you understand!" He shut the door to Dray's Trans Am firmly and jogged around the front. He got in and fired it up. I didn't know what to say to him so I stayed silent for the entire trip home. He pulled the Trans Am into the driveway and killed the engine when we got to the house. He handed me the keys.

"Don't know which one gets us in the house," he said and smoothed his hair down out of what looked like habit. I selected the correct one and he smiled.

"Excellent!" He got out and I did too, heels clacking against the cement as I went up the steps. I pulled my phone out of my sweater pocket and gripped it tightly. Reaver opened the front door and I went in. He followed and went for the fridge.

"If I gotta sit bitch with Trigger for a ride back to the club, I'm gonna drink Dray's beer," he declared. I shrugged. "You do whatever it is you do. It's your home now for all intents and purposes," he added, rooting around looking through bottles. I went into Dray's room and slipped off the heels. I changed into my pajamas and went into the bathroom to wash my face. I patted it dry and got my phone off the bed and went to the table, firing up my laptop. Reaver flopped down on the couch and turned on the TV. He flipped through channels and finally landed on MTV and Ridiculousness. I chewed my lip as I waited for the computer to finish starting up, then sat staring at it. I didn't know what to do. My leg bounced under the dining room table and I gusted out a sigh. I was too keyed up and too damned tipsy to do homework. I shut the laptop down.

I knew what I needed to do – I needed to blow off steam. I went into the bedroom and changed into tights and a leotard. I tied on a light chiffon short skirt in gray and pulled on my hard shoes. Reaver was cracking up in the living room over whatever was on television. This wasn't going to be good for the shoes, but whatever.

I snatched my phone off the table and went carefully across the kitchen floor. I clattered down the steps and put on some music from my phone. It wasn't real loud but it was enough. I set my phone on the railing and went over to the patch of driveway in front of the garage. I hadn't needed to do this since I was a kid. Whenever my da' and me got into a fight I would go out to our drive and dance until I fell down.

I listened to the measures and stood ready and let everything I was feeling flow from the crown of my head down and out through my feet. Fast, fast, fast and faster I tapped, until my muscles burned with weariness. I almost missed it when the music cut and a ringtone took over. I dashed for the phone and answered the unfamiliar number.

"Dray?" I asked, secretly hoping that I was the 'more important person' he was saving his phone call for.

"Hey, Em, how you doing?" he asked and I could hear the smile in his voice. Reaver and Trigger were sitting on the top step watching me. I blinked. When had Trigger gotten here? I turned my back on them for some semblance of privacy.

"Look at you, all badass," I said smiling, "You're the one in jail and you're asking how *I'm* doing?" I said a bit breathlessly.

"Why are you out of breath?" he asked, alarmed.

"Dancing in the driveway. Got my hard shoes on. Pounding out some frustration," I said. A towel flopped over my shoulder and I startled. It was cool, bordering on cold, out here and I was sweating pretty hard. I turned and Trigger smiled down at me. I smiled and patted my face and chest.

"Reaver and Trig there?" he asked.

"Yeah. You want to talk to them?" I asked.

"No, I want to talk to you. I just wanted to make sure they're treating you all right," he said.

"Yeah, no, they're being great." I heard a chuckle behind me and my shoes made loud metallic clacks as I took some paces forward.

"So I'll probably get out Monday. Maybe Tuesday, can I trust you to take care of Sadie?" he asked me. "I want you to be able to get to work and school and pick up your results, if you get me," he said.

"I get you," I said softly.

"Never been kissed like that," he grunted.

"Me, either," I said softly.

"I'm nobody's rebound," he warned and I bit my lip nervously.

"I don't do rebounds," I said, "I'm a good Irish Catholic girl." He snorted and laughed into the phone.

"What? I am!" I said and I was smiling broadly.

"Okay Em. Look, I gotta go, hang tight; stay safe and I'll see you when I see you," he said.

"Is it wrong that I'm picturing you in one of those awful orange jumpsuits and I think it's kind of hot?" I asked. He laughed.

"It's not a good look for anybody, I don't care what you say," he said.

"Dray?" I said after a moment of silence.

"Yeah, Em?"

"Be careful?" and I couldn't keep the anxiety from tinging my voice if I wanted to.

"Always," he promised.

"K, bye for now," I whispered.

"Bye, babe." The line went dead and I ended the call, the music picking up right where it left off, drifting out of the small speakers of the phone in my hand. I sucked in a strong, slow, steady breath.

"He'll be okay," Trigger said quietly, I turned around and tapped the screen to shut off the music.

"When did you get here?" I asked.

"About twenty minutes ago. You were tearing it up." He said it like he was impressed and sucked on the end of an e-cigarette, the end glowing blue in the darkness.

"Trying to work off some aggression," I stated simply. Reaver snorted. He was turning a knife over and over in his long slender fingers and I felt a shiver go down my spine.

"Cold?" Trigger asked, eyeing me.

"No," I said simply and I pointed at Reaver, "He's scary."

I opted for the truth. It had never served me wrong before. Reaver looked at me as if I had done something interesting.

"I had an 'uncle' like you, growing up." I put the "uncle" in air quotes. "He killed for the IRA, except he couldn't turn the cold and creepy off. He just was what he was and made no apologies for it. You," I shook my head and looked at him plainly. "You can hide it. He was scary but you two, you two are terrifying because you can blend in so well." I wiped more sweat off the back of my neck.

Reaver's smile was gone, and he looked at me with a predator's assessing gaze.

Trigger was looking at me like I was an interesting specimen, too. "Guessing by the nickname you're some kind gun fanatic?" My voice slid into the brogue of my people. He nodded slowly.

"United States Marine Corps sniper," he said. I nodded, I didn't want to press either of them any further.

"You don't have a problem with it," Reaver stated. I shook my head.

"I grew up at the knee of men like you," I said. "Good men who fought for what they believed in. I just thought you should know that I know. I'm not judging, I'm not scared, at most I am unnerved a little, but that's healthy. I just thought you'd like to know you don't have to hide from me. I won't pretend to understand it, but it's the way I grew up, and I've seen a thing or two in my time." Trigger and Reaver exchanged looks again; Reaver smiled, then Trigger did too.

"No hiding from you is there?" Reaver asked.

I shrugged.

"Shit, Dray has his hands full," Trigger laughed. Of the two of them he was the more human.

"Are you sure that isn't the other way 'round?" I asked.

"Pretty sure." Trigger grinned.

"Dray gets uncomfortable around perceptive people," Reaver said.

"I'll keep that in mind," I murmured.

"Don't, he needs a shove or two here and there," Trigger said.

I nodded and stretched. I was starting to stiffen up already. I made for the house and Reaver got up and out of my way.

"Hot shower and bed for me," I said and they both waved.

"'Night," Trigger said.

"G'night," Reaver echoed.

"It was nice meeting you both," I said and it was. They reminded me so much of my eclectic family growing up.

"It was nice meeting you too, Irish," Reaver said and smiled. I smiled back. I think we were on the same page. He knew that I knew what he was and that I was cool. As a result, he wouldn't stab me or slit my throat in my sleep. It was a pretty even trade as far as I was concerned.

I closed the back door behind me and locked it and went for a shower, and Dray's bed, in that order. Reaver had left Dray's keys on the dining table by my laptop. I'd seen them when I'd come in. As I was stripping to get into the bath, I heard a motorcycle start outside. I showered and crawled nude between Dray's sheets, breathing in deeply. I sighed in exasperation and frustration with Jerry. I hoped this would be it with him, a last hurdle. I closed my eyes and felt my cheeks burn with the memory of the way Dray had kissed me on the dance floor.

He'd as good as promised more to come on the phone and I felt my body tremble with an unspoken but resolute *'yes please!'* and I sighed. I needed to make sure Jerry hadn't given me anything before I took a single step in that direction. With as much as my mind was turning it would be a long time before sleep came.

**8**

---

**D**ray...

Spending the weekend in jail sucked balls. What sucked even more was being stuck in jail for the whole weekend with nothing but thoughts of Everett on my mind. I sure as fuck hoped that ass-bag hadn't given her anything because if he did, I was pretty much going to kill him.

God, Everett... She was different. She *knew*. She didn't go through life with a pair of blinders on. She'd grown up at the knees of killers, hell, even her dad may have been one. I stared at the underside of the bunk I'd been assigned and dared to hope. I mean, I have never been kissed like that. *Never*... and I wanted more. She'd agreed, before my lips touched hers, that it didn't have to mean anything, but as soon as I'd tasted her, I'd tasted the lie just as surely. As much as I hated liars, I couldn't blame her for it when I'd been lying to myself just as hard.

There was something about Everett Moran that I'd been missing. I craved having a girl like that in my life. She was sweet and flexible but she had an inner core of steel in there somewhere. I could see it in her eyes. She looked at you and you just knew her eyes cut right through all the bullshit. Ashton was like that, but she was softer than Everett and that made Everett so much more attractive to me.

It was Tuesday and I was waiting to be released. My club had posted my modest bail and I had a court date according to my lawyer. We were going to try and plea bargain it down so I wouldn't have a record for assault. We had a pretty good chance if I paid restitution, stayed out of trouble and volunteered to do some community service. The circumstances helped. My lawyer said that Everett agreed to enter in a sworn statement on my behalf. I was going to kiss her again just for that, but first I needed to get out of here.

"Draven Trujillo?"

"Yeah, that's me," I said and got up.

"Bond's been posted, come with me." The correctional officer held open the door for me and I went for it.

"Thanks, man," I said as I passed him.

"No problem, right this way and we'll get you processed out."

Home, shower, Everett in that order.

Around two hours later, I had two accomplished and I was resolutely heading for the third. I pulled up to a stop at a light and put my feet down walking myself and the bike up to the line. I could see her coffee stand up the block, Sadie parked nearby. I figured I'd be clever and I pulled up to the window. A blonde with way too much cleavage leaned out.

"What can I get you, honey?" she asked and I looked past her. Everett was at the coffee machine, chatting at a customer through the window opposite the one I was at. I smiled when I caught sight of her tight jean-clad ass and I thrust my chin in her direction.

"I'm here for her," I said and the blonde looked over her shoulder. She scowled at me.

"She's not on the menu," she said flatly, "but I might be." I laughed.

"She is for me," I said to the blonde, and I revved my engine and I made it loud. Everett startled and whirled around. She quickly handed the coffee off to her customer on the other side and dove for the window. The blonde side-stepped and Everett leaned her entire upper body out and grabbed my face. She planted one on me and I laughed, kissing her back.

"Miss me?" I asked and my heart glowed at the expressive way her eyes lit up.

"Hell, yes!" she said, "Haven't been able to get you off my mind."

She bounded backwards through the window said something to the blonde and motioned for me to pull around. I parked over by Sadie and shut off the bike. A minute later she came jogging across the parking lot. She had an hour left on her shift.

"My boss would kill me if he saw this," she said, and hugged herself

"Don't get caught or in trouble on my account," I told her.

"No, I wanted to tell you, our results are in at the clinic." She was smiling.

"They tell you?" I asked, she was nodding and her smile got bigger.

"I'm clean!" She did an excited little dance right there in her sneakers and it was the cutest damned thing I'd ever seen. I had left my phone back at the house, charging.

"We'll go get mine when you're off," I said. She nodded and I jerked my chin in the direction of the coffee shack.

"Go on, get," I said and she smiled and dashed back across the parking lot. I sat on my bike and people-watched. It was crisp but not too cold, overcast but not raining. Soon enough she was off work and coming back my way. She had a sexy damned walk, I realized.

"Follow me to the house and then we'll drive out to get our papers," I told her and she nodded.

I fired up the bike and waited for her to start up Sadie. What I hadn't said was that I had every intention of taking my time with her. Treating her right. I didn't want a quick fuck out of her, I wanted to go slow and easy and I wanted her right goddamned now. I knew how important having these results in hand was to her and I wanted her to know that I was clean too. I hadn't taken the test with that intent but now I was glad I had. I didn't want her to ever have to worry about me. I pulled Matilda into the garage and locked her up tight and safe inside.

"I don't have class today, only on Monday and Wednesday," she said and I felt myself smile. I got into Sadie's driver's seat, Everett settling into the passenger side. I backed out of the drive fluidly and headed for the clinic.

"Was it bad?" she asked quietly, midway there.

"No," I told her and I covered her hand with mine. She gripped my fingers and searched my face, nodding.

"Couldn't stop thinking about you, either," I confessed.

"What did you think about?" she asked.

"I like you, Em. I do casual sex but for some reason I don't want to be that with you. I want it to mean something." I put it out there, and she nodded, her steel blue eyes curious.

"Who was she?" she asked and I blinked. Wait, what?

"What?" I asked.

"You keep telling me you're nobody's rebound; someone hurt you. Who was she?" she asked. Crap. I gave myself away.

"Veronica. She and I hooked up when I was a club prospect back around when I was eighteen. I thought it was love, turns out it was for me but I was just a way for her to get over the guy that dumped her." I tightened my hand on the wheel and she nodded slowly.

"I don't want you to be a rebound," she said softly.

"But?" I asked, sensing one coming.

"I've never done this before, but at the same time... You, me... I have *never* felt anything like what I felt on that dance floor. I don't want to hurt you. I'm afraid." I turned onto Twentieth and stopped behind some traffic and thought about it. *But she was afraid...*

"Tell you what," I said gently.

"What?" she asked and she looked confused, hurt, worried, and scared all rolled into one stricken expression.

"Let's get these results. I'm going to take you out to dinner and let's let things fall into place, go with what's comfortable. Minute by minute, day by day, we'll play it by ear and see where we're at every step of the way." I didn't want this to be complicated. I just wanted a shot at her, *with* her.

She thought about it and I waited, holding my breath. Finally she smiled and it was sweet and beautiful and her lips parted and she said what I wanted so desperately to hear.

"Okay, sounds good. Except." I smiled and turned into the clinic's lot.

"Except?"

"I'd rather stay in and cook." She bit her bottom lip and waited.

"Good deal. Probably better for us anyways." I said. She smiled and I felt pretty damned good about it.

We went in together and collected our results from the front desk. This was not the most awesome way to start anything but at the same time it sort of was, at least we would know, could be sure. No secrets, no surprises. I liked that. It kept things simple.

I opened my results and, as expected, they were negative. She was looking over hers and she closed her eyes. Tears coated her lashes.

"What's wrong?" I asked and felt a frisson of anxiety. She handed me the paper and took mine from me. Her results were all negative. I frowned. Why was she crying? She looked over mine and broke into a sob and reached for me. I pulled her against me and she cried against my shoulder. "What's wrong?" I repeated, a little more urgently, unsure of what was going on, if I could fix it.

"I'm just so relieved!" she sobbed and I got it. I finally really understood just how bad she had been freaking out about this inside.

"Hey, hey, hey, it's okay." I said, "I've got you now."

I let her cry it out, helpless to do anything else. I wanted to knock out more of his teeth, chipping one hadn't been enough. I held her to me and breathed in her delicate lilac scent. She finally settled down and sniffed, wiping at her eyes. I pulled a bandana out of my back pocket and handed it to her. She mopped up and I looked her over. She was even pretty when she cried, I realized.

"Better?" I murmured. She nodded. I steered her to the passenger side of the car and put her in it. I got in the other side and started Sadie up.

"Where to next?" she asked.

"Home. You got makeup running down your face," I said. She looked into the side mirror and sighed.

"Thanks for that," she said and I smiled.

"You're welcome," I said and took her home.

Once inside the house I was hyper-aware that it was just me and her, alone. I forced myself to sit on the couch and I let her go into my room. I resisted the urge to follow her – but barely. I wanted her spread beneath me in my bed something so fierce it was turning into a deep ache inside of me. She disappeared into the bathroom and I heard the shower start and the curtain ride across the rails. I went from the couch to the kitchen but stopped when I saw the warm glow of light from the bathroom's open doorway.

*She did not just leave that door open.* I thought to myself, but she had, and I was going to take it for the invitation that it was. I took a halting step towards the sliver of light spilling out into the hall and stopped. I closed my eyes and counted to ten.

No.

I wasn't.

She wasn't in a good place, too much emotional rollercoaster and having me get into that shower would just kill it before anything really had a chance to get started. I really didn't want to be anyone's rebound. I *wouldn't* be her rebound. Something about her was different; she saw through all the bullshit, those steel blue eyes of hers cutting right through it. The thing that got me was that she was no shrinking violet around the ugly stuff. She saw it, processed it and either went with it or she didn't. So far she'd gone with it and either that made her crazy or showed an intestinal fortitude that most *guys* lacked.

I admired her, not to put too fine a point on it, and I wanted to know more about her. A quick fuck in my shower wasn't going to net me that, if anything it would snag me just the opposite with a girl like her. So, as much as I would have liked to have taken her silent invitation, I went into my room instead and changed into some comfortable flannel pajama pants. I sat on the end of the bed and mulled things over.

A little bit too long.

I hadn't heard the shower shut off and suddenly she was there, just materialized in front of me, wrapped from armpit to knees in one of my oversized midnight blue bath sheets. I looked up and met those steely eyes of hers and her somber expression dead on.

"Why didn't you join me?" she asked softly.

"I wanted to," I told her, and let her read the truth in my eyes. "But it wouldn't have gotten either one of us anyplace good." I stood up, which forced her to take a step back. I tipped her chin with my finger and smoothed the pad of my thumb over the silky skin of her jaw. Her chest stilled and I was acutely aware that we were only inches from my bed, the towel easily displaced with a flick of my wrist.

Oh, how I wanted to take away that damned towel. I could tell she wanted me to, by the look in her eyes, the stillness of her breath... I bent, closing the gap between us and kissed her softly. I closed my eyes and breathed her in, she smelled so damned *good*, warm and clean and it took everything I had in me to keep the contact we had to a chaste kiss. Her lips parted underneath mine and I damn near came undone. I pulled back reluctantly when what I really wanted to do was kiss her with a savage intensity, turn her and fling her onto the mattress, pressing her back into the covers with my body over hers, but I resisted and it cost me to do it.

I left her standing, stunned and wanting, in the middle of my bedroom, as I strode out into the kitchen, fisting my hands in my hair. I stood there and shook for a minute and tried to put the lid back on my lust, which was screaming through every single one of my veins and arteries, burning me up from the inside out. I opened up the fridge and grabbed the first beer I laid eyes on, twisting off the cap and taking a long pull.

"I think I understand why you stopped, and while I'm glad in my head that you did, my hormones think I may need another shower. A cold one this time," she said from the archway leading back to the bathroom and bedrooms.

"Want a beer?" I asked, holding mine out to her. She pushed off the wall, her steel-blue eyes never leaving mine, and plucked the beer from my hand, wrapping her lips around where mine had just been and *the way she did it*... I shuddered. *Why was that the hottest fucking thing I had ever seen in my life?* She swallowed slowly, deliberately and I couldn't tell if my blood was running hot or cold anymore. What I did know was my cock was stiff to the point of pain. She knew it too.

Her lips quirking up on one side she said, "Go sit down. I'll make dinner." I nodded slowly and wondered when the hell I'd been upstaged. I pulled out a chair at the table and sat down. I could watch her prance around my kitchen in what passed for her PJ's every night of the week and twice on Sunday. She went to the fridge and brought out another beer and held it up with a questioning look. I smiled.

"Stop being such a tease and bring me my damn beer!" I joked and she laughed. She twisted off the top and held it out to me and some of the sexual tension eased off a little bit. I took the bottle from her hand careful not to brush fingers and found myself wondering if she were as wet as I was hard. She made a great show of bending over and rifling through the refrigerator giving me an exceptional view of those long sinful dancer's legs of hers.

I drank some of my beer and decided two could play at this game. She started washing some vegetables at the sink and I crept up behind her, right behind her. She was smiling this secret little victorious smile and I couldn't resist fucking with her. I pulled her back by her hips roughly against my body and she gave out a surprised little yip that turned into this sultry moan. I slid a hand down the front of her body and let it dip below the waistband of her boxer shorts.

Oh, God, yeah. She kept her pussy smooth, shaved, just the way I liked it! The little game we were playing momentarily tipped in her favor until I could get a grip. Her breath caught and she closed her eyes, shuddering against me. I dipped a finger into her folds and teased at her clit for a moment before plunging my index finger up inside her.

God, she was wet. Her silky heat inviting and tight, oh I'd have her writhing beneath me all right. Someday, some night... all night. For now, I wanted to indulge myself a little. I pulled my hand from her shorts and backed up abruptly. She stumbled, catching herself at the edge of the sink and turned around, her eyes dilated with arousal. She watched, aching, wanting, as I brought my fingers to my lips and sucked her essence off of them. She tasted like fresh rain and spring-time. I smiled slowly, and I know it was a little cruel but she had asked for it.

"I like my dessert first," I said in my low sexy growl and relished that it had the desired effect. Her jaw dropped open and I winked at her. She stood dumbfounded, her pink lips slightly pouty when I picked up my beer and took myself beyond the dining room into the living room. I needed space. I needed distance and I needed it now or I was going to fuck her on my kitchen counter.

*That* thought had me nearly doing an about face. I flopped onto the couch in a way I hoped was nonchalant and picked up the remote. I flipped on the TV and surfed the channels without really paying attention to what was on. I could see her staring at me out of the corner of my eye but I couldn't tell you what expression she wore. Slowly she turned back to the sink and with shaking hands continued her task. I smiled and when I was sure she couldn't or wouldn't see looked over. She looked shell-shocked and in all the right ways. Her damp hair laying in tangled ropes over her shoulders and back, a slight smile played on her lips and I smiled. For a second I'd been afraid I'd pushed too much.

She handed me a plate an hour later and curled herself up on the couch next to me. The news was coming on and we watched. The food was out of this world. More of that bread she'd made the last time and some kind of casserole that was mostly rice and chicken with vegetables in a white garlic sauce.

"Damn, girl, you can cook," I said and she smiled, glowing from the praise. We ate and set the dishes aside on the coffee table for the time being. I turned and pulled her against me so we were both lounging on the couch lengthwise. She sucked in a sharp breath and let it out slowly, melting against me and I loved it. Pretty soon her soft, even breathing let me know she was asleep.

"Everett?" I asked softly. No response. I sighed. I wasn't really surprised, she'd had a long and emotional day. Sleep probably really was the best thing for her. I watched some more TV and was loathe to wake her, but I did it anyway. I nudged her gently until she started and sucked in a great breath. She yawned and stretched.

"What time is it?" she asked, voice husky with sleep.

"A little after eight, time for you to get to bed, Princess." She pouted and I knew what would put a smile on both hers and my face.

"Come on, let me up," I said and she slowly moved to comply. I got up with her and asked her where her phone was.

"Plugged in, in your bedroom why?" she asked.

"Isn't it your alarm clock?" I asked in return.

"Oh, yeah…" I smiled and walked her into my room, propelling her gently in front of me by the shoulders. I lifted the blankets and she got under and I'm pretty sure she expected me to tuck her in and leave her. Not happening. I got in with her and pulled her against me and let out a contented sigh.

"This is nice," she said sleepily against my chest, her head resting on my shoulder. I had her tucked tightly up against me, my other hand behind my head, the fingertips of the arm around her idly tracing patterns on her bare shoulder.

"Yeah, it is," I agreed.

"G'night, Dray," she murmured and I smiled.

"Sleep tight Everett," I murmured back, and she did. Me, though, not so much. I lay awake staring at the ceiling for far too long, a dull deep ache settling into my balls. She had that kind of effect on me. I smiled a little ruefully. I guess she won our little game by default. I closed my eyes but sleep was still a long time coming.

**9**

---

verett…

Waking up in the middle of the night pressed against Dray was a delicious treat. Cuddling up close and having him actually put his arms around me in his sleep rather than shoving me away, like Jerry would have, was a-freaking-mazing. The alarm shrieking at us and dispelling our peaceful cuddle calm was frustrating to say the least. I groaned and it was echoed by one of Dray's.

"This getting up before the ass-crack of dawn is total bullshit," he said. I instantly felt bad.

"I know, I'm sorry." My voice was mournful. He rolled, pinning me roughly beneath him. I gasped and his burning dark gaze trapped my own like a butterfly in a killing jar, intense and leaving me powerless beneath it.

"You're worth it, Everett," he said, his warm breath skating over my lips, a promise of things to come. I expected him to kiss me. I wanted him to kiss me but his weight lifted from me and I blinked at his retreating back as he went out the bedroom door and shut himself in the bathroom. The shower started a moment later.

*Holy crap. What was that?*

I got up and dressed quickly and quietly and went out to make sure my bag was packed with my laptop and the texts I would need for class that day. I was vaguely aware of the shower shutting off and of the bathroom door opening but I just naturally assumed he would go in the bedroom and dress not that he would come up behind me and pull me back against his body or that his teeth would find purchase in the side of my throat as he bit me gently, his tongue laving at the pulse point in the side of my neck. I gasped my muscles turning into liquid at his attentions. Icy water dripped from the ends of his slick black hair and trickled along my collarbone.

"Jesus!" I cried, as much for the contrasting sensation of his hot mouth and the cold water than for the shock of the cold itself.

"See what you do to me?" he asked, voice low and intense. "I don't like cold showers, Em." He spoke against that place where my neck met my shoulder and I swallowed convulsively.

"I can't imagine anyone does," I said, voice light and breathy with a combination of lust and anticipation.

"Pick you up from work, and we're gonna have to figure some things out," he said.

"It's Wednesday. I have class," I reminded him.

"Fuck!" he swore low and vehement. I swallowed convulsively. I wasn't afraid, just extremely turned on. I knew I was wet, I could feel it. Being near Dray was turning into a near constant state of arousal.

"Okay. I'll pick you up and take you to your school. I need to put in some extra hours at the garage to make up for Monday and Tuesday. What time your classes through?" he asked stepping back and away. I sucked in a deep breath and tried to get my body to simmer down.

"Six," I answered carefully but my voice shook anyways. I didn't dare turn around and look at him until he was dressed. I could hear the smile in his voice when he called back from the bedroom.

"Pick you up then, and I'm taking you to dinner. We'll talk then." He came back out of the bedroom pulling a black Henley over his head, his legs encased in fresh black denim that clung to the muscles in his thighs and highlighted his gorgeous and perfect ass. I tried very, very hard not to picture the feel of my palms against that ass, nails digging... He laughed and I startled.

"Good to know it's not just me," he said and shook his head.

I went in the bathroom and brushed my hair, when I came out Dray had half of his damp hair up with a tie. Too short for a pony tail but it looked really good with half of it up just the same. Who was I kidding? *He* looked really damn good just... period.

"What were you thinking about?"

"Please don't make me say it," I said, the heat of humiliation warming my cheeks.

"Oh, Em, if it gets you to blush like that, I just have to know. Spill it." He crossed his arms and watching the muscles in his forearms flex with the motion sent heat to places much lower than my face. I decided for honesty again, because it had never served me wrong.

"I was picturing my hands gripping your ass," I said and swallowed hard. He grinned.

"Oh yeah. Definitely not just me but don't say anymore. Come on, I'll take you to work." He held out his hand. I shouldered the backpack and took his hand and followed him out. His skin was still cool from his cold shower but warmed quickly where it met my own. He opened the door for me and I slid into the cold car. He shut it behind me and rounded the front end, sliding in beside me. He turned on the car and I groaned and hung my head as cold air blew from the vents.

"What?" he asked.

"I want to be back in bed, with you," I whined.

"Amen," he said, and pulled the seatbelt across my body and fastened it before doing his own. I looked at him. He smiled and drove me to work. I slogged through making other people coffee like a zombie, even after having two cups of my own. Brandy, my fellow barista, crossed her arms and cocked her head.

"That is the second order for one of our regulars you've gotten wrong this morning," she complained, tossing her blonde hair over her shoulder. I sighed. I knew she wasn't being altruistic, the only thing Brandy worried about was herself and the tip jar and her size of the cut that came from it. All morning long she complained about the hot biker from the day before and wondered aloud what I had that she didn't? Uh, let me think about that... how about *class*. I ground my teeth.

"I just have a lot on my mind," I muttered, and set about cleaning while we had a short lull in business.

"Well, knock it off! You keep it up, our tips are going to start to seriously suck and I'm not about to suffer for whatever you've got going on inside your head!" She savagely wiped down the counter by her machine and I kept my cool.

I didn't want to know what her deal was. I didn't care. I just wanted to earn my paycheck from this place and go home. I was pretty sure Brandy was shorting me on my fair share of the tips and had been for a while. Every time she counted the tip jar it was a miserable day, but every time I managed to beat her to it or another girl was here in her place, we always seemed to make out like bandits.

I sighed inwardly and decided that if she wanted to be a bitch then I would go the passive-aggressive route and just make sure I was the one to count the tips today. I was all out of diplomacy, Irish or otherwise, so I simply kept my mouth shut. It was safer than letting my temper get the best of me. I needed to keep this job and for some reason, Brandy was our boss's favorite.

I kept at it and successfully managed to make no more mistakes, and to count the tips at the end of the day. I handed Brandy her cut and she frowned but took it. I turned back to mine, organized it, folded it in half and put it in my back pocket. She was getting greedy and this count-out showed it. We had only been moderately busy and my tips averaged out almost fifty dollars higher than any of the days earlier in the week. I pursed my lips and dropped the bag with my till money in it into the safe under the counter through the heavy old-fashioned mail slot door.

"See you tomorrow," I said, and shouldered my bag.

"Yeah, whatever," she sulked, counting her tip money and I felt a tiny surge of anger. It felt like entirely too many people were cheating me lately. First Jerry, now Brandy... I went out the door and strode across the parking lot. Dray got out of his Trans-Am and leaned on his door.

"What's the matter?" he asked when I was just inside earshot.

"Is it that obvious?" I asked.

"Yep," he said succinctly. I sighed. Damn. It.

"Hey, no, what's this?" he asked. He backed off his door and shut it and pulled me in against his chest.

"I'm just so tired," I sobbed and it was true. I was tired of being screwed over, I was tired of working my ass off only to be broke, I was tired of stressing and wondering and worrying about what the hell I was doing with Dray so soon after Jerry's betrayal and I just wanted a break from my *life*. I clung to Dray's leather clad torso and he held me tight. I breathed in leather and machinery and under that the crisp scent of Dray's cologne and wiped at my eyes. I tried to get it together and gave a shuddering sigh.

"I need a vacation," I said weakly and Dray laughed.

"You ain't lyin', Em," he said and drew back to get a good look at me.

"I'm sorry," I said miserably.

"Don't be. Your life is a little upside down at the moment. We've all been there. Just know I'm here to help get you through your low and I'd really like to see gettin' you to one of your highs." He winked and I laughed at the double entendre. He leaned down and kissed me gently and I returned it but we didn't linger. I had to get to class. I got into the car and he started for the college.

"Can we stop at Renaissance?" I asked, and he gave me a sideways look.

"You just left your coffee stand. Why do you want to stop at a coffee shop?" he asked.

I rolled my eyes. "Renaissance Café is *real* coffee. The shit Eddie buys is bargain basement cheap-ass blend that tastes like it. I need *real* coffee if I'm going to get through class." He raised his eyebrows, a slight smile playing across his lips. I pulled down the visor and checked my makeup in the vanity mirror, relieved that it was only slightly blurry around the edges of my eyes and not tracking down my face. I blotted fresh powder onto my T-zone to take off the shine and repaired my eyeliner.

"Let me ask you something," he said gently, and I looked at him.

"Of course, anything," I said.

"Will stopping to get you *real* coffee make you smile?" he asked.

I smiled and answered, "Yes."

He pulled into the café's lot and I got out. I leaned into the car and gave him a bigger smile, he'd more than earned it.

"I'll be right back," I promised and jogged inside. I ordered and thrust the three drinks into one of those cardboard cupholder-thingies and went back out, handing him one.

"You look like you could use it," I said honestly and it was true. Dray was looking a little haggard. Dark circles were beginning to form like bruises beneath his dark eyes and he looked like he was in sore need of a nap.

"Yeah, thanks." He sipped from the plastic lid and blinked.

"Good, huh?" I asked.

"Yeah," he sniffed, "That'll wake you up." I smiled.

I'd ordered him a Robusta blend. Robusta beans contain more caffeine than the Arabica beans most Americans are used to. By like almost two-hundred percent. The coffee's flavor ended up being more robust and earthy and also a little more bitter than that derived from an Arabica bean but the caffeine jolt when you were sorely in need of it more than made up for the darker, richer taste. I'd added heavy cream and a little bit of sugar to try and thwart some of the bitterness and it seems to have done the trick. I figured he wouldn't want it straight black if he was more a fan of sugary energy drinks, like most of our generation seemed to be.

"You need two?" he asked, eyebrow raised, as he backed us out of the parking stall.

"No, one is for my girl Mandy. We have class together on Wednesdays." I took a drink of my coffee, usually I got a vanilla latte which was sugary and sweet but I needed the caffeine if I was going to make it through Mr. Warren's dry-as-hell lecture style in mathematics. Mandy's usual double white mocha looked a little forlorn as the lone soldier standing in the cardboard cupholder. Dray drank his coffee and drove and when he pulled up to the curb in front of the college, he turned in his seat to look at me.

"Dinner and I think we're both going to bed early," he commented dryly. I nodded.

"Sounds good," I said quietly.

"Any idea what you have a taste for?" he asked.

"Wherever and whatever is fine," I said.

He searched my face. "Be here at six," he said and I nodded.

I got out of the car, slid my coffee into the holder, kitty-corner to Mandy's, and shouldered my bag.

"You need anything, text me or call me, I'll be at the garage," he called.

"Okay." I nodded. "Hey, Dray."

"Yeah?"

"Thanks."

"Yeah." He gave me a once-over that made my blood sing and I shut the door. Once I was safely up on the curb he pulled away. I sighed and went to my classroom and set the coffee down on Mandy's desk in front of her. She set down her notes.

"The Lord bless you and keep you!" she said and made the sign of the cross with the blade of her hand. I rolled my eyes and slung Dray's backpack onto the desk next to hers.

Mandy was everything that you would expect an Irish girl to look like – without actually *being* Irish. She had a wealth of red hair in coarse tight corkscrew curls that erupted from her head in a fiery riot of color and hung past her shoulders. Her eyes were a bright green with a starburst of golden brown around her pupils that made the green that much greener. Her milky skin was scattered with a generous helping of light brown freckles that almost gave her a mottled appearance but unlike most red heads, who abhorred their freckles, she loved hers and rocked them.

"That's my line as the raised Catholic, although as a preacher's daughter, I suppose you can get away with it," I complained. She snorted.

Today she wore golden brown leggings that ended in a pair of brown ankle boots under an over-long, thick, cable-knit cream sweater. She'd pulled on a denim jacket over the sweater and looked as pulled together as a girl could get.

"So why haven't you been answering your phone?" she asked. I heaved an even greater sigh and slid into my seat.

"I caught Jerry cheating last week," I said.

"No!" she gasped.

"Yep. It was the worst day ever. Late to work, ass-chewed by Eddie, burned my hand, car broke down, left stranded at the mechanic because Jerry was in our apartment, on our couch, fucking some ho-bag stripper *without* a condom..." I shuddered in revulsion.

"That son of a bitch!" She looked around self-consciously to make sure no one had heard her and I smirked. "Wait. If you were stranded at the mechanic then how do you know..." she stopped and looked up from my face, frowning at something behind me.

"Can we help you?" Mandy asked politely.

I turned to see a slim girl our age standing at my desk. She wore black from head to toe and her short pixie-cut platinum blonde hair was parted on the side and smoothed tight to her head. Her hands were planted on her hips and her bright blue eyes were fixed on the motorcycle club patches on my bag.

"Yeah, you can tell me who's Old Lady you are," she said, and her eyes flicked to mine. Her eyes were familiar but I just couldn't place them.

"I'm no one's Old Lady," I said, frowning, and her light eyebrows shot into her hairline.

"What're you doin' with a bag with Sacred Heart patches all over it, then?" she demanded.

"The Vice President, Dray, gave it to me," I said defensively and my eyebrows knit together. Mandy bit her lower lip and her eyebrows went up.

"Dray?" the blonde girl asked, surprised, her cell phone appearing in her hand. "Now I know you're lyin'!" she exclaimed and her phone was ringing on speaker in her hand. We still had a half an hour before class but still, I was nonplussed. Not only had she interrupted the conversation with my BFF, she had called me a liar in her next breath. I was getting pissed.

"Yellow?" A male voice through the phone line.

"Hey, Cuz, you're not gonna believe this. There's this bitch in my class with a backpack covered in Sacred Hearts patches and she's trying to tell me *Dray* gave it to her!" She looked at me with cold blue eyes and it was right there at the edge of my mind.

"Mmmm, Shells?" the male voice asked.

"Yeah?"

"You got me on speaker?"

"Yeah?"

"Girl there?" he asked.

"Oh, I'm here," I said, and my voice was strained with the suppression of my temper.

"Irish!" the voice crowed, "That you?" I closed my eyes as it snapped in to place where I'd seen those eyes before.

"Yeah, Reaver, it's me." I said and put my face in my palm.

"Hey, Shells, it's totally cool! Dray licked her, she's his. I saw it with my own eyes!" He sounded entirely too happy about it and people in the classroom, including my best friend, were turning to look at me. My face flamed with embarrassment.

"No shit?" the blonde pixie-haired girl asked.

"Uhhh, do I carry a knife every day of the week?" he asked.

"'Nuff said. Thanks, Cuz!" the mysterious 'Shells' said, and hung up on him. She dropped into the seat on my other side and beamed at me.

"Reaver's your cousin?" I asked.

"Yep! Sorry, so Dray licked you and you're his now? How does that work?" she asked, all trace of hostility gone. I sighed.

"Yes, Everett, do tell!" Mandy crossed her arms.

"As I was saying, *before I was so rudely interrupted*," I said, pointedly looking at 'Shells'

"Shelly." She stuck out her hand. "I guess you could say my official title is Sacred Heart club whore; I'm no one's Old Lady, but no one messes with me on account of Reaver would flay them alive." I shook her hand and settled on doing some damage control with Mandy before she throttled me from the suspense.

"So my car died and I'm stranded at the mechanic's shop I pulled into and the mechanic – Dray –" I said for both their benefits, "gives me a ride home, where I walk into the living room to see said hooker riding him bareback on our couch." Mandy scowled and Shelly looked at her nails.

"Did you punch him?" Shelly asked, making herself right at home in the middle of the conversation.

"No." I said scowling at her. "So, I'm standing there and we're getting into a pretty good screaming match and here's Dray, with my graphing calculator in his hand, standing in my doorway. My bag ripped when I got to his shop and it fell out on the ride to my apartment." I told them.

"Did Dray punch him?" Shelly asked.

"No. Yes! But not until the next day... Hold on, let me get there." Mandy put her hand over my own. She could tell I was starting to get aggravated. Shelly rolled her eyes like I was being a drama queen and I wanted to punch *her*.

"So what happened, where did you go?" Mandy asked me and I sighed.

"I threw some of my shit into a couple of bags and Dray said he'd take me where I wanted to go, except I didn't have anywhere to go. I'd just paid rent and bills and I had like a hundred and twenty bucks. Anyways, I freaked out, he let me freak out, then he took me home like some kind of stray cat." I rested my head on my desk in abject humiliation.

"Meh, there are worse places to be than in Dray's bed." Shelly said, like she would know, with a shrug. I lifted my head and looked at her agape and blinked.

"Why didn't you call me?" Mandy asked aghast.

"You live with your parents, love, what could you have done?" I asked her honestly. She looked hurt for a moment then sighed, resigned. Her father was a preacher and I mean that in the strictest and worst sense of the word. Mandy was on ever-loving lockdown ninety-nine percent of the time. Sometimes I felt like if it weren't for me she'd have no clue how the really-real world worked, just this vague half-notion of how it was supposed to go, through her father's hard core Christian-colored glasses.

She nodded and opened her mouth to speak but the professor called for attention at the front of the class. I drank my tepid coffee and tried like hell to understand what he was saying. Mandy was holding her own but barely, then I looked over at Shelly who was rapt. She looked like this statistics crap was as easy as breathing and I think that is what tipped me toward wanting to hate her more than anything else so far.

The class ended in scraping chairs, rustling paper and the general chaos of every student trying to flee for their lives, or at least their sanity. I was no exception, unceremoniously shoving my papers, notebook, and laptop into my bag.

"Well, Sister, you've got at least one less thing to worry about now," Shelly said shoving her notebook into her bag.

"What's that?" I asked, haggard.

"I'm going to teach you and Red how to get through this with a passing grade. Call us even for me being such a cunt when I got here. Sorry about that, by the way, just looking out for the club." She smiled beatifically and it had Reaver all over it. Clearly they were related. I eyed her warily.

"Hey, if I could teach Ashton how to do her own taxes after she became a millionaire overnight, I can teach you how to do this. You've already won half the battle by even being in stats!" She stood up.

"A bunch of the Old Ladies are doing a ladies night out this Friday. You should come, we'll set something up then. Gimme your phone." She held out her hand and I blinked. I unlocked my phone and handed it to her. She added herself as a contact, sent herself a text, and handed it back.

"Call you with the details!" she sang out, and breezed out of the room.

"Why do I feel like you were just hit by a tornado?" Mandy asked me. I sighed.

"You think she's bad, you should meet her cousin," I said.

"What the hell kind of name is Reaver?" she asked and her eyes darted around to make sure she hadn't been overheard. I suppressed a laugh. She was trying to be more normal and had started with swearing but old habits die hard. It was sobering really. Her reaction every time she did it kind of made me afraid of what her da' had been up to behind closed doors. I'd seen him in action a few times, all puffed up with his righteous indignation. It wasn't pretty. I couldn't wait to get my friend out from under her parent's roof.

"A dangerous one belonging to a man who really, *really* likes his knives," I said.

"Oh my God! Evy! What are you doing with these people!?" Mandy demanded in a harsh whisper as we headed out of the classroom.

"Mandy, don't judge!" I said in a warning tone. "Dray has been taking really good care of me, driving me everywhere, and he hasn't asked for anything..." I told her everything as we stood outside my next class's door. I had an hour between classes and she stood listening, rapt, the whole time as people filtered in past us.

"And you say he's really hot?" she asked meekly. Good lord, my friend the virgin...

"Mandy, he's the sin of lust personified." I swooned and she laughed, then sighed herself.

"Look, as your best friend, I am telling you to be careful, to go slowly and to only do anything if it *feels* right. Don't close yourself off to a possibility of something with Dray because of what that jerkwad Jerry did. At the same time, don't rush into something because of it either." She made a frustrated growl of disgust at the lost and confused look that I could feel on my face. "You know what?" she said.

"What?" I asked.

"Just don't over-complicate things. Do what feels right and only if it feels right," she said and shrugged.

"Thanks, Mandy." I whispered and we hugged again.

"I'll see you after class. I want to see this guy for myself," she said and went off to the library. I laughed and sat through the next class.

Finally, at five forty-five, I collected Mandy from the library. We pushed open the double glass doors of the college building's entryway and stepped out under threatening skies.

"Will this rain never end?" she asked and I shrugged. I liked it. Dray's Trans Am was idling at the curb. Mandy eyed it.

"That him?" she asked. The driver's door opened and he popped over the roof. He folded his hands on the gleaming black metal and his dark gaze bore into me as I approached with Mandy at my side.

"I hear you met Shelly," he said flatly, and his eyes were angry, but I could tell it wasn't at me.

"Yep and you're meeting Mandy. Mandy, this is Dray. Dray, this is my best friend, Mandy," I said. He lifted his chin in acknowledgment and looked Mandy over once before his eyes settled onto me again. The heat in his gaze caused me to shiver.

"Nice to meet you, Dray." Mandy smiled and waved politely. "Ev, good luck," my friend said low and dubiously for my ears alone, and she hugged me.

"You need anything, you call me!" she ordered. I smiled at her unease. She was like a kitten, my girl, and sometimes when we were outside her daddy's sphere of influence, I felt like an overprotective mama cat. This attempt at role reversal amused me.

"Thanks, Mandy. I'll see you later," I promised. She left and I got into the car.

"You pissed?" he asked me once the doors shut.

"I'm hungry. I'm tired. I'm confused and I'm horny." I answered truthfully.

"Okay," he said, voice light and eyebrows raised, and he drove us to a nearby Mexican restaurant. When we were settled into a booth he leveled worried dark eyes on me and I leveled him with a calm gaze of my own. I was too tired to be angry.

"So, what happened?" he asked. I told him about the bag and Shelly's less than stellar introduction.

"She uh, she said there were worse places to be than your bed, so does that mean..?" He looked at me and his expression became shuttered, guarded...

"I told you I did casual sex." His hands rested on the table and I reached out and covered one with mine.

"Not judging," I said, and I wasn't. Dray had told me he did casual sex and he had already said that wasn't what he wanted from me. I took him at his word until he gave me cause not to. *If* he ever gave me cause not to. I would not let Jerry ruin my ability to trust. I just wouldn't. Dray searched my face carefully and whatever he saw there caused him to nod carefully.

"You really aren't, so what's your concern?" he asked.

"My concern is, if she's that proprietary over a few patches on a bag, then, um, does she have any of the same ideas about you?" He blinked and his mouth turned down in an expression that said that wasn't at all what he'd expected from me.

"No. Shelly is complicated. She's a club whore but sort of at an elevated status. Somewhere between a club whore and an Old Lady." He could see I wasn't exactly following and sighed.

"Look, I didn't want to talk about club politics or hierarchies tonight. I wanted to talk to you about whatever it is we're doing. We've obviously got some kind of insane attraction going on, but you just got out of a real bad situation, and I don't want a quick fuck or a short fling. You deserve better than that and for whatever reason I want to be that for you, what you deserve." He found the spaces between my fingers with his and I looked down at our interlocked hands.

Our plates were set in front of us but still I stared for what felt like long minutes at our interlocked fingers.

"Everett?" he asked and his dusky voice sounded worried.

"I don't want to overthink this," I said suddenly. "Dray, I'm attracted to you, intensely attracted to you, and this thing with Jerry, I don't know... I just don't know... but I think Mandy said it best. I should just do what feels right and only *if* it feels right. Everything else is just over-complicating things." His gaze was intense but guarded at the same time and I looked him over. He nodded slowly.

"Eat your dinner, Em," he said gently and we ate in relative silence that wasn't completely comfortable, at least not for me.

Finally I asked, "What's an 'Old Lady' to you guys, because, quite frankly, it sounds rude as hell." He choked on his sip of water and I blinked. He coughed and laughed at the same time and I felt my lips curve in amusement.

"An Old Lady is sacred, Babe. Take Ashton for instance, she's Trigger's Old Lady, that means if anyone and I do mean *anyone* that messes with her has to answer to Trig." I swallowed thoughtfully as he went on. "It's the nature of an MC that to mess with one of us, you're gettin' all of us so... yeah. Being an Old Lady is a big deal. It's an honorific we bestow only on women who are of value to us." I arched a brow at his phrasing of the last.

"You make us sound like property, like cattle or something," I said and he grinned.

"Yeah, it does, but the MC is a brotherhood and the traditions MC's follow are an age-old thing that can be full of all sorts of misogynistic douche-baggy goodness." He gave me that boyish panty-dropping grin of his and I laughed. "Seriously though, to be a patch holder's girlfriend is one thing, but to be a patch holder's Old Lady, property patch and all... Like I said, that's sacred and a real big deal to us. We take it more seriously than a wedding ring." He looked solemn all of a sudden and I really felt my eyebrows go up.

"Property patch?" I asked, my brain latching onto the phrase. He nodded gravely and explained to me that Old Ladies were given vests by their Old Men which stated that they were 'property of so and so' when they went out on runs or out to gatherings, that way the men in other MC's knew to keep their hands off. I'd blinked, astounded. It all seemed so very cavemanish and like something out of the dark ages. I mulled all of it over in silence as we ate, processing all of this new information.

Dray turned cool and unreadable and I hated it. I felt cast adrift and as I finished my meal, I felt on the verge of tears. I was suddenly worried I'd seriously offended him with my curiosity about the club's terminology and how things worked, but it seemed like it was something I should know before, you know, getting involved with a member, let alone their Vice President. He paid for dinner and walked us out to the car. I waited, hands stuffed in the pockets of my jacket, head bowed as the rain fell and he unlocked my door. I scooted inside the car and he drove us home, also in silence, his movements calculated and controlled as he shifted gears and steered through the rain-slicked streets. I went into the house and hung my jacket on the back of a chair while he did the same.

I didn't hear him follow me into the bedroom. I startled when his hands fell onto my shoulders and froze in place. He swept my loose hair over my shoulder and pulled me back against his chest. His lips grazed my ear and I closed my eyes and melted back into him, relieved. Not offended after all, simply being closed-off and mercurial Dray.

"Tell me if you need me to stop," he whispered and his hands smoothed down my shoulders, along my back, coming to rest on my hips. He kissed from my ear down the side of my neck. Barely there touches of his satiny lips against my skin. I laid my head back on his shoulder and offered my lips to his and he took the sacrifice, covering my mouth with his.

Cool air slid along the heated skin of my stomach as he pulled my shirt up over my ribs. I raised my arms and he pulled the shirt over my head and let it fall to the floor. His large work roughened hands cupped my breasts through the thin satin of my bra and he made an appreciative groan which I just ate up. He broke our kiss and sucked in air between his teeth.

"God, Em, you are so fucking beautiful!" His voice was low and intense and slithered along my exposed skin like warm, sable-soft fur. I twisted, turning in the circle of his arms. His hands pressed into my back over my wings.

"You still want me?" I asked, voice trembling.

"God, yes!" he sounded shocked.

"You just... You're so hard to read sometimes and at the restaurant you were angry and then so quiet I didn't know... I thought I offended you with all of my questions... that I broke it somehow," I know I sounded pitiful and a lot of it was insecurities based on my relationship with Jerry, and having thought I knew him... and finding out I had everything all wrong. I covered my face with my hands and scrubbed wishing that my emotional turmoil and confusion would go away with the motion.

Dray's hands grasped my shoulders and he sat me on the edge of the bed. I looked up at him and he looked down at me, his face passive, unreadable, except for his dark eyes which radiated concern.

"You got a lot going on in there," Dray said tapping me lightly on the temple with a finger. He exhaled loudly. "Stay here, Em. I'm only going to be a little bit. I promise." He went out into the hall and into the bathroom and shut the door. Water began to run. I took off my boots, waited, and after a minute or two more huffed a sigh and stood. I peeled my jeans down my legs and my socks off my feet. The sound of running water grew louder; then softer as the door to the bathroom opened and closed. Dray's shadow darkened the open doorway. Night had fallen and the shadows in the room had deepened.

"I wanted to do that," he said softly, "But this works too." He came into the room and took my hands, walking backwards, leading me towards the closed bathroom door.

"What are you doing?" I asked.

"You need to relax," he said, tone soothing, gentle. "Stop thinking about so much all at once." He led me into the bathroom which was softly lit with candles. He slipped my panties from my hips and let them fall to the floor and eased my bra straps off my shoulders but the thing that got me was he didn't look. His deep, dark soulful eyes stayed locked with my own as he took the final scraps of material from the most intimate parts of my body and let them fall.

He shut the water off and straightened, back to me, the thin material of his Henley taut across his shoulders, as he wiped the moisture from his hands. He turned to the wall, keeping his back to me to allow me the privacy to get into the tub. I stepped into the water and sucked in a breath. It was hot, almost too hot, but I think that's what he wanted. I lowered myself into the mounded bubbles and sank in up to my neck, holding my hair piled on top of my head out of the water. The water moved over me and the bubbles closed ranks. Dray snuck a glance and knelt down beside the tub. He gathered my hair in his large hands into a high pony tail and twisted it into a loose knot for me.

"Where did you learn to do that?" I asked gently. Something flickered behind his eyes and, if possible, they went even darker than before.

"Years of watching my mom do it," he said gently and the hurt in his voice made me regret asking. He rolled a towel and put it behind my neck, and turned his body, sitting down on the floor. He put his back against the wall where the faucets on the claw-foot were and we were suddenly facing each other. The candle flames flickered, casting wavering shadows on the wall and across Dray's face, which was intense as he sat and watched me.

"Thank you," I said and he nodded slowly.

"I'm not very good at this," he confessed.

"At what?" I asked, shifting a bit in the warm water. Dray's eyes widened a bit but he recovered quickly.

"At taking care of a woman. You know, being supportive. Not my usual thing." He raised a knee, booted foot against the floor and his arms went loosely around it. A defensive posture. I swallowed.

"I think you're doing remarkably well," I murmured.

"Yeah?" he asked.

"No one has ever done anything even remotely like this for me," I said. He smiled that boyish smile and butterflies swirled in my stomach.

"You looked like you needed to relax," he said getting to his knees. He brought himself close to the edge of the tub and looked down at me. I brought a hand out of the water, I felt languid, my muscles loosening under the punishing heat. He palmed the back of my hand, fingers curling around my thumb and brought my palm to his lips. His eyes drifted shut as he pressed a kiss to the heart of my palm, his tongue darting out to drink the water from my skin.

A small moan escaped my lips and his dark eyes flashed open pinning my breath in my lungs and my eyes with his smoldering look. He took his mouth from my hand and pressed it to the inside of my wrist, nipping lightly, grazing the sensitive skin with his teeth. I forgot to breathe all together and he drew back, smiling.

"Relax. I'm going to go change," he murmured and put my hand back down into the water.

I did as I was told, leaning my head back, soaking in the heat, my eyes closed. I sighed and decided that I needed to be a little less insecure, which wasn't going to be an easy task. I heard Dray's deep voice, indistinct through his bedroom wall. He was on the phone. I didn't know what time it was but my body said 'late', I was bone-weary and needed to wrap this up if I had any hope of getting a bit of decent sleep.

"Come on, Evy. Just two more days in the week and you're home free. You can get a break," I told myself. It's what I told myself almost every week at some point lately. 'Just two more days' or 'just three more days'... I tried to figure out when exactly it had been that my life had devolved into counting the days and I blinked when I realized it, too, had started with Jerry. With counting the days between paydays so I could quickly pay all the bills so he wouldn't burn through my paychecks with reckless spending.

I covered my face with my wet hands as frustrated angry tears welled in my eyes. *How could I have been so stupid?* How could I have stayed for so long and just let him walk all over me like that? I was stronger than that. My father had raised me to be and that stung more than anything Jerry could have done to betray me. That if he were alive, I likely would have disappointed my father so very much... I wondered if my da' had seen it, if he'd been silently disappointed before he'd passed and that wrenched the first sob out of me.

Hands closed around my wrists and dragged my hands from my face and around a muscular neck. I sat up as if drawn by strings and let Dray hold me.

"Shhhh, its okay," he soothed and for about the thousandth time in a week I marveled at him. He just got done telling me he was crap at this and then, almost in the next breath, was doing exactly just the thing I needed. He held me close and pressed a kiss to my bare shoulder. His voice when it came was low, warm and soothing like the bath.

"Come on, I think you're tired." He reached into the tub by my feet and pulled the drain. I nodded against his bare shoulder. I was tired. He stood me up, soap bubbles sliding down my skin and turned on the shower. I rinsed quickly and shut off the tap and he was waiting with one of those big fluffy towels of his when I pulled back the curtain.

At no time did I feel self-conscious about my nudity while he stood there in his pajama pants. He wrapped me in the towel and dried me briskly, pulling me tightly to him in the circle of his arms. He kissed me and I kissed him. We stood inside the candle-lit dark of the bathroom and I sheltered against him though how that was possible when the storm was all emotion and raging on the inside of me, I couldn't tell you. Still, I felt calmer than I had in days as he held me quietly among the flickering glow of the small candles. He smoothed his hands up and down my body, over the thick warm towel. A soothing motion that left me swooning.

"Come on, Em, time to go to bed," he whispered and drew me into the dark of his room after blowing out the winking tea lights. A lone fat pillar candle burned on his nightstand in the bedroom and plucking the towel deftly from my fingers, he let it fall to the area rug. He drew me tightly against his body and I sighed, melting into him.

"You make it hard to think," he whispered and smoothed his hands up and down my arms, my shoulders; the exposed skin of my back. I cuddled against him and relaxed under the touches. It had been a long time since anyone had touched me with any care or consideration. I couldn't help but eat it up. He turned my hair loose from the knot he'd put it in and it tumbled down my back in careless waves.

"You're so soft," he marveled and his lips came down over mine. He was an amazing and patient kisser. His lips brushed over mine hesitantly, tentatively before he deepened the kiss, lips growing more insistent, tongue flicking against the seam of my lips, which I gladly parted. Our tongues danced, our bodies melded together and I could feel the hot press of his erection through the thin cotton of his pajama pants. I felt myself grow slick between my thighs and I fought to remember why this couldn't happen right now. Dray's mouth over mine stole any ability I had to think and I was suddenly very okay with that. I pulled the drawstring on his pajama pants and it came loose. His thick fingers wrapped around my wrist and his hips jerked back.

"You do that, I'm not going to be able to stop," he growled against my mouth and oh, god, it was hot. I whimpered and sighed out and drew back to look at him. His eyes silently screamed *don't make me stop*, but the rest of him was incredibly still, incredibly controlled. I twisted my wrist in his grasp and he let it go and I captured his hand with mine. My other hand on his back, I dragged myself against his body and brought his fingers to my folds. This felt right and so I was going with it. I pressed his fingers to my pussy and let him feel how wet I was for him.

"Please, Dray? I want you," I whispered from inches away and his mouth crashed over mine, his fingers slicking through my wetness. I shoved his pajama pants to the floor and wrapped my fingers around his searing length and gently stroked him.

He threw back his head and gasped. "Oh God, Em!"

I smiled. He gripped the back of my thighs and I gave a shout as he lifted; I lost my balance and crashed, laughing, on my back in the midst of his bed. The cool air of the room disappeared as he covered me with the warmth of his body. He sucked a nipple into the warm wet heat of his mouth, and palmed my other breast and I gave a throaty moan.

My palm grew slick at the head of his cock with his pre-cum and I used it to my advantage, as I stroked him between us. I was keenly aware of how close he was to my pussy; it wouldn't take much to line him up... His hand went around mine and stopped me from stroking him. He let my nipple pop from his mouth, red and swollen from his attentions and he turned that burning dark gaze to mine and I lost all ability to draw breath for a moment.

"You keep doing that, I'm going to go, and I'm not ready for that yet," he said.

"What are you ready for?" I asked breathily. He bowed his head and cursed and reached over to fish in his nightstand drawer with his other hand. I used the one he didn't have pinned to the mattress by my hip to touch the side of his face, his stubble scratchy against my palm. He found what he was looking for and propped himself up over me with that fist on the bed and turned to look at me.

"What?" he asked.

"What are you ready for?" I repeated. I needed to hear his intentions; it was suddenly very important. He brought his closed fist between us and looked me very deliberately in the eye.

"I'm ready to make you mine in every way that counts between a man and a woman. Just like I have been from the moment you kissed me back on that dance floor. You on board with that?" He asked. We were both very still, very quiet in his bed and I nodded rapidly, not trusting my voice.

"I need to hear you say it, Em," he said uncurling his fingers, revealing the condom in its wrapper.

"I'm on board," I said and dragged his face to mine by his hair. His mouth crashed against mine and all of the pent-up sexual frustration of the last few days poured from one to the other and redoubled. We were both suddenly needy, ravenous, and neither would be denied.

He dragged his mouth from mine and tore open the condom wrapper with his teeth. He rolled it on expertly with one hand and I didn't even consider the implications. I wanted him, needed him with every fiber of my being, to touch me, to make me his. I guided him to my entrance and he closed his eyes and made an appreciative growl and sank into me and oh my god he was thick! I mean I knew he was thick, I'd had my hand around him but oh my god! I arched and moaned and gasped as he slowly, carefully worked his way in. His dark eyes burned with so many things, possession, tenderness, and care.

His eyes slipped shut and he turned his head, his expression one of pure pleasure as his body met mine and my arousal heightened.

My hands found his and our fingers laced together. He was up on his knees and fully seated inside of me. He pinned my hands to the bed on either side of my head and bowed down above me.

"You're so tight," he moaned, "I'm not hurting you, am I?" he asked. I shook my head and dragged my hands out from beneath his, and palming his ass, I pulled him into me. He kissed me and moaned into my mouth and I couldn't get enough of him.

He broke the kiss and whispered against my lips, "Wrap those dancer's legs around me." He didn't need to tell me twice, I did what I was told and the change in angle was amazing, deeper, like he touched more of me. He drew back and surged forward and found himself a rhythm of short strokes. I tightened around him and he cried out.

I smoothed my hands over the delicious rippling planes of his back, his skin smooth and warm, almost hot to the touch. His thrusts became longer, filled with a barely-contained power and urgency. My arms slid up his body and I held on to his powerful shoulders which were corded with the effort to hold his upper body off of mine to keep from crushing me.

He felt so damned *good*! Touching and stroking the most intimate parts of me, bringing me up to a fevered pitch. Our breaths came in clashing ragged gasps as he took me higher and higher into the clouds. He grinned savagely and hooked one of his arms beneath my leg. I uncrossed my ankles and he folded me upward, resting my leg along his lean muscular torso and oh my god he was going so deep inside of me! I was amazed at this new dimension of feeling, had never felt anything like it before!

I cried out in pure bliss and he took it for an invitation and thrust harder, which felt so damned good it almost left pleasure behind to become pain. I loved it! Riding that razor-thin edge between the two he upped the ante when he pressed his thumb over my clit. I came apart and was vaguely aware of screaming his name while I did it. He thrust into me a few more times and stilled, letting my leg down. He kissed me. Sweet and slow, languorously and it dawned on me that he'd had his release right along with mine.

I'd never shared that level of intimacy with Jerry. Never. I wrapped my arms around Dray and kissed him back gently, saying thank you silently with my body. He reached between us and held the condom on while he slipped from me and I made a little sound and sucked in a breath. Still sensitive. He smiled crookedly at me, that delicious little boyish grin that made my heart go soft and melt around the edges.

"You feel incredible," he growled.

I was speechless. Utterly speechless. He disposed of the condom in the trash beside the bedside table and moved out from between my legs to lay alongside me. He propped his head in his hand and trailed his fingertips along my body in a light touch that raised goosebumps in their wake. My heart slowly ceased its pounding and I turned onto my side to face him, and let my fingers do some walking of their own over his heated skin.

"Next time I'm taking my time with you," he said and I felt a thrill that there would be a next time. That he wanted that with me... The burning look he gave me in addition to his words warmed me to my toes and wrapped me in security. I closed my eyes and nodded, still robbed of speech. When I opened them he was smiling and reaching for me. He laid down and pulled me against him.

"Sleep," he ordered gently, then, "I'm making you mine again in the morning if I can." I shivered and looked up at him.

"Keep looking at me like that and I'm going to have you again right now," he warned and I smiled, but I didn't take my eyes off of him. Something flashed in his deep dark eyes and he rolled lightning fast and pinned me beneath him, one of his knees sliding between my thighs, opening me for him. Challenge accepted!

## 10

D ray...

I think Em and I both slogged through the next day, neither one of us exactly knowing how we pulled it off. I picked her up from her coffee stand, drove us home and we pretty much both collapsed fully clothed into bed. We napped from around one until her phone shattered the calm. She groped across my body and snatched the offending thing off the nightstand.

"Hello?" she asked sleepily, then, "Oh, sorry, I forgot all about it," she sighed. "I don't know, let me ask." She looked at me. "Shelly wants to know if we're going to the clubhouse tonight." I grunted. Unfortunately I had to. Church meeting tonight to decide the direction of the club. Membership had been dropping off, mostly due to retiring members or members who were patching over into chapters in other states since we'd taken a lower profile. I nodded and Everett snuggled in closer to my side and said into the phone, "He says yes." The voice, indistinct on the other end squawked out another question.

"I don't know, what time is it now?" Em asked. I raised an eyebrow and she looked at me.

"Seven?" she said, a little surprised. I frowned.

"She wants to know what time we'll be there," Everett closed her eyes and rested the ear that wasn't on the phone above my heart. She relaxed and I smiled, tangling my fingers in her silky hair and massaged the nape of her neck.

"We'll get there when we get there," I said gently.

"She heard you," she said. Her eyes had drifted shut and I swear if the girl were a cat she'd be purring.

"Hang up the phone," I said, voice low and controlled.

"Shelly, I've got to go. See you when we get there." Em pulled the phone from her ear and touched the screen to end the call. I smiled.

"I suppose we should get ready to go out," she murmured.

"Mmm," was my non-committal reply.

Church was at eight. I wanted Everett under me again something fierce but unfortunately it was going to have to wait. I looked her over and came to a decision.

"Pack a change of clothes for tomorrow and bring your dance stuff. We're staying the night at the clubhouse," I told her.

"Are we now?" she said with a smile and I could see the sleep had done her good. She had a feisty sparkle in her steely baby blues.

"Yep. We are. I have club business, then we're fucking," I spanked her jean-clad ass as a loud peal of her musical laughter split the dense air. My room was stuffy.

"Well, when you put it that way!" she exclaimed. I smiled.

"I'm such a romantic, I know." I said and smiled at her, sitting up. Her expression softened and she leaned forward and touched her lips to mine. My eyebrows went up and I couldn't help but kiss her and spend a long minute doing it. She drew back and I let her, searching her face.

"What was that for?" I asked gruffly.

"You're more of a romantic than I think you give yourself credit for," she said, voice husky with the promise of things yet to come. My cock stood at attention in my jeans and I cleared my throat.

"Yeah, well. Don't tell anybody. Might ruin my badass image," I said and she scoffed and got up. I couldn't help but smile as I watched her go, she had this perfect ass, high and tight and fucking gorgeous like the rest of her. I got up and pulled on a clean shirt that was a little less wrinkled than what I had on. Everett returned from the bathroom and picked through her pile of clothes, glancing at me.

"Just wear something comfortable. You aren't going to be in it for very long anyways," I said as I shrugged and pulled on my motorcycle boots. Em rolled her eyes at me but did what I asked, pulling out fresh underthings and a comfortable looking tee and hooded sweatshirt. I went out into the kitchen and started a pot of coffee. She came out a minute later looking a little fresher, her hair brushed out and shining around her face, some gloss on her lips that drew my eyes directly to them. She wrinkled her nose and shot a dirty look at the coffee pot and I laughed a little.

"Look, little miss coffee snob..." I started and she came up to me, her blue eyes bright with laughter. She wound her arms around my shoulders and neck and my voice died in my throat. I looked at her, really looked at her, drinking her in and she blushed faintly.

"What?" she asked a little self-consciously.

"That's one of the things that gets me about you," I said, pulling her tight up against me, my hands smoothing down her silhouette, coming to rest on her hips.

"What?" she asked, genuinely curious now.

"You really have no idea just how fucking beautiful you are to me." She gave a little gasp of surprise and I kissed her roughly. I meant to take my time with her tonight. Last night I'd lost control, the need to be inside of her, one with her, overriding my better judgment. I wanted to take my time tonight, do things right, leave her exhausted from feeling good instead of being exhausted from too much work, school, stress and whatever else she'd had piled on her plate.

I drew back a little reluctantly to look at her beautiful face and smiled at what I saw there. She glowed from the pleasure of my mouth on hers, my hands on her... from me... and that, in turn, made me feel on top of the world. It was sort of a new concept. I was used to taking from girls what I needed to feel good; I'd never felt good from giving before and I realized now that that was a sad fact. Not something to be proud of, not a mark of what a badass I was. I sighed. I'd been angry at the world for a long time, intent on burning the whole motherfucker down around me, and with it, everyone stupid enough to stick around me. For a long time I just hurt so much that I wanted everyone to hurt right along with me.

"Dray, what's wrong?" Everett asked me softly. I looked down into her blue eyes which had become deep pools of concern.

"Nothing, just some old ghosts and memories," I smiled and I knew it was sad. Maybe that was my 'connect' with Everett... Pretty had gotten me interested but really, she'd lost her dad around the same age I'd lost my mom, only a few years' difference really, and from everything I could see, he was her everything growing up, a lot like my mom had been to me.

"Hey, stop," she said gently, her hands cupped my face and I blinked and looked down into her glorious blue eyes.

"Stop what?" I asked.

"Whatever it is you're thinking that's making you look so distant and sad," she said. I nodded and jerked my head towards the door.

"Come on, I've got club business and I'm the VP, it'll be my ass if I'm late," I changed the subject. Something flashed in Em's eyes that told me I would have some questions to answer, before she nodded. I picked up her bag of dance stuff which had lightened some and I raised an eyebrow.

"Took some of the costumes out, just the basics in there now," she said and shouldered my battered old back pack.

"Plan on studying?" I asked as I herded her out the door.

"Shelly said she would help me," she shrugged a shoulder. "Besides, I don't have a purse." I barked a laugh.

"What woman doesn't have a purse?" I asked.

"Apparently yours!" she shot back and stuck her tongue out at me over her shoulder. I felt a zing of electricity race through me at her words. Teasing or not, the idea appealed to me. I watched her step lightly down the cement steps leading to my door in the dark and made the decision that I liked the sound of that so much it was pretty much a done deal.

"What are you smiling at?" she asked teasing and I looked at her over the roof of my car.

"You have no idea how much what you just said appeals to me, Em," I told her and she watched me, expression closed, considering. I threw her bag into the back seat over the headrests, she got into the car and shut the door the same time I did.

"I don't know what I'm doing," she confessed softly.

"Neither do I," I let her know, "But whatever it is, it's comfortable and I like it." Which was true. I didn't generally do anything I didn't want to do or didn't like unless it was for the club or the good of my brothers in it.

"It is, isn't it?" she asked and her smile put her past beautiful into a sphere all her own. I started the car and put it in reverse.

"I aim to keep it that way too," I told her with a rakish grin.

"Oh, and how do you plan to do that?" she asked.

By being the man my mother had hoped I would be. By serving my club to the best of my ability. By growing the fuck up and owning my past mistakes; atoning for them... and most of all by trying to be the kind of man a woman like Everett Mary Moran deserved. I didn't say any of this out loud. I didn't want to freak her out. A lot of the shit I was feeling for her was quick, out of the blue and way fucking fast to be feeling after just a week but the weird thing was it wasn't freaking me out. Instead of saying any of this to her I looked her over quickly before turning my attention back to the road.

"You'll see," I told her, with a false sense of bravado. Truth was, I was playing this whole thing by ear and I had no idea how I was going to keep it comfortable. I damn sure was going to try, though. I liked Everett, more than I've ever liked or been attracted to any other woman I'd ever laid eyes on and I didn't just want to keep her, I wanted her to *want* to stay. That was a stunner and one I pretty much brooded on the rest of the way to the club.

I pulled her bag out of the back seat and handed it to her, intent on fucking with Loyal, our latest, and pretty much only, prospect. He needed a little bit of a reminder that he was low man on the totem pole. We'd been going easy on him lately for no particular reason.

"Hey, Em," I said softly and she paused.

"Yeah?" she asked, cocking her head to the side.

I don't know why I felt the need to warn her but I didn't want her thinking badly of me about anything. That, along with my other introspective revelations, shook me up even more than I had been when I realized how much I wanted to keep her around after only a week of knowing her, insane attraction aside.

"We've got a prospect in there. You know what that is?" I asked. She shook her head. "Means he's interested in becoming a patched member of the club, to do that you go through a probationary period of a year or more to prove yourself." She tipped her head to the side.

"Let me guess? Sort of like a pledge to a frat house? You guys do and say stupid shit to him and expect him to jump through a bunch of retarded hoops to prove himself?" She smiled at me and I felt an answering one of my own.

"Smart girl." I commented.

"Would you do any other kind?" she asked and abruptly held up her hand. "Wait! Don't answer that!" She laughed a little and I shook my head. She was definitely feeling better.

I opened the clubhouse door and yelled "Prospect!" at the top of my lungs. Em blinked, an amused little smile on her lush mouth.

"Yeah, VP!?" Derek, better known to a lot of us as Loyal, jogged up from behind the bar.

"What the fuck is wrong with you, man!? Can't you see I'm with a lady?" I asked. Loyal looked confused and I fought not to grin. I crossed my arms and put on my best pissed-off face and glowered at him. "Well, don't just stand there! Take her bags!" I barked. Loyal jumped like it hadn't even dawned on him and he reached out.

"Of course, Ma'am. Sorry, Ma'am, let me get those for you." He took Everett's bags and she smiled sweetly at him.

"Thank you..." She said and raised her eyebrows, "Do you have a name or am I supposed to call you 'Prospect' like he does?" she asked. Loyal smiled at her.

"Name is Derek, most people around here call me Loyal, though.

I'm fine with either." He shrugged and hoisted the strap to her gym bag over his shoulder.

"Nice to meet you, Derek, I'm Everett, but most people call me Ev or Evy." She smiled brightly and it made her eyes seem brighter.

"If you're done hitting on my girl, there, Prospect, you can go ahead and put her bags in my room," I said ominously but shot a wink and a smile at Em when he wasn't looking. Em did her best to look solemn but the mischievous glint in her eyes gave her away.

"I wasn't..! I didn't mean to..!" Loyal was so damned gullible. He looked like he was about to piss himself until he caught sight of Em and then his shoulders dropped and I laughed at him a little. I gripped his shoulders and shook him.

"You gotta toughen up, man," I told him and slapped him on his raw cut. He had the rockers stating the club's name and location but he didn't have the colors yet. The black leather below the name rocker and above the locale rocker was smooth and blank and waiting for the Sacred Heart's emblem.

He was being sponsored by his Marine Corps buddy and our Sergeant of Arms, Trigger. With everything he'd displayed so far, it looked like he might make it. Still, he had a long way to go. Prospects typically stayed prospects for a year, sometimes more... on rare occasions, less, but a man really had to prove himself for that. I kissed Em soundly and turned her loose at the table full of women and Old Ladies and sauntered into the chapel. I dropped into the seat at my dad's right hand and propped a boot on the table. Trigger and Reaver were there, we were just waiting on Doc, who came in and shut the door.

"Alright," my dad said and let out a sigh. "Membership is dropping off. What're we going to do about it?" He looked at each of us in turn.

"Chuckie didn't end up making the cut, nobody's seen him since a few weeks after I brought my Sunshine girl in. Derek looks like he's going to make it at some point. Zander's expressed some interest and so has Squick, in becoming hang-'rounds." Trigger rattled off.

"Yeah, that's my fault about Chuckie," Doc said ruefully, "I'm afraid I'm not a very good sponsor. Kid dropped off the radar with me and I didn't exactly bother lookin'. He took up with some other club that he said had more time for him." Doc grimaced and there was a moment of silence.

"Don't worry 'bout it too much, Doc. Out of all of us you're the busiest between the club and the hospital. I wasn't too keen on the kid anyways," my Dad said. I was more interested in one of the guys Trigger mentioned.

"Squick even got a bike?" I asked, raising an eyebrow.

"No shit, he just picked himself up a 1970 BMW 75/5!" Trig answered grinning. Laughter tittered around the table. I shrugged a shoulder. It wasn't exactly a biker's motorcycle but it fit the lanky tattoo artist's style.

"Those fuckers are a rat bike if I've ever seen one," Reaver said, grinning; he used the affectionate term for a motorcycle that didn't look like much, but like a rat, just kept going and going. Rat bikes were nigh impossible to kill, just like the critter they were named after.

"Doesn't look like a rat bike," Trigger said dryly, and he was smiling like some kind of proud papa.

"Oh?" Doc asked leaning in.

"Naw, he restored it to perfection before bringing it out where anyone could see it. Did a great job on it too, looks like it just rolled off the showroom floor. He's bringing it in tonight, Zander's coming in on his custom. Thought they might like to join the party." Trigger flashed a triumphant grin in Dragon's direction. My dad shook his head, smiling.

"So I mention our membership is flagging and you bring in three of your guys?" My dad's eyes narrowed, half suspicious.

"I told you when you signed me on as Sergeant of Arms, whatever you need, Brother. You call, I answer." Trig crossed his arms over his chest and gave my dad that cool appraising sniper's look that raised the hair on the back of my arms and neck. Something silent passed between them and finally, satisfied, my dad nodded.

"I knew I made the right decision signing you on." My dad looked at me and I read it clear. Someday I would be president of this club and on that day I had better get used to the idea of Trigger as my VP because it was pretty much between him and Reaver. Both of them were great candidates, calculating and level-headed, but Trigger more so than the younger blade-loving man. I was pretty sure Trig would be my Veep and Reaver would move on up to Sergeant of Arms and we'd have to find a new Treasurer and Secretary.

Doc had been making noises about retiring for a while now. If anything, I saw him leaving before my Pops. I scrubbed my face with my hands and dropped my feet to the floor. I'd been needing to get more serious about the club for a while and I'd been failing at it. I aimed to remedy that, had been working on it ever since spring lake run. Everett had kind of derailed me for the last week or two but no one seemed to take notice or mind. Now they were all looking at me expectantly.

"You can't sponsor three guys at a time Trig. One at a time. It's in our by-laws." I sniffed and leaned back. It was time to throw my support one way or the other. My dad's suspicious look had a little bit of merit. Trig bringing in three guys would definitely sway any vote in his direction if all three of 'em ended up patched.

As it stood, we had the council of five and only three patched members in our mother chapter: Data, Gypsy, and Lucky. Lucky hadn't been around much. His folks were older and he'd gone up north to do what he could for them. The mother chapter was flat lining and a big chunk of that was aging and retiring members, the next was the fact that a lot of members had chosen to patch over into other chapters who were up for things a little less than above-board legally.

After my mom died, we'd torn ourselves apart. Burned some bridges which needed burning to the motherfucking ground and lit the way out of some bad dealings with them. We were still waging some internal battles with fringe chapters on getting out of drug-running and the illegal shit and we were in serious need of some new blood as a result.

"I'll sponsor Zander," I said at last, throwing my lot in with Trigger. He was a good man, a better man than I was, older, wiser and the club needed him. I caught a flash of triumph in my pops' dark eyes, so like my own, and felt a surge of satisfaction. My old man let me make my choices, *needed* me to make my own choices but he wanted Sacred Hearts to not only survive but thrive with his boy at the helm. I'd disappointed him for far too long and it was past time for me to grow the fuck up and change it.

"I'll sponsor Squick," Reaver threw in and his glacial gaze met mine. He was throwing his lot in with me, not Trig, even though Trig was his best friend. I gave him a nod. I appreciated that more than he would know. Still, I grimaced.

"These guys manage to patch in we have *got* to get them some better fucking nicknames," I said. There was some laughter and nods of agreement around the table.

"Next order of business?" Trigger asked.

"Nothin' official. We're heading into the somewhat quiet time of year." My dad folded his hands over his middle and leaned way back in his chair, slouching down with his legs out in front of him. It was a lazy and comfortable posture I'd seen him take a thousand times over the years but it didn't fool me. I'd also seen him draw a gun as if from nowhere, be on his feet and have it aimed in the time it took someone to blink, about a hundred times out of that thousand. I still didn't know how he did it and I really wanted to learn. Some things were just my dad's, you know, Dragon-specific, which was okay. I had a few Dray-specific things up my sleeves.

"Then, unofficially, I'd like to ask you about Irish," Reaver said, leveling me with a look.

"Ask away," I said giving him a dark one of my own. I had a feeling I wasn't going to like whatever came out of his mouth.

"She yours, or is it open season?" he asked and his smile was chilly but not cold.

"Why?" I asked and tried to come off as nonchalant, but I felt my posture stiffen.

"She's hot," Reaver said with a shrug, but I knew for Reaver to be sniffing around it had to be more than that.

"That's it?" I asked. I wanted my brother's opinions on my girl. It was important to me that they like her but not required. The way that woman felt, I wasn't keen on giving her up any time soon.

"She's perceptive, and Reaver scares her. She said as much. You know our boy..." Trigger said and crossed his arms. I raised an eyebrow. Reaver's idea of good sex involved fear and sometimes crying, maybe even a little blood. Never without consent, though. He was weird like that, and weirder still, girls went for it. Now I'm all for slapping a girl's ass when I'm doing her from behind but the shit Reaver was into was a little too hardcore for me.

"Yeah, she's mine. Hands off, Reaver." I gave him a solid look and Reaver grinned and held out his hand to my dad who slapped a twenty in it.

"Told you he'd be all over that," Reaver said.

"I thought sure you'd get tired of her after a week, son." My dad arched an eyebrow and gave me a hard stare that I wasn't getting out from under until I opened my mouth.

"She's different," I stated and hoped it would be enough. No such luck. Four sets of eyes locked with mine and every expression read the same: elaborate.

"She doesn't have her head in the sand. She's seen things and those things send a normal person running for the hills, but not her. She's solid in a way I've never seen any other girl be. I don't have to pretend around her because she sees it anyways and isn't picky about it. She seems to like me for me; I like that about her, so I'm keeping her around." I shrugged. Four sets of eyes blinked in my direction and all four expressions again read the same: incredulous.

"That's the most I've ever heard you talk about you, boy." Doc said. Which I thought was funny, wasn't I just talking about Everett?

"Son, I think you should keep her around," my dad said judiciously. A peal of feminine laughter floated through the curtained glass from the main room.

"Oh, lord," Doc sighed.

"Might have been a bad idea letting them get together," Trigger said. Reaver was grinning his head off.

*"Well if you're havin' girl problems I feel bad for you son, 'cause I got ninety-nine problems and a bitch ain't one!"* Reaver sang; I smiled my nastiest smile in his direction.

"Shelly's out there," I said simply and Reaver's face fell.

"Fuck, thanks for reminding me." Hesmoothed his hair down his forehead. If Reaver was a heat-seeking missile on a good day, his cousin Shelly was a thermonuclear device. Both of them had attitude, Shelly's was just a little over the top. Both of them kind of lived by the motto 'Listen, smile, agree, and then do whatever the fuck you were gonna do anyway.' The main difference between the two cousins was that Reaver knew how to pick his battles. Shelly was hot-headed and in it to win it, no matter what came along. She was fun in the sack, but too much of a headache for anyone outside of it, which is why she was, and likely always would be, a club whore rather than an Old Lady, which seemed to suit her just fine, leastways until she grew up some. Yeah, I was the pot calling the kettle black. No one else needed to know about it, though.

Reaver rolled his shoulders and wracked his neck from side to side. He took responsibility for Shelly most of the time but every once in a while even he was hands-off and let her sink on her own. My Pops usually stepped in and dealt with her if she got too uppity. All in all, we liked Shelly, she was fun and vivacious and a kick to be around but she had her bad spells and we tried to forgive her those. She and Reaver both had it rough growing up and both were clawing their way out of the trailer park they grew up in. Reaver was ahead of the game by age and vocation, but Shelly wasn't too far behind. The girl was smart and going to college, apparently the same one my girl was going to. I smiled at the thought of Everett and it struck me. I'd never been with a girl that just thinking about her could make me smile.

"We done here, then?" I asked, suddenly anxious to get back out there to her. I wanted my hands on her and hers on me. I promised her I would take my time with her and I suddenly felt like time, it was a-wasting. I caught my dad grinning this stupid-assed grin at me and I frowned at him.

"Yeah. We're done," he said dryly and banged his knuckles against the old battered table. We all rose as one. My dad was chuckling to himself. The rest of the men filed out ahead of us.

"What's so fuckin' funny, old man?" I asked.

"Boy, you got the same look I did every time I thought about your mother just then."

I blinked and frowned harder.

"What look?" I demanded.

"I don't know what you were thinking, but it's the same look I'd get when I thought about gettin' some. Swear to Christ, Tilly's pussy was made out of gold or something. I couldn't get enough," he sighed. "Anyways, *that's* the look you just had on your face." He smiled benignly at me and all I could give him was a horrified look.

"Dude, Pops! Okay, yeah sure, that's what I was thinkin' but god damn it! TMI! Don't ever tell me shit like that about you and Mom again!" I shuddered, for real, and shook my head. His barreling laugh followed me out into the common room. My gaze went to and fell directly on Everett who returned it with a curious one of her own, her blue eyes alive and sparkling; a cool drink of water on a long hot day.

"What was that about?" she asked when I neared.

"Don't ask, baby. Please don't ask." I shuddered again. That'd been so wrong.

"Drink?" Loyal called from behind the bar.

"Fireball, make it a double!" I called back. Everett smiled up at me and I hooked an empty chair with a boot and pulled it out, dropping into it.

"You girls having fun?" I asked.

"Yep!" Shelly quipped, "All at your expense." She wrinkled her nose at me and smiled. I raised an eyebrow and turned my attentions to Em. Shelly was just trying to get a rise and sometimes it worked, but this time it didn't.

"Ashton says she gets up early. She said she'd give me a ride to the studio tomorrow so I could let you sleep in. Cool with you?" she asked me.

I gave a nod and said "Thanks, Sunshine, the new schedule is kicking my ass." Everett shot me an apologetic look and I smiled. "I'll get used to it," I said and propped my boot on the opposite knee and jiggled my foot, both out of habit and impatience.

"Prospect! Where's my drink!?" I bellowed and the girls all laughed. He was standing right behind me.

"Should pour it on his head," Shelly muttered.

"Here you go, sorry, man." He set my Fireball cinnamon whiskey in front of me and an Irish whiskey in front of Em. She smiled serenely and smoothed a hand over my denim-clad knee and sparks shot along my nerves. I smiled at her and raised my glass.

"Sláinte!" she said and we both sipped.

"Uhhh, bless you?" Shelly said.

"It's Gaelic," Em said, suppressing a smile.

Reaver and Trigger pulled up chairs, Ashton got up and settled herself into Trig's lap and the big man smiled at her. I vaguely wondered if that might be the way I looked at Em – whatever look I'd been giving her sure had a lot of people's panties in a wad. I was surprised to find that I wasn't self-conscious about it, though. Hard to be when you had a girl like Em edging closer to you. I laid an arm across the top of the back of her chair and she immediately leaned back into the curve of it. I felt myself smile. The movement had been unconscious on her part but it spoke volumes. It was nice to know that she liked having me around.

Ashton's little friend Hayden sat quietly between Trig, with Ash on his lap, and Shelly. Shelly was chattering away at Ashton but her eyes were behind the bar on Loyal. Interesting. Ashton laughed and Hayden smiled, I wasn't paying attention to Shelly's prattle, but Everett's accompanying laugh was like music to my ears. My smile deepened, let 'em think it was at whatever Shelly had said.

Some club whores, Candy and Moira, entered the house and went to the bar. I'd done Moira a time or two when I'd been pissed off. The memories made me grimace inwardly. I hadn't really treated her well. She didn't stand up for herself. Not like Shelly. Shells would let you know all about it, if you did something she didn't like and if you didn't listen she'd set Reaver on you. I turned my attention back to the table after a long appreciative look at Everett. She was the first girl I'd ever had under me that I'd actually worried about my performance afterward. I was good in bed, I'd heard it enough times from enough chicks to believe it. I mean I wasn't a man-whore or anything, but still, I was pretty confident about my abilities in the sack. Still, after our first time, as she'd drifted off against me, I'd found myself hoping that she'd want it again. A gentle squeeze on my knee brought me out of my thoughts.

"What?" I asked, looking sharply in her direction.

"I was saying you drove us here in your car..." Everett said. I frowned.

"Why does that matter?" I asked.

"Dude, where have you been!?" Reaver asked laughing. I scowled at him.

"I'm still getting used to this getting-up-at-three-in-the-morning bullshit, give a guy a break!" I lied. Everett went very still. Shit. It had sounded better than what I'd actually been thinking. I sighed.

"What does Matilda have to do with anything right now?" I asked, using my bike's name.

"Who the fuck is Matilda?" Shelly asked and made a weird face.

"His bike!" "My bike," we all chorused and laughed.

"I was just saying, it's dry out and not too bad, we haven't done a night ride in a while and we should take a cruise down Main. Hit a bar, join the rest of society for a change then bring the after-party back here," Trigger said.

"I told him your bike was at home, you drove us here in Sadie," Everett supplied. I nodded.

"Doesn't matter," I said. I put my leg back down and slid my unfinished Fireball to the center of the table. Hadn't had more than a sip or two, I was good to go. I kissed Em, a quick press of lips.

"I'll be back in a bit." I stood up and strode out of the clubhouse, Em staring wide-eyed after me. I fired up Sadie a minute later and made the drive home. I ran into the house and pulled my old leather jacket from high school out of the back of my bedroom closet and pulled down my spare helmet off the shelf before going out to the garage to get my firstborn.

Matilda was a 2002 Harley Davidson Fatboy cruiser. I'd gotten her for a steal back in '09, when I was seventeen, at an auction. I'd been at the salvage auction with a high school buddy of mine and his dad, who was lookin' for some cheap hulks to part out of his back yard. He'd run an illegal wrecking yard of sorts for years. They'd left the auction empty-handed but had their flatbed tow truck with us just in case.

Matilda – someone had laid her down and she was in some seriously rough shape; she'd needed some love and attention. So I'd laid down seven hundred bucks and picked her up and I'd rebuilt her. My pops had been pissed off when he'd sobered up and found out what I'd done. I hadn't cared much. I'd found her after my mom had died but something about taking on the project called to me. I'd slaved in the garage over her, she was my coping mechanism.

I walked my baby out of the garage and closed it up behind me. I stowed the jacket in one of my saddlebags and clipped the helmet around the sissy bar – the passenger seat's backrest. That had been a custom piece that had cost me a pretty penny. The back rest on my passenger seat was a chromed-out Gothic cross with roses at the base. I'd had it laser cut by a custom metal shop in town. Somewhere along the line of building her, my bike had turned into a memorial for my mother.

The skin, or paint job on the gas tank and fenders, I'd had done in a glossy black overlaid with ghostly, deep red roses that were in full bloom. My mom's favorite flower. She had 'em growing all around the house and would fill vases in the house with the deep red blooms. When the sun caught the roses on my bike they sparkled; on a cloudy day they were barely there.

The exhaust pipes, engine and the like remained shiny and/or chrome but by no means was my bike, or myself, suffering from chromeitis, hell no. I kept it tasteful, that shit's just too damned hard to keep clean. My mother's rosary hung from my right handlebar. I'd taken it to a jeweler and had all of the links reinforced and soldered shut to make it strong enough to withstand being there. It was so my mom would always be at my right hand to guide me and it sort of acted like a get-back whip, flashing and fluttering to attract attention. On the back fender between the seat and tail light I'd had an artist freehand a memorial in a Gothic script.

*Matilda "Tilly" Draven*
*1973 – 2009*
*Gone. Never Forgotten.*

My dad didn't cry after my mother died. When I'd rolled my bike, completed, out of the garage and into the sun two years after I'd started her, he'd looked her over with a stern gaze. When his eyes had fallen on the memorial script, he'd paused; when he'd put his hand on my shoulder it had been with tears in his eyes and he'd had me patched in that night. A year after that he'd made me his VP.

Most clubs had a voting process on their VP; not my dad's. He'd always held true to the belief that when it came to being the leader of anything that you needed to be able to trust the man at your side implicitly. The three other positions in the club, the three votes able to sway any decision, held at this time by Trig, Reaver and Doc, those positions are up for club vote. A man could choose his successor and nine times out of ten that was who would assume the mantle of whichever given office, but the club had final say.

I started Matilda up with one kick and headed back for the club while I continued roving down memory lane. I was proud of my baby and ecstatic that I was going to have Everett warming my back tonight. I wanted to share this with her and a night ride as a club, small as we were at the moment, was the perfect opportunity to ease her onto the back of my bike. I was really hoping she would take to it.

I pulled up and hit my signal to make a left through the club's gate. Coming at me was Ashton in her Jeep. She waved through the windshield and turned up into the driveway, her friend Hayden pulled up and into the drive right behind her in some black Lexus SUV. That was Sunshine for you. Agreed to take my girl to her dancing in the morning and didn't even have her car here to do it. Swear to God that woman would give you the shirt off her back. She and Trigger were a lot alike that way. I rode up into the lot and backed my bike into its spot.

There was a small crowd forming outside the clubhouse by now. It was warmer than it had been in days but still crisp enough that my nose was trying to run from the cold of the ride. Still, it felt really damn good to be on the bike again. I shut her off and got off, pulling off my helmet and the clear-lensed, black-framed wraparounds I was sporting to shield my eyes from the wind. I tucked the glasses in my jacket and hung the helmet off one of the handle bars.

Everett glided up in that effortless walk of hers and I pulled her against me, kissing her temple while she got a good look at the bike under the flood lights. She reached out tentative fingers and I smiled.

"Go ahead," I murmured against her ear and let her slip free of my grasp. She touched the rosary and picked it up letting the ornate crucifix rest in her palm. She walked slowly around the bike and stopped.

"Am I seeing things or does it have roses on the gas tank?" She smiled at me and I smiled back.

"They're roses," I affirmed. She'd seen the bike before, outside her coffee shack but I hadn't really given her time to really *look* then. Now she could have as much time as she wanted while we waited for Trigger's boys to arrive. She trailed a fingertip reverently along the edge of the Gothic cross sissy bar and paused, bending to read the inscription below the fender rack, above the tail light. She frowned, a cute little crease forming between her eyebrows and leveled that steely blue gaze of hers, the one that I swear saw through everything.

"Matilda... Your mom?" she asked.

"Matilda is my bike," I explained. "My mom was Tilly, she hated the name Matilda and you called her Matilda at your own peril." I smiled and felt the familiar ache of loss in the center of my chest.

"You built it for her?" she asked.

"Yeah," I said shortly and one of her brows arched, the look on her face said she clearly knew the story didn't end there but then she shot a look over to the crowd of people close by.

"Will you tell me about her?" she asked quietly.

"Not something I typically talk about," I said honestly and her face smoothed into solemn lines. "Maybe, someday," I said quietly going to her and pulling her against me.

"Okay." She smiled at me and it was beautiful. I smiled back and a feminine voice cleared her throat behind me. I spooked, tensing. Only one person that freaking quiet around here.

"Yeah, Ash?" I asked, voice harder than I meant it to come out.

"I'm sorry Dray, I didn't want you thinking I was eavesdropping or creeping up on you on purpose," she said, her delicate, almost ethereal, voice drifted from behind me. I turned with Em in my arms and spied Ashton and her strait-laced rich friend Hayden standing pretty close.

"I know you don't mean it, Sunshine," I said, voice a little smoother. She'd gotten better at not crumbling under one of my looks or admonishments, which was saying something. Sometimes it was even easy to forget that she was as delicate as she was emotionally. She'd crumble or cry or have one of her hysterical fits but she always bounced back pretty quickly from them.

Em looked up at me and smiled and I didn't miss her grateful look. Seems like there was another follower in the cult of Ashton, which I couldn't really bitch or throw stones. She'd made a convert out of me, too. Hell, I'd even been instrumental in killing her husband for her. I shot a look over my shoulder to Reaver. We'd done it together. I blinked, realizing that his glacial blue eyes were fixed in our direction. For a second I was gonna get my back up thinking that he was eye fucking *my* girl but then I realized that his stare was fixed on Hayden and it was as hopeless and grim as I'd ever seen him. Em distracted me by laughing at something Ashton said.

"I don't know, I've never ridden on a motorcycle before but something tells me I'm going to learn how." She eyed me dubiously and I smiled.

I let her go and pulled my old jacket out of my saddlebag. When I'd started really coming into my own and hit that final growth spurt between sixteen and eighteen it had gotten a touch too small through the shoulders and too tight around my upper arms. I flipped up the hood on Em's hoodie and held open the jacket. She shrugged into it obediently and I tried not to think about how I'd worn it the day my mom died. It fit her near perfect, if a touch too big. It looked like what it was, that she was wearing her boyfriend's jacket and I smiled. I liked that. I liked that a lot.

"I thought it'd fit," I said judiciously. She smiled up at me and adjusted her hood on her sweatshirt so it would lay comfortably outside the collar of the coat. Zander pulled up on his custom chopper and behind him Squick on his vintage Beemer. Some cheers and calls went up from the small assembled crowd. Ashton and Hayden had moved off when I'd been fussing over Everett, and Ashton hugged Squick who leaned his tall frame, nearly folding himself in half to hug her back. Em and I sauntered over. I clasped hands with Zander and then Squick. We were all familiar with Zander's custom ride, so the talk immediately turned to Squick and his bike.

"Let's get a look at this thing," I said and smiled.

Trigger was right. The kid had done an amazing restoration job on it. The skin gleamed pearly white under the flood lights, and I mean that. The rainbow sheen of pearlessence was subtle but noticeable. He didn't have the extended seat for a passenger but that was okay. From the snippets of conversation I'd just heard he was just learning how to ride and didn't need to be taking any passengers.

Everything that was supposed to gleam, gleamed, and the sound it had put off when it had come up the drive was one of a finely-tuned, well-oiled machine, a sound my mechanic's ear totally appreciated. In short, I was impressed; it may not be a stereotypical biker's bike but fuck, who cares? It fit Squick's personality and it was a bike. Only rule on bikes in our by-laws was none of that jap-crap, and I'm not talking about sturdy Hondas, I'm talking the plastic shit. No rice or pasta rockets. ~~In short,~~ I wasn't going to be too picky, we really did need good members. The Beemer, it worked for me. My dad came out of the clubhouse with a bundle under his arm and I gave him a chin lift. He gave me one back and I nodded. Hang-around cuts.

Black denim, no-frills vests with a top and bottom rocker, a precursor to the leather cut of a prospect.

My dad's gaze lingered on Em, tucked up against my side for a split second but then he got busy strapping the material wadded in his hands to his fender rack. Em's attention was on something nearby. I followed her blue eyes to Reaver, standing pretty damn close to Hayden, who was smallish like Ashton, but still a few inches taller than Ash's five foot nothing.

"Do you trust me?" I heard him ask. She was looking past him at his bike like it was going to jump up and bite her. I raised an eyebrow. Hayden was getting hitched to some rich blowhard banker-type come summer. The dude was hardly ever around, always traveling on business and since she and Ashton had become like BFF's or something, she'd taken to hanging around with her and by default the club, whenever her fiancé was out of town. None of us minded. The woman was easy on the eyes and Trig and Reaver kept her clear of trouble. I watched fear slide behind her clear green eyes and sighed inwardly. Now I knew it was a done deal. Reaver would be getting her on the back of his bike, come hell or high water. Shelly called across the parking lot to her cousin.

"Hey, Cuz! Can I get a ride?" she asked.

He called back without taking his eyes off Hayden. "Sorry, Runt! Seat's taken!" I smirked and decided to help Shells out before she caused a scene.

"Prospect!" I barked. Em jumped in the circle of my arms, and I chuckled.

"Yeah?" Derek called back.

"You're giving Shells a ride!" I ordered.

He grinned. "You bet!"

Shelly looked at me, aghast. I knew she liked the Marine and this pretty much served her right for being such a pain in the ass on the regular.

"That was slightly mean," Everett whispered, but she was smiling this impish smile that made me laugh outright.

I explained what I expected out of her as a passenger and she listened. I didn't think she would have a problem with keeping balanced but the last thing I wanted was her counterbalancing and fucking up mine and Matilda's flow. Taking on a new passenger was always risky, though; you never knew what you were getting into with one until you were moving.

People were drifting to their machines and I got on mine. I put on my helmet and glasses and Em put her brain bucket on. I adjusted the chin strap for her and brought out a spare pair of clear safety glasses for her; she slid them on and got on behind me. I started the bike and put up her kickstand and Everett snugged close into my back, her arms twining around me. Damn, but she felt good against me. We weren't staying too long at the bar. I wanted to make good on my promise. I really did.

My dad pulled out first, me just behind to his right, Trig just behind to his left. Reaver behind me, Doc behind Trig, Data behind Doc, Loyal behind Reaver then Zander and Squick. Our tailgunner was our most experienced rider, so that would be Gypsy. We flowed out the gates and turned onto the highway, making for the center of town and the nightlife it held. We usually went to The Spot bar and grill when we had the women with us, or Sugar's, which was the local tittie bar, when we didn't.

Everett settled in behind me like she'd been born on a bike and I checked her out in my sideview. She was smiling and her smile was huge and as carefree and full of life as I had ever seen it, which was to say I'd only ever seen it on her like this when she danced, or when I'd been moving inside her. At any rate, thank you, Jesus! She liked it – no – I was pretty sure she loved it. I heard her laugh, bright and beautiful and I called out.

"You like it!?"

"I can't believe I've never done this before! Thank you!" she called back. I grinned and opened up the throttle a little more. I glanced over at Trig and Ashton and smiled. Ashton looked as calm and serene as you ever saw her. Trigger, about the same. I knew the feeling.

The ride was too damned short, only about ten minutes. There was nothing like riding in a pack with your brothers. It had a whole different feel from solo riding, though it was a tough call on which I liked better. Although riding, just me and Everett, might take the top spot. I couldn't wait to test the theory. We lined up at the street in front of The Spot and backed our bikes to the curb in the places we could find that were vacant of cars or where there was enough room for a bike or two but not for another car. Patrons on The Spot's front deck and outside surrounding bars and clubs turned and watched the main drag, leaning into one another and speaking in hushed tones.

The looks were a mixture of awe, entertainment, fear, distaste, and even some arrogance. I'd seen it a million times and didn't give two fucks what any of them thought. Neither did my old man and neither did my brothers. I helped Em off my bike and she was glowing, nose and cheeks red from the crisp cold of the autumn ride.

"I think I'm going to like that!" she stated and I laughed and left our helmets and glasses with the bike.

"Go with Sunshine and the girls and find us some tables, baby? I got some business out here." She smiled and nodded and leaned forward and kissed me, her lips cold against mine. I smiled against them.

"Don't plan on stayin' long," I said against her mouth, and she smiled.

"I'm holding you to that," she said gently.

"Be disappointed if you didn't," I called after her.

I pulled out one of my clove cigarettes and put it between my lips. I pulled a lighter out of the little pocket in my jacket meant for it and lit it, sucking in the spicy sweet smoke. Trigger looked at me with a cross between disgust and longing and took a drag off his blue tipped e-cig. I laughed at him.

"Pussy," I said and he raised an eyebrow.

"Shit you're smokin' ain't real either, bitch," he said with a grin.

"More real 'n the bitch cig you got in your hand," I said and he hooked a massive arm around my neck and shoved me forward towards the rest of our brothers with a massive hand on the back of my head. I laughed and stumbled forward. Yeah, my relationship with Trigger was greatly improved over the summer.

"Listen up!" My pops bellowed and we gave him our full attention.

"Squick and Zander here have expressed an interest in becoming official hang-around's of Sacred Hearts. I wanna put it to a fast vote. Anyone *not* in favor put it up!" No hands went up.

"Congrats, boys. You're on your first step of becoming a Sacred Heart's man." He handed them each a black denim cut. They smiled and there was a little cheering and applauding from our small group.

"You understand you need to find sponsors before becoming official prospects and that you can't have the same one," Dragon said to them and they both nodded. I looked over to Zander and gave him a chin lift, Reaver was doing the same to Squick. They each caught on and nodded back.

"Good, glad that's settled, let's get our drink on," my pops grunted and we filed towards the bar. Zander fell into step beside me.

"So how does this work?" he asked. I climbed over the railing onto the deck and he followed suit. They checked ID's at the bar here rather than the door. It was a pain in the ass getting it out every time you wanted a drink but hey, it made it easy to get shit to someone slightly underage, like Em. Twenty-one next month. I blew out a plume of fragrant smoke.

"Three to six months in that cut, then we put it to a vote; a year in a prospect's cut, sometimes less, sometimes more, depending; and then we put it to another vote. You got any questions or need any guidance you come to me, as your sponsor, first. You got a beef, you follow the chain of command; we'll get it sorted out." I sucked down another long drag. Trigger passed us with his e-cig and flipped me the bird as he skated right on in through the front door. I barked a laugh. He had me there.

"Dues?" Zander asked.

"Talk to Reaver, he's our treasurer and in charge of that shit. I can barely balance my fucking bank account." Zander laughed and I slapped him on the back and I put out my cig. We moved inside towards a set of tables near the back where the girls were at. When I reached her seat, Em smiled up at me. I put my lips near her ear.

"We're staying for an hour," I murmured and I felt her nod. I put some heat and steel into my next words.

"One drink, Em," I told her. "I mean it. I want you completely aware and to feel everything I do to you tonight." I felt her shudder against my chest and to drive my point home I put an arm across her chest and pulled her back into me where I leaned over her. I kissed the shell of her ear and let her go, stepping back. Her chest rose and fell as if she were trying to catch her breath and I felt a little self-satisfied grin curve my lips.

"Prospect, get me a beer and my girl one of her Irish whiskys," I said to Loyal, and added almost as an afterthought, "Get yourself whatever you want. I'm buyin'," and I slapped enough green into his had to make it so and leave a generous tip for the bartender. He looked to Em and got a few points for it.

She smiled. "Bushmill's, please," she called above the conversation and the band setting up on stage.

"You got it," he told her and me, and smiled, heading for the bar. I couldn't be a dick all the time. I'd been down that road and it was busted as fuck. I was still trying to find my way back with a lot of these fuckers. While things were markedly improved they weren't what they could be. Not yet anyways.

The girls laughed and talked and I let my eyes skate across Hayden, she looked vivacious and alive and I smiled. Reaver was looking at her and smiling, he looked like the cat who'd gotten the cream and I thought to myself, *good luck with that*. I mean she was getting hitched but the way he looked at her was the most human I'd seen him look at a girl in a while.

His glacial gaze caught mine and his expression startled for a second. I raised an eyebrow and he glanced at Hayden and put some space between them. Em was talking animatedly with her and the other girls and I jerked my head towards the outside.

Time for me to live up to my title some. I'd just had a cigarette but fuck, I could have another if it gave us an excuse to go out where we couldn't be heard. I kissed Em's temple and got up, she smiled but didn't say anything, and so Reaver and I went for the smoker's porch outside. Loyal handed me my beer as I passed him on his way back to the tables. He took one look at Reaver and handed him the one I'd told him to buy for himself. Good fucking man. I made serious note of that. It impressed the hell out of me. What impressed me more was that he took my girl her drink before returning to the bar to get another for himself. Reaver took a pull off his beer and we went outside.

"Dude, Reaver man, what's the story?" I asked him. He leaned against the railing and I quirked an eyebrow. He was wearing his cut, but his jacket was conspicuously absent. The leather of his vest gleamed softly in the streetlight against the deeper, light-absorbing black of his pullover hoodie. He was silent too long.

"She's getting married, man," I said in a low voice, meant to be soothing rather than accusatory.

"I know. I know!" He made a frustrated sound and scrubbed a hand over his face before smoothing his faux hawk down to the point between his eyes.

"If you know, then why you doin' what you're doin'?" I asked him.

"Can't help myself," he said plaintively.

"Well unless you plan on taking him out, which I do not recommend, I'd slow your roll Bro," I told him. He looked slightly miserable and made a face that told me to tell him something he hadn't told himself a million times before.

"Think anyone else has caught it yet?" he asked me bleakly. The question took me aback and I countered with one of my own.

"Just how into this chick are you?" I asked him. He huffed out a laugh.

"She had me the second she laid those hallowed green eyes on me when she came out the locker room behind Ashton," he confessed. I frowned, I didn't get the reference, I wasn't there but I figured it was safe to assume he meant the first time they ever met. "Couldn't get her off my mind, then weeks later she comes flying out the damned entrance to the Y with that rock on her finger and I swear to Christ it was like watching Aimee walk away all over again." I blinked. Now *that* was some heavy shit and a reference I knew all too well.

Aimee had been Reaver's first true love, high school sweetheart. His penchant for trouble and an addiction to smack had cost him that relationship and so much more. If he was comparing Hayden to Aimee then whatever he had going on in that half-cracked psycho psyche of his was serious trouble. I lit a cigarette, took a long thoughtful drag on it and leaned the arm holding my beer on the railing.

"I know that this is all spanking new to me but I think I know where you're at," I said finally. He looked me over and smiled.

"Yeah, you're all in with Irish." He was grinning and I felt an answering one of my own. I looked down at the glowing end of my cigarette.

"What do you want for Hayden?" I asked him.

"I want her to be happy..." he trailed off.

"And?" I prompted.

"I think she's making a huge mistake with this Andy guy, he's never a-fucking-round when she needs him. I got a bad feeling about it," he said.

"She's a grown-ass woman capable of making her own mistakes," I pointed out.

"I suppose you're gonna say she don't need me tryin' to ride in like some kind of white knight or some shit," he said.

"Pretty much," I said.

"You sound like Trig," he snorted.

"Yeah, well he might be big but he's not dumb," I said and the man in question shoved through the crowd.

"Whoa! I heard that!" he said and we three chuckled over it.

"What're we talking about?" he asked.

"Hayden," Reaver and I said at the same time. Trigger scowled.

"I'm tellin' you brother. Stay out of it!" the big man said. Reaver nodded.

"I said the same thing," I told him and took another drag. I held the cig out to Trigger who, no shit, looked around for Ashton first. I snorted and he took it from me and drew the real smoke into his lungs. He held it and sighed out like it was one of the best things ever. I drank some of my beer and grinned at him.

"Fuck, I miss smoking, like *real* smoking. This vaping shit is a pale fucking imitation." He made to hand me the cig back but I shook my head and let him keep it. He flashed me a grateful look.

"How the fuck did you stand it as a sniper?" I asked him. He chuckled.

"Total different mindset," he said like that explained everything, which in a way it did. I snorted. My old man joined our little deck party.

"What we talking about?" he asked.

"Pussy," Reaver answered crudely but truthfully.

"Shit, man, we got bitches a-plenty at the clubhouse lately," my dad grinned through his beard and we all laughed. Sad but true, they were starting to outnumber us.

"I see any fucking tampons in the medicine cabinets at the club, shit's gonna have to change," Trigger said. I laughed outright.

"You're the most whipped out of all of us, big man!" I pointed out dryly.

"You're right behind me, junior," he said, and I shrugged a shoulder and took a drink off my beer.

"What're they doing? Talking about doing each other's nails?" Reaver asked. My dad laughed.

"Your Irish girl is on the dance floor with Hayden and Shells. Ashton and Chandra are chatting it up with the hang-arounds and prospect. Gypsy and Doc are playing darts and Data has his nose buried in some game on his phone." Leave it to my pops to know what every one of his people were up to.

"Yeah, well, she better not wear herself out too much. I'ma bounce in a bit an' fuck her good," I said. The guys, including my pops, all nodded.

"Good plan," Reaver stated. I finished my beer.

"Yeah, I'm tired of waiting to act on it. Too much life getting in the way lately," I said and set the empty beer bottle on a table with a growing line of dead soldiers on it.

"That's my boy," my pops said and gave a mock sniff, wiping a fake tear from the corner of his eye. "You do your daddy proud!" he said with a fake warble in his voice.

"Fuuuuck you, old man!" I said laughing. He laughed along with me and we pulled each other into one another and hugged. A manly embrace. I clasped hands with Trigger and Reaver and went back into the hot, enclosed space of the bar. I wound my way through the crowd on the dance floor and located Everett. I pulled her back into me and nipped the side of her neck. I know she gasped even though I couldn't hear it and the knowledge made me smile.

She turned in the circle of my arms and wound her arms around my neck. I smiled down into her laughing face and jerked my head to indicate we were leaving. She said her goodbyes to Shelly and Hayden, who seemed much happier than she had been at the clubhouse, and we went to the table to finish the goodbyes and collect my girl's coat.

I helped her into it and led her out front. She was giggling and happy and my heart was lighter for it. She'd been having a hell of a time of it and deserved some fucking happy and I was determined to give it to her in spades. She spun once we were out the door and on the sidewalk. She wrapped her arms around my neck and kissed me and I obliged, the mixture of the cloves I'd been smoking and the whiskey she'd been drinking complimenting each other nicely.

"Oh, gawd! My virgin eyes!" My pops yelled beside us and she made to pull away. I captured the back of her head with my hand and pressed her into the kiss, keeping her from breaking it while I flipped my dad off with the other hand, which was nearer him. His barking laugh bellowed over the heads of the crowd outside and Everett smiled against my mouth.

"Take me to a bed, please? Yours would be great but if you want, his will do too." I laughed against her mouth at her audacity, and contemplated it for a minute or two. Naw, I wanted marathon sex, my bed for that. I'd get my dad back later.

We rode back to the clubhouse, just her and I, and I decided that this was a new favorite. Just Everett, me, and Matilda on the open road was nice. I wanted more of it and from the look of things in my side view, so did Everett. Awesome.

I stopped at a gas station and bought some lube and a twelve pack of ultrathin condoms. I wanted as little between us as possible. I didn't think we'd need the lube but you never knew and it was always good to have on hand. I was thick, I knew it and it was the humane thing to do so I kept it around. The clubhouse was deserted when we got to it and that was fine by me. I wanted to see how loud my girl could get when she was uninhibited by knowing people were around. I led her back to my room and opened the door, flipping on the light.

"You really like black," she observed and I smiled at her. Yeah, I'd been pretty monochromatic when it came to my club room. The carpet was black, I'd painted the walls black, the cheap ass garage sale dresser I'd painted black too. I'd mounted the small black flat screen TV on the ceiling above the bed which I had also painted black. It was going to suck if the damn thing ever came down but I didn't think it would. I'd built the brackets and mounted the thing myself.

The cables ran along the ceiling and down the corner of the wall to a triangle of shelf I'd mounted in the corner. The small cable box and DVD player sat on it, the little blue-white display reading that it was a little after ten-thirty.

The headboard of the queen sized bed was one of those cubby-style and lined with DVD's. I switched on a black iron lamp that sat on top of the headboard, setting the condoms and lube up for easy access beside it. Once I started, I didn't want to stop to wrestle open boxes or peel little safety seals off of lubricant so I made sure that shit was done, tossing the resulting trash in the bedside trashcan. That done, I flipped out the overhead light.

The glow of the lamp was pretty muted by its dark gray shade. The sheets on the bed were dark gray and the bedspread black like the rest of the room. I took Em's bags off the bed and set them on the floor in front of the dresser. I hung my jacket and cut on the hook by the door and took my old jacket from her shoulders.

"I want you to keep this," I said and she turned and looked at me, nodding softly.

"Okay," she breathed. I hung it on a hook to the side and slightly lower to the one I'd hung my coat on.

I put my hands on her hips and brought my lips to hers. I was careful, soft and gentle with her. I wanted to make this last. I wanted to show her she was more than a quick fuck for me. That she was special and I started by kissing her... letting my hands slide beneath the hem of her sweatshirt and the tee beneath it. I palmed her smooth and sexy skin and ran my hands over her stomach and ribs. She moaned softly into my mouth and I swallowed the whimper whole.

God! I could eat this girl like ice cream. Slow and decadent, one lick at a time... *Okay I needed more skin.* I lifted her shirts over her head, both at the same time and she raised her arms, her necklace tumbling free and hanging tantalizingly between the globes of her breasts. I was as hard as I could get and straining at the fly of my jeans. Her hands pushed under my shirt and her fingers were deliciously cool against my heated skin. She slid her hands up my stomach and across my chest, letting them come to rest on my shoulders. I pulled the shirt off from over my head and let it fall. She sucked in a breath and looked me over, her blue eyes near-boiling with the heat they contained. I loved that she liked what she saw. I turned her and sat her down on the edge of my bed and knelt in front of her. I pulled off her shoes and socks and stood and pulled my own boots off.

"All of it," she whispered, desperation tinging her voice and I smiled.

I flicked the tongue of my belt out of the loop holding it flat and opened it up. I watched her, her gaze transfixed by my hands and what they were doing, and the look of raw need on her face, in her eyes, had my desire for her ratcheting up several notches. I unbuttoned, unzipped and slid the denim over my boxers and down my legs, peeling out of my socks when I reached the bottom. She wasn't getting the full Monty. Not yet.

I reached for her waistband and she let me. There was something so sensual, so erotic about peeling the tight denim from her long dancer's legs. She lay back for me and lifted her hips so I could do it and the fact she was wearing one sexy-as-hell matching bra and panty set underneath her plain comfortable clothes damn near did me in. I didn't miss that the dove gray satin at the apex of her thighs was much darker with her wetness.

I felt a surge of fierce joy that she was as turned on as I was. Once the jeans were off, her scent lightly perfumed the air with pheromones that I had no intentions of trying to resist or ignore. I wanted Everett Mary Moran more than I had ever wanted any other girl in my life. That included the bitch that had used me as a rebound. I had to take a moment. I stopped and stood over Everett, laid out across the black covers in her gray satin and lace bra and panty set. She was so fucking beautiful, but there was more. I felt a slow wicked smile curve my lips and fought to keep the press of laughter down.

"What?" she asked smiling, her voice trembling with a giggle of her own, I didn't answer right away and she sat up, turning so she was on the bed, head towards the headboard rather than laying across it. "What's so funny!?" she demanded and I waved a hand in a sweep from her head to her pretty French-manicured toenails.

"You match," I said and the laughter spilled out. Black and gray, that was my room and her dove gray bra and panty set matched my sheets almost to perfection.

She looked around the room and then down at herself and the giggle poured out of her lovely mouth. She pressed a hand over it to stop the girly sound and I laughed some more. I motioned for her to center herself better on the bed and she obliged, moving over. I sat down beside her hip, facing her, and bent, kissing her softly. I touched her silky cheek and trailed fingertips in a barely-there touch down the side of her throat, across her shoulder.

I loved her whiskey-flavored kisses. Her tongue boldly stroked across my own. I loved that she wasn't afraid to be an active participant when we kissed, her hands cupping my face, smoothing across my shoulders. Her arms curving around my back and igniting my desire for her, like pouring gasoline on a bonfire. I got the bra off of her and cradled her breasts in my hands. God, she was a perfect gorgeous handful! Creamy skin and rose-colored nipples. I broke our kiss to take one into my mouth and she arched into me, moaning my name in a breathy push of air that drove me absolutely wild! I teased the other between thumb and forefinger and she writhed a little beneath the attention.

I traded sides and lavished the other with the same attention and her fingers tangled in my hair, holding it off my face. She captured my eyes with her heated blue gaze and I couldn't help but picture a steaming mountain hot spring when she did it. The steel blue-gray waters surrounded by freshly fallen snow. I got up on my knees while I sucked at her breast and hooked my fingers into the waistband of her panties. I kissed down her body and moved the soaked satin fabric off of her as I made my descent and she eagerly raised her hips to let me get them off.

I used my hands to push her thighs apart and let my gaze wander her pretty, freshly-shaven pussy. God damn, it was a thing of beauty! The light pink petals of her sex slightly lighter than the rose color of her nipples and glistening wetly, ready for me in the soft lamp light. I put a hand just above her mound and pushed back, bringing her clit to the fore. It was engorged and begging for my attention and I so wanted to go there.

I got between her thighs and scooted down the bed. I'd been wanting to do this and take my time savoring her since that first taste in my kitchen. I looked up the length of her lean body, her chest heaving in deep breaths, her eyes were almost panicked, frantic with her need for me to touch her and I loved that I held this kind of power, this kind of sway over her. One of these nights, if she were up for it, I wanted to play my orgasm game with her. Tie her to my bed, finger and lick her until she came and see how many times I could make her come. How long it would take until she begged me to stop, then how long it would take after that until I could get her to cry from the sheer overload of pleasure.

That wasn't for tonight though. I lowered my mouth agonizingly slow to her silky wet pussy, never breaking eye contact, and watched the anticipation in her eyes build. She wanted this, she wanted it bad and I was going to give her not only what she wanted but what I could tell she needed tonight. I smiled slow and lascivious, and I know it was a little cruel but I wanted to hear it. I craved the high of hearing her sweet voice beg me to do it and she didn't disappoint.

"Please, Dray, touch me!" Her voice lilted with her desire. I had her worked up and it showed, her breath coming in an unsteady cadence, eyes dilated, hips rocking unbidden. I teased her opening with a light touch and her eyes closed. I slid my middle finger up inside her and her head fell back with a moan. I looked on in wonder at the grace of her honest responses and teased around inside her looking for that spot. Her cunt spasmed around my finger and her hips bucked when I stroked deep and I smiled at the freshly gleaned knowledge. Unlocking Em was turning into seriously fun times.

I let my breath wash over her skin, over that sensitive little nub and she cried out, a soft little gentle pleading cry that gave me a wicked surge of triumph. I smiled and stroked that spot deep inside her adding my index finger to the middle; she was so hot and ready for me both glided in easily. With one last appraising look at how my girl was doing I lowered my mouth to her body and took my prize, giving her a long, slow, lick.

God she tasted good! Fresh and clean, like sunshine after a spring rain. She fisted the comforter to either side of her hips when I did it and arched her back, her head tipped back.

Looking up the long sensual curve of her body was a picture of grace and beauty I'll never forget. I think that was the point I could admit to myself what everybody else had probably been seeing from the moment I put my lips on hers on that dance floor...

I was in love with Everett Mary Moran.

# 11

Everett...

Oh my god, oh my god, oh my god, Dray was driving me insane! I felt full but not stretched as he probed me with his fingers. He'd found that place deep inside me and was coaxing pleasure from it, a slow draw, a slow pull, his tongue touched me and I felt like I was pulled off the bed as if with strings. Velvet and hot, it teased across that bundle of nerves and I felt things low in my body tighten and constrict around his invading fingers. I tangled my fists in the covers by my hips and tried to hold still. I wanted this, oh god, I wanted him to make me come, I wanted the sparks flitting through my body to roar to life and consume me in a raging inferno of an orgasm and it was headed that way! I gasped for air and cried out his name and he sucked on my clit. Oh god, it felt good but the fires slightly cooled with the change.

"Oh God Dray! Oh please, oh I'm so close!" I forced out through my rapid panting. I felt him smile against my body and he took his mouth from me.

"Not yet, baby, just a little bit longer. I'm gonna make it feel so good, I promise." I moaned a low passionate wail, his words spoken so close to me that the vibrations of them sent a different sort of thrill through my tortured nerves. He'd stilled his fingers as he'd spoken and now he resumed their gentle rocking. The motion awakened that ember of sensation deep inside me anew and with a little more ferocity than it'd held before. I clutched the covers and looked down the length of my body between my breasts... straight into the deep and lovely dark eyes of Dray, which smoldered with heat and intensity as he observed my reactions to his ministrations.

The look stole the breath from my lungs and sent me sailing over the edge, I plunged into the deepest orgasm of my life, the sensations unfurling in a rapid tide from my center, washing out through my limbs, colliding with my edges and washing back in, filling me with bliss. Sight stopped, sound stopped, the whole world stopped and narrowed down to Draven Trujillo's mouth on my clit and his fingers deep inside me. He was eking out every bit of pleasure he could from my body until I felt light and heavy at the same time.

The bed became cloud nine and I lay boneless, panting for breath, my throat was raw and I didn't know why. Dray shifted over me, his fingers slipping free of my body, the heat of his mouth replaced with the cool kiss of air from the room and I shuddered again with an aftershock. My whole body had come alive, I let my eyes drift shut and reveled in these new and intense sensations, the rest of my senses slowly coming online from wherever Dray had sent them.

I heard the rustle of a wrapper, a tearing sound. I hadn't even been aware of him removing his boxers but my eyes flicked open to reveal him kneeling between my legs, which twitched faintly. His dark eyes were glued to my face as he rolled the condom securely around the base of his thick cock and my breath caught in my throat. The sight of him making himself ready to take me was erotic to the nth degree.

He smiled down at me and the curve of his lips was borderline cruel and for some reason that turned me on too. I reached for him and he situated himself, collapsing forward over me, holding his upper body off of mine with one arm while he positioned himself with the other. I wasn't sure I was quite ready, I still hadn't caught my breath but that didn't matter to Dray, he was apparently determined to keep things going, because he pushed his hips forward and slid into me with barely any effort at all. God, I must be wet and who wouldn't be after an orgasm like that!?

He folded down over the top of me and with our heights being nearly the same, it made missionary so very close and intimate. His eyes held mine as he stroked in and out of me and he smiled tenderly down at me. My hands found his shoulders and I curved my arms around his neck and opened myself more completely to him, winding a leg around his, spreading the other a little wider. I closed my eyes for a second and just allowed myself to feel what he did to me, to drink in his spicy sweet smell and the warmth of his body against mine.

"How you doing, baby?" he asked, his voice husky and deep with passion.

"You feel so fucking good!" I breathed back and he growled and adjusted his thrust so he went deeper and a little harder. I gasped and cried out, clinging to him tighter. I couldn't get enough of his skin against my body and finally dragged his mouth to mine. I could taste the salt of myself on his lips and I didn't care. He took his time loving me and I did everything to love him back just as fiercely. I'd barely had time to recover from my last orgasm but already another was building. He rocked into me expertly, finding and reaching all the right places like his body was built to fit mine.

He broke the kiss to lean up and change angle again and I wrapped my legs around his lean hips, dragging him deeper still. I nipped his shoulder and he growled against the side of my neck and licked that sweet spot that sent a wash of goosebumps across half of my body.

"Oh god, Dray, I'm almost there!" I gasped.

"Good," he growled, "I wanna feel that pussy come around my cock. Don't disappoint me, Em, you disappoint me we're going to try again until you get it right," he said with a playful edge of challenge in his voice. I laughed and then moaned as the head of his cock found the same spot his fingers had so lovingly exploited a little earlier. My womb grew heavy with the delicious threat of another powerful orgasm and I squeezed my muscles around him.

"Oh god, yeah! That's it, baby!" he said and drove into me steadily.

"Oh, Dray! Oh! Oh! Oh...!" I came apart underneath him. It was like he pulled the loose thread that unraveled all the best parts of me in all the best ways. I shook and held onto him as if he were a rock in a storm-pitched sea as I came and I don't know what he did but it was like he kept it going, rolling it out as long as possible for me until I was a panting, nerveless, quivering, beautiful mess beneath him.

It was so intense, too intense! I clung to him, overwhelmed by everything I was feeling and then some. Tears stood out in my eyes and he smiled an entirely too-satisfied smile and held me close.

"You okay?" he asked. I didn't know but his wide grin was reassuring.

"I don't know," I said and my voice broke on a terrified little girl sob.

"Shhhh, you're okay, baby, just a little intense, yeah?" he asked. I nodded against his shoulder and he kissed my forehead.

"Hang on, because I'm not done and it's about to get worse... or better... depending on your perspective," he said between breaths. I blinked and he hooked an arm beneath my knee and folded it upwards and started thrusting all over again, sure strokes that stoked the fires of my passion for him all over again, sure, but even and surprisingly gentle strokes.

I didn't know if my body could take it, but Dray wasn't going to give an inch. I liked that. I liked that a lot. He made me come at least two more times before taking his own satisfaction. I lay sweat-soaked and trembling beneath him and I wasn't sure how well I would be dancing in the morning. My body felt like it had been through a thorough workout by the time he was through. Parts of me tingled with the memory of the pleasure, other places felt numb, others were so fatigued I didn't know if they would ever work right again!

Dray looked entirely too satisfied with himself as he disposed of the condom in the trash. He gathered me up, as boneless and nerveless as I felt, and cuddled me close, getting the blankets up and over us, nesting us down in the surprising softness of the bed. I closed my eyes, exhausted, but not before catching him looking at me like I was his long-lost treasure. That, more than anything else, is what made my night. No man had ever looked at me with such love and adoration. As much as my da' had loved me, not even he came close to a look like the one Dray was giving me.

"I think I love you for looking at me that way," I said in a softly-lilting voice that was half dreamy at this point.

"Aww, sleep, baby. I wore you out," he said gently and I laughed.

"That's true... but I'm still pretty sure I love you," I whispered.

"Good, because it would really suck to love you as much as I'm loving you and not have it returned," he said. I relaxed just that much more and he gave me a squeeze.

"You love me?" I asked and I could hear his smile.

"Yeah, Em. I think I do... I *know* I do. It's the only explanation for what I've got going on inside." He sniffed and cleared his throat like he was getting choked up. I opened my eyes and craned my neck back to look at him.

"I'm not going anywhere, Dray," I whispered and something flashed in his dark eyes. "You don't find a connection like this very often," I whispered, "What I'm feeling for you, I don't know," I gave an exasperated sigh, words failing me.

"Goes way beyond incredible sex?" he hazarded a guess.

"Yes! God! Way beyond. What I feel right now is the stuff of fairy tales... You showed up out of nowhere, a knight in armor and swept me off my feet, and now you're stuck with me!" He barked a laugh.

"My armor's not white or shiny, baby," he said.

"Well, if you're a knight who really knows your way around a sword, it's kind of impossible to keep your armor shiny isn't it? I mean you'd be fighting in it all the time..." I yawned at the end of the observation. My father had raised a pretty practical daughter and that *is* what seemed practical in this certain analogy. Dray chuckled and changed the subject.

"Em?"

"Yeah?"

"Why you fighting so hard to stay awake?" he asked. I blinked and relaxed into him and thought about it and the answer startled me a bit.

"I don't want to wake up and find out that this is just a really good dream..." I said.

"Aww, well, sleep tight, babydoll, I'll most likely love you in the morning," he said sweetly.

"I don't know if I'll have it in me to go another round so soon," I said honestly.

"I didn't mean physically, babe," he said and his tone was gently chiding. I absolutely melted and drifted safe and warm against him in the deepening night. He reached up and switched out the light and I feel like my consciousness blinked out with it.

My phone started ringing a minute later. I threw myself out of bed and felt through my clothes until I located it in my hooded sweatshirt's pocket. I looked at the screen and groaned inwardly as I silenced the alarm. I had a bevy of bright-eyed girls and a couple of boys to teach in an hour and a half. I looked over my shoulder back at Dray, he was giving me a tired but amused look.

"'Morning," I said softly. He gave a luxurious stretch.

"'Morning," he grunted. I got to my feet slowly and he smiled, those deep, dark, lovely eyes of his hooded with satiation coming alive with lust as they traveled over my nude form.

"Guess what?" he said.

"What?" I asked softly, my smile growing.

"It's morning, you're awake and..." he looked me over again and I cocked my head to the side.

"And..?" I prompted. Oh god, I wanted to hear it, I *needed* to hear him say it.

"...and I still love you," he said and my apprehension drained out of me, through the floor and disappeared into oblivion.

"I love you too," I murmured softly and he gave me that beautiful, heart-stopping, boyish grin that I absolutely adored.

"Got some towels in the top of the closet there, you know where the bathrooms are at?" he asked. I nodded and fetched down the towels, taking up my bags.

"'K, come here and kiss me so I can go back to sleep," he ordered and I didn't mind at all. I went over and kissed him and he brushed fingers across my cheek.

"See you when I come pick you up," he whispered.

"Okay," I whispered back and wrapped up in one of the towels. I peeked into the hall but it was deserted and I made a break for the nearest bathroom with a shower.

I was sore in all the right places which were, unfortunately, all the *wrong* places for a dance instructor to be sore the morning she had to instruct. I hoped the hot shower would help and it did. I took some Aleve out of my dance bag and swallowed them with some water from the tap. I did not pass go, I did not collect two hundred dollars, I did get dressed directly in my dance stuff and hauled ass out into the common room.

"Please be up, please be up, please be up..." I chanted under my breath and sure enough she was, bright eyed and ready for the day not a hair or stitch out of place. Thank you, Jesus!

"Running late?" Ashton asked at the look on my face and I laughed.

"Not exactly. I have *got* to stop for coffee on the way in. Robusta or bust," I said, and hoisted my bags higher on my shoulder. I had chosen black leggings, black leotard and a deep forest green chiffon skirt over the top. Ashton smiled.

"Is there a place you usually stop at on the way?" She asked.

"Renaissance. You know it?" I asked.

"Absolutely! Let's go." I followed the smaller woman out to her Jeep and got in. The interior was crisp and still held that faint new-car smell.

"Nice ride," I said surveying the tan interior. the Jeep's paint was a deep rich red, the color of a really good ruby. She smiled.

"Dray helped me pick it out," she said brightly.

"Surprised it's not black then," I said and she laughed.

"No, he lost on color." She turned the key and shifted out of park and into reverse. She was very careful and meticulous in her driving.

She drove us to the café and I ran in and bought us coffee. She was singing when I came out and when I opened the door I was surprised that it was her that I heard outside the Jeep and not the radio as I first suspected. She was so small and so quiet all the time I didn't think she got much above a whisper.

"What is this?" I asked.

"Phantom of the Opera," she said and I gave her directions to the studio.

"Do you mind if I watch?" she asked.

"Sure, you should like it, it's the advanced class this week."

"Thanks," she said following me into the old building, "Trigger and Reaver, when they get up, will likely go work out and there isn't yoga on Saturdays." She made a face. I laughed. I didn't have the patience for that crap, but I wasn't about to call it that to her face. If yoga did something for her, then awesome, it just wasn't my cup of tea.

I downed my coffee and got on my soft shoes. I stretched and warmed up after putting on some music and my students started showing up and dropped into doing the same. God, I was sore! I wouldn't trade the night before with Dray for anything though. I sighed.

"Everett Mary Moran!" I turned to see my best friend, hands on her hips, looking pretty put out with me.

"Mandy, what's wrong?" I asked.

"You!" she exclaimed in a hiss when she got close to me. I frowned, perplexed, and she huffed out a sigh.

"You didn't answer any of my calls or texts last night. I was worried!" I leaned back and felt a furious blush overtake me as my face fell. Several of my students laughed.

"Oh. My. God." Mandy said and turned a brilliant shade of red herself. "Okay! Um, oh my god, okay. You were busy. Got it!" She looked flustered and I closed my eyes. Thank god all my students were eighteen to twenty-somethings today. I know *I* was still an eighteen to twenty-something but I was also just that damned good to be teaching them.

"Mandy," I said when she really started to babble.

"Yeah, Evy?" she asked meekly, and I led her over to the line of chairs against the wall and Ashton.

"Mandy, meet Ashton. Ashton, Mandy is my BFF when I'm not busy being horrible and self-absorbed. Mandy, Ashton is Trigger's Old Lady and knows Dray pretty well. I have a class to teach." I gave a pleading look to Ashton and she smiled sweetly.

"I'll tell your friend all about Dray and how he's *not* an ax murderer," she said, reading my look correctly.

"Thank you." I turned on the class.

"Places please!? First number. I want to do a run through and for anybody still laughing you can stay after and do two." The faces fell into careful lines of not-laughter and I smiled sweetly.

"That's what I thought."

We took it from the top and mid-way through I saw Ashton on her phone. Mandy was smiling and taking pictures with hers. I laughed inwardly and pushed my class. They were getting ready for a community theater fundraiser for the homeless and some were even getting ready to try out with some troupes for tour.

It was the end of class and I was standing with John McGuigan, one of the best male dancers I'd ever been able to pair with, when I felt that burning stare of Dray's on me. I looked up and my smile faltered when I saw jealousy slide through his dark gaze. Oh, boy. I could fix that, though. All I needed to do was get John to talk. He was gay and had a very effeminate way of speaking.

I went over to the surprising crowd of onlookers. In addition to Dray was his father Dragon, Reaver, Trigger and the lanky young tattooed man everyone had called Squick the night before, as well as the other hang-around, the one with the custom chopper. I hadn't gotten his name.

"Wow. Where did you all come from!?" I exclaimed, laughing. Ashton looked sheepish. Ah, ha.

"Came to see what all the fuss was about. Ashton mass-texted everyone," Dragon laughed.

"Ahhh, well!" I blushed. I really didn't know what to do with all of this.

"Hi, I'm John," John waved at everyone and Dray had the grace to look embarrassed. It was Squick's reaction, however, that was somewhat priceless. He looked at John, I mean *really* looked and it looked like he liked what he saw. I smiled at him and he startled and checked to see if anyone else had noticed.

Oh.

Ashton winked at me and hugged Squick. Interesting; so she knew, and it was a secret. I filed that away. Mandy was looking at me and then at all of the delicious man-candy and smiling at me with her 'I am so going to get you, bitch' smile. Probably for not sharing sooner. I smiled back and shrugged a little. I'd been horribly wrapped up in Dray. I made introductions until I got to the man whose name I didn't know. He gave me a one-sided grin and supplied it for me.

"I'm Zander. Nice to meet you, Ev," he said and shook my hand.

"Evy, baby, do you think we could do one last run of the third dance?" John asked. Show off that he was, he picked the most difficult, but also the one that his partner was having the most difficulty in.

"Trying to figure out what she's doing wrong?" I asked.

"Oh, I know what it is, but I want to be sure," he waved a hand as if waving off a fly. "You know how she is." I rolled my eyes.

"Yep. Do you guys mind?" I asked, and people started finding seats, grinning at my expense.

"Guess not. Okay!" I kissed Dray and he kissed me back, I sat down and switched back from my hard shoes to my soft shoes while John checked his laces on his hard shoes. I put on the music, took place and went for it.

I swayed and spun and leaped and stepped and did what I did to the very best of my ability. Not because I had an audience but because it was how I always danced... but I would be lying if I said I didn't put in any extra effort knowing that Dray's eyes were on me. We danced a number that was clearly one of those 'anything you can do I can do better' type of dances between a man and a woman, which was a lot more complex than it sounded given him being in hard shoes and me in soft.

Midway through the number he had his solo and I got to change shoes which I only had a finite amount of time to do and do right. I pulled it off and was out and on the floor and tearing it up, *proving* the way it was meant to be proven that I indeed could do it better. I loved numbers like this. I'd had a lot of high-level and cocky male students that thought they were hot shit and didn't need to listen to me until I had them dance this number with me. I made them eat their egos once I had the hard shoes on and outpaced them. Machine gun fire from a fully automatic weapon had nothing on me when I really put my mind to it and my hard shoes to hardwood.

John and I finished our number to the last set of notes and stopped cold in the correct position breath heaving. His hand slid from my waist and he fell to his knees, hands clasped together and wailed.

"Please, Evy! Don't make me do this number with Kayden! I'll do anything!" he begged. I rolled my eyes.

"She's not that bad!" I exclaimed.

"She is!" he insisted, and got up and I was sensing one of John's famous temper tantrums about to erupt. I battened down the hatches of my resolve and crossed my arms and let him go. Everyone else was in stitches by the time he was through. A lot of people mistook John being just plain mean for him trying to be funny and I'm not going to lie, he *was* hysterical, but I wasn't having any of it. The only time I stepped in was as an understudy in case of injury or illness.

"Are you done yet?" I asked him, and caught the towel Dray tossed me and mopped up. I needed a shower and I was starving and I was about to get medieval on John's ass if he kept having a tantrum between me and getting some food. He sulked and threw up his hands.

"You're not listening to sense!" he said.

"Nope, I'm just not listening to you, sweetheart. I'm starving and I need a shower so if there isn't anything else, I'm hitting the locker room and letting my man over there take me to lunch." I raised my eyebrows and he looked from me to the pile of man-candy on the opposite side of the room.

"Which one?" he asked.

"The dark one," I answered.

"Isn't he a little old for you?" he asked picking out Dragon, who barked a laugh.

"The *other* dark one," I said simply. Dray's eyes sparkled with amusement. John looked him up and down and turned to me.

"Damn. Find me a gay one," he said.

"I'll work on it," I said and he hugged me.

He sighed, "You're dooming me to fail up there with her."

"Quit being such a fucking drama queen and take your skinny ass home," I ordered. He flashed a grin at me and sat down to take off his shoes.

"Be out in a sec," I called to my crowd, still marveling at how many people were here, and I went back, showered in record time and redressed even faster, in jeans and a tee. I went back out to applause and whistles and I took a mock bow.

"Okay, I'm free! What's next?" I called out.

"Food!" Everyone shouted back at me and we all shared in a laugh.

"Weather's holding," Dragon commented, "We're ridin'." It wasn't a request. Ashton took my bags from me while Dray helped me into his jacket, well, mine now, I suppose, since he'd given it to me.

"Where you guys going? I need some time with my BFF. I'll meet you," Mandy said.

"I said we're riding," Dragon winked at her.

"I've got room, Red," Zander offered up. I smiled at Mandy.

"You should take him up on it," I said. "It's unbelievable!" My best friend chewed her lip indecisively. She was dressed well enough for it in jeans, riding boots and a cream-color cable knit sweater. She had on her brown leather jacket over the sweater so she should be warm enough. It wasn't her dress giving her pause though. *What would my father think?* scrolled through her eyes like a reader board.

I had on jeans and a pair of black ankle boots that laced in the front, along with a ladies'-cut black tee, which was funny because Dray was pretty much dressed identically. I raised my eyebrows at my best friend in my best, 'you're going to be a chicken aren't you?' look. Her back went up like I knew it would.

"My car is safe here. Why not?" she said. Zander grinned at her and held out his arm. She swallowed nervously and linked hers through it.

"I'll lock your stuff in the Jeep, Ev," Ashton murmured and Trigger took the bags from her.

"Damn right, I want you on the bike as often as I can get you there. We'll come back for it later," he said. She giggled. Everybody was parked in the lot next door and got ready at their own pace.

"Trigger, take tail-gunner," Dragon ordered and I raised a brow in question at Dray. As he explained it to me, tail-gunner was always the most-experienced rider, which by the looks of things today, was Dragon, wasn't it?

"Dragon's our Pres. He'll always ride at the front, but the most experienced rider should always take the rear guard, I'm the next experienced rider but I have an inexperienced passenger, so Trigger is the next for the distinction," Dray explained quietly. I nodded. Practical and true on all accounts. He grinned.

"What?" I asked.

"That's what I like about you, Em. Most girls would get all snarky about it going out there that they're inexperienced. You, you just take it as it is and move right the fuck on. It's sexy." I smiled at him.

"You know what won't be sexy?" I asked, buckling on my helmet.

"What?" Reaver asked.

"When I turn into a raging fucking bitch because nobody has fed me!" I complained. There was some laughter and Dragon fired up his bike; I saw Mandy jump out of the corner of my eye and smiled at her reassuringly. Zander helped her onto his bike behind him and she looked good there. I snapped a picture with my phone to Facebook later. I shoved the phone into an inside pocket of the coat. It had my ID and debit card in the case so I didn't need to carry a wallet.

"You gonna stand there snappin' pictures all day or you gonna get on so we can go? Shit! You were the one bitchin' you were starvin'!" Dragon bellowed, his slight smile betraying that he wasn't being serious. I got on behind Dray and snugged up tight against him.

"Looks like we need to feed the Dragon!" I yelled at him over more bikes firing up.

"Shit yeah! Move out!" He called back and gave the signal. Everyone fell into place behind him.

It was crisper than the night before, colder... the fall temperatures dropping back into what was normal for this time of year. We followed Dragon twenty minutes to the other side of town and into the lot for Gino's Pizzeria. The place was just opening for lunch and was mostly empty, which was fortunate for us, such a large party showing up unannounced as we were. We managed to get a table, no problem, and what was more, the staff seemed genuinely happy to see us.

We settled around several four-seat tables that had been pushed together into a long row. Mandy made sure to sit next to me and I smiled at her. Her eyes were bright with excitement and I was happy she was having fun. Zander sat across from her and I took the opportunity to get a better look at him; the dim light in the bar the night before hadn't afforded me much of a look.

He wore a red baseball hat backwards on his head but I sort of recognized the logo. It was for an NFL team in Florida, a red pirate flag flying off a cutlass, the Buccaneers, I think. Couldn't tell you which city. His hair was black from what I could tell, and closely buzzed to his scalp, like a kiss of stubble along the skin where it peeked out from under the hat.

He had warm brown eyes that reminded me of chocolate caramels and was built solid, his shoulders wide and imposing. He was a solid wall of muscle and completely proportionate all the way through. Still, even though his eyes might be warm and his smile equally so, his chipped front tooth and crooked nose said he was no stranger to holding his own in a barroom brawl or late-night tussle. He smiled at my best friend and his smile, like his nose, was crooked but endearingly so.

He held one large fist inside the other and propped his elbows on the table and leaned his mouth against his hands. He had modest black gauges in both ears and a piercing in his eyebrow, which both bore scars from past fights, now that I looked at them. His arms were inked from elbow to wrist, one arm a riot of color: oranges, yellows and reds; the other simply black and white. I let my eyes skate along his skin. It almost always took me a moment or two to decipher such thorough tattoo sleeves and his was no exception. I blinked in surprise when I realized that the colorful arm was a depiction of a devil- and demon-riddled hell while the soothing black-and-white arm was a host of beautiful female angels.

"Is that Ashton?" I asked, my eyes locking on the upside down face of an angel on the outside of his forearm near the elbow. His grin got wider.

"Perceptive," he drawled and then answered my question. "Yeah, it is. She was the right kind of pretty, so I had Trigger ink her in." He smiled wider and cocked his head to the side and considered Mandy.

"Wouldn't mind puttin' Red here on my leg, pin-up style," he said, patting the outside of his thigh. Mandy blushed and tried to engage me in conversation, pointedly ignoring Zander. He winked at me when she wasn't looking.

"So, have you found a place yet?" she asked. Dray leaned back and looked at her from around me with one of those burning looks of his.

"She's cool," he said and tried to soften the look with that boyish panty-dropping grin of his. "When we get home we're going to find space to get all her stuff put away off our bedroom floor." Mandy blinked at him wide-eyed and then looked at me, but I wasn't going to help her out. I was too busy grinning at his use of the word 'our'. My friend tipped her head to the side and tried to read my face. Finally she sighed in defeat.

"Okay, look. As the best friend it is my obligation to tell you that if you hurt my girl, I'ma have to find you and cut your balls off." She crossed her arms and said it so sweetly and matter-of-factly the entire table busted up laughing. A waitress came by and we ordered our drinks.

"You catch up to her ex yet?" Dray asked Mandy speculatively. Her expression darkened.

"No, but if I ever do, boy, he better look out!" I believed it. Mandy had a sharp tongue and was a master at emasculation via verbal assault; she was just so sweet and unsure of herself it took her a long time to get there but once she did, woo boy! We ordered pizza a-plenty and the conversations wove in and out of what people did for a living, where they came from, and a general way of everyone getting to know each other.

"What do you do?" Mandy asked Zander and it was just this side of shyly.

"Tattooist and piercer. I own Open Road Ink along with Trigger, Squick is our new-school artist, I mostly do portraits and cover-ups. Trig is a jack of all trades, portraits, new-school, old-school, he does it all and does it well. Damn fine at cover-ups too." He shrugged one shoulder. "Ashton runs the counter. Sets up appointments, finishes out the billing and rings people up. Took to it like a fish to water." Trigger smiled proudly and rubbed a big hand up and down Ashton's back while she blushed under the praise.

"You're just happy you don't have to pay me anymore," she said faintly in a teasing tone.

"Why not?" Mandy asked, frowning.

"My husband... passed away.... When he did, I got a lot of what was left," she shrugged.

"Oh! I'm so sorry to hear that..." Mandy said sympathetically and I squeezed her knee under the table, she looked at me startled.

"What?" she asked.

"Don't be sorry," Ashton said and her expression was solemn. "I'm not," and she put on a brave smile. Mandy nodded and I could see she filed it away for later. I would explain quietly much later. Mandy would see to it.

"What about you, Ev? What do you do?" Squick asked.

"I'm a barista over at Quick Stop coffee shack. I work the early shift. It's just until I finish school, though." I took a bite of pizza.

"What are you going to school for?" Zander asked.

"Mandy and I, both, we're going for business. I'm really into coffee, she's a fabulous chocolatier and we want to open a coffee and chocolate shop together." Mandy and I exchanged smiles.

"We dreamed it up in high school. I have a bunch of these family recipes. My grandparents were confectioners, chocolatiers. I want to open a shop and be like them. Gran and I always had so much fun in the kitchen when I was growing up." Mandy smiled. Ashton was looking at both of us thoughtfully, but remained silent.

"Well, you know a great interior designer now," Reaver said.

"Oh! That's right!" I exclaimed, and told Mandy all about Hayden.

The lunch concluded, there wasn't much leftover pizza and it was wrapped in plastic wrap for us and put into grocery bags so it would be portable on the bikes, pizza boxes being too unwieldy. Everyone split off from the pizzeria. Zander, Mandy, Trigger, and Ashton went back to the studio for their cars. Dray and I went with them to keep Mandy comfortable. I didn't want to just ditch her with people she'd barely just met and I didn't know Zander from Adam yet, so, yeah.

I loved that Dray was cool with it, I didn't even have to ask. I stuffed my backpack from Ashton's car into my dance bag and slung it across my chest and Dray took us home. I got off and he backed Matilda into the small garage and locked her in.

"I meant what I said. I figured we could find some comfortable clothes and get all your stuff put away. You don't need to be livin' off our floor." I pulled myself against him and he kissed me.

I drew back. "I love that you call it 'our' floor. Shows me that you really do want me here, in your life." He smiled at me and smoothed some stray hair off my face.

"Yeah. I do," he said and a gust of wind swept our hair across our faces into our eyes. I looked up. Dark clouds were starting to roll in. I sighed.

"Looks like the weather reprieve is over for now," I said.

"Yeah, let's get you inside. It's gettin' fuckin' cold out here." We went inside and I put on some coffee.

"I need to do laundry," I said.

"You and me both, put something comfortable on before we get started."

He eyed me up and down and I smiled. By the time we were both changed, me into what passed for my pajamas and Dray into some lounge pants and a black wife-beater, the interior of the house had become downright gloomy. He switched on the bedside lamp and opened his closet. I gathered my dirty pile and went for the mudroom. Unfortunately, the way the house was built, it hadn't been done with the modern convenience of a washer and dryer in mind. The house was from well before that time. So, in order to reach the washer and dryer in the basement, you had to go out the mudroom, down the back stairs on the outside of the house and then down another set of concrete stairs to the basement door.

I was surprised when I went into the basement. I expected it to be musty with a cracked and uneven dirty concrete floor, exposed beams overhead... what I found was a comfortable and completely-finished basement.

The floor was concrete, but smooth and even. It had that paint stuff on it that you could mop clean like a linoleum floor, which was really nice. The water heater sat in one corner and the electrical panels for the house were down here as well, set into completed drywall painted a uniform light gray, like white with just enough color in it to make it gray.

The washer and dryer were flanked by cabinets and shelving. Above the washer and dryer, a shelf hung with all the supplies needed to do the laundry. There was even an ironing board and iron set up down here. The cabinets held canned goods and bottled water, basically an emergency storehouse. The shelves held all manner of dry goods and there was an extra freezer down here too and I blinked in amazement.

I started a load in the machine and just as I switched it on, my ears were assaulted by the dull pounding of the rain. I dashed outside and up the steps and back into the house and managed to only get half-soaked to the skin.

I found Dray standing in the bedroom. He was still and holding something in his hands, and when I stopped in the doorway I realized what it was. He was holding my da'. More specifically, the stainless steel urn that held my da's ashes in it. I rocked back on my heels and bit my lower lip between my teeth.

"I didn't want to freak you out," I said and grimaced. A ghost of a smile flitted across his lips, his deep dark eyes held sorrow. He held out a hand to me and I stepped forward to take it. He pulled me into his side and hugged me with one arm, placing a kiss against my bare shoulder.

"You didn't have to hide your dad under a pile of your clothes, baby," he said gently.

"I'm sorry," I said quietly.

"Don't be, just... where would you like to put him?" he asked, and I looked up at him.

"Someplace safe," I said.

He smiled at me and led me out into the living room. There was a shelf in one corner. The kind that you bolted to the wall, with wrought iron accents. The kind that held two votive candles on either side of it. Another urn sat on top of it and I blinked. I hadn't noticed it before. He carefully, reverently, slid the smaller urn to one side, and asked, "Okay with you?"

I nodded mutely and he set my da' next to his mom. He swallowed hard. There was a picture of a small woman with long brown hair and laughing brown eyes on the wall above and behind the shelf. I went back to the room and found the picture of my da' and my mom when they were young in the silver picture frame. There was just enough room to put the smaller photo behind and to the side of my da's urn.

Dray looked the photo over and pulled a lighter out from behind the TV. He lit the candles and we stood for a long time drinking the image in. My dad, his mom... their children standing in front of them in silent introspection... thought and prayers... Dray put an arm around my shoulders and I leaned into him. The only sound in the house was the pulsing rain on the roof and outside.

"I miss her," he said.

"I miss my da'," I said, and it was all that needed to be said. We were two human beings united in perfect harmony by our shared grief. It was one of the most profound and intimate moments of my life and I think it was for Dray too, because neither one of us ended it right away. We let it go on for several somber moments until a flash of light and a crack of thunder dashed it to pieces. We exchanged a look and laughed nervously.

"Guess they've had enough of us doing that," he said smiling.

"I think so!" I agreed and we went about finishing what we'd started.

"Tell me about your dad?" he asked me, while he was shifting things aside in one of his dresser drawers. I handed him some neatly folded tees.

"My da' was a slender man. Tall and willowy with big hands," I said. I handed him the last photo my da' and I had taken together, him in his Dockers and button-down shirt, me in one of my dance costumes after one of my competitions. His hair had been freshly cut, business-like and his round spectacles perched smartly on the bridge of his nose. Pride shone in his eyes as we both smiled for the camera, a trophy clutched between us.

"What did he do for a living?" Dray asked softly, his gaze roaming the photo in his hands.

"Worked in a warehouse, loading and unloading trucks and trains," I said softly.

"My mom..." he paused and took a deep breath, "My mom was a bank teller when my dad met her. She left that to run the front office and the books for the club and the shop," he said.

I smiled. "My da' was tough on me," I murmured. "He had grand plans for me, wanted me to be whatever I wanted to be, but wanted me to be more than him, you know? More than blue-collar, working all hours in a warehouse or factory. When I told him what Mandy and I wanted to do he wasn't all for it at first. I convinced him."

I smiled, remembering. We'd had one hell of a row over it at first and finally he'd relented, on the condition I get a degree in business. I hadn't argued the point, accepting it as more than fair.

"My mom was like that too. There was nothing second rate for me, everything was first rate and she'd be damned if I would be treated as anything less... that I would accept anything less for myself. She loved me, she loved my dad and she loved the club. She was proud as hell when I said I wanted to be a mechanic like my dad..." He rubbed the back of his neck and I could tell that our conversation pained him.

"What do you miss the most about her?" I asked, "For me, it's the way my dad would explain things. He was a great philosopher that one, always thinking. Always encouraging me to think, to look below the surface, to lift the stones and people's hearts and to look at what was underneath. 'Never take what you see at face value, Evy, always look underneath. It'll keep you safe and you might be surprised at what you find' he'd always tell me." I looked at Dray and he looked at me.

"My mom always knew how to get me to talk about it," he said. "She saw though all the layers and all the bullshit and knew just what to say to pry whatever was bothering a person free. She'd always listen and then she'd find a way to help you fix it. Or some piece of wisdom would come out of her mouth like it was as effortless as breathing." He swallowed and coughed like he was choking up and handed the photo of me and my da' back to me. I leaned way across the bed and set it up on the bedside table he'd declared mine.

I returned to his side where he sat, shoulders hunched and I put my arms around him. I didn't know what to say, so I just held him and said the only thing I could.

"I love you, Draven." He turned his head, dark eyes flashing when they captured mine.

"Love you too, babe," he said and we held each other close for a time before resuming integrating each other into one another's lives.

# 12

**D**ray...

"Fuck me!" I exclaimed. Everett blinked her pretty blue eyes in mild surprise herself. I tried turning Sadie over one more time.

*Click!*

Nothing.

"Battery?" she asked.

"Or starter. At least it's dry today, come on. We're going for a ride." I got out of the car and she followed suit.

"I can tell you are just so broken up over that!" She grinned at me but her smile faded when I didn't quite return it. I didn't know what my problem was today but I had this, just, nagging bad feeling.

I wanted to lock Em in the house, pull the blinds; *keep her safe.* It was crazy and didn't make a damn bit of sense.

"Dray, what's wrong?" she asked. I didn't want to sound crazy so I grimaced inwardly and lied.

"Nothin', babe. Car's just pissin' me off." I smiled and she looked at me with those steely baby blues as if she were trying to decide if I was lying. *Let it slide, let it slide, let it slide...* I chanted in my head and finally her shoulders relaxed as I slid up the garage door. She bought it, but grudgingly so.

"Okay," she said and put on her helmet and glasses. She slid the straps of the backpack over her shoulders and shut the garage door behind me as I rolled Matilda out. It was dark and cold and the ride was going to be a biting one. I fired up my bike and Em got on behind me.

"You good!?" I called over the growling thrum of the engine.

"Yeah!" she called back. She settled her thighs around my hips and her arms around my chest and gave me a squeeze with her whole body. I smiled. I couldn't help it when she did things like that. I moved us out of the driveway and onto the street and took my girl to work.

It had been a couple of weeks since the night ride and Em and I had settled into a routine. Life with her in it was amazing. To have someone to hold at night, to wake up with her tight against my back, her arms around me. To come home on the days I had to go back into the shop after bringing her home, and find dinner bein' set on the table. To have someone love me, care for me, worry about me, support me... Fuck, man, it was an amazing ride.

I pulled right up to the shack and frowned when I caught sight of the blonde bitch she worked with. Em had told me how the broad had been cheating her out of tips. She had even gone so far as to whine to their boss that Everett was cheating the tip jar to throw suspicion off herself. Em got off the bike and pulled off her helmet. She'd keep hold of it and the glasses for when I picked her up. Didn't have to worry about leaving them out on the bike. She gave me a quick kiss goodbye and I pulled her into it, making it last, letting it linger a touch longer.

"I love you," she said against my mouth. I smiled. We didn't say it often enough and I never got tired of hearing it.

"I love you too, baby," I said, and let her go. She smiled and disappeared into the brightly lit interior of the little drive-up coffee spot. I rode to the shop, my feelings of unease growing, the more pavement passed beneath me. Finally, I pulled up in front of one of the bay doors. I shut off the bike and got off, taking my keys. I unlocked the padlock holding the bay door down and lifted. The thing went up about half a foot and jammed tight.

"Fuck!" I screamed into the silent dark. I fiddled and wrenched on the damn thing until I stood in front of it, breathless and defeated. Something bright captured my attention from the edge of my vision. I looked over and the bright light cut across my eyes again.

I watched the crucifix from my mother's rosary swing and sway from my handlebar. I stared at it as the cross spun on its length of beaded chain. It twisted slowly; the blue-white light of the shop's floodlight illuminating the parking lot caught it just right and the silver metal blazed. I put up a hand and frowned. The street was suddenly eerily silent. So still, so quiet you could hear anything and everything. I felt something. Deep down inside, somewhere out in the dark, in me, around me, and the cross flashed silver at me once more.

"Mom?" I asked softly... I knew it was crazy but...

That sense, that crushing unease I'd been feeling since I woke up, swamped me full force. Hit me square in the chest and squeezed the breath from my lungs.

Everett.

I didn't know what the fuck it was but I wasn't about to argue with it anymore. I threw a leg over Matilda and put my helmet on. I barely had it fastened and I was firing her up. She roared to life and I swear to Christ I heard my mom's voice, whether it came from inside or outside my head I couldn't tell you but it said one word and it was all I needed to know I was making the right decision.

"Go."

And I went.

Like a bat out of hell, I rode. Back the way I came, back to Everett, because something damn sure wasn't right–

## 13

Everett...

I sighed as I entered my workspace and shut the door behind me, twisting the lock. Brandy gave me her customary dirty look and I smiled back. I wouldn't stoop to her level; if anything I would do my utmost to use the Irish diplomacy my father had taught me growing up.

Irish diplomacy, unlike regular diplomacy, was pretty much the art of telling a person to go to hell in such a way that they look forward to taking the trip.

I hung my backpack and Dray's spare helmet on the coat-rack peg with my name written on a piece of masking tape underneath it. I tucked the safety glasses into one of the backpack's side pockets. Brandy and I didn't speak. I set about arranging my barista station the way I liked it and made sure everything I typically used was stocked. About ten minutes into this a young man walked up to my window. I slid it open and told him,

"I'm sorry, hon. We're not allowed to serve walk-up customers." He was lanky, his hair hung greasy and he wore a faded band tee shirt under a leather jacket and motorcycle cut, but it wasn't a Sacred

Heart's cut. The colors were wrong, not white with blue writing but white with red. He looked left and right and pulled a small pistol out of his pocket and pointed it at me.

"Well, you're going to serve me," he said and the whole world slowed. I saw Brandy give me a triumphant look out of the corner of my eye but then she put her hands up like you would in a movie hold-up. Palms flat and facing out to either side of her face. I swallowed and stared at the gun. A serenity fell over me, a calm I couldn't even begin to describe. I nodded slowly.

"Okay, friend, what can I get you?" I asked.

I kept myself still. My chest felt tight and my blood raced through my veins but that sense of calm persisted. *Don't make any sudden moves, Evy, m'girl. Nice an' quiet-like, jus' do what the boy tells you.* I blinked slowly. Now was a really strange time to hear my da's voice in my head... or had that been out loud?

"Open the cash drawers," he ordered and I complied. "Good, good. Now open the safe," he said.

"I can't do that," I said. My voice felt thick, sluggish, coming out of my throat and I realized that tears were threatening. I really couldn't open the safe. None of us could. Only Eddie, our boss, had the combo.

"Jesus, Ev! Do what he says!" Brandy said frantically.

"I can't," I repeated and something flashed in the young man's eyes. He lowered the gun and I sighed out in relief, but then the world erupted in a riot of sound. There was a flash and the smell of hell poured out into the small shack and something bit me, hard, in the middle of my left thigh. The ethereal calm that had fallen over me moments before shattered.

I fell backwards onto my ass and looked at my leg. Red welled and soaked the light denim of my jeans and I clapped a hand over the wound. A scream split the air and I looked helplessly at Brandy who had her hands clapped over her mouth. She looked down on me in a mixture of horror and revulsion. I turned my head to look at the young man who was screaming at me.

"Open the god damned safe! Open it! Open it now, or the next one will blow your god damned head off! You hear me bitch!? You hear me!?" he was screaming.

Brandy started screaming at him. "Jesus, Ronnie, what did you do!? You weren't supposed to fucking shoot her!"

I sobbed, the fire in my leg unbelievable. I couldn't believe what I was seeing, couldn't believe what I was hearing! I dragged air into my lungs through a throat raw from screaming and wept.

"Please don't, please don't kill me..." I begged piteously and he turned back to me from screaming at Brandy. Something flashed to the right of the window and the boy, man, I don't know, disappeared. His face connected viciously with the stainless steel shelf on the outside of the window where we set drinks and I heard something metal skitter across the blacktop, under the kiosk.

He disappeared again and I closed my eyes. I opened them again to see the door to the stand shudder in its frame. The young man's back fetched up hard against the glass by the door and the visage of a king, like one on a playing card, filled my vision. Brandy went out the window on the other side of the stand, leaving me bleeding on the cheap linoleum floor.

"Everett!" I heard Dray's voice scream and I screamed back.

"Dray!"

The young man who'd shot me slumped to the ground outside the window to reveal Dray, who stood heaving in desperate breaths.

"Oh, god! Oh, shit!" he yelled and went for the door, but I'd locked it.

The door shuddered once, then twice in its frame, as Dray viciously kicked it before it finally gave way. It exploded inwards and I was peppered by shards of wood as the frame shattered around the lock. Dray slid in the door along the tile on his knees and came up next to me.

"Oh god oh baby it's okay it's going to be okay..." He looked at my leg and I turned my tearstained face up to him.

"It hurts..." I complained woefully. Dray got behind me and I leaned back into his chest, he put an arm across my chest and pressed his phone to his ear.

"Goddamn!" A familiar voice with a southern drawl made me turn back to the broken door. One of my customers, a trucker by the name of Mark, went to his knees on the side where I'd been shot. "Hold on, Evy, help's on the way," he said and pressed his big hands tight over mine. I cried out from the pain and Dray, on the phone, glared at the man.

"Army medic, back in 'Nam," Mark said. "Gotta keep pressure on this." Dray relaxed marginally and kept talking into the phone.

"No, no, she's awake. Just get me a fucking ambulance, bitch! She's fucking bleeding!" He turned those dark intense eyes, so full of panic, to my own and rested his forehead against mine. I closed my eyes and fresh hot tears tracked down my face. We could hear sirens.

"You're going to be okay, baby. You're going to be okay, baby. I'm here. We're going to get you to the hospital, we're going to get you fixed up. You'll see. Just don't fucking go anywhere on me." I sniffed and cried tears of relief.

"I'm not going anywhere," I said, "I love you, Dray. I love you." I sobbed out.

"I love you too, baby. I'm right here. I love you too..." He cradled me tight against his chest and I closed my eyes.

Dray was here. I was safe. Dray was here... Oh, God, it hurt so much.

# 14

**D**ray...

I held Em's hand in my own. As soon as we'd gotten to the hospital they'd rushed her into a curtained area. Doc was on duty, thank fuck, and she was under his care. After a quick look, he'd sent her to x-ray, and now we waited.

She was in a hospital gown the nurses had put her in after cutting off her pants. Pillows were under her leg and gauze had been wrapped around the wound. The back of the bed was up so she was sitting, but she looked pale and wan against the pillow behind her head.

She was alive. *Thank you God, thank you Mom... she was alive.* I was glued to her side, once they'd let me back to see her. I'd called my pops while they'd worked on her and he'd shown up in about fifteen minutes flat. Doc pulled aside the curtain and stepped in, looking all official and strait-laced and shit. It was weird as hell for me. We all knew he was the local ER doc but we didn't see it often enough for it to really hit home.

"Cavalry is in the waiting room," he grunted. Em opened her eyes and frowned. Her eyes were tight with pain. They'd given her something for it but it had barely taken the edge off. Doc looked at her and frowned, then riffled though her papers. He cursed and went out. We could hear him chewing someone a good one but couldn't hear what he said. He came back and put something through Everett's IV and everything smoothed out, her body going lax after a moment or two.

"Who's here?" I asked.

"Your dad, Trigger, Ashton, Reaver, Hayden, Loyal, Zander, Squick, and Data," Doc said. He smiled down at Ev, his blue eyes sparkling. "Looks like you got yourself a fan club," He finished.

"Everett!" Mandy, her best friend, skirted around the curtain in her pajamas. "Oh, my God!" Large hands landed on her shoulders and the redhead jumped.

"Easy, Red. Let Doc do his thing," Zander had a hold of her.

"Mandy?" Ev said, confusion tinging her voice.

"Yeah, babe, I'm your emergency contact, remember, you didn't think Jerry was up to the job..." Everett nodded and closed her eyes. Tears slipped out.

"I'm okay, Mandy," she said.

"What happened?" her friend demanded.

"Brandy set it up... she knew him. Called him Ronnie..." Em swallowed.

"She was robbed, he shot her. I got him though. Cops have him," I said.

"Everett, I need to talk to you about some things before the drugs kick in too hard," Doc said. Mandy nodded to me and let Zander take her out to the waiting room.

"You're lucky," Doc said flatly. I snorted and he ignored me.

"You were shot with a .22 long rifle round. It's still in there and I got to dig it out. But no surgery. I should be able to give you a local and go in, right here. Okay?" Ev nodded and tears sprang to her eyes.

"Nothing's broken, baby, we're just gonna keep you for a few hours and make sure you're good before I let Dray take you home." He rested a hand on her shin and smoothed over it with a thumb and she nodded.

"Will I dance again?" she asked in a tremulous voice, and Doc's posture eased.

"Oh, honey, yeah, a week or two on some crutches and probably a couple of months in physical therapy. It might pain you some when it gets cold, but yeah, you should make a full recovery." He smiled and she sucked in several breaths. I leaned over her and let her have her meltdown.

She had herself a deep ugly cry, weeping out all that pent-up fear and negativity onto my cut and I smoothed a hand through her hair and let her do it. I was just glad she as here, I was just glad she was alive, not like my mom... not like my mom. Doc went away while she worked through things and came back as she was finishing up.

"Better?" he asked. She nodded. "Sorry, I gotta do this. Dray, you may want to lay over her and hold her some. This shot for the local is a bitch." I nodded and did what I needed to.

"You scream, you cry, you do whatever you need to do to let me get this done, Everett. I've heard it all before from people a lot less pretty 'n you." He said and she nodded a little too rapidly. God, it broke my heart. You'd like to think Doc was killing her with that shot. He waited about five minutes. She couldn't see him, her face buried in my chest as I held onto her.

"You feel that, Evy?" he asked and she shook her head.

"No," I answered for her.

"Okay, good," he said. A minute later there was a metallic-on-plastic clack as he dropped the bullet into one of those disposable kidney-shaped pink dish things.

"Almost done," he told us. He said something to a nurse standing beside him, then he cleaned, stitched, and bandaged my girl's leg.

"Okay, hon, relax. You're all done. Dray, I'ma talk to your old man," he said.

"Yeah, thanks, Doc," I said. I pulled back slowly from her and looked into her dazed blue eyes.

"I don't understand..." she started.

"Shhhh, we'll get it all sorted out later, baby." I kissed her forehead and her eyes drifted shut. The sound of the curtain on the rails had me turning around. A man, late-forties, early-fifties, stood there, holding my old pack and my spare helmet. I glared at him.

"Who the fuck are you?" I demanded.

"I'm Eddie," he said and my frown deepened.

"He's my boss," Everett whispered and closed her eyes.

"You want him here, babe?" I asked.

"It's okay," she murmured.

"What do you want?" I asked.

"I just wanted to bring Everett her things." He held up the pack and helmet and set them aside on a chair against the wall. "She going to be okay?" he asked, concerned.

"The fucking lying twat you had her working with had her shot trying to rob the place with her boyfriend! What do you think?" I demanded. We'd already had the cops come by. The man who'd shot Everett was in custody down the hall. They'd gotten the full story from him after he'd woken up. They'd had to bring his ass to the hospital after I'd knocked him out. ~~The man~~ Eddie flinched.

"Please, don't call her that. She may have behaved that way, but she's still my niece." He gave me a pleading look and I snorted. I didn't give two shits who she was at that point. All I kept seeing was the glint of neon off the fucking gun in the dude's hand... I'd seen it from almost two blocks away. I was half a block away when he shot her, the crack of the gun and the most godawful wounded-animal scream... I gritted my teeth. Her screaming was the only thing that had held my shit together. If she was screaming, it had meant she was alive. Meant that I'd had time...

"Dray, I know you're mad. I'm okay. Really." Everett's voice was gentle, and wavered with her drug-induced high, snapping me out of reliving the nightmare. I looked from her boss down into her eyes. Her pupils were dilated to the point there almost wasn't any blue. I smiled down at her.

"Doc gave you some good shit," I said and she smiled tremulously.

"Nothing hurts anymore... I'm fine," she half-said, half-sang. Eddie looked stricken.

"Yeah, she quits. Fuck your two weeks' notice." I told him and the look on my face was enough to make him shit himself. He nodded a little too rapidly.

"Yeah, no, I understand. Thank you. You may not believe it, but I like Everett. I'm glad you were there, that she's okay. Have her call me, if she wants to..." he said, backing out of the curtained area. I gave him a chin lift. Everett was sound asleep. I had a nurse tuck some warm blankets around her and went out to give everyone the news. Mandy stood up as I entered the waiting room.

"How is she?" she demanded.

"Easy, Red," I told her, adopting Zander's pretty-fucking-unoriginal tag for her.

"Doc says she's gonna be on crutches for a couple of weeks and then physical therapy for a couple of months but after that she'll be just fine. Dancing shouldn't be affected." I said, my shoulders slumping. Mandy came up and hugged me. I stiffened. I wasn't really one for this kind of crap.

"Thank you so much for getting there when you did," she sobbed and I softened, patting her back awkwardly.

"Yeah, no problem," I said, capturing my dad's gaze. I'd told him what made me go back and I was more than a little bit surprised that he actually believed me. He nodded and I nodded back. Mandy went and sat down, Ashton hugged her and said something to her in her too-quiet ethereal tone.

"So, what happened? For those of us late to the party..." Reaver asked.

"Look, they're going to keep her for a few hours and then let her go. I want to take her back to the clubhouse for now. Easier to get around than the house. More open. We need to have a club meeting about this anyways," I said. "Dude that shot her was wearing a cut. Colors I've never seen before," I said. Trigger's eyebrows went up.

"Get a name?" he asked.

"Yeah, Suicide Kings. King like on a playing card as their emblem, colors look to be yellow and red. I want to get back with Em. Sadie wouldn't start this morning, I left Matilda near her coffee stand." I looked at my Dad.

"Keys," he grunted. I tossed them to him.

"I'll give you a ride," Ashton murmured. She rose and a bleary-eyed Mandy rose with her.

"Can I go back with you?" she asked me. I nodded.

"I'll hang out here if you need anything," Zander said and gave her a crooked smile. She looked him over and nodded slowly.

"Okay..." she trailed off. "Thanks." She went with me back to Em's room. My girl was still out cold.

"She looks so exhausted," Mandy said and took the stool by the bed. I leaned back against the wall. I knew the feeling.

**15**

___________

Everett…

Whatever pain medicine they had given me at the hospital had worked a little too well. When I woke up, it was only for a little bit; I had a vague memory of Ashton's Jeep and then nothing. When I woke again, it was in Dray's bed at the clubhouse, a pair of crutches leaning against the wall by the head of the bed.

I blinked and tried to sit up. My leg was raised on a pile of pillows and I couldn't get my arms under me to push myself up without pain tearing through it. I closed my eyes. I was alone in the room but the door stood wide open. My mouth felt full of cotton and I tried to work up some spit to lubricate it. It wasn't happening.

"Dray!" I called out and Ashton ducked into the room a moment later, just as I opened my mouth to call again.

"He's in the Chapel with the others," she said softly. I struggled into a sitting position, despite the searing pain in my leg. Mandy bounced into the room and around Ashton.

"Whoa, whoa, whoa! Easy!" Mandy said. The two club hang-arounds and the prospect looked in. The prospect, Loyal, came in and put one arm behind my back and the other behind my knees and slid me carefully, wrestling me so I could sit up. I gasped out a 'thank you'.

"Time to take one of these," Mandy put a white round tablet into my hand. Ashton handed me a glass of water.

"Prospect!" I heard bellowed from somewhere out into the club. The three men disappeared. Mandy sat down on the edge of the bed by my knee and watched me, a worried crease between her brows. I obediently swallowed the pain pill.

"How long have I been asleep?" I asked.

"It's around ten o'clock," Ashton said.

"At night," Mandy clarified. I closed my eyes and my shoulders sank.

"I'm sorry..." I said.

"For what!?" Mandy asked, "Evy, you got *shot*," she said and crossed her arms. I blinked and shook my head to clear the lingering confusion.

"I want to press charges!" I said, and Ashton laughed, a high, musical sound.

"Honey, when somebody shoots someone, the police do that for you. Some detectives want to talk to you when you feel up to it though." She took the empty glass of water from my hand and I realized I really had to pee. I sighed.

"Crutches?" Mandy asked, figuring out my predicament. Dray appeared in the doorway when I finally got to my feet, the crutches under my arms.

"Bathroom?" he asked and I nodded; he stood aside but kept pace with my slow going. My leg hurt abominably. I managed to take care of business on my own, getting up and down no small thing.

I wore a sexy satin nightgown. Black, so I know it had been chosen by Dray, it clung to my body, held up by thin spaghetti straps and only hung to just below where it would be considered completely indecent. My left mid-thigh was wrapped in a snowy white bandage that was stark against my peaches-and-cream skin, made even more so by the fringe of black satin above it. I sighed and used the crutches to get back to the door. I reached for the handle and the door opened. Dray's dark eyes raked over me, assessing.

"You go shopping?" I asked and he smiled faintly.

"Yeah. I wanted you in something that would make getting to your leg easy. Something you didn't have to keep running over it with every time you needed to use the bathroom," he said, keeping pace, spotting me on my return to the bedroom. I smiled.

"An oversized tee shirt would have done the same," I pointed out gently. He shook his head.

"You deserved something beautiful," he said and I smiled even more. Most girls get hurt, their boyfriend brings them some flowers, I get hurt and Dray gets me sexy lingerie. I let him help me back into bed. Mandy elevated my leg with the pillows, careful of me.

"You guys, really, you don't need to fuss!" I said.

"Let us. You were shot Evy... Shot! Okay?" Mandy's eyes misted, the green becoming luminous and she sniffed. Dray looked grimmer than I'd ever seen him; so still, so quiet. Ashton took Mandy's hand.

"We need to go," she told my friend pointedly. Mandy looked at her, confused, but whatever she saw in Ashton's golden eyes convinced her. They slipped out of the room, leaving me and Dray alone, the door shutting softly but resolutely behind them.

Dray seemed to fold in on himself. He sat on the edge of the bed by my hip and closed his eyes bending forward at the waist. His hair fell into his face, curtaining his anguished expression, his shoulders shook and he sobbed.

"Oh, my god! Here!" I said and reached for him. He collapsed into my arms, careful of my leg and sobbed into my chest. His arms went around me and he held me tight as if at any moment I might disappear.

"It's okay..." I soothed. "Shhhh I'm here. It's okay..."

He wept his fill and looked up at me, his deep, dark eyes full of sorrow mixed with relief and tinged with a bit of gratitude. He covered my mouth with his own and I welcomed his kiss, drank him down. I was so incredibly grateful to be alive, to be here with him.

Our lips parted and I asked him, "How did you know?" I sniffed. I hadn't realized I'd been crying with him.

"My mom. I swear to God, Em, my mom told me to turn around. Sadie breaking down was the first sign. When I got to the garage, the bay door jammed and it was the damnedest thing, I swear *I heard her tell me to go.*"

I smoothed the tears from his cheeks with my hands. "I believe you," I said.

He captured my wrists with his hands and pulled them away from his face.

"You don't understand Em, *my mom was shot*, she died right in front of me... Em, she knew, she knew it was going to happen. I had a bad feeling all morning. Baby, I'm so sorry I didn't get the message sooner." Fresh tears tracked down his cheeks.

"I heard my da'." I confessed. Dray kicked off his boots and stretched out next to me. I laid my head on his shoulder and we stared at the ceiling and the blank television screen bolted there.

We traded our stories and marveled that our parents, both of them, had come together and guided us both, that they were instrumental in rescuing me that morning.

"Should we keep this between us?" I asked after a long silence.

"I told my pops. I had to... He believed me but I think we should keep it on the down-low with the rest of the club," he said.

"I might tell Mandy," I said, and I felt him nod.

"You know her better than I do, Babe." He turned his head and kissed me.

"I guess this means your mom approves?" I tentatively ventured.

"Baby, I know she does," he said and smoothed his hand down my arm. I closed my eyes, the pain meds starting to take effect.

"What was the meeting about?" I asked. Dray had told me about the club and how it operated, just not what the closed-door meetings were about. He'd said, in the interest of there being no secrets between us, seeing as what Jerry had done, that he would always tell me what he could and if he couldn't he would simply tell me so.

"The man who attacked you was twenty-three. His name is

Ronald Fortin and the meeting was about the colors he was flying," he said.

"You mean the patches on the back of his cut?" I asked.

"Yeah, you see 'em?" he asked.

"Yeah, when you slammed him against the window by the door." He gave me a little squeeze.

"Yeah, I beat the fucking brakes off that fucker," he said, savagery in his tone.

"I know, thank you," I said.

"Not bothered by the fact I fucked him up?" he asked.

I snorted. "Hell no! He shot me!" I exclaimed and he chuckled.

"Do you remember the patches?" he asked.

"Yeah, the top one said Suicide Kings and the middle one was the King of Hearts, from the playing card. The bottom one was the one that confused me, it said Nomad." I rolled my head back and to the side so I could look at him. He looked down at me.

"'Nomad' patch on an individual might mean that they lead a solitary life and don't want to claim allegiance to any particular chapter within a club. Or it could mean that the club sporting the nomad patch doesn't have territorial roots, or that they don't have enough members in a particular area to put down roots for a chapter. In any case, the boy in question seriously pissed in Sacred Hearts' Wheaties, doin' what he did on Sacred Hearts turf." He cuddled me close and sighed.

"How do you know it was the King of Hearts specifically?" he asked, frowning.

"My da' was a bit of a cardshark. The King of Hearts is known as the Suicide King because it looks like he's driving his own sword into his head on the card, same as the image of the King on the back of his cut. Well, that, and the name 'Suicide Kings.'" I explained.

"Oh, good to know... Trigger's gonna reach out. See about having a meet-and-greet with some of their guys. Lay down the law, see what they're about." He shifted.

"What if they don't care?" I asked.

"They're going to want to care. If they're smart, they'll care a lot,"

Dray said, an underlying threat to his words. A long silence ensued while I lay in his arms.

"Hungry?" he asked when my stomach let out a very audible squeal of displeasure.

"Yeah," I said, laughing.

"Let me slide out from under you, and I'll fix you somethin'." I sat up as best I could and he got out from under me. He opened the door to his father on the other side, poised to knock.

"Got food out here, boy," he said.

"Yeah, I'm gonna get her something," Dray said and slipped by him. Dragon leveled me with his gaze, so like his son's, and I smiled.

"I'm glad my wife likes you," he said. I smiled wanly.

"I am, too," I said, and he grinned and stepped into the room.

"You need anything?" he asked and it touched me that he would ask.

"To heal and to get back out on the dance floor," I said, smiling.

"Yeah," he agreed.

"Thank you," I murmured.

"You bet," he said and sat down in the chair that had been brought in.

"Dray tell you how Tilly died?" he asked.

"Yes, just now," I said.

"Good," He grunted. A long moment of silence. "You know, since he met you he's been a different person. More the way my son was before his momma died..." The big man swallowed and I stayed silent, letting him speak. "He was so angry when she went. He turned inside of himself. I've heard Tilly a time or two before but never heard Dray speak on it. I was beginning to think he never would." He sighed and smiled a little sadly, but then the smile brightened.

"Then there was you." He leaned forward in his seat and kissed my forehead. "Thank you for bringing me back my boy," he whispered and I sniffed, tears running into my hair at my temples. "I know yours is lookin' out for you, but this daddy is too," he said and got up, moving out of the room, the heavy tread of his boots echoing further away as he walked back towards the common room. I blinked and rolled my eyes heavenward.

"Thank you," I whispered, grateful for the blessings that had been heaped upon me. Mandy spoke up from the door.

"Yeah, sure, Dray told me to tell you there's an emergency club meeting." I looked over.

Ashton closed the door behind them, turning to me to say, "Womenfolk are banished back here for the time being," with a soft smile. They helped me sit up so I could eat, Mandy setting a plate of food in my lap. Ashton opened the DVD player and turned on the television on the ceiling. She put on a movie for us and she and Mandy flanked me on the queen-sized bed.

"What are we watching?" Mandy asked, curious.

"Ethan bought me this, I don't know what it is," she said honestly.

"Oooo, Magic Mike!" I exclaimed and Mandy giggled. I laughed, I'd told her about it but hadn't been able to get her to watch it. "It's about male strippers!" I exclaimed.

Ashton giggled. "Oh boy!" She rolled her eyes. We all three laid back to watch.

## 16

**D**ray...

I didn't want to be out here. I wanted to be back in my room with Em, but we'd decided to call a full club meeting, and opened it to the hang-arounds and prospects, too, which was highly unusual. We were gathered in the common room and the girls were conspicuously absent. The mood in the clubhouse was sober and holding that edge of anger, that threat of violence. Or maybe it was just me. I stood to the right and a little behind my pops; Reaver, Doc, and Trig ranged out behind us on the small stage. Our brothers sat in neatly-lined chairs in front of us. My pops addressed the room. Now was a time that he was my president and not so much my father and I was cool with that.

"Everybody here knows that my boy's Ol' Lady, new as she may be, got shot this mornin'," Dragon started. Yeah. Em was mine, I totally claimed that and everything that went along with it. There were grunts of acknowledgment and nodding heads around the room.

"What everybody might or might not know by now is that some other club calling themselves the Suicide Kings is in town and a boy flyin' their colors is the one that did the shootin'." Again there were nods and unsurprised looks among our small gathering.

"Now, I know we're small right now, what with membership flaggin', and honestly, that's no one's fault but mine an' my cabinet's, but we've been doin' our best to stay true to each other and turn a new leaf and all of that. What I'm getting at is we're gonna try and make contact with these Suicide Kings an' see what they got to say for themselves, both for bein' on our lands without givin' us the customary heads-up, and for what happened with our VP's girl."

"Some of us are new," he inclined his head towards Loyal, Zander and Squick. "That bein' said, now's the time to decide if you boys are in it to win it or if you want to get off this ride here. Things have the potential to get real ugly, real quick when it comes to these kinds of dealings. We're gonna try some diplomacy first... This is our territory, though, and our diplomacy looks a lot like 'they better damn well play by our rules while they's in it'." Cheers went up around the room, a smattering of applause with it and I felt a wicked smile curve my lips. "We may be small, but we pack a punch. Shit gets heavy, we got to stick together." Dragon scratched his chin through his dark beard.

"Shit gets heavy, it ain't no where I haven't been before. Count me committed," Loyal said and crossed his arms.

"Sounds about right, and y'all know I love a good fight," Zander said and grinned, showing off the chip in his tooth. I heard Trigger chuckle.

"Why would I want to leave when it looks like the party's just getting started?" Squick asked, but he looked grim. I think he liked my girl, he sympathized with wanting to serve up a beatdown.

"Okay." My dad looked secretly relieved, but quickly covered it by turning to Data.

"Get us what you can on these Suicide Kings. I want a number for their Prez by morning. If the bastard were smart he'd have called me long before now, so let's just hope he doesn't want to be in any more hot water. We'll hold off on contacting surrounding clubs about the trespass, but notify the surrounding Sacred Heart chapters. Let 'em know, no violence for now, but that could change, depending..." Data was already making notes and as soon as my dad finished and gave him a nod, he was up out of his chair and making strides for his media room, which was really just a converted janitor's closet.

My pops went on to remind us that this was a brotherhood and to give props to the men assembled for sticking it out, weathering the storms, both in previous years and against this new threat. He reminded us that we lived the lives of outlaw bikers while walking the straight-and-narrow. That just because we lived clean, that it didn't mean that trouble would never find us from the outside. Such was the life of flying our colors and living under the Sacred Heart's banner.

It was really nice, touching, even, and I was proud of my old man, proud to be his son, proud to be the vice president of this club and to be a part of such a brotherhood... yet at the same time I was damn near crawling out of my skin with the need to be back with Everett. I forced myself to stick around, answered some questions from Zander, and made my presence as VP of this club clear. I stayed as much as to prove that I wasn't dicking around anymore as to prove that I had a real loyalty to this club despite having such a personal stake in this particular situation.

Finally, my dad clapped me on the back. The sound of his hand slapping was amplified by the leather I wore. I jumped slightly because I hadn't seen it coming. He trained his burning dark eyes onto my own and I read clearly what he was trying to say before he opened his mouth.

"Go on, get back to your woman. We'll let you know when we got anything," he said. I nodded and hugged him.

"Thanks, pops." I let go and he grinned at me and I went back into the farther reaches of the clubhouse. The building was old and there were more rooms to it than just the council of five's but they needed some serious work before they could be anything. We were fixing the place up little by little and hoped that someday we would have a room available for each man in the club. We had the space for it, it was just bringing the rest of the place up to code.

I opened my bedroom door and smiled. My girl lay on her back, Ashton on one side, her best friend on the other, watching something on the TV. Ashton looked over and raised a brow.

"Meeting done?" she asked.

"Yeah," I said. She got up and smiled at me, brushing past and ghosting out the door. I turned back to the bed. Mandy was looking at me, indecision on her face which was half-illuminated half-blue by the flickering light of the screen, the other half cast in shadow.

"She's asleep. Pain pills," she said finally. I went over and sat on the edge of the bed. Sure enough, Everett was out, her face tight around the edges, drawn into lines of pain, her brow slightly furrowed despite her slumber.

"She's going to be okay," I said and the relief finally, really, set in. I let out an explosive breath and raked my hands through my hair, holding it back from my face and bowing my head as I watched her sleep.

"I want to be mad at you," Mandy said and gave a little one-shouldered shrug.

"Yeah?" I asked and eyed her warily. No sense in flying off at her until I knew what was what.

"Yeah. I look at you guys and I see 'bikers' and I look at her laying here, shot..." she sniffed and took a deep breath, overcome with emotion. I knew how she felt and it should scare me but it didn't. It just felt right that I should feel what I did for Em and so I didn't try to fight it, rather, I just went with it.

"But it's not your fault," she said, getting a hold of herself. "You guys aren't like that – but you are. I don't get it, it's weird and confusing." She stopped, and I drew in a long, slow breath.

"We *were* like the dude that shot her," I said quietly.

"But not anymore?" she asked.

"Not unless you push us and this was a pretty damned good push. We're going to try and solve this one through some diplomacy, but trust me, Red, I want to burn their whole motherfucking world down for this." I curved fingers around Everett's prone hand where it lay beside her hip.

"I've known Evy since we were in the second grade," Mandy said. "Yeah?"

"She's always been this powerhouse, you know? Outgoing, knows how to take all comers and win, mostly by outsmarting them. There isn't anything in the world outside this girl's reach. When I told her it was my dream to be a chocolatier in junior high, she pushed my ass to be a straight 'A' honor student all the way up through high school, dragged me along in her wake like it wasn't anything." Mandy looked at me, her green eyes penetrating right to my soul in a pale imitation of Everett's cutting gaze. Still, different as it may be, it had the same effect. I was listening and I was listening good... I nodded, once, that she should go on.

"Everett made my dream hers and didn't even think twice about it. She had it all planned out. Put it inside my reach and wouldn't you know it? We're almost there!" She chuckled and shook Everett's other hand gently where it rested in her own.

"She got me grants and not only put me through business class right along with her but she also found a way to put me through culinary school at the same time. Talked my parents into letting me live with them, which admittedly, was the easy part, I'm an only child... anyways. Everything I have is because of this girl right here. She's like my sister from another mister." I laughed softly.

"So I want to be mad at you guys for this, but I can't... I know it wasn't *your* biker gang that did it and I know that you guys don't do that stuff but I feel like I have to say it... if you hurt her, or any of the shit you get into gets her hurt, I'm'a find you and cut your balls off!" She stabbed a finger at me and I nodded solemnly. She couldn't hurt shit, but the same time, I figured it'd be best to let her have this one. I wanted Em's BFF to like me. I wanted to keep the peace in Em's life.

"Understood," I said and looked at Em.

"That's the other reason I can't be mad at you," she said and sniffed.

"What's that?" I asked her carefully.

"The way you look at her is... I don't know... it's indescribable. You'd do anything for her, wouldn't you?" she asked.

"Probably as much as you, Red," I told her. I set Em's hand down on the bedding and got up with a sigh. I shrugged out of my jacket and cut and hung them on the hook above the jacket I'd given her. Her boss had stuffed it in her backpack which hung underneath it. I was tired. It'd been a long-ass day. I glanced over my shoulder at Red and my girl, and decided *fuck it*.

"I'm changing for bed," I warned her as I pulled off my boots, and when she looked disappointed, I softened a bit. I could tell she wasn't ready to leave Em's side, and you know what, my girl needed all the love and healing energy she could get.

"Just do me a solid and keep your eyes to yourself," I grunted and stripped my Henley and wife-beater undershirt over my head in one fluid movement. Mandy obediently squeezed her eyes shut and covered them with her hand. I smirked with my back turned and quickly changed my jeans over to a pair of comfortable black cotton lounge pants.

I stripped out of my socks and went back to the bed. Em was pretty much dead-center. It would be a bit of a tight fit for three, but with her leg propped up like it was, I wasn't about to go moving her anyways. Red could stay on her other side.

I settled into bed and laid an arm across my girl's trim waist and kissed the side of her neck, breathing in her lilac scent, which was slightly overlaid by antiseptic hospital smell and a coppery hint of spilled blood. Her blood. I sighed and she stirred.

"Dray?" she asked sleepily.

"Yeah, babe, I'm here," I said.

"Mandy?" she asked.

"I'm here, too," her friend said softly from across her body.

"Good," Em said, and slipped back into sleep. We sandwiched Everett in a cuddle and not too long after I fell asleep, vaguely aware of my door opening. Mandy said something to whoever was there but I was unconcerned. Nothing but the brotherhood and their women in the house. I was out like a traffic light inside three minutes.

# 17

---

verett...

My leg *hurt*. It was way past time for another pain pill, but I didn't like the way that they made me sleep. I opened my eyes and realized that it was daylight outside the Venetian blind shuttered window. The light seeping in around the edges was enough for me to make out the room and the people in it.

It was a full house.

I lay snug against Dray's hard body on one side and against Mandy's curvaceous one on the other. I smiled faintly at them both and then blinked in surprise. Sitting on the floor of the bedroom, back against the wall, was Zander. His feet were crossed at the ankle, and his chin drooped onto his wide, muscled chest. His hat was still on backwards and his face was surprisingly at peace in his sleep.

I realized with a light start that, though he smiled when he was awake and his eyes laughed silently, there was a tightness at the very edges of his expression, all the time, a tightness that I only now noticed... because it was gone.

Dray sucked in a long deep breath and stirred; I turned my head at a slightly odd angle and his dark eyes blinked open and met mine.

He smiled slow, lazily and stretched, much like a cat, one of those luxurious full-body stretches that made me realize I was in dire need of one, too. I'd been in a deep, drug-induced sleep for so long I felt as if when I got up, there would be a permanent impression of my body left behind in the mattress.

"Hi," he said softly and I smiled.

"Hi..." I returned. He drank in my features and I felt myself blush faintly.

"You all right?" he asked.

"Um, no," I ventured. He pushed himself up from where he'd been laying on his stomach.

"What's wrong?" he asked, alarmed.

"Oh, nothing, I just really have to pee!" I admitted and then frowned.

"Everett..." he said derisively, in a tone that more than anything told me to spill it.

"My leg really hurts, I should take something, but I'm sick and tired of sleeping." Dray stood up and carefully helped me into a sitting position on the edge of the bed, which woke Mandy.

"What's wrong!?" she asked. I rolled my eyes. It was going to be a domino effect, I could just feel it...

"Nothing, I have to pee and my leg hurts." Dray brought my crutches and Zander startled awake. He stretched his big arms over his head and yawned.

"What's wrong?" he asked.

"Nothing!" I laughed.

"Her leg hurts and she has to go to the bathroom," Mandy supplied.

"I get what you're sayin' about the meds, Babe. Mandy, can you go cut one of her pain pills in half for her?" Dray asked. "I'll help her to the bathroom." He helped me get on my feet and I got the crutches under my arms. Oh, good lord, I was stiff! I groaned a little, my bladder screaming for immediate attention, and got myself going. Dray paced me. I made it to the bathroom and did what needed doing, grateful I hadn't embarrassed myself.

"Feel better?" Dray asked when I came back out.

"Much," I said but tears were starting to stand out in my eyes from the pain. How could something feel dull and sharp at the same time? That's what it felt like though, a dull, deep, sharp, grinding ache that just could not be ignored.

"Come on, let's get you out to the bar. Ashton's cooked breakfast for everyone and you should eat with your pill." His voice was soothing and sympathetic and I let him pace me out there. An old brown leather recliner that had seen better days had appeared from somewhere and Dray led me to it. I sank into it and he put up the footstool, and Mandy appeared with pillows.

"Morning, Evy," Doc said and knelt down by my leg. He looked ragged.

"You look so tired," I said, concerned, and he smiled at me.

"Twenty-four-hour shifts at the hospital; I'll go to bed as soon as I see to this leg and get you square for the day." He smiled kindly at me and opened up a big, boxy, padded bag It held all manner of medical stuffs.

He gently propped pillows strategically under my leg, snapped on some gloves and brought out a pair of trauma shears, cutting through the bandages. He stuffed the soiled bandage in a plastic grocery bag and tied it off. The prospect made it disappear. The wound was angry and red and spikey with black stitching thread. It had a sheen over the top from antibiotic ointment. Doc looked it over through his glasses and nodded.

"Looks good," he declared. He cleaned it up carefully and I hissed through gritted teeth and even yelped a few times. People looked on with interest. The girls' and a couple of the guys' expressions were sympathetic; some of the men's expressions, including Dray's, clouded over with anger.

Doc doctored me up and re-bandaged the leg. Mandy handed me a napkin and I wiped my eyes and blew my nose. The prospect made that disappear too. Ashton handed me a plate of food and Dray stood by with a pill and some water.

"Eat a few bites and I'll gladly hand it over," he said, and I obeyed.

As much as I hated the oblivion and fuzzy feelings the pill brought, I wanted so badly to dull the pain in my leg I would do just about anything. I swallowed the bitter-tasting pill quickly and went back to the rest of my food before I lost my appetite. Everyone else ate, scattered around at tables or the bar behind me.

"Got it," Data handed a piece of paper to Dragon, who took a swallow of coffee before setting the cup down and plucking the bit of white out of Data's long fingers. He read over whatever was on it and picked up his phone from beside his plate. A hush fell over the room. He dialed and put it on speakerphone. The ringing was loud in the silence between people.

"*Hello?*" came out of the phone.

"This Sparks?" Dragon asked.

"*Yeah, who's this?*" the voice demanded, surly.

"The fuck you think it is?" Dragon asked. A long silence ensued on the phone.

"*The fuck you think I'd be asking for if I knew?*" the voice bit back.

"This is Dragon, President of the Sacred Heart's MC," Dragon said. "We need to sit down and have ourselves a little chat," he went on before the man on the other end could say anything.

"*Oh, yeah? Why we need to do that?*" the voice asked.

"Well, it seems your crew is running around in Sacred Heart's territory. One of your feller's caused a hell of a mess yesterday. Shot our VP's Old Lady. Think that might be something worth having a little sit-down over?" Dragon asked.

"*Shhhit! Fuck!*" came over the line softly, it sounded like the phone was being jostled and the man on the other end changed his step to Dragon's tune in a really big damned hurry.

"*I had no idea, man! Is she all right?*" he asked, and maybe the drugs made me a little fancy-free, but I couldn't help it.

"No, I'm not bloody well all right! He shot me!" I blurted. Some low chuckles swept the room and Dray's hand descended on my shoulder. He gave me one of his burning scowls and placed the index finger of his other hand to his lips in the classic sign for 'shhh'.

"When and where you wanna meet about this?" The man on the other end sounded pissed. Hard to tell at who or what over a phone though.

"This afternoon. Neutral ground," Dragon said.

"Sounds good, you know the campground off State Route 62?" the disembodied voice asked.

"Yeah," Dragon said.

"Can you do it in an hour?"

"Make it two. No more than three men," Dragon ordered.

"Just gonna be me and my VP," the man said. "No weapons. If one of my guys did this – and I'm pretty sure I know which one you're talkin' about – last thing I want is a war with your boys. See if we can make this right." The grip on my shoulder eased marginally and I breathed out. Well, that was something.

"Two hours. We'll be there," Dragon said.

"Two hours," Sparks agreed and Dragon disconnected the call.

"Trigger, Dray, you're with me. Get ready to roll," Dragon said, and finished his coffee in one large swallow. "Prospect, hang-arounds, you got anything immediate you need to be doin'?" he continued.

"Don't need to open shop until two," Zander said.

"I make my own hours," Loyal supplied.

"Good. You're stayin' here with Ev. Keep her comfortable. What about you?" he leveled his gaze on Squick.

"Nowhere until two, like Zander says," Squick explained.

"You're her errand-girl then," Dragon said. He looked at me. "You need to square anything with your school or whatever, send Squick," he said. I nodded a little too rapidly.

"Thank you," I said.

"Mmm," he got up, and Trigger and Reaver made to follow, but not before Trigger kissed Ashton soundly.

"Be careful," she whispered against Trig's mouth.

"I'll be in the hills or the trees, Baby. No place safer." He smiled a one-sided smile and went to get ready. I looked up at Dray and he looked down at me. He kissed me.

"What do you want, Baby?" he asked.

"I don't want anyone fighting, if his people didn't know what he was up to... I mean, it's really bad to be kicked out of a club right?" I asked.

"The worst," he said.

"That's what I want. He gets kicked out of his club and goes to jail and I'll be happy with that," I said. Dray smiled down at me.

"Reasonable girl," he said and sighed. "I want his balls on a fucking plate but I'll do it your way." He leaned down and kissed me and it was full of heat and promise.

"Just be careful," I said.

"Trig will have our backs. Don't you worry about nothin'." He kissed me one more time and moved off back towards his room for clothes. I watched his muscled, well-defined back as it departed and let myself mope that he had to go. Ashton came over and sat down with me and Mandy.

"They'll be fine," she said with certainty and winked at me, her golden-yellow eyes full of sunlight and confidence. Mandy looked at us both dubiously.

"You need anything from your school or from Dray's?" Squick asked me.

"I need my phone from Dray's room and to call my school before anything," I said. He nodded, head bobbing eagerly, and disappeared.

"You need anything, Sugar?" Zander asked.

"I don't think so," I said and shook my head.

"'K, we're here if you do," Loyal put in, and they took themselves just inside earshot from our group of girls. Doc had disappeared, as had Data, Doc presumably to sleep and Data back to wherever it was that he went.

Squick came back with my phone and wandered over to where Loyal and Zander sat. I called my school and spoke to my professors about why it was that I had missed class the day before. They were very understanding, and I say that with total sarcasm. The head office explained to me that as soon as I supplied a doctor's note, the absence would be excused. I was fuming by the time I got off the call.

They wouldn't let Squick or Mandy pick up my school work either. I had to come in. Well, fucking fine!

"Mandy, help me get dressed," I said.

"Sweetie, I don't think you have any clothes here," Ashton said gently. Well then, by fuck I'd wear something of Dray's!

I got up on my own, my anger propelling me upward and onward. My crutches were loud as I hobbled down the hall, the boys and girls following me like helpless little lemmings, trying to stop me and talk me out of my temper. Well, all except for Mandy. She knew better than to try when I got like this. I pushed open Dray's door with my crutch and he turned towards me, rubbing a towel over his wet hair, shirtless and barefoot and totally delicious in just a pair of boxers and his jeans.

"I need to borrow some clothes," I said.

"The fuck you do, babe! You need to rest," he said incredulously. I started going through things. I picked up his discarded lounge pants and threw them over my shoulder. They had a drawstring waist; they would work. I found a clean, black, if faded, short-sleeved Henley of his and picked that. Mandy was explaining to him what had lit the fire under my ass and he was glowering.

"Prospects," he said, giving my all three of my appointed guardians the title, "take my girl to her school, help her get shit done, and get her ass back here so she can heal," he ordered. I nodded in his direction and he came over and kissed me gently.

"Give 'em hell," he said and I nodded, resolute.

"You too, if you have to," I said. He smiled at me and ducked out into the hall; he'd finished dressing while we'd talked.

"Out! Unless you want an eyeful," I ordered the boys. Squick damn near tripped over himself. Zander and Loyal grinned at me.

"At least one of you is a gentleman." Mandy snorted.

"Nah, Squick's gay." Zander said. Loyal looked at him with wide eyes.

"I am not, you douchebag!" Squick shouted from the hall. Zander's grin got bigger.

"Watch it, Puddin'! I'm still your boss!" he called out, and he and

Loyal left the room, closing the door behind them. Ashton was frowning.

"He is," I said, softly. "I saw it when Johnny started talking at the dance studio; he was interested." Ashton looked a little stricken and sad.

"Not our secret to tell," Mandy said and sniffed.

"He doesn't want anyone to know, he's afraid they won't let him patch in," Ashton said.

"I'd be more afraid of lying," I stated dryly. Dray had caught me up on a lot of the club politics and how things worked in the last couple of weeks.

"I think more people know than he realizes, they're just waiting on him to come clean," Mandy said.

"Something Zander told you?" I asked her and wrinkled my nose and smiled at her. She pursed her lips.

"Say no more, Sis," I told her and Ashton held the pants for me. I stepped into them carefully. I didn't care how wrecked I looked. Hell, the worse I looked, maybe the better off I'd be when I showed up at the school. Fucking assholes! Once satisfied Squick's secret was indeed safe with us, Ashton slipped out. She was going after my doctor's note before Doc got too far into sleep. She said he was likely reading, that he never crashed right away. Mandy helped me finish getting dressed. She slid a shoe onto my foot and tied the laces.

"Something there?" I asked her.

"I don't know," she hedged.

"Well, if there is, he better treat my bestie right or I'ma find him and kick his ass." She laughed at me.

"He's twice your size!" she exclaimed.

"I'd cheat," I told her.

"I believe you, Ev," she said, laughing.

"I know you'd do it for me, too," I told her and she smiled impishly.

"Heard me last night?" she asked.

"Yup." I said, popping the 'p'.

"Meh, I love you. Don't go getting all emo over it," she said and we both laughed. When it was just me and her and no one else, Mandy lost a lot of her shyness.

A half hour later I was in my school's office, raising ever-loving hell about their shitty bedside manner, flanked by Loyal and Squick, Mandy and Zander. Ashton had stayed at the clubhouse to clean up the breakfast mess. I got my school work and assignments for the rest of the semester, an assurance that my absence the day before wouldn't be a mark on my otherwise-perfect attendance record and the okay from my professors to have either Mandy, Shelly, or Squick come and turn in my work until I was able to get around better. In short, I gave the college hell and then some for me having to drag my ass out to it the day after being shot in the leg!

Afterwards, I was exhausted and all I wanted to do was go home... home being the clubhouse, for the time being, I suppose. Loyal and Zander helped me into Mandy's car, a cute little blue Ford Focus that had been a gift from her parents on graduation day. Squick had ridden with us and folded himself into the back seat. Zander and Loyal had ridden, both in front of us. It was strange having a biker escort but I was simply too damn tired to really ruminate on it too much.

I went straight for the recliner the moment we returned to the clubhouse. I needed clothes. Real clothes and not skimpy night-gowns... all though the satiny material *had* felt really nice on my skin. It had made me feel both beautiful and cherished when Dray had told me he'd bought it for me. Shelly was at the club when we got there and she dropped into a chair beside me.

"I suppose now is as good a time as any to catch you and Red here up on statistics seeing as you can't run screaming from it," she joked. I glowered at her.

"What? Too soon?" she asked with a grin. I opened my mouth and Mandy covered it with her hand and laughed.

"Watching you do math on drugs. Sounds like fun times!" my best friend said, looking down into my face from her standing position. She took her hand away from my mouth and I frowned at her. I frowned harder when she handed me my glasses. Ashton floated over with a glass of water and another half of a pain pill. I debated for a moment.

"Don't we have just, like, Tylenol?" I asked meekly. Ashton smiled serenely.

"I'll find some," she said but left the pain pill nearby in case I changed my mind.

"Thanks," I sighed out in relief. I needed a break from the effects of the painkillers. Oxycodone was so not my idea of a good time. Shelly and Mandy broke out the textbooks and calculator and I felt mutinous. Ashton returned with the Tylenol and I took it, but finding a way to comfortably sit and do math homework was almost as futile as trying to understand the math homework itself.

Reaver came out of the back and raised an eyebrow at his cousin, who was enthusiastically untangling the mess that was statistics for me and Mandy. I think I fell a little in love with Shelly, then. When she explained things, they made sense. At least one thing other than Dray was going well for me in recent history. I sighed. I missed him and I was beginning to worry the more as time dragged on. I hoped he was okay.

**18**

---

D ray...

This time of year, the middle of the week, the campground was deserted, making it pretty ideal for our little meet-and-greet. Trigger was set up somewhere in the hills. I'm pretty sure that knowledge alone is what caused the itching between my shoulder blades. I wondered vaguely to myself, how many times now I'd been in his scope? How many times could he have ended me with a twitch of his trigger finger? How many times had he wanted to, but refrained?

It was a morbid line of thinking. Once upon a time I wouldn't have cared. He could've put a bullet in every major organ in alphabetical order and I wouldn't have given two shits about it. Now there was Everett... Em, who loved me with everything she had. Me. Broken, twisted fuck that I am, she loved me and wanted to be with me and I'd almost lost her before I'd ever really had her because of one of the brotherhood that was walking across the expanse of pine needles towards us.

"Easy, boy," my father said in that low and controlled way of his. It was like slipping a leash on my anger, immediately bringing it to heel.

I'd seen him use it on more men than just me and I wondered briefly if it was a trick I would ever learn. The thought was fleeting, because the men of the hour, Sparks, the president of the Suicide Kings and his VP were drawing up within feet of me and my father.

Sparks was a lanky, bald guy that had been around a block or two in his lifetime. His jacket was worn but I noted that his cut looked relatively new. His president's patch wasn't even worn. My dad and me, our cuts looked ancient in comparison, and they probably were. I don't think Sparks had been in his even a year yet. He had blue eyes that weren't anything to write home about, not the steely blue like my girl's. He *did* have a wicked looking scar that ran from the corner of his right eye back over his ear to disappear around back of his shaven head. Whatever it was had taken off the top of his ear and it gave him this feral alley cat look.

His VP was a big bear of a man. No joke, the dude looked to be close to three hundred pounds. It was fat, sure, but you could tell there was a shit-ton of hard muscle underneath the padding. He had a yellow bandana wrapped around his forehead, sweatband style, in a wide swath. His hair hung long down his back in a curling salt-and-pepper ponytail, while his beard hung full and rounded at the bottom to his mid-chest. The name patch on his denim cut declared his road name to be Grizzly. He looked like a grizzly bear.

Like his president, his patches looked new, but the denim they rode on was hardly fresh off the rack. It was as dirty and roadworn as the leather jacket underneath. His chaps and boots spoke of a hard life on the back of the bike, and I caught myself wondering what the fuck he was doing following the younger bald man.

*"These two fucking kidding?"* It was a rhetorical question that growled low in my ear and came from Trigger. My Bluetooth was on an open call to him, hidden up under my hair. He was waiting for a signal from me or my pops in case something happened down here that he didn't see. Which, Truth be told, that wasn't fucking likely. Trig had eagle eyes. We squared off across from the Suicide Kings men and spent a minute getting each other's measures.

"Your girl the one Spaz shot?" Sparks asked me. I inclined my head and gave him my hardest withering look.

"Dray," my father warned.

"Now, I don't mind him bein' hostile with the looks, so long as that's as far as it goes. Not sure I'd be so understanding if it were me in his place," Sparks said.

"I 'preciate the understanding," I said and managed to keep the sarcasm out of my voice. Grizzly chuckled.

"Look, the shit Spaz pulled wasn't sanctioned by me or mine," Sparks said and put up his hands.

"Your girl lose the leg?" Grizzly asked.

"No. The dipshit shot her with a .22 long rifle round, must have been packing a pocket pistol or something. Doc says she'll be okay in a couple of months with some intensive physical therapy, but she's a dancer. Not sure if she'll be able to do that again." I lied about the last part, but I wanted my girl's terms met.

"Which club?" the big man asked.

"Jesus, Griz, does it matter?" Sparks asked with a scoff.

"Not that kind of dancer, friend," Dragon growled, and it was when he growled like that he was Dragon my Prez, not my pops.

"Mind me askin'?" he asked.

"My girl's Irish, she does that Riverdance shit. She was good at it too," I sniffed and crossed my arms. Sparks grimaced.

"We don't want any trouble with your crew," Sparks said. "You got a rep and it's a rep we don't want no part of. We just set up shop outside your territory and were hoping to meet you and yours when the time was right–" My dad interrupted him.

"That was your first mistake, then. Never should have 'set up shop' so close without contacting us first. You know the first thing about runnin' a club, son?" My dad pinned the younger man with a stare, though the dude wasn't that much younger... maybe forty-something to my dad's fifty-something.

"Told yah, Sparks," Griz grunted under his breath.

"*What the fuck, over?*" Trigger muttered in my ear. He had that right.

"Fair enough. I deserved that," Sparks said, taking the insult in stride, though you could see by his sour expression he didn't much like it. My pops was the master at this shit – knowing just how many licks he could get in before a dude would blow his stack. It was a skill we shared. Sparks wasn't at his limit by half, still my old man took it down a notch. "What can we do to make this right?" the King's President asked.

"Heh, don't ask me, ask the boy. It's his girl you shot!" My pops crossed his arms and Sparks looked at me. I think he was expecting something unreasonable; here's to hoping my demands weren't what he'd consider out of pocket.

"I want him dead, but–" I stopped him when he opened his mouth. "My girl is a lot more lenient and the slug was dug out of her leg, so I asked her what she wanted." Griz laughed under his breath. Probably thought I was whipped. I didn't give two shits what he thought. "She wants him to go to jail, which, let's face it... that part is out of all of our hands."

Sparks looked at me shrewdly. "That all she wants?" he asked, suspiciously.

"She wants him Out Bad with your crew." Sparks and Griz exchanged looks. I'd talked it over with my pops. Telling another crew how to conduct their business was pretty much the height of rude, and enough to start a war over by itself, but seeing as why we were here... it was a fair trade. My dad spoke up.

"Way I sees it, your boy, Spaz you call him?" Sparks and Griz nodded carefully. "What he done is a pretty hard betrayal of your brotherhood. Now I don't pretend to know your business but if what you say is true and you don't want a war... I'd consider it a pretty reasonable trade. Seein' as our reputation precedes us an' all." The other two men exchanged shrewd looks.

"We do this and we're square?" Griz asked.

"And then some. We might be able to even call you 'friend' for reals." My pops grinned.

"A moment." Sparks said, and they retreated towards their bikes, heads bent. They talked it over; a minute, then two going by, before finally coming to some sort of agreement. They stepped back towards us.

"You got yourself a deal – on one minor condition," Sparks said and sniffed.

"Oh? What's that?" my pops asked, raising an eyebrow.

"I wanna meet your girl. See with my own eyes what kind of shape she's in. If she's as you say she is, then Spaz'll be Out Bad like she wants." He crossed his arms. It was well-played; we insulted him, told him how to run his club in not-so-many-words, and he comes back calling us liars in not-so-many-words. My pops looked to me. She was *my* girl.

Everett probably wasn't going to be too happy with this. That, and it would give these yahoos a chance to scope us out, see what our numbers look like, unless...

"Fine. You can accompany us out to our clubhouse. Has to be now or never." My pops' eyebrows went up, but I had this in the bag. Sparks' mouth turned down at the corners. It was the middle of the week; if he came now, we'd have a only few MC members at the clubhouse but people gotta work for a living. I was betting most of *his* club were at their nine-to-fives now, too. They wouldn't be able to tell how many of our guys *weren't* there.

"Deal. We ride together under a banner of truce." He put out his arm. My pops looked at it for a moment, then clasped it.

"Follow us," he said simply and we went for our bikes.

Sparks and my pops rode even, and I fell in beside Griz; about a mile up the road, Trigger fell in behind us as our tail-gunner. Griz shot a surprised look into his sideview and I gave him a feral grin.

"The fuck he come from?" he shouted over the wind.

"There's a reason why we have the rep we do!" I shouted back, and it was true. We were the Boy Scouts of the outlaw biker world – always fucking prepared, come hell or high water. Griz shot me a look of solid respect and I counted it as a small victory.

The gate was open when we got back to the clubhouse, and we pulled up the steep drive. Trig, my pops, and myself backed into our customary spots while Sparks and Griz backed into vacant places left by some of the Sacred Hearts brothers.

Zander's chopper and Squick's Beemer were absent, as was Ashton's Jeep. I saw Reaver's, Doc's, and Loyal's bikes, but my girl's BFF's ride was gone. Shelly's car was parked in the far reaches of the lot and Data's bike was missing. I knew Gypsy was at the garage – somebody needed to keep us going on that front. That pretty much accounted for everybody. *Shit,* we were in a sorry state membership wise.

Sparks and Griz wandered over and unabashedly eye-fucked Matilda. She was beautiful; I'd worked my ass off to make her that way.

"Who's Tilly?" Griz asked, softly.

"My wife." "My mother." My pops and I simultaneously answered. Sparks and Griz exchanged looks.

"Sorry for your loss," Sparks said.

"Did a damn fine memorial to her, son," Griz said. I nodded.

"Thanks, man."

My dad led the two men into the clubhouse. I followed and Trigger followed me, his soft case containing his disassembled rifle slung over his shoulder. Shelly sat at a table with textbooks and note-book paper scattered in front of her, pencil moving across the page. Loyal sat across from her, a semi-automatic pistol in pieces in front of him as he cleaned it. Sparks let his eyes linger on Shelly a little too long and my pops grunted.

"Shells, c'mere an' give yer old man some sugar," he called. She looked up sharply and smiled. Her cool blue eyes, so much like Reaver's, skated over our guests and she smiled brightly. Loyal tried very hard not to watch her sashay across the common room and into my father's arms. It was for her own good. She kissed my father, long, slow, and deep, and put on an amazing show of it. Sparks and Griz looked both impressed and a little jealous, as well they should be. We had some damned fine women associated with this club.

"Hey, Prospect, where's my girl?" I asked.

"Pain was getting' to her. She's in your room layin' down. We couldn't get her to take any more of the strong stuff; she's tryin' to cope on Tylenol." He slid the barrel back into the gun and let his eyes rove over our guests. They were mostly curious with an undertone of hostility, but he earned himself some serious points by not commenting.

"Cool, thanks." I jerked my head at Sparks to follow me and led him back into the private quarters.

I took a deep breath outside my door and motioned for him to wait a sec, and opened it. Everett was laying on her back in the night gown I'd bought her. Her hair was clean and dry and brushed out in a silky wash over the pillows behind her head. The girls must have helped her clean up some. She stared sightless at the ceiling, tears tracking down to dampen the hair at her temples. She didn't look over right away. I think she was ashamed I caught her crying. Her eyes slipped shut and she took in one of those hitching breaths and my heart broke for her. I went to her, not even giving two shits that the President of what could turn out to be a rival club looked on.

"Hey, Baby, what's this?" I asked her. I sat down on the edge of the bed and picked up her hand between both of my own, laying a kiss on the backs of her knuckles.

"I know Doc said I would dance again but I'm scared. I don't know what kind of person I would be if I couldn't dance anymore," she said, and the brutal honesty, the face of her fear, made me want to rip the little douchenozzle's guts out. I scowled and it was a fierce one.

"Baby, try not to think about that right now," I pleaded.

"It's all I can think about, Dray, I close my eyes and all I can see is that man. All I hear is that God-awful sound and my leg – it hurts. I'm swallowed by the fear, and the pain, and the noise, and the blood all over again!" I pulled her tight against me and rubbed her back as she sobbed into the shoulder of my cut.

"I don't want to be this weak, paralyzed thing, Dray! My father didn't raise a weak daughter! I don't come from a weak people!" she cried, and I pulled back and speared her with my gaze.

"You're not weak, baby. You've had a lot of really horrible shit happen in a real short amount of time. You're tired, you're hurt, and you're in pain. Meltdown was imminent. It doesn't make you weak. Just makes you human." I kissed her forehead and held her tight, strands of her silky smooth hair tangling in my fingers. Sparks cleared his throat from the doorway and I looked over.

"You got your wish, Sweetheart. Spaz is Out Bad as soon as he makes bail or gets out of jail, whichever comes first." He looked murderous and my respect went up for him a notch or two. Everett drew back from me and looked over at him, confused.

"Who're you?" she asked.

"Baby, this is Sparks, he's President of the Suicide Kings MC." I told her and her steel-blue eyes roved his cut. She shuddered in my grasp and I held my breath.

A war was going on all over her face and finally she said, "I wish I could say I was pleased to meet you and mean it... But honestly, I don't really know how I feel." It was probably the most graceful and perfect thing she could have said under the circumstances.

"I get you," Sparks said and smiled.

"Baby," I said, but her eyes were far away for a second too long. "Em," I tried again. She looked at me.

"Yeah?" She looked exhausted, deep lines of pain engraved around her mouth and eyes.

"Fuck, baby, I know you don't like 'em, but, take a pain pill for me? Sleep some?" I asked her.

"For you," she said, nodding.

I got one out of the little orange pill bottle and handed her a glass of water from the nightstand. She drank the pill down obediently and handed me back the glass. I eased her down so she was reclining, stuffing some pillows behind her to make her comfortable.

"Thank you," she said and I smiled, smoothing back some of her hair. Sparks looked on but said nothing.

"I'll be back soon, baby," I murmured and kissed her lightly. Her fingertips grazed my face as she returned the kiss and when I drew back, her steely blue eyes were filled with a vulnerability and practically begged me not to go.

"Just escort me back out to your common area and I'll let you get back to your girl," Sparks said.

"Thanks, man," I said and got up. I took him out and nodded to my pops and left them to do whatever they wanted. Right now, Everett needed me, and damn it, I needed her too.

## 19

Everett...

Dray left the room with the scarred biker president from the club whose member shot me and I swallowed hard. I scrubbed at my face with my hands and let out a shuddering sigh. I hadn't meant for anyone to catch me mid-meltdown. I tried to keep things like that under wraps and to myself.

Dray slipped back into the room and shut the door behind him. He slipped off his jacket and cut with a sigh and it was like he stripped the burden of his Vice Presidency that came with it off, too. He hung it on the hook by the door and turned to look me over. He looked as tired as I felt, anxiety radiating off of him like heat from a summer sidewalk. I swallowed hard again, my throat squeezing tight with guilt at being the cause of his discomfort.

"Don't," he said and his voice was hard. "Don't do that, Em, don't cry," he said and he trudged the few short steps across the carpet to sit down beside me on the bed.

"I love you and it kills me to see you cry," he said and I sniffed back the threatening tears, nodding a little too rapidly. He pulled his shirt over his head and let it drop to the floor before bending to pull off his boots.

"What are you doing?" I asked.

"Getting into bed with my woman," he answered back, succinctly. He dropped his pants and lifted the blankets and spent several minutes getting the pillows out from under my leg and both of us tucked in. He held me close and let me find a position that was comfortable, or as close as I was going to get to it, with my leg the way it was.

"I'm not going anywhere or doing anything else, baby, so just relax," he said into my hair. I closed my eyes and held close to him.

"I missed you," I said thickly. The pain medicine was starting to severely blur the edges of my consciousness.

"I'm here now," he said, and it was true. He was, and I drew strength from having his hard body up against mine.

I fell asleep, much more restfully than when I'd tried to on my own, wrapped up warm and safe against Dray's chest, his hands playing along my body, rubbing up and down my arms, my back, through my hair, just anywhere he could reach. It had been a long time since a masculine presence had comforted me. Probably since before my da' had died. Jerry hadn't really tried to understand the depth of the hit I'd taken losing the only parent I had ever really known.

Dray, even though he still had his da', he understood. We connected on a sub-level, the very fibers of our being weaving together into a beautiful tapestry, two broken halves made whole. I knew it, deep down where it counted, that we were somehow meant for each other. I think he did too. He didn't say it, he didn't have to... he telegraphed it just as surely with every look, every touch and with every little nuanced thing he did for me, from opening doors, to carrying my bag, to holding me close and smoothing away my tears.

Draven loved me just as surely as I loved him, and that, in and of itself, would go a long way in healing my hurts. Jerry and life in general may have burned me but good in recent memory. However, meeting and loving Dray was a soothing balm to my soul. It made all the nasty bits bearable.

I was vaguely aware of the bedroom door opening. "Go away. I'm with my girl," he said, without even opening his eyes, and I smiled.

The door shut and we slept some more and I felt much better for it. We woke sometime in the evening. There was a light rap at the door and it opened. We turned to look and Ashton poked her head inside.

"I fixed a late dinner. You should both eat," she said gently. I smiled.

"Thank you," I said. She nodded and ducked back out.

"I take it that means you're hungry?" Dray asked with a vague smile in the dark. I nodded.

"How's your pain?" he asked, expression darkening.

"Okay. I should probably take something more," I sighed.

"Yeah, well, let's get you some food." He extracted himself from beneath me and I nodded. He found my crutches and switched on the bedroom's lamp on the back of the headboard. The little clock radio glowed that it was after eleven-thirty. I yawned and he helped me get up.

"Hey, look who's up!" Doc said as we went into the common room. Dragon was sitting at a table with him and they were eating. Ashton brought two plates to their table and set them down. I sat by Doc, Dray across from me by his dad.

"So, what's the word?" Dray asked.

"Sparks and Griz left out of here right after you brought him back out." Dragon took a drink of his beer before going on. "Said they'd be in touch as soon as they had their house in order." He shrugged.

I tucked into warm mac and cheese and sighed in pure bliss. Ashton knew how to cook! I smiled at her when she and Trigger set down plates beside mine and Dray's and pulled over another table. They joined us and we ate in silence for a time.

"Your red-headed friend came by while you was asleep. She said Dray told her to get lost and she looked a little butt-hurt about it. I told her I'd have you call her when you got up," Dragon said.

"Ah, so that's who it was. I didn't look," Dray said. I smiled across the table at him, but secretly feared Mandy's feelings were really hurt. She was sensitive, God love her, and I had no clue how she managed to be as awesome as she was, with her father the way he was around her.

Gravel crunched out front but no one seemed concerned. I guess they were used to people coming at all hours, but all of our heads shot up when a light rap fell at the door.

"Who the fuck is that?" Trigger asked no one in particular. Chairs scraped as he, Dragon, Doc, and Dray stood up as one.

Dragon pulled a gun out of the back of his waistband and went for the door. Doc had a gun of his own in hand and Trigger went with Dragon. Dray stood, hands to his sides, held slightly away from his body in a fighter's ready-stance. Ashton looked surprised and we traded alarmed and helpless looks. Knocking was something to be alarmed about?

Trigger palmed the door handle and ticked off three fingers. On 'three', he jerked the door open and stood behind it, Dragon aiming his handgun out the open portal. He aimed the gun up.

"The fuck you doin' back here unannounced?" he asked.

A throat cleared and a pair of meaty hands held skyward appeared inside the door frame.

"Was hoping to talk to your VP and his girl. My club has a little present for 'em."

The gun came back down and aimed at a great big bear of a man I didn't know. "What kind of present?" Dray asked.

"A peace offerin', if you'd be so kind as to come with me. Bring who you want. I drove in my grocery-getter so the girl can come, too." Trigger patted the man down while he spoke.

"He's clear," the blonde Viking declared.

"Trig, step out and keep an eye on him." Dragon addressed his Sergeant At Arms then leveled the big man with his dark stare.

"Can't be too careful, you understand," he said.

"That I do. Not tryin' nothin', my lips to God's ear. We want to make things right between us." The man put one palm down and held the other in its place as if he were swearing on a bible and took a step back. Trigger followed him out and the door closed.

"Lot of balls to come back here that quick," Doc muttered.

"Who is he?" I asked softly.

"That's Griz, he's the Suicide King's VP," Dray answered.

"Do you think he meant what he said?" Ashton asked softly, fear evident in her golden eyes as she stared at the closed door her man had just gone through.

"I think so," Dragon said thoughtfully.

"Been a minute since we've had to play inter-club politics," Doc observed, then swore. I could swear I heard him mutter "I'm getting' too old for this shit."

"What could they possibly have for us?" I asked.

"Think along the lines of your dad's friends for me, babe," Dray said pointedly, and I swallowed.

"Nothing good, then," I stated dryly, "but not necessarily bad for *us*." I mulled things over and looked up at Dray. "What will happen if we don't go?" I asked.

"Mm, maybe it's an insult too big for these boys to swallow. Could start a war," Dragon mused. I mulled things over further, Dray watching me, his face schooled into an undecipherable mask, cool, appraising.

"If it's up to me, I say we should go," I said at last.

"Why?" Dray asked.

"If they are on the level then it's nothing that will hurt us, and if we refuse it's war and they'll have a legitimate gripe and ability to vilify us. If they *aren't* on the level, and it's war as a result, it will be war on a wrong done to *us*. We'll have the moral high ground and you can always recruit soldiers to your cause when you have the moral high ground." I looked up at all the semi-stunned faces.

"What? It's nothing I haven't heard before… I come from a land of martyrs and cutthroats all in the name of freedom-fighting. My fairy tales growing up were of Irish car-bombs and foul English overlords," I said, my voice full of derision.

It was a double-edged sword, growing up around the people I

had. On the one hand, I didn't have any illusions about the way things were in situations like this; on the other hand, I didn't have any blissful ignorance either. I sighed out. This was making me tired. I ate another bite of food.

"Does that mean you're going?" Ashton whispered.

"Yeah," I answered, suddenly annoyed, my backbone coming back from wherever it'd crawled off to. "It also means I've about had it with these Suicide Monkeys and after this I hope they'll leave me the hell alone!" Dragon's booming laughter filled the common space of the Sacred Heart's clubhouse and he looked at his son.

"Boy, she'll make you a damn fine Queen someday," he said.

Dray was smiling a slight little smile that told me nothing of what he was thinking. He looked down at me from where he stood and I could swear there was a glint of fierce pride in his deep, dark eyes. "Yeah. I think you're right, pops," he said.

And so it was I found myself back in Dray's sweats, in the back seat of Griz's land-yacht of a 70's Caddie with my fucked-up leg across Dray's lap. Doc rode in the front passenger seat, and Dragon and Trigger followed behind on their bikes, as we drove into the next county over, to the Suicide Kings' modest clubhouse out in the middle of some industrial area.

I felt my heart thundering against my ribs hard and harder as Griz shifted the old beastly car into park. A Suicide King with a red and yellow Mohawk opened my door and Doc was there with my crutches. It was awkward, getting out, but once I was on the crutches and on my feet with Dray beside me I felt a little bit better, a little bit more in control. I took in a deep, silent, cleansing breath and let it out slowly. I was surrounded by Dragon, Dray, Doc, and Trigger and it wasn't lost on me that they acted as a living shield. Sparks, the scarred bald man from earlier, came out of a worn old heavy-looking door and held his hands open wide in greeting. He shook Dragon's hand.

"This way, please." He motioned and we went through the door into a wide-open space with a large round bar and scattered tables and chairs. There was a loft area to one side and metal steps leading up to it. Chains and metal were everywhere and it looked like something out of the old post-apocalyptic Mad Max movies my da' watched with me when I was a kid.

"Nice place you got here," Dragon uttered and he sounded impressed.

A crowd of bikers in Suicide Kings colors turned toward us and we stopped in the center of the great expanse of room. My skin prickled with unease.

"So, our boy Spaz made bail today," Sparks said and turned to face us. I swallowed hard and the mass of black leather and chains undulated a little and the bikers in front of us parted, spewing the man who'd shot me to the cement floor at our feet. I jumped slightly. Dray's hand automatically went to my lower back and rested there. I felt steadier and grateful for him, but didn't dare take my eyes from the man sprawled at our feet.

His wrists were bound behind him with sturdy industrial zip ties and were turning purple with the length of time they'd been like that. A yellow bandana was clasped between his teeth and tied tight against the back of his head. Drool soaked it and ran down his chin. His brown eyes were wide and wild and his breath sawed in and out of his chest in great panicked gasps.

"You want him Out Bad, and truth is, sweetheart, we do, too," Sparks said and I raised my eyes to meet his. His eyes sparkled with cold mirth and calculation. "I want this to be a lesson to all of you!" he shouted over his shoulder, back at his crew. "We don't cause trouble with other clubs! We don't go pulling petty crimes, robbing coffee stands for drug money and *we don't go shooting innocent girls!*" Griz stepped forward and hauled Spaz by his collar onto his back and dragged him back a few paces. A gun appeared in Spark's hand from beneath his cut as he turned and everything happened in slow motion.

*Steady, Evy, m'girl. No emotion. Just steady as she goes.* I heard my father say but it wasn't like in the coffee stand, this was simply me replaying his voice in my own head for my own benefit. Dray's hand pressed harder into my lower back and the whole world slowed down to nothing. Sparks aimed the gun slowly but surely and pulled the trigger. The world erupted in a riot of sound and light. Blood flew from the man who'd shot me— from his leg, same as mine— I stared down at him dispassionately and couldn't say it bothered me one whit. My ears rang from the shot and sound slowly returned to me and it was of a deafening silence that slowly backfilled with the muffled screaming and crying of the man on the ground in front of me.

I turned my head and met Dray's eyes, so sad and dark, and he met mine. Something passed between us in that moment. An acknowledgment of just how monstrous and barbaric our standing here bearing witness was... and an equal acknowledgment, at least to each other, that this was the natural order of things in our world. I looked down at the man writhing on the floor one more time and turned my eyes up to Sparks.

"Are we done here, then?" I asked, my Irish brogue out in the fore.

"You accept our apology?" he asked, smiling. The bastard.

"Aye, tha' I do," I said, and he nodded.

"Doc," Dragon said and the single utterance was weighted. Doc sprang into action and I closed my eyes, sending up a silent prayer of gratefulness to whatever power that be that he was here. Trigger's face was carefully neutral as he helped Doc stem the bleeding.

"What you got in there?" Doc demanded.

"Thirty-eights," Sparks responded mildly.

"You don't want him to die, you best drop him at an ER," Doc said harshly.

Sparks nodded to several of his MC minions standing by and they dragged Spaz's limp body out. I felt hot and cold at the same time watching the blood smear across the concrete but I knew, I just knew, that the men I was with, Dragon, Dray, Trigger, and Doc needed me to put on a good show, needed me to be tough as nails on the outside. I could freak out later. Right now I just wanted away from all of this. What do you know? Apparently watching the man that shot me get shot back *did* bother me.

"My leg hurts. I'd like to go home now, if you please," I said to the men and my voice was steady and calm which was not at all how I was feeling on the inside.

"We square then, brother?" Sparks asked Dragon.

"Yeah. We're square," Dragon said and held out his hand. They clasped arms.

"Glad t' hear it! Griz, take the lady home," he said and yelled out, "Prospect! Clean up this mess!"

We turned and followed Griz out. He took us back to the Sacred Heart's clubhouse. I went inside and held all emotion in until the goodbyes had been said and the door was safely shut behind us. Then I hobbled to the nearest sink, which happened to be the kitchen's, and I threw up Ashton's lovely meal. Dray was there, a cool hand pressed to my forehead, the other rubbing uselessly up and down my back. He said nothing and I gasped for air and fumbled for a glass of water. Trigger was on my other side and pressed a full glass into my hand. I rinsed out my mouth.

"Sorry! Sorry! Sorry!" I blurted out.

"Don't be, Baby," Dray said quietly and he was as shut down as I had ever seen him. I was grateful I wasn't the only one effected; we just handled it differently.

"Been a couple years since we had to be privy to something like that," Trigger commented dryly. Ashton looked on, her golden eyes worried as she looked over her man, who had blood on his hands.

"What happened?" she asked.

"They shot him," I said breathlessly. "The man who shot me, they shot him in the leg," I said and wiped at my mouth.

"Oh," she said and markedly relaxed. A hysterical bubble of laughter escaped my mouth and I slapped a hand over it.

"It's okay," Dray said and held me from behind, keeping me upright, pinned between him and the counter. I nodded rapidly.

"There's a difference," I said breathlessly, "Between hearing about it all your life and seeing it up close and personal..." I said.

Yeah, there is," Dragon agreed, "but you handled it like a pro, Darlin'. You did your man and this club proud tonight," he said. They left me and Dray in the kitchen, his leather-clad arms tight around me, gripping me to his chest as if he were afraid to let go.

"I understand if you don't want to stay," he said quietly, voice anguished. I closed my eyes. What woman in their right mind would wish to after seeing something like that? I smiled a little to myself.

"I don't feel bad that he shot him," I said softly, and Dray was silent, waiting for me to continue. "I feel bad that I don't feel bad... Is that crazy?" I asked. While watching the brutal act had bothered me, the fact that he'd been shot, that he'd had to endure what I had, that didn't bother me in the slightest. I fought down another wave of nausea. Oh God. What kind of monster did that make me?

"If it is then I'm fucking nuts," Dray stated sardonically. He sighed.

"You're not nuts... I think we're both the product of our upbringing," I said. I had to rationalize this somehow... He turned me in his arms and looked me in the eye. I wrapped my arms around his neck and shoulders and stared him in the eyes.

"That mean you're sticking around?" he asked lightly, but his eyes told me the true cost of what it was for him to ask me, to give me the choice. I pressed my lips to his in a chaste kiss. I wouldn't subject him to my mouth after he watched me puke, not without brushing my teeth.

"That's the second time you've watched me puke and the third time you've seen me at my worst and you're still here..." I said practically.

"No place, I would rather be than by your side, Em. Question is, can you handle bein' by mine?" He searched my face and whatever he saw there must have reassured him some because his hold on me lessened.

"I love you Dray; good, bad, or indifferent, and there is no place I would rather be than with you," I said and his eyes closed as if he were savoring my words.

"Still, before you commit you should know it all," he said and my heart dropped. He opened his smoldering dark eyes and it was as if the fire had gone out, they were drowning in such deep sorrow.

"Okay," I whispered reluctantly, wondering, *did he really have to do this right now?*

"Come on, let's get you laid up and we'll talk," he murmured. I nodded mutely, unsure if I could handle any more truth and consequences tonight.

Dray led me through the common room and into the back. Everyone was quiet and I almost felt as if I marched towards some kind of death. What could he possibly need to tell me? What was possibly so important after seeing such things? I swallowed hard and tried not to be afraid, because whatever it was... whatever it was, if it was worse than what I'd just seen, maybe ignorance was bliss. Maybe I was better off just not knowing.

He shut the bedroom door behind me and helped me into bed. My leg hurt and my face felt hot and my stomach still churned and Dray sat down on the bed by my hip and looked so fucking solemn I wanted to scream at him to stop, that whatever it was he didn't have to tell me tonight, that it didn't matter, but I could see it in his eyes he needed me to know whatever this terrible truth of his was, that he needed to unburden his soul and for whatever reason the time was now.

"It's not always like this, Baby," he said and took my hands in his, smoothing over the backs of my fingers with his thumbs.

"I know, Dray. Look whatever it is you don't–" He cut me off.

"Yes, I do, you need to know that it's not always like this, but when it is, when the shit gets heavy, and it *will* get heavy from time to time, you need to know what I've done, what I'm capable of, and that I'll do it. I'll use it to protect you and the people of this club." He was so earnest, I simply nodded mutely and let him have his say.

"I've done worse shit than what you saw tonight. Just last spring in fact." He held his breath and I blinked. Worse? Worse how?

"W-wh-what did you do?" I stammered.

"I helped kill Ashton's husband. I mean I was there, I... I hid in the man's own damned panic room all fucking day and I held him down while Reaver shot him up with heroin. I helped get him into the tub and just stood there and watched while Reaver fucking toyed with him. Reaver fucking stood there, and told him why he was going to die and then he cut his wrists and I just fucking stood there, Em. I just fucking stood there and watched the man bleed to death."

I stared at him and blinked. "Why?" I asked.

Dray blinked at me and confusion flashed across his face.

"'Why?', what?" he asked, caught off-guard.

"Why would you do that?" I asked and we stared at one another across a chasm of silence for what felt like forever.

"It was either him or Ashton... and I needed to do it, because I did something terrible to her, Em." He swallowed hard and his shame spilled out of him. He told me everything. About how he'd treated Ashton when she'd first arrived at the MC; about the spring Lake Run, whatever that was; and how he'd gotten drunk; how he'd wanted to scare her off but also... how he'd wanted her for himself. How his father had intervened and how he'd taken his beating from Trigger and just, all of it... Every single sordid, dirty detail. I stared at him, completely shocked.

"Please say something," he pleaded, and I did, probably the worst thing I could have possibly said in that moment.

"I think I just want to be alone right now..."

## 20

Dray...

Her words hit me like a hammer-blow to the center of my chest. I stared at her numbly for a second and nodded dumbly and got up. I slipped out the door and shut it behind me and moved back out into the common room. Just about everybody had gone except for my old man. He took one look at my face and his crumbled in sympathy. He kicked out a chair across from him.

"Sit down before you fall down, Boy." I took the seat and he poured a shot of tequila. I grimaced as the phantom smell of blood invaded my nose, but picked up the shot anyways and downed it.

"I told her everything," I said and my pops raised his eyebrows.

"Sure that was the smart thing to do?" he asked.

"No, dad... No... I don't know." He poured another and I downed it.

"What'd she say?"

"She said she wanted to be left alone." I poured the next one and downed it. He slid the bottle out of reach and leveled me with a smoldering look that made mine look like puppy-dog-eyes.

"No screaming?" he asked.

"No."

"No crying?"

"Uh, there were tears, but not like wracking sobs or hysterics or nothing." I frowned, the world beginning to swim as the alcohol hit; I had a pleasant buzz going but I needed more than that, *this* called for a roaring drunk.

"She just needs time to think, boy. Sort out everything she's feeling. Give her time," he said sagely.

"How do you know?" I asked hollowly.

"Yer mom was the same way. If she started screaming and crying all hysterical-like I was up shit's creek without a paddle. She did the quiet stuff, it was kind of fifty-fifty on if my hide came out of whatever it was in one piece." His words were cold fucking comfort.

I put my head in my hands.

"What if I fucked this up past fixing, Pops?" I asked and his hand descended onto my shoulder.

"You love her?" he asked me. I looked up at him and didn't even fucking care that the tears showed.

"I've never felt anything like what I feel for her, it's like it's just... too huge for words. Like they don't make a word big enough or grand enough for it. I don't know how this fucking happened. I gave this girl my whole damned heart and I don't even know when I did it." I looked at him and I think he flinched in the face of my raw pain but then my alcohol-addled brain realized he was looking behind me. He must have had the good shit on the table. I turned, dreading seeing Em standing there, but the person who actually was made it somehow worse.

"Fuck, man, really?" I asked and laid my head on my arm on the beat-to-shit table. Trigger hooked a boot around one of the chair legs next to me and pulled it out, dropping his tall bulk into it.

"Your girl's cryin'," he said. "My girl's in with her."

"Fuck, I fucking broke the best thing I ever fucking had," I moaned and Trigger chuckled.

"Don't count my Sunshine Girl out. Ev just went through a hell of a thing and you, my young friend, just piled it on. It was an honest mistake, Dray, just give her some time to process. She may surprise you yet." Trig clapped me on the back and I held out my hand. My Pops put another shot into it and I drank it down.

"Last one there, Junior. You need to slow your happy ass down," I heard my dad say, but my head was back on my arm. I was already grieving the loss of the first girl I think I've ever loved, though I think the booze was helping that along to some extent. I don't remember ever feeling so... squishy.

"That's a good word. Squishy," I mumbled aloud and the two other men laughed a little.

"Oh, lord, he's feelin' that tequila," I heard my pops say. "Between his momma and me I'm not sure how we popped out such a lightweight."

"He'll be feeling it worse in the morning. I'll have Doc hook him up to an IV, last thing he needs to deal with is a killer hangover. I think he's been punished enough."

Trig was wrong. So wrong, this was too much, the potential of losing Everett for good, after her being the first really good thing I've ever had in my life... it was too short; it was too fleeting! I had to do something, I had to do something drastic. I stood up abruptly and swayed on my feet. Trig was suddenly up beside me, hand on my back, the other on my chest. I looked down at his tattooed arm and blinked in confusion.

"What're you doin?" I asked. Wait, did I just slur?

"Uhhh, question is, what're *you* doin'?" my dad asked, and he had his amused look on his face.

"I gotta fix thish." Yeah, okay, I was definitely slurring, I'd only had like three shots! What was in that fucking tequila?

"How you planning on doing that, son?" my dad asked and leaned way back in his seat, crossing his arms.

"I'ma ask her to marry me," I declared and both of them busted up laughing at me. "Aw, fuck you guys!" I tried to shake Trig off and moderately succeeded but then my dad was there.

"Sit down, boy," he ordered and I dropped back into my seat. He poured a round for the three of us.

"I ever tell you about the time I almost lost your momma?" he asked me. I blinked at him owlishly.

"She musta kicked your ass out a half a dozen times when I was growing up," I said and it was true. My dad scowled.

"True enough, I deserved it." He drank down his shot as if to clear a bitter taste from his mouth, "Of all the times she did though, she always said the same thing... 'I love you Dragon, you and only you and this isn't forever just until... ' and she'd lay down the law. I'm talking about the time I almost lost her for good, before you were even thought of." He grew real quiet and I shook my head and widened my eyes to try and get 'em to focus.

"You an' mom were always tight, there wasn't any time like that... was there?" I asked. This night was getting to be too fucking much for all of us.

"Sacred Hearts was a few years old, I met your mom at the bank where she was workin' an' it took me weeks to convince her to take a ride with me. Anyways, we were hot 'n' heavy..." I interrupted him.

"Ew, gross that's my *mom* you're talking about, asshole!" and my dad barked a laugh and reached across the table and slapped me upside the head.

"Don't interrupt," he schooled me, and then went on. "Anyways. I guess she'd just found out she was knocked up with you and I was heavy into the drug-running and the rivalry with the Wraiths and I went out and got m'self shot." I blinked at him. My dad had taken a few bullets in his time, most of them before I was born, only one in the time I could remember.

"Mom freaked out?" I guessed.

"To put it mildly. I'm up on the bar at the old club and Doc is pulling a slug outta my chest," he slapped a hand over his chest, up near his shoulder and grimaced with the memory, "and Tilly's a standing there crying all silent, and looking all lost, and then it was like something just flipped her switch. She starts screaming at me about how she isn't going to raise no baby like this and I'm wondering what the fuck she's on about but before I can say anything she's telling me it's over and done and she never wants to see me again, she's moving back in with her ex-boyfriend and she's out the fucking door."

"What'd you do?" I asked.

"I let Doc finish what he was doin' and got fucking drunk. That's what."

I blinked. "How'd you get her back?" I asked.

"I didn't, I let her go. She came around a day or two later and we talked. Your momma loved me son, I don't know why. I sure as hell didn't deserve a woman like her, but all the same, she loved me and I loved her enough to let her go. Just, fate, God, or somebody had a different idea, and fuck if I don't regret it every day because it was my stupid shit that got her killed." His words broke on a sob and fuck the glass, he took a fortifying pull right off the bottle. I blinked stupidly and he passed the bottle to me. I took a pull.

"Naw, dad. The fucking assholes that killed her got her killed and we killed them," I said.

"Doesn't matter, Son. It ain't gonna bring her back," he said and dashed at his eyes with the back of his hand. This was the most emotional I'd ever seen him get over it; I felt like I'd seriously just been sucked into the motherfucking Twilight Zone!

"So what're you sayin'?" I asked, "That I should just let Em go? Push her away so nothin' can happen to her?" I asked.

"No. I'm sayin' you don't do what I did. Don't fucking waste the time you get with her, you keep her, you protect her; you spend every waking fucking moment you can devote to her by her side. Don't you backslide into that shit no matter how appealing the money, you keep your woman and this brotherhood together and safe against all comers. Boy, we ain't got any fucking control over what happened to your girl, her getting shot in the leg was the damnedest thing and had nothing to do with us but we fixed it the best we could. This life ain't easy for any of us but we got each other. You lean on me, you lean on Trig, an' Reaver, an' the rest of your brothers when shit goes sideways. You take comfort from your woman and when you have 'em, you give a future to your kids." He looked at me and we stared at each other for long minutes.

"I was just trying to be upfront about all of it. Honest about what kind of man I've been–" Trig stopped me.

"That's the problem, Dray. You're focusing on the man you've *been, were*, past tense. We've all done some terrible fucking things. We all got our ghosts and our skeletons and shit, but that's the past. Instead of focusing on our past, young brother, we should be focusing on our *future.* Doesn't mean we should forget what we've done, because Lord knows, we may need to be those men again, like we were tonight, but the difference is why. Before it was for all the wrong reasons... Now it's for all the right ones. We got people we love, people who care about us. We gotta stay whole for them and keep them in one piece too. Carve out what little bit of happiness we can in this life before it's over." Trig clapped a hand on my back reassuringly and I stared for long minutes at the scarred wooden table top, the wheels turning in my head.

This is what they had been trying to impress upon me for a really long time, but before Everett I didn't have anything I cherished, worth protecting other than the brotherhood, but even then... I was young. Hell, *I* am young and behind on the fucking curve. The heat of my anger curtained me off from everything for far too long. If I'd spent a little less time raging internally about the unfairness and injustice of it being my mom who'd had to die instead of me or any of these other guys... I scrubbed my face with my hands.

I would give Everett her alone-time. Give her the night. I wasn't laying down without a fight though. If my mom and dad could make it work, then we could too. I had a lot to fucking think about.

"I got a lot of shit to catch up on and learn," I said at last and sniffed, tears burning my eyes. "Thanks, Trig. Thanks, Pops," I added.

"No thanks necessary, boy. You have a way of carryin' yourself. I think Trig can agree that sometimes we all forget you're only twenty-two, then shit like this goes down and it reminds us. We've all been here with our women at one time or another. Feeling like it's the end of the world and it's broke past fixing... I gotta say though, you picked a damned fine one in that Irish girl. Something tells me she's gonna get past this, you two got some talking to do for sure but this ain't the end." My dad put a cigarette between his lips and handed one to Trig. Trig smiled and took it, I pulled out one of mine. We were silent save for the clicks and flicks of lighters as we lit up and sucked the smoke into our lungs. My dad blew his first drag out his nose and I smiled.

"I remember when I was a kid and you used to do that," I said and smiled fondly.

My Pops chuckled. "Had the whole damned club calling me "Puff" for a year or two," he said to Trig and the big man laughed.

"As in Puff the..." we all three chorused the last, "Magic Dragon!" We stopped and smoked some more.

"I'm not singing that shit," my Pops said.

"Me, either."

"Yeah, no, breaking out into song is my girl's thing... and maybe Squick's." Trig said.

"What is with that, anyways?" I asked.

"Squick's gay," Trig said and I raised an eyebrow.

"Figured as much," my dad mumbled. I looked from one to the other of them.

"I ain't got a problem with it as long as he doesn't go hitting on me, but how's that going to work? If he wants to patch in, that requires honesty and loyalty of the highest order, can't have him hiding that kind of shit." I took a smaller pull off the bottle, I was finally evening out. Drunk, sure, but I felt like my wits were more about me. A little too much too quick at the beginning there. Fuck of a head rush.

"He don't come clean, he don't patch in. It's as easy as that, anyone has a problem with it we settle it with an old school ass-kicking. Let 'em face off," my Pops said.

"Squick may be lanky as fuck, but the kid's quick and what he lacks in the ability to dish when it comes to heavy hits, he's not a-fucking-fraid to fight dirty. I've seen him do it," Trig said.

"Meh, we'll cross that bridge when we come to it," my Pops said on an exhale, the smoke curling heavy around the three of us. We sat quietly, smoking, drinking and just generally trying to wind the fuck down from being wound tighter than a fucking Timex.

"Think there'll be more trouble with this new crew?" Trig mused aloud.

"If there is, we'll handle it," I said quietly. I felt like I was back in the driver's seat when it came to my emotions, which made me in turn realize just how under my skin Everett had gotten but I couldn't be sorry. I'd been angry and depressed for so long it was like she breathed color and life into my otherwise gray world. Everything had been strictly black and white before and it was like seeing in color for the first time. I swiped a hand over my face and tried not to think about it, tried not to worry about whatever decision she'd come to, even though I felt my heart pick up with panic at the mere thought of her leavin'.

"That was some bullshit and we all know it," my Pops said with a gusty sigh, as he leaned back in his seat as far as it would go.

"Agreed, since when does any club worth two shits involve bitches and Old Ladies in the club politics?" Trig's expression was dark.

"Since we did first, I think," I said. Another mistake I'd made; I never should have presented it that *Everett* was the one that wanted the dude that shot her Out Bad. Fuck! I'd fucked up! Dragging her into this was our fault as much as the Suicide Kings' fault. Trigger echoed out loud what I'd just been thinking...

"Yeah, well. Irish was the one who got shot, so it was only right she have a say. We fucked up showing that particular card, we should have presented it better. Fuck. We opened the door and they just walked right on through! She never should have had to see that." Trig shook his head and took a thoughtful pull on his cigarette, the tip flaring bright.

"And the wheel makes another turn," my dad said, snapping me out of what was promising to turn into a full-scale brood.

"Yeah," Trig agreed somberly and they were right. With a new crew in town, the odds were that things would change. It was the nature of MC's that you could only stay friendly with another one for so long before some kind of beef came up. Could be weeks, months, or years before it happened, but reality dictated that eventually, some shit would go down between clubs and we wouldn't be so friendly anymore. Our 'friendship' with the Suicide Kings couldn't really even be called that. At best we were aware of each other and Sacred Hearts was merely tolerating their presence near our territory in order to keep an eye on them and their activities near our lands.

"On that depressing note..." I said and stubbed out my cig in the glass ashtray across the table.

"Where you gonna sleep?" my Pops asked.

"Out in the car, I've done it before," I said.

"Take my room. Ash and I'll take Reaver's, he won't mind us in there," Trig said. I looked at him, we were total opposites in looks, him all bright and shiny and Nordic and me all deep and dark and Latin. I'd never seen the inside of Trig's club room.

"Thanks, man," I said and he held out his hand. I clapped my hand into it and gripped it the way you would if you were going to arm wrestle before letting it go.

"That's another thing we gotta do. Get the rest of this place in shape to house everybody. I'm tired of it being only a third of the way livable," my Pops complained. I nodded wearily. I heard that.

I trudged in the direction of Trigger's room and paused outside the door to mine. I could hear Ashton's voice muffled and so very mouse-quiet as she spoke to Everett.

"I love him," I heard Everett say, and my heart lifted. "I just wish he'd told me another time, either before all of this, or not at all... I don't know, it's just too much right now." I rested my forehead against the door frame and let out the breath I'd been holding ever so slowly. Maybe my dad was right and this could be saved, maybe he wasn't; either way I wasn't going down without a fight. It wasn't the Sacred Hearts way. I trudged to Trigger's door and opened it, hitting the overhead light.

Jesus. The man was a fucking minimalist. He hadn't painted, changed the carpet, *nothing*. The bed was neatly made, if shabby, the sheets white and the blanket one of those thin, institutional felt ones. Whatever. A bed was a bed, and I was fucking beat. I flipped out the light and flopped across it on my stomach, comforted by the weight of my jacket and cut. The club, my father and my brothers would get me through if shit went south with Em, of that I had no doubt. Maybe I was being fatalistic that things wouldn't work out but I could say one thing for sure, if I lost her, she'd be taking one hell of a chunk of my heart with her and I knew I would never see it back again.

Strange thing was, I was totally cool with that, but that was something to be analyzed another day. Oh, say, when hell froze over. I closed my eyes and passed the fuck out within a couple of minutes, welcoming the oblivion with open fucking arms.

**21**

———————

**E**verett...

I lay there, staring at the ceiling for a long moment after he left. He'd looked so destroyed when he'd gone, like a little boy who'd just been told there was no such thing as miracles, and I hadn't meant that. I'd just meant that I needed some time to process everything. I thought too much had been happening with Jerry and his cheating and suddenly finding myself homeless and wanting another man so quickly... I never dreamed I would be shot! I never dreamed that in less than a full day I would be shot, that my ever being able to dance again would be torn from me, that I would be given that hope back, be under the care of an outlaw motorcycle gang, see another man shot, and have the person I loved the most in the world decide that as soon as I was done losing my dinner over that, that it would be a good time to tell me plainly that he'd killed another man.

My thoughts broke and my mind scattered and I cried, the first ugly wrenching sob tearing out of my chest. I covered my face with my hands. God! I was so sick of crying! I suddenly missed my da' with a fierce deep ache and wanted so badly for him to be there, to give me some of his practical wisdom to cling to, to ruminate over, to fit all of this into nice neat little compartments so it didn't seem so big, scary, ugly and confusing. Mostly I wanted to wipe that broken look of pain from Dray's face as he'd gotten up abruptly and left me.

*Oh God what had I done!?*

"Oh, honey, no, what happened!?" Ashton's soft voice broke through my noisy crying and her slight weight dipped the edge of the bed. She hugged my head and shoulders to her chest and I collapsed and just gave myself over to the howling, raging crying clawing its way up and out of my throat.

"Gonna find Dray," I heard Trigger say from the door and then heard it shut. Ashton smoothed my hair and rocked me.

"It's okay, Everett," she said gravely, "Just let it out, just let it all out." So I did, in great hiccupping sobs, my face painted red and blotchy, salty and slick with my tears. My nose started to run and Ashton thrust tissues from the box on the nightstand into my hand. I blew my nose and the emotional shitstorm started to abate.

"What happened?" She asked me, her face stricken with the need to make it better. Ashton would make a beautiful mother someday.

"He told me everything! Just, everything and it's too much! It's just too much!" I cried.

"Shhhh, shhhh, shhhh. What did Dray tell you?" Ashton asked gently and I quailed.

"Oh. He told you about that, then," she said and I swallowed.

"He said he killed your husband. Him and Reaver." I sniffed and Ashton nodded.

"Yes, but they did it to protect me," she said and shifted uncomfortably.

"I don't understand, I guess I don't fully understand why... or what happened," I said truthfully, hoping desperately against hope that it would make a difference. How could I have not seen that Dray was a killer too!? I'd grown up around them all my life, I should have seen it! Shouldn't I? I mean I'd suspected at one point but... I sighed. Who was I kidding? I hadn't wanted to believe it. Not really. Ashton took my hands in hers and sighed too.

"Chadwick Granger was a beautiful monster..." she started. She told me all about it. How she and Trigger had met on the side of the road, how he'd brought her here, seen to her injuries at the hands of her husband, sheltered her, protected her, fed and clothed her, how he'd taken her on as a project and had given her everything she'd needed to grow outside of the shadow of her husband, but also about how that shadow was impossible to escape.

"He sent people impersonating police to our door to tell me Ethan was dead, they sent men to hurt Ethan, and he and Reaver had to fight them. Finally, my husband's head of security broke down our door, beat me bloody, broke my bones and tried to take me back to Chadwick and he succeeded." She swallowed before continuing.

"I don't remember most of it, he injected me with something in the car on the way over, but Ethan, Reaver, Dragon, and Dray; they came and got me. Took me back. It was what made us decide that Chadwick was crazy, the things he said to them... He wasn't going to stop. I was his property and he would hurt or kill them all and... and..." she pulled some tissues from the box and wiped her eyes, taking in a deep breath. This still affected her as much as hearing it was affecting me. Her hands shook as she placed them in my own and we clung to each other as we weathered the storms our emotions wrought within us. I suddenly need to hear this, all of it because if what Ashton was saying was true, and it rang true to my ears, Reaver and Dray had done the world a service. Cold? Yes, but also practical and true.

"So, Dray killed this man in order to save you?" I asked.

"Honestly, Everett, I don't think they saved just me from Chadwick. They saved everyone in this club. Chadwick was crazy and the more his perceived power grew, so did his insanity. He left me on the side of the road the night Ethan saved me fully expecting that I would meet his unrealistic expectations, that I would walk miles and miles home, barefoot in a skimpy party dress, and that I would make it there by morning. That life would go on and it would just be another of many corrections I was forced to endure because I didn't quite fit the framework he had laid out for me in his mind... If Ethan hadn't come, I would have never made it. I would have died of exposure. That never occurred to Chadwick, or if it did, he didn't care. What's more, he never even dreamed someone like Ethan would come along. He was more furious about his image being ruined in the local media than he was about whether I lived or died. Like I said, I was simply property to him. Like a car, or a piece of furniture." She shrugged and looked so sad.

"This was on the news?" I asked.

"Some of it. Not all." She nodded.

"You'll have to forgive me," I murmured, pulling my laptop into my lap. Ashton gave me a brilliant smile.

"Not at all, it's smart of you to check your facts, and I understand completely. The story is pretty fantastical. At first, when I didn't turn up, it was Chadwick who went to the media stating that I had disappeared after we'd had an argument. It was last March." I did a Google search and Ashton's smiling face, tight around the edges, came up on one of the local news station outlets. The first story was as she'd said, Chadwick spinning tales about how he and she had argued and she'd demanded to be let out of the car. How he'd driven off angry and returned to find her missing.

She slipped out of the room and returned quickly as I went to the next article, one proclaiming that Ashton had gone to the police and charged her husband with abuse. She sat down beside me and handed me photographs which she pulled from the inside cover of a handwritten journal.

"These were taken by Ethan and Doc the night he found me," she said and they were horrible. Her feet were bloody and scraped, her dress a barely-there affair providing nothing in the way of cover against the elements. Her lips were tinged blue from the cold in the photos and the swelling and bruising painted her pale skin in splotches of purple and black that made my stomach roil. I swallowed hard and handed them back before I looked through them all. I couldn't finish. She took them and I went through news articles and a few more television interviews about his suicide. He'd apparently been a fairly prominent defense attorney in the area.

I closed the lid of my laptop and scrubbed my face with my hands, Ashton set it on the floor within reach, beside the bed for me. I looked at her.

"Why tell me all of this?" I asked her. She sighed.

"Can I ask you something first?" She chewed her lip.

"Go ahead."

"How do you feel about Dray?"

"I love him," I said, and it was true, that hadn't changed not at all. "I just wish he'd told me another time, either before all of this, or not at all... I don't know, it's just too much right now." Which was true too. Ashton smiled like she'd won some sort of prize.

"Dray is a good man at the heart of it all, and I think you two complement each other quite well." Ashton grinned, "We just really have to work on his timing of things." I laughed and her expression grew serious again, all levity gone.

"Dray doesn't open up to many people, Everett. I've barely scratched his surface and that's okay. We love Dray for who he is, still, he needs to open up to somebody, and if he loves you enough to do it... please take that into consideration before either of you do anything drastic." I stared at her dumbly.

"Ashton, I... I love Dray. I don't give up that easily. Hell, I was with Jerry for four years! Dray is a million times the man Jerry ever was. I'm just... overwhelmed... and when Dray decided to tell me every-thing... well, it was one straw too many for this camel's back to hold." I sighed out, a harsh exhalation of air. A slight knock came at the door and Trigger poked his head in.

"Everything okay?" he asked. Ashton smiled at him like he was her whole world and then some, and it was a beautiful sight to see. I had a sudden and new appreciation for the big man.

"Is Dray all right?" I asked and chewed my lower lip apprehen-sively. Trigger smiled like suddenly *he'd* won the prize.

"Drunk as fuck and sleeping it off in our room. I was just poking my head in to tell Ashton we're staying in Reave's," he said. I sighed out in relief and he continued, "Not going to lie, pretty girl, you scared the fuck out of him. He thinks it's all over between you two and he broke it past fixing. I think you two need to have a talk in the morning."

"Give me my crutches," I demanded and his eyebrows went up.

"Where are you going?" Ashton wondered aloud.

"Your room," I said and started leaning over the side of the bed, reaching for the smooth aluminum of the nearest crutch. Ashton sat frozen, speechless I think, but I'd made up my mind and once I've done that, good luck getting me to change it! Mandy would have given me the damned devices without a backwards glance. I missed her.

"If you don't freaking give me the damned crutches I'm going to combat-crawl my way over there! See if I won't!" I snapped and Trigger laughed and opened the door wider.

"Here, stop, you're going to hurt yourself!" I pushed my way back up onto the bed and gasped. Too late, my leg hurt like a bitch! Ashton got up and moved out of his way.

"Careful, Ethan, she might bite you," she joked and I smiled.

"Here, girl, put your arms around my neck," he ordered and stooped. I did and he slid an arm around my back, the other beneath my knees and lifted with his legs like I weighed nothing. My eyebrows went up.

"I feel sorry for the poor bastard you have a need to hit in the face," I commented dryly. Trigger grinned.

"I'm a pacifist, Baby. God made me all big and scary 'cause I'm all marshmallow inside." I snorted.

"Me da' would say 'bullshite' and 'if God went around hugging liars, he'd break every bone in your body.' You go ahead and keep telling yourself whatever you want to believe though," I said as he moved us out into the hall, sideways through the doorway. His footfalls were heavy as he moved to his door. Ashton opened it for him, the rectangle of light falling onto Dray who lay on his stomach, the patches on his cut illuminated by the light from the hall. I grinned.

"Isn't that a picture?" I asked. Trigger laughed a little.

"Go easy on my VP. His heart is missing in action, says he gave it to this girl, the whole thing, and doesn't even know when it happened." I blinked at him and his expression wasn't joking anymore. "I need to set you down so I can move him," he murmured and I contemplated the situation and shook my head.

"Just set me down at the foot of the bed there, I'll scoot myself up and you can lift his head for me," I said. Trigger shrugged a shoulder and did what I said. I sat at the foot of the bed and was grateful I'd been shot in the left leg so I could do what I wanted. I scooted up until my back rested against the wall. I took several deep breaths and waited for the pain to subside before putting a pillow behind my back and another in my lap.

"Lift his upper body," I said and Trig slid an arm under Dray's shoulders across his chest and lifted. I scooted over just a bit and laid Dray's head on top of my right thigh. He was passed out cold and didn't even stir.

"You good, Irish?" Trig asked.

"Yes, thank you." I smoothed Dray's hair back out of his face and rested my head back against the wall. It was going to be a long night but I needed to be near him as much as he needed me.

"'Night," Trig grunted and shut the door behind him and Ashton. I was plunged into darkness absolute, lap weighted where Dray rested against my thigh. He didn't move all night. I slept off and on, and thought about things when I was awake. The room lightened with the rising sun where it seeped in around the blinds and it was early still when Dray stirred. He started with a little jerk and a sharp intake of breath; I petted his thick hair, smoothing my hand over it, and he looked up at me with bleary eyes.

"Hi," I said softly.

"Hey," he said back and looked around to make sure he was in the right room.

"You're stupid," I told him flatly and he frowned.

"Why?"

"I love you, you dumb asshole! Just because I need a minute to sort through the dumptruck of shitty emotions I'm feeling – which I might add, your timing on adding to them sucked balls! – does not mean that I'm leaving you or that we're broken. It just means I need a minute to be alone and get my shit together." His lips curled into a smile and he laid his head back down carefully the way it'd been which meant he was looking away from me.

"You're right on one thing, Em," he said dryly.

"What's that?"

"I'm a dumb asshole. A very sorry dumb asshole. Forgive me?" he asked. I huffed a small laugh.

"Yes... Why does this feel like our first fight when we aren't even fighting?" I asked.

"Uh, let's see. I'm used to what went down last night, you aren't, and instead of being there for you and making it better my dumb ass decided 'No, wait, this is the perfect opportunity to get this off my chest', which just shoved you away and made things worse. I'd say you've got the right to be mad about that, babe." He sighed, and I felt it rather than heard it.

"Sounds like we're on the same page then," I said cautiously. He pushed himself into a sitting position and I almost mourned the loss of contact but it was short-lived. He leaned forward, reaching for me and I did my best to meet him halfway. His fingers found my hair, tangling in it, pulling my mouth to his and he kissed me savagely, possessively, so strongly I was left breathless and in awe.

He broke the kiss and said against my mouth, "I'm glad, because I need to get something straight with you. I fucked up last night, I own my mistakes and I'm going to make more of them but one thing I've done that's no mistake is I've given you the keys to the kingdom Em. I've given you my heart, and I go where it goes, so you're fucking stuck with my dumb ass." His dark gaze bored into mine, smoldering and hot and enough to make my blood boil with its intensity from mere inches away. He continued his little tirade and I was okay with that, I wanted to hear what he was saying more than I ever wanted to hear anything in my life.

"I can't promise you sunshine and roses all the time, baby, but what I can promise you was that last night isn't a common occurrence. I can't promise you bad shit won't happen but what I can promise is that I will never lie to you, I will never cheat on you, and I will never intentionally hurt you. What I will do, is love you, and be with you and protect you and if that means I need to pull out my motherfucking badass to do it, I will. If it means I have to punch a guy in the mouth or shoot him in the leg, or fucking kill him in the most insidious ways you can imagine to keep you safe and whole I won't hesitate. I love you that much." I blinked stupidly, I didn't know what to say.

"Say something," he said.

"I..."

"Just tell me you're on board," he said, desperation in his eyes, lacing his tone.

"Yes, I'm on board! Oh my God, I'm on board! What woman in their right mind wouldn't be on board after that, Dray!" I hugged myself to him and his arms curved around me. What he offered, what he said, it was all I had ever wanted... Dray was a hell of a Prince Charming but then again I wasn't exactly a Disney princess. I'd always prided myself on being a self-rescuing princess if there ever was one, but Dray... I kissed him.

"So we're okay?" he said hopefully.

"We're okay," I said breathlessly.

"You gotta promise me, Em, you start to freak out or get overwhelmed, to talk to me. Don't shut me out, baby, it damn near gave me a heart attack," he said, and I nodded.

"Okay. We can make this work," I said.

"Damn straight we're going to make it work." He smiled. I closed my eyes, a weight lifted from my shoulders. When I opened them Dray was searching my face.

"Tired?" he asked.

"Yeah," I admitted.

"Were you like that all night with me?"

"Yeah." I smiled.

"Why?"

"Because I love you and there wasn't any way I was going to let you wake up thinking we weren't going to be okay," I said with a gusty sigh. "I think, the more I'm with you, that we were made for each other. The way I was raised, the people I was raised around, I think it was all to prepare me for a life with you. Believe me, I know it can get ugly, I just let myself get overwhelmed with so much happening all at once, so close together. After thinking about it, I think I can handle it. I know I can handle it, because not handling would mean I couldn't stay... would mean a life without you, and I don't want to face that probability." He was looking at me, his dark eyes roving my face, his expression so serious.

"What?" I asked finally.

"Now I really feel like we're on the same page," he said and I smiled because it felt incredibly good. Dray got up on his feet beside the bed and stretched.

"Where are you going?"

"*We* are going back to *our* room and getting some decent fucking sleep. Trig's bed sucks and you look like you need a good sleep."

"I need to be held, by you," I admitted.

"Cool, I can do that," he said and lifted me. I wrinkled my nose.

"Can you take a shower first? You smell like an agave farm." He laughed and took me back to his, excuse me, *our* bedroom and settled me into the bed. He showered quickly and joined me cuddling me into his embrace and I felt, that despite the wild and weird sequence of events that brought me here, that I was home.

# 22

**D**ray...

I straightened up from under the hood of the old Charger and looked out the bay door, my breath fogging in the cold air. After the night my girl got a full dose of the ugly side of club life we'd settled into a pretty decent routine of work, school and for her, doctor's appointments and physical therapy.

Fall had worn on into winter and she and Mandy both had finished out their semester. She'd passed that damned math class, her and Red both, thanks to Shelly, and earned their degrees. Now, she and Red were pulling up at the garage after lunch with Ashton and both of them looked shell-shocked. I grinned. They got out of Red's little Ford Focus and walked across the parking lot towards me. Em didn't even limp anymore and had been slowly but surely, in addition to her physical therapy, been getting back into her dancing.

"Hey, girls." Gypsy said and waved at them both before disappearing into the office. I wiped my hands on an old rag as they approached.

"Have a good lunch?" I asked, and Everett raked me with her steel blue shrewd gaze.

"Did you know Ashton was going to do it?" she asked me.

"Uh, yeah," I said carefully, grinning. Mandy still looked like she'd been cracked across the skull and was seeing stars.

"Holy crap, this is really happening!" Red blurted and sat down right on the ground where she stood. My girl was grinning from ear to ear and God was she beautiful.

"What's happening?" I feigned innocence.

"Ashton is fronting us all of the money required to start our business. She wants to be a silent partner!" Red said and I laughed. Everett shrieked in excitement and flung herself at me. Her long dancer's legs wound around my hips and I was instantly hard. I held her up and kissed her fiercely and laughed with her, sharing in her joy.

"Well, she has all that money, might as well use some of it for something. She can't take it with her." I shrugged nonchalantly.

"Oh my God!" Red leapt to her feet. "I'm not dreaming. This is really happening!" She spun in place and let out an explosive breath.

"Celebration at the clubhouse tonight?" Everett asked me.

"I think that can be arranged." I grinned and she slid down my body to her feet.

"I love you," she said.

"Love you too, babe," I said back.

She kissed me one more time and she and Red went off to do whatever it was they did while I had to work. Closing time couldn't come fast enough and eventually it moseyed on down my way. I closed up the garage with Gypsy and walked Darlene, our front-office girl, to her car across the lot. The sun was going down and I was ready for a hot shower. I climbed into Sadie and drove home. When I went in the front door I was immediately aware of the mouthwatering smells coming from the kitchen. I smiled.

Everett stood at the dining room table and set down a plate, a feral, way-too-sexy smile curving her lips. I went very still and drank her in from the high heels on her feet, up the long stems of her legs, my gaze skating over the frilly, 50's housewife apron and along her smooth creamy skin. The apron was all she wore and god damn it! I was achingly hard.

"Welcome home," she said in a sultry purr. Candles glowed on the dining tabletop, warm and inviting, and the food looked almost as spectacular as my woman. I groaned. I didn't know which appetite I should assuage first.

"Do I have time for a shower?" I growled. She bit her lower lip in that way that drove me nuts and shook her head very, very slowly.

That was it. I went to her and snatched her into my arms bringing my mouth down on hers wildly. The skin of her back was warm and silky beneath my dirty work-roughened hands and I gloried in it. I turned her so her back was to the table and crushed her petal softness against it. She moaned when she felt my thickness up against her through my jeans and I let myself lose it. I swept an arm across the table. Silverware and plates crashing to the floor with placemats and glasses. Good thing there wasn't any food on anything yet; that was still on the kitchen counter.

The candles snuffed out and rolled to the side and I laid her back across the table. I fumbled at my belt and fly and she produced a condom out of the apron pocket. I growled low in my throat.

"God, I love you!" And she smiled, tearing the packet open. Somehow between the two of us we got it on me and I fit myself inside of her. She was wet and ready and cried out in pure bliss the second I was fully seated. She gripped my shoulders and looked deep into my eyes.

"Make it rough. God, please, I want it hard!" she cried and hell yeah! I was up for a round of rough and dirty sex on my dining room table, what guy wasn't?

I gripped her hips with near-bruising force and thrust into her wet heat like I was going to come out the other side. The entire table, which was a sturdy piece, shuddered with the force of our coupling, and she cried out, writhing beneath me so beautifully I couldn't make it last if I wanted to. I bowed over her and crushed my mouth over hers before straightening to a standing position again. I smoothed a hand across the dip her hips took between the sharp curves of her hipbones and slicked a thumb down into her wetness and up over that sensitive bundle of nerves at the top of her sex.

I may not be able to last for longer than a couple of minutes with how turned on she'd made me but I damned sure wasn't going to come without her either going up and over first or going along for the ride. Her body bucked sharply under me and she moaned, a throaty wail that had my balls tightening. I kept myself from going off by sheer force of will and gritted my teeth.

"Come on, baby, I want to hear you sing," I said and rubbed her clit just the way I knew she liked, fast light little strokes up and down. She squeezed down so tight and delicious around my cock and just when I was sure I couldn't stand it anymore she exploded around me and underneath me, emitting a sharp, piercing cry that was a cross between triumph and ecstasy. I lost it completely, my hips losing rhythm, my cock jumping wildly as I spilled myself into the condom inside her. I collapsed over the top of her and kissed her shoulder, the side of her neck, panting in great gasps against her warm, moist skin. She laughed and wiggled her hips just a bit and it was too much after coming so hard. I jerked back out of her with a small strained cry of my own and she laughed again.

"Can we have dinner like this every night?" I asked her and chuckled. I hauled my pants up my legs.

"Go wash up," she ordered breathlessly. "I'm just," she swallowed, "I'm just gonna lie here a second." I went into the bathroom and took care of things, flushing our offering down the porcelain goddess. I washed up and took a warm wet washcloth out to her and cleaned her up carefully.

She moaned a little, her eyes closing in bliss.

"I'm never going to be able to sit at this table again without picturing what we just did," I stated dryly and she struggled into a sitting position.

"Good," she said. I went and got the broom and swept up while she saved the rest of our dinner from burning in the oven.

"You're fucking irresistible, woman," I growled into her ear, pulling her nude back against my clothed front.

"Mmm, do we have to go to the club?" she asked quietly.

"Your girl Mandy going?" I asked her.

"No, she's celebrating with her parents. She's still going to be stuck there for a while until we can start turning a profit and..." I turned her around.

"What if she moved in here?" I asked.

"What? What about your dad?" she asked.

"You seen his room lately?" I asked her.

"Nooo..." she trailed off. I took her by the hand and led her to it and opened the door flipping on the light.

"When did he move out!?" she asked. I grinned at the four bare walls and furniture-less room.

"Apparently when you weren't lookin'!" I said she turned around and crushed herself to my chest. God, I loved the feel of her against me.

"Are you sure?" she asked apprehensively, chewing her bottom lip.

"Does the Pope shit in the woods?" I asked borrowing a favorite saying of Reaver's. She snorted, getting the joke and I kissed her.

"This house was –and is– full of ghosts of my mom for my dad. He was pretty much moved into the new clubhouse the day we took it over. He only stored shit here and came to crash so I wouldn't be living alone, he worried about me being on my own... but I'm not alone anymore. I got you, and when he figured out you weren't going anywhere he moved the rest of his shit out." She gazed up at me adoringly and smiled.

"You're stuck with me, you know," she said and I smiled.

"Better be," I said.

"Oh, you are, mister..." she said, dragging me back into the bathroom I raised an eyebrow.

"What're you doing?" I asked her.

"Making love to my man in the shower," she answered and let go to turn on the tap. She shouldn't have presented that heart-shaped ass to me so nicely. One, because I slapped it and two, because after snatching the condom out of my wallet, I took her again, bent over the tub.

I loved her. I loved living with her and when the time was right... I had every intention of making E.M.M., E.M.T. and heaven help me, she kept it up, I was going to need a medic!

# ALSO BY A.J. DOWNEY

***The Sacred Hearts MC***

1. Shattered & Scarred

2. Broken & Burned

3. Cracked & Crushed

3.5 Masked & Miserable (a novella)

4. Tattered & Torn

5. Fractured & Formidable

6. Damaged & Dangerous

***The Virtues***

1. Cutter's Hope

2. Marlin's Faith

3. Charity for Nothing

***The Sacred Brotherhood***

1. Brother to Brother

2. Her Brother's Keeper

3. Brother in Arms

4. Between Brothers

5. A Brother's Secret

6. A Brother at My Back

***Indigo Knights***

1. Her Thin Blue Lifeline

2. His Cold Blue Command

***Paranormal Romance (with Ryan Kells)***

1. I am the Alpha

2. Omega's Run

3. Hunter's End

# ABOUT THE AUTHOR

A. J. Downey is the international bestselling author of The Sacred Hearts Motorcycle Club romance series. She is a born and raised Seattle, WA Native. She finds inspiration from her surroundings, through the people she meets and likely as a byproduct of way too much caffeine.

She has lived many places and done many things, though mostly through her own imagination...An avid reader all of her life, it's now her turn to try and give back a little, entertaining as she has been entertained.

facebook.com/authorajdowney

twitter.com/authorajdowney

instagram.com/authorajdowney